SILENCED

SILENCED

JENNIE ENSOR

This edition produced in Great Britain in 2021

by Hobeck Books Limited, Unit 14, Sugnall Business Centre, Sugnall, Stafford, Staffordshire, ST21 6NF

www.hobeck.net

A CIP catalogue for this book is available from the British Library.

ISBN 978-1-913-793-54-8

Cover design by Jayne Mapp Design

https://jaynemapp.wixsite.com

Printed and bound in Great Britain by Clays Ltd, Elcograf S.p.A.

❦ Created with Vellum

PRAISE FOR SILENCED

Hobeck Books has a team of dedicated advanced readers who read our books before publication (not all of them, they choose which they would like to read). Here is what they, reviewers and other bestselling crime writers have said about *Silenced*.

'A crime thriller with depth. It's heart pounding, addictive and intelligent. It's rare to come across a rollercoaster read that has heart, but this is it. A must read.' Barbara Copperthwaite, bestselling psychological thriller author

'With authentic voices, a believable storyline and characters that you can really relate to, this is one of my favourite books of the year so far – gripping, fast-paced, poignant, and, most importantly, REAL!' Liz Mistry, author of the DI Gus McGuire and the DS Nikki Parekh crime thriller series

'Sally Rooney meets Lynda La Plante in this dark tale of teenage experiment and adult shame. Ensor shows how our childhood traumas shape and break us, with sometimes devastating consequences. This is a tale of cruel violence where each player is forced to confront their vulnerabilities and question their own integrity. Breathtaking and gut wrenching in equal measure.' Kerensa Jennings, author of literary thriller, *Seas of Snow*

'An absolutely thrilling, rollercoaster read, so cleverly told and so immensely authentic. I ws gripped from start to finish. This is storytelling of the highest order and I can't wait for Jennie Ensor's next book.' Alex Day, author of *The Best of Friends* and *The Missing Twin*

'A savage and powerful novel that exposes the dark underbelly of gang culture, the self-destructive actions of those caught in its web and the shattering consequences for all that it leaves in its wake. Crime fiction at its best.' Ian Skewis, author of *A Murder of Crows*

'Mesmeringly good...haunting, heart-wrenching and thought-provoking - this book stayed with me for a long time after I had finished it.' Linda Huber, author of psychological fiction

'The story holds you right to the end.' HART reader

'Well what can I say about *Silenced*. Such a great read.' Joe Singleton

'...was wonderfully crafted and the story was gripping: in fact, I read it in one fell swoop.' Janet Pole

'Wow. Brilliant!' Emma Hardy

'This tense thriller and police procedural throws back the curtain on gang life...a tense and well-researched thriller.' Karen Eisenbrey

ARE YOU A THRILLER SEEKER?

Hobeck Books is an independent publisher of crime, thrillers and suspense fiction and we have one aim – to bring you the books you want to read.

For more details about our books, our authors and our plans, plus the chance to download free novellas, sign up for our newsletter at **www.hobeck.net**.

You can also find us on Twitter **@hobeckbooks** or on Facebook **www.facebook.com/hobeckbooks10**.

For all the teenagers struggling to find their path in life

PART ONE

A girl, alone in the glare of afternoon.

She's humming *Seven Seconds*, which she heard on the radio at breakfast while her mother packed her lunch. She wipes the beads of sweat off her brow with the back of her hand and rolls up the sleeves of her white shirt. She'll be at the estate soon.

She's short for her fifteen years. A fuzz of black hair is drawn behind her head with a scrunchy. The small turquoise rucksack on her back bobs from side to side as she hurries, nimble-footed, along the pavement. Inside it, among the exercise books is a copy of *I Am Malala* and a leftover apple. In the zip pocket are her keys, coin purse and a tube of raspberry lip gloss that her best friend gave her, not yet worn outside her room.

Three kids in school uniform dawdle towards her. A boy spurts past heading for the bus that has pulled up in the distance. She pays them no attention.

Her thoughts turn first to what she might buy her sister for her birthday – a journalling book maybe, she still can't decide –

then return to what Mrs Kostic said about her history project. *That's a super idea, Solita. You've put so much thought into this.* The words of encouragement bloom within her, leaving a sliver of resolve. She will get good grades in her GCSEs next summer, then she'll take her A levels and go on to uni and study to be a social worker. She isn't going to end up like her brother, wherever he is now, always scowling and getting into trouble.

In the distance, two young men slouch against a wire fence. Their dark clothing merges into the shade of a nearby tree. One is thin, his shoulders hunched. A rucksack is snug at his side. His hood hides his face. The other is bigger in build and heavily muscled, also hooded. He wears disposable gloves.

The thin man pulls a phone from his pocket and puts it briefly to his ear. He straightens, nods to the other.

Solita walks faster. She can't wait to get home. She imagines her mother's smile when she hears what the teacher said and the deep-violet shade of the summer pudding waiting in the fridge.

The muscled man nudges off his hood and reaches inside the rucksack that the other has opened. Thirty seconds go by; a minute. The girl passes him, unaware of his pale, unblinking eyes tracking her. His breaths are slow and controlled, his trainers make no sound. He's closing in on her. His fingers curl tightly around the handle of a zombie knife.

She glances behind, sensing someone. Her mouth falls open and her eyes widen. She sees a man with a face that looks like a skull, then the glint of a vast, jagged blade. It's aimed straight at her. The blade slips through her chest without difficulty, entering her heart and emerging on the other side, only stopping when it can go no further.

CALLUM

15TH JULY

IT WAS ANOTHER BAD NIGHT – FRAGMENTS OF SLEEP CHASED BY thoughts I didn't want and memories I'd give anything to forget.

Around four in the morning, as I was about to drift off again, I heard it. A repeated knocking, getting louder. The sound of something being struck against glass – knuckles, or a fist. Was someone trying to break in? An acrid taste filled my mouth and the smell of burning clogged my throat. A flash of horror went through me. No, someone was trying to get out. The shed...

I opened my eyes before the rest came. The knocking kept on, like echoes in a haunted house.

This isn't real, I told myself. It's only the past stuck inside your head.

The noises had come once before when I'd been under severe stress at work. I'd read up on what might be happening. It was a flashback; auditory and olfactory rather than visual.

I sat up, turned on the bedside lamp and took some deep

breaths, visualising palm fronds swaying as waves rolled gently onto white sand. But no way could I go back to sleep now.

———

I pushed my hands deeper into my pockets and walked faster, head down, into the rain. Proper rain now, not that half-arsed drizzle like walking into a cloud that you often get around these parts. I trod carefully along the stony path to avoid the piles of horse shit and occasional dog, sheep and goat turds.

Up here in the Welsh hills, the air carried the scent of animals, not diesel, and I was glad of it. I'd had enough of London. I needed a break from the young men – kids, as they often were now – who bled to death on the streets every week, suspects who refused to cooperate and requests for information met with silence. It was eerie how a whole community could decide to keep its collective mouth shut, out of fear of what telling the truth might bring. Not even the largest rewards would dent the resistance to informing on associates, neighbours and friends. People would rather justice wasn't done than risk an all-powerful hand striking down them or their loved ones.

I kicked a stone hard and watched it tumble over the edge of the path and plummet towards a bank of wildflowers.

Ahead, clouds hugged the upper valley. Sludgy grey clouds merged with sludgy grey land – no vivid greens today. The weather suited my mood. I needed to stop thinking about work and all the things I did not have the power to change. If I didn't switch off from it all for a while, I'd be in big trouble. I was heading downhill already, wasn't I? Running away from the job last week had hardly been a career-enhancing move.

Operation Tiverton had been a chance to show what I could achieve. The DCI had taken a back seat and let me 'run with it'. But it hadn't worked out like that.

It had been another apparently senseless killing, most likely gang-related, the sort of thing happening in cities all over the country. Four males in hoodies had stabbed a seventeen-year-old youth. The incident had been witnessed by many but no suspects were ever identified. No one knew anything, no one saw anything.

One week ago, it had become clear that there was little likelihood of ever putting away those responsible. Once again, the criminals were going to get away with it. Something inside my brain had seemed to slip from its position, like the first stone of an avalanche. I rushed out of the office to my car and sobbed, head on the wheel, overcome with a sense of utter uselessness. What was the point of my job? I'd joined the Met's Homicide and Major Crimes squad because I'd wanted to make a difference, however unfashionable that might be. I'd wanted to help stop young men wreaking havoc on their communities with ever more extreme violence. But I had failed my first big test since joining the murder team, end of. Staff were being pulled from the inquiry, which soon would be only a memory.

Despite the lack of notice, the DCI hadn't made a fuss about me taking annual leave. *Take a week or two off, Callum, get some sunshine and relax.*

The sunshine had proved elusive though, not to mention the relaxation.

I arrived at a dog-leg in the path. Below lay a field of inquisitive sheep. As usual, some poked their heads over the fence to study me as I approached. I stared back. I should enjoy this place while I had the chance. My respite would be over before I knew it – unless I didn't go back.

What if I quit the murder team and did something else? I could grow apple trees and learn to fish, spend more time listening to Sibelius and actually go on that trip to Norway. No more getting up in the middle of the night to look at broken young bodies. No more chasing invisible criminals who would do anything to keep on corrupting those they came across. Instead, I could work on mending the relationship with my son, maybe even save my marriage...

Thank God, the rain was almost gone. A break in the clouds hinted of a return to sunshine. This incessant dampness always got to me after a while. Why the hell had Kate and I bought a holiday home in the rainiest part of Britain?

I turned and headed back towards the cottage. The path descended steeply. I tried to ignore the twinge of pain coming from my left knee. I wasn't in bad shape for a bloke past forty, though niggling pains kept reminding me that I'd probably reached my halfway point. Time and tide wait for no man, wasn't that the saying?

A loose stone under my foot wobbled. I regained my balance, just in time.

At the stile, I stopped. The clouds were shifting – suddenly sunlight turned the smudge of distant mountains into crystal-sharp peaks. I let out a long breath at the beauty of it all, and my thoughts came into focus. How could I quit the Met? What was I thinking? I was a police officer and a damn good one, most of the time. I loved my job. Despite its recent toll – Kate leaving and Brendan blaming me for it – no way was I going to give up. I needed a breather, that was all.

Back in the house, I removed my jacket and boots and went to find Brendan. He was sitting at the kitchen table, scrolling through his Instagram feed.

'How's it going?'

He ignored me. I shrugged and headed to the armchair opposite the fireplace, looking forward to a nap. I was knackered after my night's sleep. The sounds I'd heard during the night – experienced might be a better word – had stayed with me for hours, a ghostly presence that couldn't be exorcised.

It's the stress of the job, I told myself. I'm not losing my mind.

The stress was setting off the shit inside my head again. All this week my mind had kept on returning to the day my childhood ended; that day I'd give anything to be able to change.

Outside a hawk screeched softly, then all was silent. It was a silence I still hadn't got used to.

I picked up a long strawberry blonde hair from the seat cushion. It was weird being here without Kate. Would we ever spend time together again, except to wrangle about children and finances? I needed to face up to it, I'd lost her. She was making a new life for herself, without me.

———

Recoiling from the blare of sirens emanating from it, I picked up my phone intent only on shutting it up.

'Hello?'

My head was thick with unfinished sleep. My nap had been broken first by Brendan's acid house, and now by my damned iPhone.

'Sorry, boss, is it a bad time?' DS Harper's tone was anxious. Sam could never hide how she was feeling, one of the things I most liked about her. 'I wasn't sure whether to call. But you said you wanted to know if anything came up.'

'That's OK, I can sleep later.' I shifted myself upright and tried to focus. 'What is it?'

'There's been a fatal stabbing, about an hour ago. A fifteen-year-old girl, Afro-Caribbean origin, attacked near the council estate on Effra Lane. She was on her way home from school. It was daylight, there were people around, kids getting off the bus. Jon and I are just back from the crime scene.' The barest of wobbles entered Sam's voice. 'She was stabbed in the chest. Paramedics found her lying on the pavement in her school uniform in a pool of blood.'

'Jesus.' Anger flared inside me, making my shoulders rigid. Who the hell had done such a thing? A girl so young, slaughtered in broad daylight. Such a killing was exceptional even for a city as inured to knife violence as London.

'You said to let you know if anything happened.'

'Thanks Sam, I appreciate it. Anything else?'

'Several witnesses saw two males run from the scene into the estate. They were both wearing hoodies and their faces weren't visible. Oh yes, one wore a skull mask under his hood.'

'A skull mask?'

'Yeah, a black balaclava or ski mask. It had a skull design over the lower part of the face.'

The Skull Crew – could they be responsible? Based on the Effra Lane estate in a deprived part of the borough of Haringey, the gang was one of London's most violent. Its members were rumoured to plant human skulls on doorsteps to intimidate people; there'd been complaints from shop owners targeted for extortion. A girl killed next to the council estate they controlled, and one of her killers wearing a mask that looked like a skull...

'The other thing, DCI Coleman was asking around just now, wanting to know when you're coming back from your leave.' Sam coughed. 'Are you coming back, boss? We all thought you'd done a runner.' A giggle came down the line. 'Escape from Stalag 55.'

I thought of all the reasons I should say no. This was my first leave in goodness knows how long. I needed another week to properly unwind. I needed time to reconnect with my son, time to be alone to connect with myself and step back from the edge. I didn't know if I'd ever be ready to come back.

But MIT55 was difficult to escape.

'I'll be back soon, I'm sure. I'll let Andy know. Thanks for keeping me up to date.'

'You'd better not be away too long,' Sam added in a mischievous tone. 'DI Pierce was using your desk fan yesterday. He reckons you nicked it from him.'

'God's sake,' I muttered, ending the call. Pierce was a continual thorn in my side. He never missed the opportunity to have a go at me about something, since the night he was enlightening us all with his far-right views. I'd had a few too many pints when a few descriptive phrases had slipped out, *You total tosser* among them.

Sunshine streamed through the kitchen window. Brendan was sitting at the table crunching toast. As I sat down, he got up, put his plate into the dishwasher and walked out of the room.

Another snub. This was his usual pattern now. Ever since Kate had announced she was leaving home our easy companionship had vanished.

I thought again about that girl and how she'd died. Was it a case of mistaken identity, or had she been targeted? If so, why? To stop her from talking about a crime that a gang member had committed? Revenge, perhaps? But what could anyone have done that was bad enough for a fifteen-year-old girl to end up dead?

I picked up my phone.

'Hello, boss. Callum here.' I raised my voice to be heard over the background chatter at the other end. 'I wanted to update you on my situation. I'm sorry if I've caused any—'

'What *is* your situation? Are you sick or just taking a break?' The DCI sounded as if he'd had a long day.

'I'm not sick, sir.' I hesitated. 'The frustration of not making any headway was getting to me.'

'Stress can get to everyone, you know. Maybe you should consider having a word with the counsellor.'

I mumbled something dismissive – I had no desire to tell a

stranger about my messed-up mind.

'Do you need to take more time off?'

'No, boss, I don't. I heard about the latest incident – the girl stabbed outside the estate. I want to play my part in the inquiry, sir.'

A pause; worryingly long. The click of a door closing, then quiet.

My heart sped up. Was the DCI going to accuse me of being unfit for duty and send me for a psychological assessment? It had happened to my mate in SO19. *Go on sick leave and get your mental health sorted.*

'I have to go into hospital soon for a major operation,' the DCI resumed. 'I'm announcing it to the team tomorrow. Afterwards, I'm supposed to be recovering at home. I'll be out of action for a couple of months, more if the missus has her way. How would you feel about leading the new inquiry? Officially, this time. Looks like it could be gang-related, so right up your street.'

'You mean the inquiry into the girl's murder outside the council estate? You want me to take over from you as SIO?'

'That's right, you'd be SIO of Operation Rye. The girl's name is Solita Milton. Martin will be stepping up to acting DCI, he'll manage our other live inquiries and keep things ticking over while I'm away.' A long exhale. 'I completely understand if you're not up to it. Martin would love this one too. But to be frank, you're the best man for the job.'

'I'll do it.' Even with Martin Pierce as my temporary boss, this was a no-brainer.

'You'll probably need a chance to think it over.'

'I don't need to think it over. I'm saying yes.'

'This will be stressful, you know. The brass will be on your back, not to mention the media. They'll be all over this one.'

Another long exhale. 'If you're not in the right place to take on the job, I'll need to know now.'

It was time to be honest with myself. I was struggling to cope as it was. But the thought of Pierce getting his mitts on the investigation and ballsing it up... In my view, the bloke would be hard pressed to tell a gang leader from a counter assistant at McDonald's. I couldn't turn this down. If I did, the girl's killers might never be brought to justice.

'I've made up my mind,' I said. 'I know it's the right decision.'

'OK, Callum. See you at eight tomorrow morning. I'll get the paperwork done, then you can brief the team.'

'Thanks, boss.' I hesitated. 'Can I ask what's wrong?'

'Angina. The doc says I need a coronary bypass, I can't put it off any longer. Now, I've things to get on with. Get yourself a good night's sleep.'

Excitement bubbled through me. Senior Investigating Officer – for real, this time. The only downside was Pierce. How on earth had he managed to land the acting DCI slot? DI Martin Pierce – or 'Smiley' as some preferred – was knowledgeable, I had to admit. But there was something off about the man.

I headed into the house to tell Brendan the good news.

'Brendan! Where are you?'

On the kitchen table was a note.

Gone for a walk

Guilt pressed on me. I hadn't considered Brendan in coming to my decision. As SIO, I'd see even less of my son – how was I going to mend things between us now?

I decided to forego a celebratory glass of Prosecco, and set to work on my beard. Everyone in MIT55 would run away in fright if they saw me looking like this.

A discreet layer of stubble restored, I ran a comb through my wayward hair and assessed myself. Annoyingly, a few more grey hairs had sprouted among the dark brown ones. The remnants of handsome were clinging on, if you overlooked the deepening shadows around my eyes and my less-than-angular jaw. But at least now I looked the part.

Half an hour later Brendan hadn't returned, so I sat down on the bed, logged on and checked the crime scene photos on my laptop. I swore under my breath. The overlay of blood couldn't conceal the massive slice into the girl's chest or the brownish sludge dribbling out. What knife had caused such a wound? It had cut through her flesh as though it was a piece of sodding cake.

'Hey, Dad.' Brendan stood in the doorway.

I slammed the laptop shut. 'How was the walk?'

'Working again?'

'A new case.' I got to my feet. 'Let's go downstairs, I've got something to tell you.'

Over the kitchen table I explained about my new job, which would mean more responsibility and longer hours – and that I'd need to leave for London later the same day.

'What do you think, Bren?'

'It seems like a good opportunity. You don't need to turn it down because of me.'

'You're really OK with this?'

'Of course.' His tone was terse. 'It's your career, isn't it?'

He picked up his phone and started swiping the screen. Once again, I was left floundering. Almost everything Brendan said seemed laced with indifference, if not irony, sarcasm or outright aggression. If only I had Kate's ability to navigate the emotional complexities of family interactions... Though even she had had problems communicating with our son lately.

'There's no reason for you to cut short *your* holiday,' I pointed out. 'If you want to stay on here without me—'

'Nah, I'd rather be back in London anyway.' He kept on swiping. 'See my friends, do stuff.'

I nodded, letting go of my hopes for an honest conversation, even a modest celebration. The boat we were sailing in was definitely letting in water – could I mend the hole before the vessel was scuppered? The thought of losing Brendan, too...

'I'll get on with my packing,' I said, 'and make us a bite before we leave.' I'd have to leave soon to arrive home much before midnight.

'Do you think you'll catch them?' Finally, Brendan met my eyes. 'Whoever killed this girl.'

'You know I can never predict—' I stopped myself. 'I'll have to.'

As I zipped up my suitcase, doubts began to surface. Was I ready to throw myself into something that could take me further away from my son – and stretch me to my limits?

On a good day, I knew I was one of the best detectives in MIT55. But what about my attacks of insomnia? What about my bad dreams, irritable moods and angry outbursts? They were becoming more frequent, even if – so far – I was the only person who'd noticed. And how would I handle being held responsible for every aspect of a murder investigation? The ramifications of every questionable decision I made would come down on my head, sooner or later. What if I couldn't cope with the pressure? What if I wasn't up to the job?

LUKE

I'M SITTING ON THE FRONT STEP WATCHING OUT FOR KEVIN. He'll be here soon. He's always straight home after work. The air is heavy and wet: a big invisible sponge sucking up human breaths and lorry fumes and cat pee. It's like breathing soup. Lots of people pass by. Girls in skinny jeans pushing babies, old women pulling shopping. Kids in school in uniform arsing about, kids in hoodies on bikes, up to no good.

Our place is a few minutes' walk from the estate. You can see the high-rise tower from my bedroom window. Rows and rows of tiny windows. When we had nothing better to do, me and Kirsty used to spy on the people behind them with Kevin's binoculars. I always wondered what it was like in there.

Those fuckin' crackheads, Kevin says whenever anyone mentions the estate. *Thank Christ we're not living in that rabbit warren of misery and mayhem or I'd top myself.* Some people on the estate look like they're on smack or crack – skinny with dark hollows for eyes, always shuffling and scratching. I don't see how living there could be much worse than what it's like now though, inside this house. We're in a bigger hutch, that's all.

We've got three bedrooms, a lounge, a bathroom, a kitchen and a back garden full of weeds. It never gets any sun. Mum tried to grow flowers there but they all died. Our front garden is a thin strip a few steps back from the main road. It's full of bins now. Kevin is always telling us what bin to put things in. He works for the council's waste management service and says it's a waste of his life. Mum put a plant in one corner but it didn't flower and Kevin wanted to dig it up. They had a fight about that. Then three days before she died, five curly bright-red flowers like toilet brushes popped out. I told Mum. She said the plant was waiting for the right time.

Kirsty hurries out of the kitchen looking stressed.

'I can't find the can opener for the beans!'

'OK, Pixie. I'll come and look.'

She's got Mum's apron on. It hangs too low on her flat little chest. I adjust the apron so it's actually gonna be some use. Her hair's short again which makes her look about ten, though she'll be thirteen soon.

Kirsty and me both have Mum's wild hair and sad brown eyes. Soulful eyes, Kirsty says. We're only half- brother and sister as we've got different fathers. But in my head, she's one hundred per cent my sister.

'Need me to get something from the shop?'

'That's ok. There's five burgers and I'm doing the mash now. I'll have a go at roasting the chicken at the weekend.'

I wipe my eyes in case she sees them watering. It's not fair, my little sister having to do all this. Kevin tells me to keep out of the kitchen, cooking is woman's work. My job is to repair this place. Every week I'm supposed to do tasks in the house – sanding window sills, putting in light bulbs, fixing all the broken things he never gets round to fixing. He wrote them down for me:

Blinds in kitchen
Loose strip on back door
Shed door
Mould on bathroom wall

Mum liked me helping with cooking. Pastries, stews, curries.

Last week I was in the kitchen peeling potatoes. Kevin found me and grabbed the peeler out of my hand. *Are you trying to replace her or summin? We're gonna do things different from now on. Your mother ain't here to take your side no more.* He went on about how I must respect him now and do what he tells me. I told him I wasn't trying to replace Mum, I thought Kirsty might be getting hungry. No one had cooked dinner for us since the night before Mum died, except McDonald's and the chicken shop and Rita from next door. She came round with a pumpkin pie for us, said she didn't like to think of us going without. Kevin threw it in the bin and said we didn't need no one's help, or people sticking their beaks into our business.

I feel sorry for Kirsty for having him as her father. Mum tried to make me call him Dad, but I never did. He never called me 'son' either, just 'Luke' or 'boy' when he was angry at me. I was five when he moved in. I've no idea where my real father is. Mum said he went away after she told him about me. He came back to see me when I was eight but I was away on a school trip.

Now Mum's gone, the house has a big hole where she used to be. Singing to herself while she cooked and cleaned. Dancing in the kitchen, yakking to her friends about TV, recipes and living with teenagers.

All the time he's not at work, Kevin's sat on the sofa drinking Heineken and staring into space. Mum was taken from us for a reason, he told us, to punish us all for taking her for granted.

———

Kirsty's trying to keep the burgers warm in the pan but they're crisp and hard now. I turn the oven on and shove all the food in there. We've already set the table. I put the glossy purple flower I found in a garden down the road into our vase. Mum used to do that. Not get flowers from other people's gardens – she took any nice ones she saw from the park or along the canal. She said it was a waste to pay out for shop flowers.

Thinking of her doing her best to pretty up this place makes me well-up, I have to pretend there's something in my eye. I still can't get Mum outta my head. She comes into my dreams at night and pops in and out all day.

'You OK, Beamer?'

I go over to the table and take her hand. She's sitting in Mum's seat, the one without the knife and fork, doing her home-work. Her writing is way neater than mine and the words make proper sense. She's getting top grades still. It's weird how Mum dying has made her work harder and me the opposite. Things don't stay in my head anymore. All the things we have to remember for exams fall through my brain like sand in a sieve.

I miss Mum, I say.

Kirsty looks sad. I go and hug her. I close my eyes and wish for things to get better. When I let go, Kirsty's eyes are wet too. She squeezes her lips together and looks at the door.

'Do you think he'll like this meal?' Her eyes look up at me like I have all the answers, like I could make things right again.

'Who cares? If the food's fucked, it's his fault for being late.'

I wonder if Mum knows what's going on, wherever she is now. She said it's not anywhere we can find, like a house or a town. It's in the gaps of the real world, in quiet moments when the traffic's gone and you can hear the birds sing and a hush comes over your soul. Then you'll hear a soundtrack running beside the everyday things where everyone you've lost will come back and dry your eyes and whisper sweet words into your ears.

Me and Kirsty were sitting either side of Mum's bed in hospital, holding a hand each, when she said that. The day after she died, Kirsty saw a robin hop into our garden and start singing, and thought it was Mum come back.

———

It's gone half six when Kevin gets home. He clomps down the hall into the kitchen. I smell the fags before I see him. And the Hugo Boss aftershave to hide the pong of his sweaty armpits and garbage bins. He's in his suit, the one he wore to Mum's funeral.

'Hey, Dad,' Kirsty says in a careful voice, closing her books. 'We didn't know you'd be late. Dinner's in the oven. We waited for you.'

'I had a job interview, din I? Thought it might lead to summin better than this council lark.' His picks up the glass of water on the table and slams it down. Water slops out. 'Fuckin' waste of time, it was. One looked at me funny and the other wrote summin down. They asked four questions, that was it. Four measly questions!'

He stares at us. A frown is gouged into his brow like a tractor has run through it.

'They didn't give a hoot what I said, they'd made their minds up the job wasn't goin' to me. The whole thing was over in less than twenty minutes, then the blonde said, "You can go now, Mr Foster." She couldn't even get my name right, silly bint.'

He takes off his jacket and drops it onto the table. His belly flops over his trousers. There are dark stains on the back of his shirt.

He scowls at me. 'What are you starin' at?'

Kirsty gets up and takes her homework off the table. When we were waiting, I made the table look nice – added a square of folded kitchen roll next to each knife and fork, and a pot of mustard for him and ketchup for us.

While Kevin washes his hands, I give the *take care* signal to my sister – a cross made with the first finger of each hand. She nods and starts bringing the food over. Kevin sits down last, wincing as he lowers himself into the chair. His back has been playing up lately.

Suddenly, there's a noise above the house like a giant fan whirring. A police helicopter, I know without looking. They're always scooting about, looking out for criminals and escaped prisoners.

'Someone's been killed right outside the estate,' Kevin says. 'There's a tent on the street and tape up, cops everywhere. I saw it on my way past. Fuckin' hoodies up to their tricks again.'

I don't reply. I wonder who's been killed and who did it. I'm glad I never joined the gang on the estate.

'I tried to pick off the burnt bits,' Kirsty says. She serves Kevin a plate with two beef burgers, a pile of mash and peas. He looks at the food and sniffs it. Takes a mouthful of potato and starts to eat. He hasn't noticed the candle Kirsty got from the bathroom. Or the flower.

When the helicopter's gone, there's other sounds. Car engines revving, kids yelling. A wail starts up from next door – Jade's latest baby. Kirsty farts and giggles. I frown at her and she clamps a hand over her mouth. Kevin ignores us.

Something's wrong. My sister is looking at me with raised eyebrows. I shrug. I don't know what's up.

Kevin's staring at the vase. He points at the flower with his knife. At the top of the main stem is a big mauve flower, the lush kind you'd see in Africa or Jamaica. A yellow stamen pokes up through the middle of five petals. There's a splash of red at the bottom of the petals, like the flower is bleeding.

'What's the matter, Dad?'

Kevin looks at Kirsty then me. 'What is that? Who did that?'

My mouth goes dry. I feel the press of pee wanting to escape. I don't understand what's wrong.

'It's just a flower,' I say. 'I picked it from someone's garden.'

'It's a bloody hibiscus, knob end. Did you do that to wind me up?' He points his knife at me. 'Did you?'

'I thought it would look nice. I wanted to brighten the place up, like Mum used to do.'

He drops the knife. It clatters to the floor. He stands up, pushing his chair. It falls over.

'Your mum ain't fuckin' here, is she?' He digs me in the chest with his fingers. I've never seen him this angry before. 'She ain't comin' back, don't you understand?'

'It's only a flower, Dad. He didn't mean anything.'

Kevin jabs a finger at my sister. 'Shut your mouth, girl, unless you want a good hiding.'

He's never talked to Kirsty like that before. I can't believe it.

'Leave her alone, you bastard!'

I realise what I've said, sit frozen in my chair. My stepdad stares at me, his mouth open and his eyebrows meeting in the middle. His face is a weird reddish-purple, the colour of the flower.

'Jesus! What did you say?'

He pulls me to my feet, his burger breath in my face, draws his arm back. He's going to punch me. Years ago, Mum said she'd leave him if he hurt me again, and he stopped.

'Get outta my sight, boy.'

He pushes me hard in the chest. I stumble backwards. A shooting pain at the back of my head. My knees collapse and everything goes black.

I open my eyes. There's a *boom boom boom* inside my ears. Bright sparks appear in blackness. I'm hallucinating – or have I gone blind? A chink of light turns into a fuzzy patch of room. I see my sister kneeling in front of me, her eyes huge, her hand up to her open mouth. I can only hear the booming in my head.

Kevin's gone. I'm sat on the floor against the wall, a blanket over me. I move my hand up to where it hurts. My fingers come away sticky. The back of my head is numb. I'm floaty, coming back from somewhere far off. My thoughts are tangled up like a lump of overcooked spaghetti.

I can see the overturned chair behind Kirsty now. I lean forward to take my sister's hand. Pain shoots through my neck.

She looks scared.

'What happened?'

'Dad pushed you and your head hit the wall.'

Footsteps coming towards us, heavy. I stop breathing. His legs loom in front of me. My heart is a huge hammer that won't stop. What's he going to do now?

But he just puts the washing up bowl on the floor and sits down beside Kirsty. He pulls out a sponge and squeezes water out.

'I'm not gonna hurt you.' He brings the sponge up to the back of my head. 'Move your head down a bit, will ya?'

The sting of the sponge makes me gasp.

'It's OK, it's only a bit of water and Dettol. Keep still for a minute.' His voice is different. He sounds like the stepfather I used to know, the one who took us camping and to football matches, who wouldn't hurt me in a million years.

The water in the bowl goes a sludgy red after the sponge has been back a few times. Kirsty stares at the bowl and bites her bottom lip. She looks like she's going to cry. She doesn't, just a sound every so often like a sniff crossed with a hiccup. I wonder why he's doing this, if he feels guilty. I wish he would leave me alone.

He goes away. The kitchen light blasts into my eyes. I shut them and lower myself over my knees. I feel sick. The burgers don't want to stay inside.

'Luke. What's the matter?' Kirsty scans my face. 'Luke.' Her voice is high, shaky. 'Shall I call 999?'

'No need for that. We'll take care of him here.'

Footsteps from behind her. His cauliflower ears are still red but the rest of his face is back to normal. I vomit on the floor. Little turds of burger spew into a puddle.

'Kirsty, get the mop and clean this up.'

She comes back with the cleaning stuff and holds out a damp cloth. I wipe my face.

'Careful not to touch that stuff,' I say as I pass her the cloth. 'It might give you the lurgy.'

'Yeah, looks like it might.'

Kevin's back with the first aid box, a determined look on his face. He picks up the fallen chair and holds out his hand to me. 'Come sit here.'

I get to my feet without taking his hand, steady myself on the table. The room won't stay still. He guides me onto the chair, starts getting things out of the box and putting them on the table. Kirsty stands to one side.

'Don't just stand there! Get the gel pack.' Kevin tends to my head while Kirsty rummages in the freezer.

Kevin presses a gauze pad onto my injury. He tells me to hold it in place as he cuts up a bandage from the box. He wraps the bandage over it and round my head. He told me he had plenty of injuries in his boxing days. He was British amateur middleweight champion one year and became a pro boxer for a while, but he got hurt and had to stop.

'That'll sort you out, me boy.'

He looks concerned, like a real father would. But he can change in an instant. Usually, he makes do with banging his fists into his punch bag. When I was younger and I said or did something he didn't like, he'd belt me. One time, Mum stormed in and said she'd kill him if he ever touched me again. Afterwards, she told me he was angry at everyone because he'd had to give up boxing, even though that wasn't their fault.

Kirsty frowns at my stepdad. 'What if he's got concussion?'

'He ain't got fuckin' concussion.' Kevin rolls his eyes. 'Go and make us some tea, will you. That's a good girl.'

She opens her mouth like she's going to argue, then reaches for the kettle.

————

That night, I lie in bed listening to Kevin snoring in the room next door. Moonlight slants in through the gap in the curtains, bathing the room in cold white light.

The pain at the back of my head is only a throb now, like toothache. My neck hurts less but I can't get my head comfy on the pillow. I've taken all the ibuprofen pills Kevin gave me.

What did he hurt me for? I don't even know what I did. I think about what I'll do to pay him back. Horrible things. What if he has a go at me again? With Mum out of the way, he can do whatever he wants. I feel like one of those spare kittens people dump in the canal. I'm trying to swim but the bag won't open and the water's sucking me down.

————

Next morning, Kevin comes in early to check on me. I've got a headache and my neck is still sore. He says to call him if I feel any worse. Then he gets Kirsty up for school, leaves the bottle of painkillers out for me and goes to work.

'Hey.'

Kirsty comes into my room after I've dozed off. She's in her school uniform. Purple blazer, pleated skirt, white blouse. Her tie is on properly but her hair's a mess.

She speaks quietly. 'I'll stay and look after you. I don't need to go to school.'

I tell her I'm feeling better, she doesn't need to miss her lessons. She bends down, touches the bump on my head.

'What will you say at school about this?'

'It'll go down soon. No one will know.'

'What about your neck?'

'If anyone asks, I'll say it's whiplash, I was in a car accident. Like your dad said.'

'But it wasn't a car accident.' Her eyes flash with anger.

'No. But if we tell anyone what really happened, they might take us away from him. We might have to go into care. We'd be separated, more than likely. You might get fostered but no one wants to foster a sixteen-year-old boy.' I'll be sixteen in October, anyway.

She lowers her head, doesn't speak.

'Kirsty? Do you understand?'

'I know, we can't tell on him. But I can't bear for him to hurt you.'

'He won't hurt me anymore. I promise. Go on, get to school. You'll get in trouble for being late.'

We go to the same school, John Berriman Academy. They send letters to parents for the slightest things, if you're late more than three times a term, or you get a detention. Mum used to question us about any letters we got, tell us we were messing with our education. Kevin used to back her. Now, he doesn't seem to care.

'What do those tossers want now?' he said last week when a letter from the head of year came. I pulled it out of the kitchen bin. It said I hadn't done my homework recently and the school was concerned about me and wanted to know how I was adjusting after the loss of my mother.

'What is it, Kirst?'

Kirsty's lost in something again, something only she can see.

'There used to be those flowers in the garden,' she says. 'Remember?'

'What flowers?'

'The ones you put on the table.'

'Sort of.' But I don't care about the flowers.

When Kirsty's gone, I take out the photo from my *British Wildlife* book. I put it there so it'll be safe from Kevin. My real father left me a picture of him in his Marines uniform, the time he came to visit and I wasn't home.

You can't see his face properly, there's too much shadow. But you can tell he's proper handsome, he could be an actor with his blue eyes and moody stare. I get why Mum fell for the guy. She said she loved him more than anyone she'd ever loved, only he didn't love her like that.

On the back it says, *To my son, may you grow into a fine young man*.

I don't know why he didn't write my name, just *my son*. Maybe he has so many other sons, he forgot my name. Once I asked Mum why he didn't come to visit again and she said, 'He knows where we are, Luke. I'm not asking any more of him.' I looked at her. 'You can't always get what you want in life,' she said.

Sometimes, I dream he's come back and he takes me away from here.

As if. I'll have to find another way out.

CALLUM

THE 'STALAG' WAS AN ANONYMOUS THREE-STOREY BRICK building on the outskirts of Wood Green, where Major Incidents Team 55 was based. I arrived at an ungodly hour, nabbed a parking space then hauled myself to the top floor and shoved my box of granola bars into a drawer in a secluded corner desk inside Major Incident Room One.

'I expect to be back in three to four months,' DCI Andy Coleman explained at the 8.30am murder team briefing. 'DI Pierce will stand in for me as acting DCI and DI Waverley will take over as SIO for Operation Rye'. After a spate of concerned questions about his imminent surgery and good wishes for his recovery, Andy thanked everyone for their support and left the room.

DI Pierce was up next. I sat at the front table watching the startled, less-than-pleased faces as he turned to the rows of police officers and civilian specialists, and promised to do his best to fill the DCI's shoes. 'Though it will be difficult, I imagine,' Pierce muttered, looking down at his notes.

He wiped his brow, which shone moistly under his receding hairline, managing to look both stern and awkward at the same time. He finished his spiel with a hope that we would all 'pull together' while Andy was gone. Stony faces greeted him.

'Thank you, everyone. I'll let DI Waverley get on with the Operation Rye briefing.'

A dozen or so people stayed behind. I strode to the spot Pierce had vacated, hoping the Rye team would overlook the fact that only a week ago I'd thrown a giant wobbly and fucked off. Nerves churned in the pit of my stomach. The rooms on the top floor were, as usual, hot despite the air-con. I gulped a breath.

'Good morning, everyone. Most of you know me already, so I won't beat around the bush.' A lightning smile as I carried on, nipping in the bud any jokey asides. 'I'm pleased to say that I'm definitely back in action and keen to get going with Operation Rye. It's an honour to be picked to run this one. I hope I'll do the DCI proud – I hope we all will.'

Andy, I meant of course, not Acting DCI Pierce. But everyone seemed to know who I meant. I caught a smirk from DC Perry – known to everyone in the murder team as 'Ferret' because he kept two of the creatures as pets – and his mates in the back row. DS Harper gave me a warm smile. DS Freeman – his iPhone temporarily out of reach – gave me a thumbs-up and DS Rowan tentatively raised his eyebrows. I'd worked with all three sergeants before, without any problems arising. But this was going to be a very different experience.

I scanned the room, checking Smiley hadn't stayed on to surreptitiously observe the proceedings. The briefing would be difficult enough without him picking holes in my performance.

'Let's get down to the incident yesterday afternoon. It was a brutal attack in broad daylight, just a few miles from here.'

Quiet settled on the room as I put up the first slide – a photo of a girl lying on her back on the pavement. Details struck me. The small rucksack poking out from underneath her shoulder, its zip pocket decorated with a dolphin. The whiteness of her rolled-down socks against her black legs. Her hair, unstraightened and unbraided, neatly fastened into a pony tail with a white scrunchy decorated with red spots – when I'd first seen them on my laptop, I'd not realised they were blood.

I stared at the spots; aware I was breathing hard. This close to the extra-wide high-res screen, every detail of the girl's demise was horrifically apparent. Heat flared in my core. What psycho nutjob thought they could get away with something like this? I pushed the anger down as best I could. Control rods definitely needed.

'The victim was Solita Milton,' I said, hoping no one could hear the quiver of emotion in my voice. 'She was fifteen years old. Her mother identified the body yesterday. The girl was seen walking home from school shortly before she was killed. Two males with their hoods pulled up were spotted about fifty metres from the main entrance of Effra Lane estate outside a nearby park, shortly before four o'clock. Witnesses at a nearby bus stop saw the bigger of the pair pull out a zombie-style knife and stab the girl in the chest. He was wearing a balaclava or ski mask with a skull image on it, which hid his face. Solita screamed and collapsed.' I took a deep breath. 'The killers were seen running into the estate's main entrance. Emergency services were called at 4.02pm and Solita was pronounced dead at 4.08pm. A search of the estate was conducted as soon as officers arrived, but failed to locate the killers.'

I turned to DS Freeman. 'Any response yet to our appeal for witnesses on the website and social media?'

'No more witnesses have come forward, sir. No one admits to

seeing the offenders on the estate in the minutes following the stabbing. No one saw their faces or knows who they are.'

That was hardly a surprise. I pressed on.

The next slide was a map of north London gang territories. I pointed to a close-up of an area just over a mile north-east of central Tottenham.

'A gang called the Skull Crew are based on the Effra Lane estate. My guess is that the killers were members of this gang. As I understand it, the Skull Crew split off from a larger gang a few years ago and became the dominant gang on the estate and in the immediate area.' I glanced at heads nodding and pens scribbling. *My team*, I thought, with pride and a spike of trepidation. 'But someone else knows a lot more about them than I do. Over to Sandra, our newly arrived gang expert.'

I nodded to a woman in her early thirties with short black hair and functional glasses that didn't conceal the thick dark sweep of her eyebrows. She wore a high-necked top with a knee-length skirt. DS Sandra Hanna had recently transferred to MIT55 from Walthamstow gangs unit. She had joined Operation Rye at Andy's request and supposedly knew everything there was to know about gangs.

'There's a lot we don't know about this gang,' she began in a quiet voice. Her manner was reserved – nerves, or something else? Her skin tone and features suggested Middle-Eastern, perhaps North African heritage. I wondered how much border-line racist shit she'd had to deal with in the Met. She wouldn't have any of that on my watch, not if I could help it.

'What we do know... Intel suggests that their members are male, aged roughly twelve to thirty, mostly British-born, of different ethnicities. Drugs are their number one business. They sell class A drugs on the streets of north London and towns all over the south-east. The gang is believed to be behind several brutal assaults. They are known for the intimidation of all those who get in their way. They've used a variety of methods, including death threats. Lately they've made serious attempts to control the local area. Residents of the estate, and local business owners, have faced extortion – unfortunately, they're usually too frightened to come to us with information.'

'Do we have any gang members' names yet, boss?'

I glared at DS Rowan, who looked as lean and modelish as usual. His cocky swagger hadn't gone. Thanks for putting me on the spot, smart arse.

'Yes Jon, I'm sure we do. And if we don't, you'll sure as hell need to come up with some before too long.' Sniggers from the back row. 'Sandra, do you want to comment on that?'

'Michael Gabriel is one of the elders – street name 'Angel' – he's been in prison for GBH,' DS Hanna said in a more confident voice. 'We know of a few others who have been arrested.'

She gave further names, then looked pointedly at Rowan. 'Unfortunately, most gang members do their best to keep well out of our way.'

'Thanks, Sandra.' She had handled that well. 'On to the PM.'

The attending officer updated us on the post-mortem, not yet finished. Early results suggested that the cause of death was acute heart failure from a traumatic aortic rupture when a single stab wound to the chest penetrated the heart.

'As far as the knife goes, the blade is estimated to be thirteen inches long. It was pushed in to the hilt and passed right through the victim's heart. From the extent of the damage, it was probably serrated on the upper edge.'

A hush fell over the room.

'OK, our main lines of enquiry.' I gestured at the screen, showing a map of known CCTV cameras in the Effra Lane council estate and nearby streets. 'Can we have an update on the CCTV?'

Only two of the council's cameras were working, according

to the balding DC usually known as Combover. 'They've picked up the two offenders. Three others didn't pick up anything because the lights nearby were broken.'

Combover played the first CCTV segment marked 'Camera 1'. It was rubbish quality, showing two blurred figures in balaclavas running towards the estate. One was carrying a rucksack; the other was a big guy who looked like he spent all his time at the gym. You couldn't see much uncovered skin. What there was could have been black, white or purple. Video from the other camera, taken a minute or two later from outside the estate's housing office, showed two males walking towards the central area. It didn't look like the balaclavas were on but their hoods were still up, hiding their faces.

After more low-res stills of the men, I couldn't supress a sigh of frustration. Why were council cameras so shit? How would anyone be able to identify the killers from this?

'Any thoughts?'

DS Freeman, clad in his usual grey cords and fading polo shirt, waved his huge paw at me. 'The bigger one is white, I'd say. The one carrying the rucksack looks black.'

'The bastards know where the cameras are,' DS Rowan observed. 'And the smaller one doesn't shave.'

'Hmm.' DS Harper put down her coffee cup and blinked at the screen.

I clicked up stills from the next video. The same two men were strolling past a lamp post, their hoods up. The quality was even worse.

'That's from the camera at the Effra Lane recreation ground,' Combover said. 'It's the only camera outside the estate that the offenders have shown up on. This is close to the spot they were seen waiting for the victim.'

'The question is, did her killers know Solita would be passing the park on her way home from school?' I sipped my coffee, the foul machine brew. 'Was this a planned attack? Or was she in the wrong place at the wrong time?'

DS Harper jiggled her hand. 'Solita called her mum around three fifteen yesterday to say she'd be late home. She talked to her history teacher for about fifteen minutes after class about a GCSE project and ended up walking home alone, rather than with a friend as she usually did. Looks like she unexpectedly ended up walking home alone – and her killers pounced.'

DS Rowan's hand shot up. 'But why would they attack her outside the estate while a load of kids were getting off the bus, rather than inside it, where there'd be fewer witnesses?'

'Maybe fewer cameras outside?' DS Harper suggested.

'Not necessarily fewer witnesses.' DS Freeman pushed his bulky six feet three inches frame up from his chair. He was the biggest member of MIT55 and made the biggest belches. 'We were told there were kids hanging around inside the entrance. Also, there were people walking between the blocks. At four in the afternoon, the estate would have been crawling.'

'Let's have the stills sent to the local team and the gangs unit, see if anyone recognises these two.' I looked around for the PolSA. 'Have the search team found the murder weapon yet?'

''Fraid not, sir. All communal areas of the Effra Lane estate have been searched, plus nearby streets, towpaths, so forth. We did find a few interesting things on the estate though. A bag of cannabis was stashed underneath the slide in the children's playground and some underwear was found behind the bin area.' The older redhead paused, her face deadpan. 'A matching dark blue lace set from John Lewis.'

'The wrong size?' remarked DC Perry. Laughter from the group beside him.

'That's enough, ladies and gents.' I perched on the table and took another sip of tepid instant coffee. 'How's the house-to-house going?'

'Nothing of interest yet. It'll take a week at least to get to everyone, I reckon,' the house-to-house enquiries coordinator replied. Her team were going door-to-door on the estate. 'The council told me one thousand four hundred and thirty-five people live on the Effra Lane estate. I reckon it's closer to two thousand.'

'Any indication as to who these two might be?'

'No one's given us any names, though a kid of ten said, "try asking the crew." I had a feeling some know exactly who the offenders are but they're either scared to say, they don't trust us or they just don't want to help. Lots aren't even bothering to answer their doors.' She rolled her eyes. 'Can't be arsed to get involved.'

Feeling a twinge of déjà vu, I pressed on. 'Where are we with forensics?'

'No prints or fibres have been found. We're still checking DNA samples from the victim's body and nearby,' came the crime scene manager's reply.

With any luck, the DNA testing would yield some clues as to the offenders' identities.

'Sam, you've been talking to the victim's mother?'

DS Harper nodded, tucking a long strand of dyed auburn hair behind her dainty ear. The pink streaks were almost gone, after DCI Coleman had complained they didn't look very professional. Sam was of Pakistani origin and had naturally black, glossy hair. Though she encouraged everyone to call her Sam, her first name was actually Samaira.

'I talked yesterday to Bev Milton. She was distraught, I couldn't get much out of her. She's a primary school teacher. She lives on the estate with Solita and her other daughter, Leonie. Her husband died six years ago. Solita had lots of friends and was doing well at school. She was a keen member of the Scouts and had planned to study social work at uni.'

Sam blinked and dabbed at her eye. Her contacts often seemed to cause her trouble; I guessed that wasn't the problem this time. I turned again to our gangs expert.

'Sandra, any indication that Solita was involved with gangs?'

DS Hanna rubbed the nape of her neck, her diffident manner back.

'Not Solita herself. But her older brother Jayden popped up on the local matrix. He's twenty-four, also known as "Doc". Her eyes flicked to her notes. 'He was put away six years ago for possession of an offensive weapon and served eighteen months. Back then he was believed to be gang-affiliated. There's no intel on current gang membership.'

As DS Hanna sat down, DS Harper spoke up.

'Solita's mum told me she thinks Jayden used to be in a gang, but she doesn't know what it's called or anything about it, or the names of any of his friends or associates. I got the feeling she was lying.'

Could Solita's mother be covering for her son? I made a mental note to ask her a few questions myself.

'We need to find out if the brother has any connection to Solita's death,' I said, turning to DS Freeman. 'Rob, see if you can dig up anything on social media that might help us find him, and keep an eye out for any gang members posting about the murder. But please don't fall down the Instagram rabbit hole.'

Laughter rippled around the incident room. DS Freeman's phone constantly pinged with social media notifications. Work-related, he insisted. He could play the fool at times, but I liked him.

'We know the Skull Crew are based on the local estate,' I carried on. 'I don't want to exclude alternative theories so early on, but it looks to me as if they're involved in this. Sandra?'

'I agree, sir, they're the most likely to be behind this. This gang is ruthless and they want people to know that. They want to be seen as beyond justice, to spread fear in the community so people won't come forward about their crimes. That helps with recruitment, too.'

I nodded. 'Now, the motive. Why was Solita killed? Could she have been mistaken for someone else? Did she witness a crime and have to be silenced? Could it be a revenge attack? We know Solita's older brother was gang-involved. If he went missing due to a beef with the Skull Crew, could his sister have been targeted for retribution?'

'Absolutely, she could.' DS Hanna spoke up. 'Revenge attacks by gangs on gang members' family are increasingly common,' she said, 'often targeting brothers and male cousins but sisters some-times if those aren't available.'

'Unusual for a young girl to be murdered,' a DC called out. 'Someone must have been pretty hacked off.'

DS Rowan chimed in. 'Maybe she saw something she shouldn't have? Hard to believe that someone would do some-thing like this just because she was a gang member's sister.'

I interrupted. 'We'll need to keep working on the motive. Right, next steps. I want to identify and track down the two suspects asap...' I tasked the remaining actions on my list, including a talk to Solita's friends and classmates. 'Any questions?'

DS Rowan jabbed his hand in the air.

'If this is planned, how would the killers have known that this girl was going to come home alone yesterday?'

Another good point – or was it designed to trip me up?

'Maybe they didn't know. They may have watched her leave school every day for weeks, waiting for when she'd be alone. Or maybe they got lucky first time and went ahead when they saw she was alone. Maybe they would have killed her anyway, even if she hadn't been alone. We just don't know at this stage.' I caught

DS Harper's eye. 'Any particular reason Solita was in the habit of walking home with her friend?'

'Her mum told me she was worried about Solita coming home alone as some girls on the estate had been harassed and threatened by boys – a girl was assaulted behind the bin shed a few months ago. But it could be that she was worried for a more specific reason.'

'As in, she thought her daughter might be targeted by members of her son's gang?' It was a chilling thought. I got to my feet. 'Let's get down to work. I have faith in all of you, I know you're going to do your utmost to get Solita's killers put away.'

I headed outside to get a proper coffee. The air was mercifully fresh. Relieved to be out of the hothouse, I strolled along the narrow street behind our building to Lorenzo's.

So, I'd survived the first test of my new job. Apart from Rowan's terrier-like interjections and a handful of detectives trying it on at times, nothing stood out as a cause for concern. Going by the engaged faces and the absence of whispering and snickering, the Operation Rye team had reacted well to me. They were a capable bunch. If luck was on our side, this investigation should go well.

16TH JULY: AFTERNOON

I hurried away from the mortuary towards the Ford Mondeo, wondering if I should have eaten two granola bars for breakfast at my desk. My stomach wasn't happy, to say the least. The post-mortem had been worse than I'd expected, despite the dab of Vicks up my nose. No matter how many times I attended one, that sickly-sweet smell of putrefying flesh always got to me.

This time, it hadn't only been the smell. It was Solita Milton's small, helpless body, exposed to all those probing eyes and sharp instruments. It was the ripped-open chest, the blood congealing in the hollows of her throat, the expression of disbelief imprinted on her face.

Air-con up full blast and air rushing in through the opened windows, I drove to my next destination as fast as traffic allowed, through avenues of once-grand three-storey houses. Below crumbling facades, litter drifted. People too, had an air of melancholy – not surprising, given this end of the borough had one of London's worst figures for serious violent crime. It was home to an array of gangs and drug dealers, along with organised criminal networks which imported much of the heroin supplying them.

Effra Lane itself was a drab mixture of terraced houses and low-rise blocks. I parked in a side street and walked towards Effra Lane estate. It was unpleasantly fumy and hot; the early afternoon traffic flowed in a steady torrent. That conversation in Wales which had brought me here seemed like weeks ago, not yesterday.

The police cordon took in the width of the pavement and a broad slice of the main road. Its centrepiece was a bus stop. At the end closest to the estate's front entrance, a female PC stood guard. Behind her, heaped against the wall, a shrine was growing – flowers in plastic wrappers, candles and handwritten messages. I took in what I could, telling myself that this wasn't prying.

To darling Sol, love you always
RIP Solita, you were the best
To my gorgeous friend, luv u forever
Fuck SC you didn't deserve this

'How's it going?' I showed my ID and told her who I was.

'All quiet now,' she replied. 'There was quite a fuss yesterday. Reporters blocking the road. Lots of the public too, having a gander.'

I suited up in the mobile SOCO unit and walked the length of the cordon. Inside the forensic suit, gloves, face mask and hood, sweat boiled off me. The stretch of pavement beside the tiny front gardens of a row of terraced houses looked ordinary enough but for the dark, ragged stain on the pavement. A few metres away, the bus stop and shelter were out of action. The sign indicated that three bus routes stopped there.

I wondered again at the audacity of the killers, striking beside a well-used bus stop, practically outside a busy estate as a bus was pulling up, at one of the busiest times of day. Had there been an element of impulse, even desperation, in the stabbing? Or had the crime been executed as planned, the killers counting on no one coming forward to identify them? The second option seemed more likely, given the skull mask. Whoever had done this wanted to send a message to the area's residents: *This is what you get if you fuck with us.*

After a further stroll around to visualise the geography of the scene – the cordoned-off front entrance and the park entrance a stone's throw further on – I was ready to expire. I de-suited and headed through the pedestrian entrance of Effra Lane estate.

I'd visited the council housing complex a few times for a serious domestic violence incident, back in my first months as a detective with the local CID. The estate wasn't far from the Spurs stadium and roughly the same size, though rather less pleasant to visit, it had to be said. I must have looked a good deal younger back then – a kid had asked me if I smoked anything. I'd been teased for weeks after that. DS Freeman assured me that not much had changed; the estate's dealers were happy to provide weed, crack or smack for the cost of a few bars of chocolate. They were a bit more careful who they sold to these days, though.

The footpath took me through a grassy area flanked by tatty four-storey blocks, with flaking sills and discoloured walls, a playground flanked by a low fence and untidy shrubs, empty of children. Rust and graffiti covered much of the play equipment. Dismal, all of it. The further I went inside, the more I had an urge to turn around. Behind the taped-off area, lay a central strip – the housing office, residents' centre and a shoebox-sized barber's with no one inside. I hurried past. Above, the estate's two high-rise blocks peered down. A group of youths, white and darker-skinned – school age, roughly – stopped kicking a football and stared at me from an area of withered grass. Their backward glances ranged from wary to hostile.

I skirted the first block and headed to Luther Tower. Inside a cubby hole on the ground floor, an overweight man in uniform slumped over the *Daily Mail*.

'No one's allowed in, unless they're—' He'd seen my warrant card.

The lift smelt of chips and piss. A teenage girl approached. I stepped further inside, expecting her to get in. She glared at me, shook her head and darted off.

The ninth-floor corridor stretched out ahead. I passed doors of various colours, my footsteps sinking noiselessly into the material coating the floor, and stopped outside the pale blue door belonging to Bev Milton.

A girl in her early teens wearing a floral dress opened the door. She was as tall as her mother and as skinny as an eight-year-old.

'Hello, Leonie?' I said through my hastily donned mask. 'Is your mum in? It's the policeman to see her. I called earlier.'

The girl nodded and hurried inside. A woman returned, in her forties, somewhat overweight with short, straightened black hair and red-framed glasses. The black skin of her brow glistened. A loose T-shirt hung over her jeans and flat sandals.

'Mrs Milton? Hello, I'm Detective Inspector Callum Waverley. I'm leading the investigation into Solita's murder.' From instinct I started to offer my hand, then dropped it. Damn Covid.

Bev Milton looked at me, face uncomprehending.

'Oh, I'm sorry, I'm all over the place today. Hello, I'm Bev Milton. Solita's mother.' She spoke softly with precise diction.

'Pleased to meet you, Mrs Milton. I'm sorry to intrude on your grief. I wanted to introduce myself, I won't keep you long.'

I followed her into the narrow hall. She moved sluggishly and paused at the first doorway, gesturing inside. I took a seat in the nearest armchair. Bev Milton sat in another armchair, on the other side of the fireplace. The modestly-sized room was neat, clean and smelled of flowers. Bookshelves covered most of one wall.

Leonie peeped around the door. 'Shall I put the flowers in the vase?'

'Thanks, love.' Bev Milton looked back at me. 'You'll have to forgive me if I'm not totally coherent.'

'No need to apologise, Mrs Milton. I can hardly imagine what you're going through.'

She tapped beside her mouth. 'Don't wear that on my account, I'm double-jabbed.' I removed the mask. The woman stared at a spot on the floor, her shoulders slumped. 'How could they have done that to my little girl?' Her sobs were quiet and small at first. Her chest and shoulders began to heave, tipping her pendant on its side. 'She's the kindest, gentlest girl you could ever imagine.' She plucked a tissue from a box on the floor. 'I'm sorry. Please, carry on.'

This was one of the worst parts of the job; having to witness the grief of bereaved families. I yearned to feel less useless in the face of their misery, and could never quash the sense that it was wrong to see them as anything other than victims.

Bev Milton dried her face and composed herself. She confirmed she'd given Mihai, the family liaison officer, a photo of

Solita for the press conference later in the afternoon. Mihai was a cheerful chap who instinctively knew what to say to grieving families. He'd told her that we had two suspects.

'Neither have been identified as yet,' I said. 'But we're doing our best to discover who they are and to find them.'

My eyes rested on a framed photo on the mantelpiece, of a serious, grey-haired black man strumming a guitar.

'That's my late husband, Lou. He passed three years ago.'

Further along, a photo of a young man with similar features. 'Your son?'

She didn't reply immediately.

'That's Jayden, yes. I told your officer yesterday, I haven't seen him recently.' A defensive tone had entered her voice.

'My colleague said you believed Jayden was involved with a gang,' I ventured. 'Can you tell me anything about that?'

'Nothing more than what I said before. I don't know the name or anything about it. He was on the fringes of gangs for a few years when he lived with us.'

'How long ago was that?'

She frowned. 'Before he went to prison... Seven, eight years ago.'

'What work does Jayden do, Mrs Milton?'

'He trained to be an electrician. He hasn't done that since he got out... He's been going through a difficult patch.'

'Has he been in any trouble with anyone, as far as you know?'

Another pause. 'Not as far as I know.'

'Do you have any idea where Jayden might have gone?'

'I don't know, I'm sorry. I haven't heard from him since early June. He said he was heading out of London for a bit, he needed to sort himself out.'

She wasn't going to help us. 'OK, Mrs Milton—'

A fleeting smile. 'You can call me Bev.'

'Thanks for your help, Bev. I'll be off now. I'll update you as soon as we have any news.'

'Do you think you'll find him?'

'Him?' Who was she talking about? She knew there were two suspects.

'The men who killed her, I mean. Do you think you'll find them?'

'I'll do everything in my power to find whoever killed your daughter and bring them to justice,' I replied, searching her face. Whether or not she was lying, she was definitely holding something back. 'Do you have any information at all that might help us find them, Bev?'

Her hands clutched each other in her lap and she opened her mouth as if to speak. Then her face closed down.

'I don't, no. Sorry Callum, I can't help you.'

This probably wasn't the right time, but I might as well get it over with.

'You told DS Harper that Solita usually came home from school with a friend, because you were worried about her safety?'

'Girls were being threatened on the estate.'

'By gang members?'

'That's what people say.'

'There was nothing else you were concerned about?'

She cocked her head, squinting at me. 'What else would there be?'

I got up to leave, saying I'd see her at the press conference later.

At the end of the corridor, on impulse I took the door to the exterior walkway and peered down over the guardrail. Tiny figures moved over the concrete below. I felt myself sway. Heart racing, I pulled back. I'd never manage, living up here. Luckily, I didn't have to.

I took the stairs down. Small piles of dirt and broken glass had been swept into the stairwell's corners. Outside, hip-hop blared from a portable sound system on a bench. The group of young men clustered around it watched me, expressions closed off, suspicious. As I strode away, I saw graffiti on the tower's side wall. At eye level, words in white aerosol:

DON'T LET THEM GET AWAY WITH IT

Beside that, in smaller, bright-red letters:

DONT SAY NUTTIN
OR YOU WILL BE DEAD TOO

Beside the last word, sprayed in white paint, a representation of a skull. I hurried towards the exit, my queasiness growing – a feeling of icky unease, not simply the after-effects of vertigo, or having to watch the body of an innocent girl being manipulated with cold instruments in front of detached professionals. It was the whiff of complicity that permeated this place.

———

Back in Wood Green, I managed to track down the covert ops manager to a small, untidy office. DI Nigel Kenyon was well over six-foot and seemed too tall for the space. He stood up from his desk and gave a brisk nod.

'Good to meet you, Callum.'

'Good to meet you too—' I'd been about to say 'Nigel' but it seemed wrong to use his first name. He was pushing sixty and had an odd, fusty manner.

'Make yourself comfortable.'

I sat down in a scuffed leather armchair, deciding not to beat around the bush. This was all new to me; the DCI had handled all meetings relating to intel gathering. But I wasn't going to let DI Kenyon intimidate me.

'I need a surveillance team based on the estate, to identify and trace our two suspects asap,' I began.

His right eye twitched as he studied me. 'It's the obvious place to start looking.'

Torn-off pieces of paper skittered under a desk fan. DI Kenyon's long frame wilted over his desk, making me think of an overgrown plant. I waited for him to say something else, but he didn't.

'I'll also need to find out about their roles in the Skull Crew and more about who's running it, where they live and so on.'

'Sounds about right.' His eye twitched again.

We went over the details and agreed that the team would need to work undercover, given the risks of deployment on a council estate.

'A separate undercover officer would be useful to gather intelligence,' I added.

He nodded vigorously. 'Of course it would.'

'Well, that's great... Thank you.' What a weirdo. 'Will you get me an estimate of the cost and I'll run it past the superintendent.' Whatever. I had no idea how all this worked.

Eager to escape, I sped down the corridor. Back at my desk I emailed Pierce's boss, Detective Superintendent Bailey – I didn't want Pierce to somehow scupper this – with the gist of what DI Kenyon and I had agreed, asking for a decision asap. It wouldn't take too long, I hoped. In the meantime, we'd have to make do with local officers keeping an eye out on the estate.

Driving home at the end of my first day as SIO, I was knackered.

The day's final hurdle had been the media briefing held at the crime scene. Bev Milton had started to read out her statement but had broken off at the end of the first sentence, sobbing. Mihai had read out the rest.

'My life has been shattered by the death of my daughter. She was a beautiful angel, the light of my life. I don't know how I will carry on without her. I pray that the people who did this will be caught.'

We were doing everything we could to identify the killers, I told the crowd of reporters. Anyone with information that could help us find Solita's killers should contact the inquiry team, no matter how insignificant it might seem. Regarding the motive, we were keeping an open mind while pursuing key lines of enquiry. The attack appeared to be highly targeted and there was little risk of further attacks on members of the public.

'Are you confident you'll be able to find the killers?'

I didn't hesitate, though the clean-up rate of gang-related murders in London was significantly lower than the overall rate.

'Yes, we'll find them. Make no mistake about that.'

Then, surprise, surprise, DI Pierce had turned up in a suit that wouldn't have looked out of place on an investment banker, introduced himself as acting DCI in overall charge MIT55 and proceeded to get his smarmy smile snapped by a brace of reporters.

Afterwards, Pierce had come up to me.

'Well done, mate. You've been boning up on press briefings, I see. You'll be the MIT's shining star, soon.'

Shining star, my arse. I bit hard into my Mars Bar, which collapsed satisfyingly in my mouth. I'd be home soon, thank goodness. I was looking forward to pounding the hell out of the running machine – it might help get me forget about that man long enough to relax.

What was it about Pierce? Ever since his transfer into MIT55 two and a half years ago, we'd rubbed each other up the wrong way. I disliked his racist, homophobic views but those weren't exactly rare in the Met. It was something else. Beneath Smiley's charming demeanour lay – I would put money on it – if not duplicity exactly, a certain sneakiness. I'd have to watch him.

I pulled up outside the house, yawning. Brendan's light was still on upstairs. It was way past dinnertime, but at least I'd have a chance to say goodnight.

LUKE

LATE JULY

It's baking. I'm standing under one of the lime trees near the community centre. Except for worn areas of grass, they're the only green things on the estate. A tower stands over us, windows glinting like dirty jewels. It's another world in here. From this part you can't see anything beyond the estate.

I've been coming here a while, on and off. It's somewhere to go on days when Kirsty is doing something in the house and Manny can't come out and I don't feel like being alone. Last summer, me and Manny were together all the time. Now, most times I call by he says he has to study or his mum will kill him. I know studying is just an excuse. His mum has told him I'm bad news.

'Yo, Luke. Wah gwan, man?'

It's Minty, the small darkskin kid. Always chewing spearmint gum when he's not talking or taking the piss. He's on his bike today. Keeping his bum on the saddle, he leans the bike and plants a perfectly clean Nike on the ground.

We spud.

'Where you off to?' I ask.

'Got a job to do.' He raises his eyebrows like it's a furtive mission for MI5. 'A delivery.'

'Wanna play footy later?' I don't like soccer that much. But Minty likes to practise with anyone who's up for it. I'm bored too. The holidays are going on too long and I need something to take my mind off Mum.

'I dunno. Gotta go home now and look after me little bruv.'

Minty bumps his trainer in the patch that used to be grass. Dirt puffs up in a cloud. He seems serious for a change. Minty's always messing around. He hides behind walls and jumps out at visitors when they're studying the signs showing maps of the estate, and calls out rude things at residents who complain about hooligans taking over the place. He lives in Godwin House with his mum, uncle, grandad, brother and sister. He's in the same year as me. He goes to the Catholic boys' school near the academy. Used to, anyway. He was excluded for stealing phones. He's soccer mad, always kicking a ball around and talking about his hero, Dele Alli. He's got a try-out at Spurs soon, for their junior team or something.

'Has your stepdad hit you again?' He peers at my eye, blood-shot since I woke up this morning.

I make a face. 'Course not. If he touches me again, I'll kill him.'

Minty looks like he doesn't believe me. 'You should roll with us, bruv. The crew will keep you safe. We won't let no one touch you.'

He's one of the Skull Crew youngers. He's been rolling with them about a year, since his sister got sick and his mum had to take a second job. He says he gives all the cash he earns to his mum, except for what he needs for football kit.

I shrug, awkward. I don't want to turn down his offer but I don't want to be part of the gang and I can't say, My mum would kill me if I got in with your crew. I'll never forget what she did when the gang on the estate tried to recruit me. I was thirteen. One of them kept offering me tenners to do things for him. She found them, prised it out of me, all the details, said didn't I see turkey written across my head, they were grooming me to be a drug dealer. If I didn't want to be dead in five years, I'd better keep away from them. Then she made me gargle with soapy water for saying we could do with the money.

'See ya, then.' Minty rolls gum around his mouth.

'Yeah, see ya.'

He cycles off.

My eyes stray to three guys in the distance. Two darkskins, one white. They're older than me. Their chests are sculpted under their vests. The white guy – the biggest one – has a dark brown buzz cut, a thick gold chain round his neck and wears military style trousers full of pockets. He looks mean.

I can't take my eyes off the lazy sway of their walk, how their faces give nothing away. They have to be gang members.

There's a white girl with them. She's slightly ahead, on the outside of the group. She says something and smiles and the white guy says something back. She's younger than them, my age. I know her from somewhere. From my school, that's it. The girl who turned up halfway through last school year.

She's pretty. Shiny dark brown hair falling down her bare back. Strappy top, shorts, sandals and big yellow plastic sunglasses. A small leather bag on a gold chain hangs at her hip. She doesn't seem the kind of girl who would live round here.

They go and sit against the wall of the community centre, in the shade of the tower. One brings out a roll-up. They pass it between them. The girl takes her turn and passes it on, resting her head back against the wall as she exhales. A scent of weed drifts over. I want to stay watching her but I turn away before they see me.

CALLUM

2ND AUGUST

'I'M GETTING A RIGHT BLOODY EAR-BASHING OVER THIS GIRL'S murder,' Bailey said, before I could sit down. We're in his office at New Scotland Yard. I watched his foot jiggling up and down under his desk. 'Everyone wants to know how long it's going to take for us to nail the killers.'

It was our first meeting to discuss the progress of Operation Rye. Detective Superintendent Bailey, a milky-faced man with bushy ginger eyebrows, matching moustache and over-shiny shoes, gave the impression of an old-fashioned army officer.

'I understand you're curtailed by a lack of evidence.' He twirled his moustache disconsolately. 'To be frank though, I could have done with further signs of progress.'

My instinct, as always, was to fight back. There was nothing I would have done differently; I was facing external factors beyond my control. I took a deep breath. There was nothing to be gained by retaliating or defending myself. Bailey knew the situation.

Nearly three weeks on, we had yet to arrest anyone for Solita Milton's murder. We hadn't even identified our suspects. So far, all lines of enquiry had led to zilch. House-to-house visits had yielded no further sightings of the suspects around the time of the murder, and no one would tell us who the two men were. We hadn't managed to find Solita's brother, Jayden Milton. He hadn't posted on his Facebook in two months – DS Freeman had tried to track him through mentions in friends' posts without success. DNA testing had reached a dead end – no foreign DNA had been found on the victim's body. The only hard evidence we had was the CCTV footage of our two suspects.

Nor did we have any motive for Solita's murder – only the fact of her brother's recent disappearance and his possible link to the gang that were based on the estate where she lived. None of the leads we'd checked out had provided any reason why someone might have wanted Solita dead. We'd talked to friends, classmates and contacts. We'd gone through the phone numbers she'd dialled and calls she'd received in the months before her death and nothing suspicious had been found. Solita had been well liked and seemed to have had no troubles beyond the normal worries of an adolescent girl.

Bailey leaned over his large, neat desk.

'You still think she was killed because of the brother, rather than it being a random attack?'

'I do, sir.' Despite the lack of evidence, I was convinced that the reason Solita had been killed was connected to her brother. 'It was some sort of twisted revenge, maybe. Nothing else makes any sense.'

The super's formidable eyebrows met, forming a ginger hedge above his stern gaze. His foot started jiggling again.

'I very much hope we'll be in a position to charge the suspects soon, Callum.'

'So do I, sir. I'll keep on giving the operation my utmost.'

I left the building swearing under my breath, my gut twinging ominously. I'd been prepared for this meeting. Of course, a high-profile investigation like this was going to be accompanied by hectoring from above, and I knew well enough that I didn't react well to twats in authority. However, I wasn't prepared for the reality of being chastised for something beyond my control. It stuck in my craw. What the fuck did the super want me to do – manufacture the bloody evidence myself and pin it on some random men on the estate? The operation would take as long as it took.

From habit, I took out my phone and started tapping out a text to Kate.

Having a crap day...

Shit. How had I forgotten? My wife didn't want to hear from me anymore.

I put the phone away.

———

Back at Wood Green, acting DCI Pierce looked pleased about something when we crossed paths outside the men's room.

'Been in with Bailey?' His eyes gleamed as he looked me up and down. Up close, they looked sunken inside their sockets. 'You look stressed.'

I shrugged dismissively.

'Don't let him rile you.' Pierce smiled his most insincere smile. 'Save it for villains.'

'Thanks,' I said briskly. 'Good advice.'

Fuming, I went back to the incident room, hoping no one

would try to speak to me. From his desk nearby I overheard Rowan say to Freeman, 'Grumps is in a mood, I wouldn't bother.'

I pretended I hadn't heard – Grumps, my nickname since my Hendon days, was probably more appropriate than I liked to admit – and immersed myself in Operation Rye. Fortunately, my requests for an undercover officer and covert surveillance had both been approved.

The surveillance team, led by PS Colin Jacobs, a black officer in his early thirties, had set up long-lens cameras in a flat with a good view of Delius Tower and the communal areas most frequented by gang members. They also had access to the council's CCTV cameras on the estate and had planted listening devices.

Recently, the team had observed a hirsute male with similarities to our second suspect, on the eighth floor of Delius Tower, and overheard him being called 'Wolf'. Wolf had left the estate on foot before he could be pursued and hadn't been spotted since. They hadn't sighted our number one suspect, whom the Rye team had christened 'Muscleman'.

At 4pm I went over to DI Kenyon's bunker for an update on the undercover op. The undercover officer assigned to the operation hadn't yet found out anything significant, it appeared.

'The top boys are hiding out, waiting for the storm to blow over,' Kenyon read from a page he pulled out of a manilla folder.

'That's not a lot of help.'

Kenyon stretched out his long legs, a wry smile on his face.

'These things take time.'

Before heading back to the incident room, I managed to wrangle a few details about the undercover. DI Kenyon read out a snippet from his legend. 'Dan' had been allocated a flat in Godwin House, one of the grimmer buildings on the estate. He was posing as 'an alcoholic and heavy cannabis user from Newcastle'. I sneaked a glimpse at the photograph of a straggly-haired, thin-faced white man in a dirty, weary-looking tracksuit top, over equally dirty, weary-looking jeans. How long would it take for him to gain the trust of his fellow residents, I wondered.

Around five o'clock, feeling a sugar craving coming on, I went to the kitchenette for a granola bar. I usually kept the packet in my desk, but the yoghurt coating couldn't withstand the recent heat.

I stood blinking in front of the fridge. Arranged prominently on the door were four tiny skulls, somewhat over an inch in each dimension. I plucked one off and examined it. The thing was made of concrete. What the fuck?

Skull magnet raised, I stormed back into the incident room. 'Who put the skull magnets on the fridge? Is this someone's idea of a joke?'

Everyone stopped tapping into their computers and looked at me.

'Dunno, sir,' shot back one of the DCs closest to me. 'They were there this morning when I came in.'

'I don't know who did it, boss,' protested another. 'I only saw them this afternoon, I hardly use the kitchen.'

'God's sake, this is ridiculous,' I muttered, feeling like a teacher in a classroom of badly behaved kids. I marched up to DS Freeman's desk. This was exactly the sort of boyish prank that Freeman would get up to. His giant hand hovered over his iPhone. He glanced up, mid-tap.

'Rob, was this you?'

His face reddened. 'I – er – I thought it would be a laugh, boss.'

'Well, it isn't! Get rid of the rest of them.' I tossed the skull magnet onto Freeman's keyboard. 'Honestly, you lot are the end.'

Admittedly, I wasn't in the best of moods. Catching DS Rowan's smirk and DS Harper's sympathetic smile at Freeman, I realised I was acting a little over the top. Maybe there was a funny side, after all. Oh, well. I'd apologise to everyone in the morning.

————

I arrived home in time to prepare an evening meal for me and Brendan. Nothing complicated, just breaded haddock, peas and mash. I'd bought a tub of his favourite ice cream for dessert. As usual, Brendan said little in reply to my questions about his day.

'What about your trip? Any more ideas where you might go?' Brendan was planning a visit to the Scottish Highlands with two mates later in the school holidays, with a detour to the town where I'd lived for several years as a child before my father's death. The handful of times I'd taken my family on trips to Scotland, I'd made sure to avoid the area.

'Not really.' He toyed with his ice cream.

'Tell me what's the matter,' I persisted, with a twinge of despair. 'What's upsetting you?'

'Nothing's the matter. I just don't feel like talking.'

'Fuck it, Bren, I'm on your side, don't treat me like your enemy! I'm your dad and I love you.'

He met my eyes. 'Why did you make Mum leave, then?' His voice was thick with pain and anger. 'It was your fault, wasn't it?'

'I'm sorry for what's happened. I know it's been hard on you.' I got up and tried to hug him but he pulled away.

'Leave me alone.'

With a scrape of his chair, he was gone. Was his honest response a good sign – or had I made things even worse? I forced myself to get up and clear the table.

I, too, wanted Kate back; I missed her more than I could

have imagined. But it wasn't going to happen. She had a new home in Dublin to go with her new HR role – and she'd made it clear she didn't want to see me for the foreseeable, or even talk to me unless it was 'urgent'. Kate's angry words came back to me, from the evening she'd told me she was leaving. I'd replayed them in my head too often, lately.

For all the time we've been together, you've put your job first. If there's a thing you have to do at the office, a criminal you have to chase or you have to work twenty days and nights in a row so you can put someone away, you'll do it. I'm the one who's taken our sick children to hospital, who's given up chances of promotion so I can be there for our family.

I hadn't argued. I knew very well I'd not been around enough for my wife and son – and my daughter Lucy, before she left home. It wasn't only the long hours at work that Kate had objected to, though. I'd sat in helpless silence, knowing what was coming next.

You shut me out, Callum. You never talk to me about what's going on with you. You tell me it's because you're a cop that you can't talk about things. But that's not true, is it?

From Brendan's bedroom, the insistent thump of bass turned up louder than the human ear could withstand. I unloaded the dishwasher and dumped in the dirty dishes.

I should have confided in Kate; I knew now it was too late. Not just about my work and how it was impacting on me – often badly – but all the things about my past that I'd needed to keep hidden. Rather than lie, it had been easier to say nothing at all.

I sat back down at the table. The words that had cut the deepest she'd saved for last.

I love you too. But I can't carry on living half a life.

I looked around the darkening room. Somehow, I would have to keep on without her. Carry on doing my job as best I could and be there for my son, if and when he needed me.

JEZ

BADGIRL

ZOM PASSES ME THE SPLIFF. I TAKE A LONG DRAG.

I'm used to smoking dope now. My mum would go nuts if she could see me getting high, lying in my skimpiest underwear beside a guy with tatts all over, made of solid muscle. The old Mum would, anyways. The woman she's turned into wouldn't give a fuck if I smoked crack every night and offered myself to each of the boys in turn.

We're watching Netflix in Zom's dead uncle's house. His uncle got gunned down in Kosovo, something to do with a business deal. There's mirrors everywhere and a bathroom with gold taps.

I met Zom in the spring term. He took me in when I turned up last term like little girl lost, not knowing anyone and everyone looking at me sideways. He and his mates Wolf and Angel were cruising around the streets in his BMW looking out for boys to recruit as 'soljas'. I was having a quick fag one lunchtime on the green. Anyways, we got chatting. I started hanging out with them lunch times and after school. Zom told me I was the sexiest girl he'd ever met. The first time he took me out, he said, 'Ain't been with no man like me before, have ya, girl?'

His parents are refugees from Kosovo. They came to London in 1998 on the back of a lorry. His brother and sister nearly died. Zom was born the year after. He told me his dad used to aim a rifle at his mum's head when she upset him, that's why he's turned out a bit wild. Zom likes to act mean, the ultimate badman; but I know he's a softie underneath. I've seen him tear up at the sad bits in films and he squeezed my hand when I told him about my dad telling me he couldn't stand to be in the same house with me anymore.

'What's the matter?'

He's tense, in a mood.

'I got a job to do soon.'

'A job?'

'You don't wanna know.'

'Yes, I do. Why can't you tell me?'

He puffs out a cloud of ganja. 'We're gonna put the fright'ners on this old woman from the endz.'

'Why?'

'The bitch lives next door to Crew HQ. She told Wolf she knows what's goin' on, she's not gonna look the other way no more. If it don't stop soon – the loud music and people comin' to the flat late at night – she's gettin' the feds onto us. So, the boss asked for volunteers to give her a little shock, a reminder of who she's messin' with.'

I don't want to know any more.

Zom winks at me. 'Wanna see my blade?'

Before I can reply, he opens a drawer in the base of the bed and pulls out a knife.

It's scary. The handle is fluorescent green. The blade is over a foot long with SLAYER etched into it. It has jagged teeth on top and little red marks that look like blood. Or *are* they blood?

'Oh my god.' I pull away.

He laughs at my shock.

'Have you ever used it?' Dumb question. Of course he has.

'Best believe, girl.' He swipes the blade through the air. 'Anyone who crosses me had better watch their step, know what I mean?'

I can't stop a giggle. But underneath I'm like, who is this dude? If I thought about it too long, it would totally freak me out.

'You ain't scared of me, sweetheart? You think I'm crazy?'

'Of course I'm not scared of you. But you are crazy!'

'Takes one to know one. Total psycho bitch you are, I reckon. You should come with me next time I go out on a job.'

I laugh and take another drag on the spliff.

———

That's as far as I've got.

Miss Collins in English gave me the idea for this last term. She said we could put the things we can't tell anyone in a journal. It's like talking to a friend, only better. So, as I've got zilch friends to tell anything to, I'm going to put all my secret bad-girl stuff that I can't share on Insta in here.

CALLUM

FOUR WEEKS AFTER SOLITA'S MURDER, I WENT TO SEE BEV Milton to inform her that the second post-mortem had been done and her daughter's funeral could now go ahead. Since my first visit, the woman seemed to be shrinking. Her body was thinner, her voice quieter, and her words less frequent.

'I'm sorry, Bev. I know this isn't what you would have wanted.'

Of course it bloody wasn't. On top of a murdered daughter who'd not yet been buried, she'd had to cope with the thought of Solita's body being subject to a second intrusion.

She looked at me wordlessly and gave the slightest nod.

'Mihai will be on hand to help with the funeral arrangements,' I said, squirming in my seat. 'Let me know if there's anything else you need.'

The delayed funeral symbolised our lack of progress. No charges had been laid against anyone yet, therefore the body hadn't been released, as per the regulations – what's more, a second independent PM had been required. No matter what my suspicions were about Bev Milton withholding information, I had to face up to 'the conspicuous lack of progress being made by Operation Rye' in Superintendent Bailey's words earlier that morning. He'd said little but conveyed plenty, leaving me in no doubt that whatever I'd been doing so far, it wasn't enough.

That afternoon on Radio London, I appealed again for information.

I need to know who's done this murder and why it happened. Someone out there knows. Please come forward and give us that information, for the sake of the victim's mother and sister.

The interview produced a flurry of phone calls but few useful leads on the identity of the two suspects, their motivation for the crime, their movements before and after the killing or their current whereabouts. They were beamed up by a starship orbiting Saturn, for all I knew. One caller mentioned two men getting out of pink rabbit costumes in the stairwell of Dylan House soon after Solita's killing. Another claimed that six members of the Green Mob had strolled into the estate playground five minutes afterwards, brandishing machetes and taking selfies of themselves on the climbing frame.

DS Freeman showed me the Skull Crew's latest YouTube video, which showed a group of males inside an underground car park. Various coverings adorned with skull images hid their faces. Below the video, some comments discussed the identity of the killers. Suggestions included 'Your local hitman', '@grrlpower', 'the N17 squad' and 'Psychokiller'.

13TH AUGUST

Dazzling sunshine blessed the Spiritual Church on the morning of Solita Milton's funeral.

I stood a few rows from the back with DS Freeman, as clumps of mourners listened to the pastor. We'd both scrubbed up. I wore one of my slimming black linen outfits; Freeman wore suit trousers instead of his crumpled corduroys.

Videos of a bubbly, photogenic girl were shown, then friends and classmates got up to pay tributes to Solita. Bev Milton stumbled through a few sentences. Younger sister Leonie said she would never forget Solita. Her form teacher said that, although inclined to be talkative, Solita had been a joy to know. She had been awarded a certificate for being the year group's most helpful student. By the time an Ethiopian boy read out a heartfelt poem he'd written for his classmate, I was ready to join in with the outbreak of sobbing. Dabbing my eyes, I was disconcerted to see Freeman shifting his bulk from foot to foot while probing an ear with his pinky.

After the service everyone milled around outside while doves were released from a basket. Many mourners gave us a wide berth while casting curious glances in our direction. I hadn't spotted either Solita's missing brother Jayden, our two unidentified suspects, or anyone I'd put down as a gang member. Of course, no one was likely to turn up at a funeral in hoodies and trainers. But some gang-affiliated young people have a certain look around adults, challenging yet brittle, as if they've encased themselves in glass.

While Freeman disappeared into the queue for the toilet, a solemn-faced youth in a school blazer came up to me and asked if I was a policeman.

'Is it that obvious?' I replied with a grin. 'I'm Detective Inspector Waverley, by the way.'

The boy grinned back. 'I'm Jamal. I want to be a police officer too.'

He was a school friend of Solita's. 'It's scary what happened to her,' he added. 'None of us could believe it.' I asked if he had any ideas who might be responsible. Jamal shrugged.

'Not really. I knew Jayden was in a gang, it wasn't a secret. But he didn't talk about it. Not with me, anyway.'

'Thanks for info,' I said with a wink. 'I'll look out for you in a few years' time.'

I was about to round up Freeman when a man with greying hair in a three-piece suit caught my eye and stepped closer. 'It's a dreadful business,' he said in a low voice. 'My niece shouldn't have died like that.'

'It's a tragic waste,' I agreed. 'She had so many years ahead of her.'

'You're in charge of the police investigation?' He glanced over his shoulder.

'That's right. I'm DI Callum Waverley, the Senior Investigating Officer.'

'I'm Ray Milton, Solita's uncle. Her late father's brother.'

'Pleased to meet you, Ray.' I kept my hand at my side. 'My condolences. Solita was well loved by everyone, it seems. It's hard to understand what could make someone want to kill a girl like that.'

'Her brother's to blame for what happened.'

'Jayden Milton?' I waited.

'He was running with this gang. There was a disagreement between him and the boss man.'

'Did you happen to hear the name of the gang?'

'Skull Gang, Skull Kids, something like that.' He rubbed the nape of his neck. 'Anyhow, this beef was going on for months. I reckon it got out of hand. Jayden came over to ours a couple of months ago to borrow my car. I told him no, I needed it for work. That was the last time I saw him.'

I nodded. Ray Milton's jaw tensed.

'If he'd had the guts to stay and face the music, those thugs wouldn't have killed my niece... That's my view, anyhow.' He glanced over his shoulder again and lowered his voice. 'Don't tell Bev I said anything, will you? She's worried about the family saying too much, in case someone else gets killed. But I want whoever killed my niece to pay for what they did.'

'If you come across anything else...' I gave him my mobile number and went off to find Freeman. He was hovering awkwardly near Bev Milton, who was now wrapped in an older woman's arms, her eyes closed and cheeks wet. My heart went out to her.

'Come on, let's get back to work.'

The procession to the grave was about to start. I'd intended to join it, but impatience was getting the better of me. Every minute spent here was another minute that could be spent working on bringing the murderers to justice.

On the way back to the office, I considered the information from Ray Milton. Its implications buzzed around my head. Was Mrs Milton scared of the Skull Crew – or someone in the gang – enough to jeopardise the investigation into her daughter's murder?

I slammed the car door and jogged into the building ahead of Freeman. The heightened emotions at the funeral galvanised me. I had to break through the shield of apologies and denials that people kept thrusting at us.

———

I ducked into the DCI's office for privacy. Pierce was nowhere to be seen. I closed the door, sat down behind the desk and took out my mobile. To my relief, my call was answered four rings in.

'Hello, Paul. DI Waverley here.'

A grunt at the other end. It might have meant hello but sounded more like 'piss off'.

Paul F was a former nightclub bouncer who lived on the Effra Lane estate, and my only contact there. He'd supplied me some gang-related intel in the past, for which he'd been paid in line with other unofficial informants. I suspected he was in touch with active Skull Crew members but, despite my repeated requests, Mr F maintained he knew nothing about the Skull Crew or what they were up to. Lately he'd stopped answering my calls.

'You know what I'm after,' I said. 'Have you heard anything?'

'Sorry,' he wheezed. 'I'll let you know if I do.' He was on sickness benefit, due to a lung condition.

'I need to know why Solita Milton was killed and who gave the order.'

'Can't help you with that, mate, sorry.'

His pat delivery triggered something in me. The 'mate' didn't help. Any residual sympathy I had for the man drained away.

'Look, Paul, I know you're struggling to get by. But to be frank with you, if you want to stay in our good books, I suggest you start to tell me what the fuck is going on.'

It was a total bluff. I've lost him, I thought as his silence continued. He's going to tell me to fuck off.

'These people, they don't like to be crossed.' His voice was low, measured. 'If I tell you anything... it can't have come from me.'

'I give you my word. Nothing you tell me will ever be traced back to you.'

I waited, tension tightening every muscle of my body. His

level went down a notch, so I had to concentrate like hell to make out what he was saying.

'Word is, one of Skull Crew's top tier, name of Jayden Milton, stole two boxes of sniff from the main man. V was divvying it up between Jayden and the other two – he'd just bought it off this new supplier. There was this big bust up between him and Jayden. Jayden lost it, accused V of taking advantage, pulled a gun and took off with the white.' Mr F took several wheezy breaths. 'I'm not saying V was the one that went after Doc's sister. But if you put two and two together...'

I thanked Mr F and told him a payment would be on its way.

'You wouldn't know V's real name by any chance? Or where we might find him?' There was no harm asking. I knew practically nothing about the gang leader.

'No, can't help you with either, I'm afraid.'

On the way to the Effra Lane estate with DS Rowan, I mulled over what I'd learned. It looked more and more as if Solita had been murdered in retaliation for a falling out between her brother and the leader of the Skull Crew. We now had both a motive for the murder and a clear indication of the man ultimately responsible.

'Think we'll get anything useful, sir?'

'I hope so, Jon.'

For the past week the Rye team had been visiting the remaining residents who'd indicated they might know something useful. They'd spoken to all but two. So far, there had been little to justify the hours officers had spent trudging around the estate trying to engage with residents who wanted to help but knew nothing of value, or knew something but weren't prepared to talk. Whether or not it would make any difference, I needed to speak to the last two residents myself.

I took the risk of parking in a visitor's parking space beside the low-rise Godwin House. Getting out of the air-conditioned car into the sunbaked concrete space felt like stepping into a sauna. A few mothers and small children sat in the shade.

First, we called on Aydin Tas. He seemed pleased to see us and told us we didn't need to wear masks. He was the former owner of a kebab shop on the High Road half a mile up from Tottenham nick, and lived on the fourth floor of Godwin House. He apologised for not being in on previous occasions when officers had called; he and his wife had been at work.

'My wife is out, but she has left something – she makes here.' His broad smile revealed two missing crowns.

The three of us stood at opposite corners of the kitchen waiting for the contents of a metal coffeemaker to boil. The coffee it produced, Turkish style, was strong but tasty. Mr Tas sat us down at a sunny table and cut three hunks of delicious-looking syrup-soaked semolina cake, which I didn't have the heart to refuse.

'So, Mr Tas,' I began, 'you said you had information that might help us with the investigation?'

'Last year, two men were harassing me. They were from the gang here. They tell me I owe them five thousand pounds in fees, I need to pay to keep my business going. I tell them no, I can't afford. In the morning, I find a skull outside my shop... I borrowed the money to pay them and I do not hear from them again. Afterwards, I sold up. I am scared to deal with people like that.'

'Understandable,' I said. 'Was the skull – er – human?'

His dark brown eyes locked on mine. 'It was human, I would say. I am not expert. It was small for adult. I thought it was a girl's, maybe.'

'What did you do with it?'

'I throw in the garbage.'

'Did you get the names of the two men who visited you?'

He hesitated. 'They do not say.'

'Did they look like either of these two?' I showed him the photos of the suspects. He said no.

'Thank you for talking to us, Mr Tas, I appreciate it very much. And thank your wife for the cake.'

He dipped his head. 'She does not want me to talk to you. But I tell her we must help to defeat evil.'

We walked over to the incongruously turquoise-painted Ridley House, got the lift to the fourth floor and masked up. Trudi Lamont, a bony young white woman, came to the door with her hair damp and a towel around her neck, scowling.

'Miss Trudi Lamont?' DS Rowan flashed his badge and introduced us. 'You gave some information to the officer who talked to you during our door-to-door enquiries, that we'd like to follow up. In relation to the Solita Milton murder inquiry.'

'Right.' Her tone was wary. My hopes faded.

'Can we come in please, Miss Lamont?'

We were shown into an unkempt room.

''Scuse the mess.' Miss Lamont sat herself in the armchair opposite, giving her hair a rub and exposing a heavily tattooed forearm. 'I've been babysitting my niece.'

There were no other free seats apart from a hair-strewn sofa. Rowan and I exchanged glances then simultaneously sat down at either end. Rowan's mask had slipped under his chin. A matted cat sprang into my lap, as thin as its owner.

'So, Miss Lamont,' I began, cautiously petting the cat's head, 'you told the officer you had some information in relation to Solita's murder?'

Miss Lamont's jaw tightened. She folded her arms across her chest.

'I don't know if I can help you, sorry.'

'Please, Miss Lamont.' I pressed on. 'A fifteen-year-old girl was stabbed in the heart outside this estate. We need to catch her killers.' The note of desperation in my voice wasn't fake. 'If you know anything at all, no matter how small, I need to know what it is.'

Miss Lamont's scrunched brow softened a fraction. I glanced at DS Rowan, who had produced a dazzling smile.

'Anything you can say to help us will be very much appreciated, Trudi.'

Miss Lamont looked from Rowan to me and back again. 'All right then.'

DS Rowan leaned forwards with an encouraging nod.

'I know who it was that did this.'

Her gaze darted to the floor, as if she was having second thoughts. We waited.

'Go on, Trudi.'

She shrugged. 'I used to be friends with this guy who lived on the estate. He used to hang out with The Marsh Boys about six or seven years ago. He went off to form his own crew, the one that's in charge of this estate.'

'The Skull Crew?'

'That's right.'

'What was his name?'

A long pause. 'Vinny Edwards – Vincent.'

I glanced at Rowan, who raised his eyebrows at me before he carried on.

'How did you become friends with Vinny?'

'He used to live down the corridor.' She gestured to her right. 'My best friend Dawn and I was friends with him when we was teenagers. She was closer to him than me. She had quite a thing for him, actually. Her mum didn't like her seeing him cos he was quite a bit older than us – plus he was half black – but Dawn never took no notice. He was always so charming, so polite, 'til someone went against him. You'd never guess the stuff he got up to – drugs, robberies... Crazy it was sometimes. Dawn let him into her place once to hide out from you lot – her mum was working night shift at the hospital. She was up for anything in those days, she didn't mind all the weird stuff. It creeped me out though, to be honest.'

I posed the next question.

'What do you mean, 'weird stuff'?'

'People used to say he was into spells and black magic. I heard about him cutting off this chicken's head before going to mash up his enemies. The boys went to the cemetery up the road on Halloween and Vinny got some of them to rub its blood over their faces... Then he made this potion with the blood and told them to drink it.' She screwed up her face. 'It was for a—' She made air quotes with her fingers. 'Spell. None of them was s'posed to talk about it but we found out from this boy at school. He said he poured out his cup and Vinny found out, told him to go home and stab his pet rabbit through the heart and bring it to him.' She rolled her eyes. 'I know, gross. There was always rumours going round about the crazy things Vinny did. You never knew if any of them was true.'

'When did you last see Vinny?' DS Rowan asked.

'I was sixteen, in my last year at school. So, it must be four years ago. He moved off the estate soon after and we didn't see him no more.'

'Do you know where he went?'

She looked past DS Rowan to the door, as if someone might burst into the room. 'I heard he was living at his cousin's place in Tottenham a few years ago. That's all I know.'

I thanked Miss Lamont and tried to dislodge the cat from my lap.

'Do you think you'll get him for that girl's murder, then?' The young woman fixed me with her eyes. 'The one that was stabbed outside of here?'

'We're doing our best to bring the killers to justice,' I replied. 'Including whoever gave the order to kill Solita.'

'It was Vinny who ordered it.' Miss Lamont got to her feet, frowning at me. 'He's the one that gives the orders, everyone knows that.' Her voice hardened. 'You've gotta go after him. He's gotten away with it for too long.'

'We're doing our best. If you come across anything else that might help us...' I left my card on her coffee table.

DS Rowan aimed the key at the Mondeo. As he drove away from the estate, I opened the glovebox intending to have a munch on a Trail Mix bar. Instead, my fingers found a hard, rounded object.

'What the fuck.' I brought out a scaled-down human skull, the size of a paperweight.

DS Rowan peered at the object; his brow scrunched. 'What's that doing in there?'

'It looks like a paperweight.' It had a flat base and was heavy enough. 'As to what it's doing in there, your guess is as good as mine. Stop the car, will you?'

Rowan pulled up in a side street. I held the object in one hand and rooted around in the glovebox with the other, finding only the folder with insurance papers and the car's handbook.

'Did you lock the door when we parked, Rowan?'

'Yes, sir. And it was locked when we got back to the car, anyway.'

'So, who left this? And who took my fucking granola bars?'

DS Rowan looked at me with a hurt expression. 'I don't know, sir. When did you last see them?'

'This morning,' I snapped. 'I left two in there on the way to the funeral... Get me an evidence bag from the side pocket.' I dropped the skull paperweight inside.

'Could be that the car was left unlocked by someone else,' Rowan said. 'And someone sneaked it in there before we set off. Or maybe I *did* forget to lock it earlier.' He was on a roll now. 'Maybe someone broke into the car while we were doing the interviews with one of those unlocking devices, planted the skull and locked it back up. Car parks are notorious—'

'Who the fuck would want to plant a fake skull in my car?' My consternation was growing, along with my anger. Was someone trying to wind me up? Or was it something more sinister?

Rowan kept his eyes on the dashboard. 'I don't know, sir. A member of the Skull Crew, maybe?'

'Hmm. They must have a taste for granola bars.'

'Maybe it's just some idiot messing around.'

'Which idiot would that be – any idea?'

'No, sorry, sir. No idea whatsoever.'

After sending the fake skull off to Forensics for tests, I phoned Detective Superintendent Bailey and told him what I'd found.

'A fake skull?' I pictured his thick ginger eyebrows merging.

'I've just sent you a photo. It's a paperweight.'

He rang me back after an hour and told me to come straight to his office. When I arrived, Bailey was standing staring out of the window, sipping a cup of tea. He nodded at an empty chair facing his large, gleaming desk.

'Do you think this could be intended as a threat from someone in the gang we're targeting? Isn't leaving skulls with potential victims their *modus operandi*?'

'That's right, sir, and yes, it could be a threat from the Skull Crew. But if anyone from the gang was going to threaten me, would they do it with a fake skull? Some kid on the estate put it there for a laugh, probably. Or someone on the murder team put it there as a prank, and is afraid to own up to it. Every detective in the Wood Green office has access to that car.'

I decided not to mention the skull magnets on the fridge – I didn't want to land Freeman in it. Nor the two missing granola bars. That would make me sound totally nuts.

'Have you asked anyone in the MIT if they put a fake skull in the car?'

'I talked to the officer who was with me when we found it and one other, that's all. I didn't think it appropriate to ask, generally.'

Bailey shook his head, tutting.

'I very much doubt any officer in MIT55 would stoop to such a level.' He frowned. 'Please don't accuse anyone else until you have evidence.'

––––––

'What's up, Jon?'

DS Rowan took that as an invitation to rest his butt-cheek against the back of my desk.

'Boss, I've had an idea. Given all this skulduggery...' Rowan grinned and waited for my groan, which didn't come. 'With what Trudi Lamont and the Tas guy told us today about V, I thought maybe we should search Tottenham cemetery and the local graveyards and see if we find anything dodgy. Disturbed graves, pentagons, goats' hooves or whatever.'

'It's pentagrams, not pentagons. Didn't you read Dennis Wheatley?' I let out a sigh. 'Do you know how big that cemetery is? No way is Pierce going to authorise a search team. Or the super.'

DS Rowan stayed where he was, looking hopeful. I thought for a moment. Bailey had recently removed a sergeant and three DCs from Operation Rye to MIT55's newest inquiry, telling me Pierce needed all the officers he could get. Pierce – and the superintendent, for that matter – wouldn't be overjoyed to learn of a large search team trawling through Tottenham cemetery for signs of nefarious activities. The cemetery hadn't been searched for the murder weapon though, given it was outside the radius of the search area.

'But if you want to go for a nosey around the cemetery for the murder weapon with a few DCs...'

'Thanks, boss.' Rowan flashed me a grateful grin.

The search struck me as a sign of my rising desperation. I doubted Rowan would find anything without dogs and a proper search team, but I hated to quash his enthusiasm.

———

After a feeble attempt at yoga and being unable to settle to Sibelius, *Coasts of Britain* or *Great Continental Railway Journeys*, I switched everything off and sat staring into space.

I was alone – Brendan was still out with his rugby club friends. A late dusk had fallen, bathing the room in semi-darkness. The shadowy corners seemed darker than usual, and the house seemed larger and emptier than ever. A tube train rumbled beneath the earth on its way to East Finchley station.

A loud creak from upstairs set me on edge. My mind flitted back to the paperweight in the glovebox. It was some kind of bad-taste joke, I'd thought at first; Freeman had already admitted putting up the fridge magnet, but when I'd taken him aside, he'd strenuously denied having anything to do with the one in the car. The fact was, as I'd told Bailey, anyone in MIT55 could have put it there. The Ford Mondeo was one of several cars used by many officers and there were two sets of keys. One set was kept by the officer manager for whoever the car was allocated to. The second set, ever since Pierce had taken over from Andy, could usually be found somewhere in the DCI's office. He could have even planted it himself.

God's sake, what was I thinking? Pierce might be an obnoxious twat, but no way would he do something like this to a fellow officer. So, if it wasn't someone at work... Was it only coincidence I'd found the skull so soon after we'd visited Aydin Tas? Could V, or someone in his gang, have something to do with this?

A shiver went down my spine. What would be the point of such a thing, though? To toy with me, to taunt me, show they were in control? I was hardly going to stop doing my job because of a skull paperweight left in a glovebox.

I got up, closed the curtains and turned a lamp on. Its yellow warmth banished the shadows.

Resisting the temptation to pour a whisky, I fetched my laptop and set up a new document 'V' on the hard drive, so it wouldn't go into the case management system. In it, I summarised what we knew about the leader of the Skull Crew.

V
Name: Vincent/Vinny Edwards, aka V
Age: 28
Nationality: British
Bio: Expelled from secondary school (Catholic)
Criminal record: Aged 17 convicted of possession with intent to supply and possession of an offensive weapon; served 4 years
Current address: Not known
Last known address: Ridley House, Effra Lane Estate. Possibly lived in Tottenham with his cousin
Gang history: Member of The Marsh Boys since approx. 2013; started offshoot the Skull Crew around 2017
Believed associates: Michael 'Angel' Gabriel, Jayden Milton aka 'Doc', 'Wolf', 'Muscleman'
Habits/hobbies: Voodoo/spells/cutting off chickens' heads

I stared at the screen. The gaping holes in what we knew

were only too apparent. But Vincent Edwards was the key to this investigation, my gut told me. If we could get to him, we would bring the whole show crashing down.

20TH AUGUST

DS Harper scanned the draft beers on the menu. She wore one of her usual black trouser suits, flattering on her slim figure.

'A pint of lager, please.'

'And a pint of London Pride,' I added, and paid for our drinks.

We were seated at a discreet table in the corner of the room, at the first pub within walking distance of the office, past the Green Man: the down-at-heel local boozer where most of our colleagues would be. It was the end of another long week. I'd invited Rowan and Freeman for a drink too, but both declined due to prior engagements, leaving me and Sam.

I was glad it was only us two here. She was an attractive woman and I enjoyed her company.

'This is nice.' Sam smiled at me. She had lipstick on – which she never wore inside the stalag – a frosty raspberry shade. I had a sudden desire to kiss her.

'Isn't it? I've been looking forward to a pint all afternoon.' I raised my glass. 'Cheers.'

Sam gulped at her pint. 'Any news about the skull?'

I hesitated. Everyone on the murder team knew about the skull I'd found in the Mondeo's glovebox – there'd been a few quips about the 'granola thief' too. I'd not told anyone except Detective Superintendent Bailey about the test results, though.

'Nothing much. It was a 3D print job, most likely.'

Forensics hadn't found any fingerprints or fibres, or anything else of note. They told me it was made of PLA, a plastic often used in 3D printing. The things could be made without much difficulty and were available from Amazon.

Sam pushed her hair off her face. Its auburn tint caught the evening sunlight.

'So, who do you think put it there? Do you think it could have come from someone on the team?'

'I don't know. It's possible... Then again, it could have been put there by someone else who managed to get inside the car.'

'Like a member of the Skull Crew?'

'It's probably just some kid having a go. They can sniff a cop at a mile off.'

'I suppose. Let's hope no more skulls turn up.' She sounded worried.

'Do you think Jon or Rob might have put the thing there for a laugh?'

It wasn't the approach I'd normally take, and wasn't exactly conducive to team building. But Sam had worked closely with both men for five years and knew them better than I did.

'Absolutely not, sir. I'm sure neither of them would have put it there. Jon is a cocky so-and-so and Rob hasn't grown up yet, but they're both decent blokes. Though I suppose you never know for sure... People can always surprise you.'

'Thanks, Sam. Don't let slip that I asked, will you?'

Sam smiled. 'Don't worry, sir, my lips are sealed. And if I come across anything from anyone, I'll let you know.'

I took in a large dose of bitter. My mood was lifting. I'd needed to share my concerns with someone, and I trusted Sam as much as I trusted anyone.

'As we're off duty... don't bother about the sir.'

'Right oh, sir.' A smile wrinkled the corners of her eyes. 'Callum, I mean. I'll try to remember.' She chuckled. 'How's your son getting on? Brendan, isn't it?'

I groaned. 'He's back this evening from his holiday in Scotland. I hope it's cheered him up. He's been missing his mum.'

'Oh?'

'Kate and I have separated. I don't think I said.' I definitely hadn't – I hadn't even told my sister. But it was about time I talked about it. And Sam was right here, unlike Marcia. 'She got a transfer to Dublin for a year.' I took another generous swig of brew, feeling my tongue loosening.

'Sorry to hear that.'

'Things have been difficult for a while. Work got in the way of our relationship, I guess. I didn't make enough time for her or the kids, and she resented having to do everything.'

'You'd not be alone in that, Callum. My life is littered with the carcasses of guys who've given up waiting for me to get home.' A half-smile lingered on her face.

Tempting as it was, I decided to avoid going down the path towards more intimate chat. Relationships with colleagues, especially junior ranking colleagues, had for a long time been a no-no, as far as I was concerned – including the sex-centric affairs favoured by DS Rowan and several others in MIT55. Anyway, my heart wasn't entirely free of Kate.

'So, what are you up for the rest of the weekend?'

She rolled her eyes. 'Catching up on my ironing, watching TV, having a long soak in the tub... How about you, Callum?' The corners of her mouth lifted as she looked at me over her glass, a tad flirtatiously.

'Shopping, cleaning, cooking.' I gave a dry titter. 'Got to keep the house in order now I'm a single dad.'

Sam gathered up her jacket and bag. 'Have a good one.'

When I got home, Brendan was in boxers and a T-shirt munching on a piece of peanut-buttered toast and singing along to whatever was pumping out of his headphones. His rucksack lay on the kitchen table.

'Hi Bren,' I said cheerily.

He nudged the headphones off his ears. 'Hey, Dad.' He held up a packet of shortbread biscuits. 'I couldn't carry the whisky.'

I nodded. 'How about a beer?'

'No thanks, I've got to get my stuff sorted.'

'How was your trip?'

'Good, we did everything we wanted.'

'What did you think of Kirkcudbright?'

'It's a nice place.'

'Did your boots hold up OK?

He scowled. 'Sorry, Dad, I'm tired. I'm not in the mood for talking right now.'

Brendan reapplied his headphones, gathered up his rucksack and disappeared upstairs. Though tempted, I stopped myself from yelling, *Don't be such a rude git!* With any luck, he'd be more talkative over the weekend.

LUKE

SEPTEMBER

THE JAY SCREECHES WOKE ME AGAIN THIS MORNING. I SAT UP in bed with a start, in a cold sweat. In my dream their cawing turned into the sound of a hideous creature summoning me to its lair. I found one of them yesterday in the back garden, tiny and stiff on the grass below their tree. Must've got toppled from its nest by a gust of wind.

It's double English later. My first lesson in Year 11 with Miss Collins. She was my favourite teacher last year.

I remember the first lesson with her. She looked scared, her hands literally shaking. The lesson was on poems. She asked if anyone wanted to read this poem to the class, one of her favourites. No one put their hand up, so I did. The poem was called *Darling*, Jackie Kay wrote it about her mother dying. It was the only poem I'd ever read that made me feel something. It was like Miss Collins had chosen it just for me.

Miss Collins is talking about Romeo and Juliet. She's trying really hard to keep us interested. Juliet was only fourteen, younger than the girls in this class. The star-crossed lovers were done in by fate – or luck, coincidence whatever – and the world they lived in.

We take it in turns to read parts of the play but I can't get the words or much of what's going on. I watch the bright yellow beads at the ends of her braids.

Miss Collins's voice brings me back.

'Ruby! I won't ask you again. Get your backside over there beside Damon or you'll be in detention this lunchtime!'

I've never heard her sound so angry. She's pointing to the front row. Ruby picks up her exercise book, pen and bag, and swaggers to the desk. Her black hair is mostly escaped from the band.

Miss Collins asks us what is going on in the play. I've no idea. Nor does anyone else, it seems. I dig into my desk with a finger-nail, hoping Miss Collins won't pick on me. Her eyes rest on me for a millisecond then shoot past.

'This Shakespeare shit is doing my head in,' Ruby says.

'Please don't use language like that, Ruby, it's not acceptable. I'm sorry you don't like this topic but it's part of your exam.'

I look around the classroom, catch Aden's eye. He screws up his face, making it even uglier. He has a drainpipe nose and life-less eyes. I always try to stay out of his way. He's a troublemaker, worse than Ruby.

Miss Collins writes on the whiteboard. Ruby chucks a Coke can. It hits Miss Collins on the shoulder blade.

'Who threw this?' She holds it up.

'Mickey Mouse, Miss!' Ruby smiles, full of herself.

Miss Collins's cheeks go red. 'Ruby, I've had just about enough of your behaviour. For heaven's sake, stop being such a baby!'

Ruby stares at Miss Collins. Aden slaps the desk.

'Right on, Miss! Time she was told what's what.' Another boy joins in. 'Yeah, Miss, let her have it!' Smirks, titters and hoots of laughter spread around the room.

Ruby gets up. She has tears in her eyes.

'Fuck you, Miss Collins!' She sweeps the things on her desk into her bag and rushes out. The slam echoes in the corridor.

'Right, the drama's over. Let's get back to Shakespeare, everyone.'

I go back into my own world. Thoughts come and go. Mum making me read aloud to her when I was small. The girl from the estate. I wonder if I'll see her in the next English lesson. Jessamine Robbins, I think she's called. Her name was on the register but she isn't in class.

Once or twice I sense Miss Collins's eyes rest on me. They move away before she says anything, though. I guess she knows I don't want to answer questions all the time like I used to.

The end-of-period bell goes and everyone starts packing up. As I go past the teacher's desk Miss Collins raises her hand to stop me.

'Luke. Can I have a word?'

I grip the strap of my backpack. I shoulda said something in the lesson. She's gonna tell me off for not paying attention.

'I'm sorry about your mum,' she says.

She looks serious, not like how she used to be with me. She's wearing an orange shirt, black skirt, black tights and black ankle boots. Her braids are tied back in a loose band. Miss Collins is the best dressed teacher in the school, easy. She's cool too. Last year we spent the whole lesson looking at rap and hip-hop. She said it's modern poetry.

'If there's anything you need to talk to me about…'

I shrug. I don't want to be a pity case.

'If you're ever having trouble with the lessons or your homework, let me know.' She smiles quickly and her face goes serious again. 'Given your situation, I can make allowances for you. You were doing so well last year and it's easy to get behind.'

'Yeah, OK, Miss. Sorry for not paying attention.'

'Never mind. Given what you've had to deal with...' She pats my arm. Teachers aren't meant to touch us without asking first but I don't mind if it's Miss Collins. 'Have you been to see the school counsellor?'

I tell her I'm going every week but I can't talk to her. Miss Collins nods.

'I know how hard it is when someone you love dies. My brother died a year ago. I'm still not over it.'

'How did he die?'

'In a skiing accident. He was a daredevil, always going too fast. He lost control and collided with someone. They had to airlift him off.'

'That's so sad, Miss.'

She's blinking like she's trying to stop herself from crying.

'One of the things that really helped was writing. I wrote down all the things I couldn't say to anyone.'

'I am already,' I say.

'I'm so glad, Luke, I hope you keep going with it.'

She sounds sad, though. There's voices outside the classroom. Miss Collins glances nervously at the door and picks up her bag like she's worried someone has seen us doing something we shouldn't.

———

The sky is blue when I wake up, the kind of sky you'd have if you lived on a tropical island I reckon, though I've not yet stepped outside of Britain. Sunlight bounces off the tower block windows into my room, nearly as bright as the real sun.

At lunch break, the girl I saw on the estate is pretending to be the head of academy, Mr Swinton. She's shuffling along, snorting and squealing and stamping her foot while some kids watching hoot and whistle. I stop crossing the playground and watch too.

She ends the show with a surprised smile. I go sit on the bench under the beech tree, where I go when I don't want company, most of the time now. I get out my phone, stick in my earbuds and zone out.

'You're Lucas, aren't you? I think we do a class together.'

She's in front of me. A tang of licorice on her breath. Her accent isn't like anyone's at school. It's the way a posh girl talks.

'Yeah, we're both in art and English this year. It's Luke, by the way.'

She sits down beside me like this is where she always sits. Tosses her long hair behind a shoulder. It's dark brown and makes her skin look vampire-white. A gold chain dangles between her breasts where her blouse isn't buttoned.

'Luke, I'm sorry.'

'It's meant to have a *c* like it is in French, but no one can spell that.' I don't know why I say this.

She raises her eyebrows. 'Are you French?'

'A quarter French, I guess. From my mum. She died in July.'

I look into her eyes. They narrow at the ends, Asian style. They are weirdly pale, like chinks of sky.

'Was she ill?' She doesn't go all sad on me, which helps me to keep sounding normal.

'She had cancer. She didn't find out 'til it was too late.'

'What a bummer. Is your dad still around?'

'My stepdad looks after us. Me and my half-sister. I never knew my real dad.'

She brings a green apple out of her large white leather bag

and munches into it. The designer's name is tagged in gold letters: *Balenciaga*.

'Sounds like you could do with cheering up, Luke.'

'You can try.' I grin. 'You're Jessamine, aren't you?'

She pretend-scowls. 'Jess, please. Or my friends call me Jez.' An arc of teeth, neat and straight and shiny in the sunshine. Something like jasmine floats off her.

'Good to meet you, Jez.'

'It's good to meet you too, Luke.' A crunch of apple. 'I don't know too many people here yet. It isn't ideal to join a school halfway through Year 10.'

'You came here from Alexandra Park Girls, didn't you?'

'Yeah, they kicked me out. None of the other schools in the borough would let me in.' She unfolds her long legs.

'Why did they kick you out?'

'Oh, some ridiculous thing.' She shrugs. 'I got into a fight with another girl. They made a big deal about it. So now I'm here.'

I'm about to say I saw her on Effra Lane estate, only she gets up. Her shoes are flimsy-looking ballet pumps.

'See you in art, then'. She tosses the apple core into the bushes and hoists her bag over her shoulder.

I notice the empty playground. I didn't hear the bell ring for end of break.

———

I don't get a chance to speak to Jez again 'til the end of the lesson. We sit on separate tables. The lesson is on mosaics. After looking at examples from the Greeks and Romans, we try our own. I can't concentrate on mine. The two or three times I look over, Jessamine is engrossed in cutting out or sticking down coloured shapes. Her hands move fast. She isn't talking to anyone on her table.

When everyone starts getting up from their desks at the end of the lesson, she looks round and catches my eye.

'Hey, Luke.'

'Hey.'

'Doing anything later?' She raises her eyebrows.

'Not really.' My check list for this evening? Go home, eat dinner and wait for my stepfather to get angry with me again. Not do my homework.

A couple of boys give us a curious look on their way out.

'We could go somewhere, what do you say?'

We walk to the park. I often cycle through it to get to the canal. Past the café, through the gate to the towpath. It's warm and the trees are green. A man is fly fishing. Boys throw stones at ducks. It feels like summer still.

'Let's sit here.' Jez sits without waiting for my reply like she's used to getting her own way.

I lie on my back, propped up on my elbows. She's straight-backed, cross-legged, yoga style. Groups of teens in school uniform go by, none from John Berriman. Jez's shirtsleeves are pulled up, so is her skirt.

'Where are your parents from? Were they from, I mean.'

I explain my mother was from Martinique, my real father was American and my stepfather is from south London.

'Interesting! My parents are both from England. Surrey and the Thames Valley. Good old middle-class commuterville.'

'You don't get on with them?'

'My dad's pissed off with wifey number two. They live in Jersey. I only see him during the school holidays or when he's had a fight with Blondie. I live with my mum most of the time. She's got a few issues, you could say.' Jez swivels her eyes, sighing. 'So, what GCSEs are you doing?'

We chat about school. The sets we're in, the subjects we like best and worst, our favourite teachers. Jez is in the second lowest set for everything except art and drama, the only subjects she likes. I'm the top set for Spanish and French, and the second or middle for the other subjects.

'Clever clogs! You'll be off to uni then.'

'Don't think so. Not at the rate I'm going.'

'What do you mean?'

'I dunno. I can't focus on lessons anymore. It's like trying to grab hold of a bit of cloud.'

'I guess with your mum 'n' all...' She touches between her breasts, showing denim-blue nails. 'That would take anyone's mind off lessons. Do you have friends at school? I don't think I've seen you with anyone.'

'I don't hang out with anyone much these days. You grow apart from people, don't you?'

'I know what you mean. When my mum's drinking got bad, I couldn't talk to my friends. I tried to share stuff with them but they were like, "Oh my god, you're the daughter of an alchie! You're not one of us anymore."' She gives a snort and hugs her knees, rocking herself backwards and forwards. 'That really fucked me up, on top of everything else... Jeez, I'm talking too much. Let's get a beer or something.'

Her eyes open wider than ever, so do her lips. Another flash of teeth – she must get them polished monthly. She's coming on to me, no one could mistake the signs. Something about her warns me to be careful.

'I don't think there's anywhere round here that sells booze,' I say. 'Anyway, they might not sell it to us.'

'There's a Sainsbury's near my place, they never ask for ID. You can get other stuff for free too, through the scanning machines. I've nicked loads. The staff are so busy chatting to each other they don't notice a thing.'

She puts her hand on my thigh. I enjoy the feeling. It feels like a long time since Deb and I split up. I'm not in a hurry to find another girl though. You can't just replace people.

'What about we go to mine? You can stay over if you want. There's a spare room.'

I think about it. She gives me a look like I've trodden on her foot.

'Are you worried about your stepdad finding out, is that it?'

'I don't care what he thinks. Yeah, I'd like to go back to yours. If that's OK with your mum.'

'She won't even realise you're there, probably. By dinnertime she's usually out of it.'

It's nearly six thirty when we get the bus. I text Kirsty I won't be home for dinner and won't be back tonight as I'm staying with a friend, can she pass it on to Kevin.

———

It takes ages to get to Jez's place. She says the bus is quicker in the morning.

Walking along the street she lives in, I realise her house will be different from mine – Kevin's place, I mean. It's a wide road called something Avenue, full of trees, near the centre of Muswell Hill. Alexandra Palace peers down in its grey goofiness.

I already knew this was an expensive area – it's ripped with poodle parlours, boutiques and beauty salons. But it's like we've entered a portal into another world. The houses have proper front gardens and the hedges look like they've been sculpted.

A guy bursts out of a gate in front of us, trying to keep control of two Dalmatians and a bunch of terriers. Jez waves.

'That's our old dog walker,' she explains. 'He used to take Rolo for walks. Our labradoodle.'

'He died?'

Her voice goes quiet. 'Yeah, he was only six.'

'What happened?'

'Mum got really out of it after Dad went off to live with his girlfriend. She never noticed when he ate stuff off the floor. The dog, I mean. Rolo got this allergic reaction and had to be hooked up to oxygen. The vet thought he must have eaten her pills. She takes about ten different kinds, I'm not kidding: anti-depressants, painkillers, sleeping tablets... It's a fucking pharmacy in our place.'

We stop outside a semi, huge like the others. It has a shiny green door with stained glass panels either side. An old silver Merc sits opposite the front gate. I wonder if it's her mum's.

She brings a keyring out of her bag, smiles teasingly. 'You're about to see chez Jez in its full glory. Mumsy might be about too, you never know.'

I follow Jez through the massive hall, all click-together wooden floor and arty walls, spray-painted to make them old. This space alone is as big as our kitchen.

'Dump your stuff anywhere.'

The kitchen is like you'd see in a magazine. There's a table with steel chairs in the middle and glossy white cupboards all around.

'You hungry?' She opens the fridge that's hidden behind a cupboard door, and stands looking inside. Then she takes out two cans of Stella and a packet of ham, a packet of bread and a tub of butter. 'You're not a vegetarian, are you?'

'I'm easy.'

'We're a bit low on supplies at the mo, this'll have to do...' She tiptoes to reach the top shelf of the cupboard. 'Ah, here we are. Mum's left us some crackers. And nuts, yay!' She brings out a bag of roasted peanuts.

I glimpse inside the cupboard. There's sod all, a few tins of peas and tomatoes, some Sultana Bran and Cheerios packets and about ten Boots the Chemist prescription bags lined up. Two boxes of rapid flow Covid tests, unopened. Stuck onto the front of the cupboard is a photo of two small girls, heads together, brown hair to the shoulder and front teeth sticking out. One's grinning, the other's glum. They have to be sisters.

'Which one are you?'

'Mum put it up.' She twists her mouth. 'To remember the good old days.' She puts a beer can in my hand, swigs on hers. 'Take that, come with me. I'll bring the rest.'

We go into a massive room and eat with our hands, side by side on the sofa, the food on the coffee table in front of us. Jez rolls the ham into parcels and crams them into her mouth, scarcely chewing before swallowing. Folded slices of bread without butter and Jacob's crackers go the same way. She catches me looking at her and giggles.

'Sorry, am I being a pig?'

'It's good to see a girl enjoy her food.'

I take another bite of the sarnie I've made, looking the room over. There's not enough furniture for the space. Two sofas, an armchair and a coffee table. No lamps or anything. Finger tracks on the dusty table, a stinky ashtray.

'Fancy a spliff?'

I shrug. 'Sure.'

She clears the table and returns with a lighter, Rizlas and a bag of weed. She rolls a thin spliff and draws on it a few times then passes it to me. I take a drag. There's not much baccy in it. I pass it back.

'Tell me something about you,' I say, suddenly shy. She isn't peaches-and-cream pretty. But there's something about her face, the dainty turn-up nose and sky-grey eyes. If I look too long, it might put a spell on me. 'What do you watch on TV?'

'Reality shows like *Strictly*. I don't have much time to watch

TV though. I'm always busy with something. Dance classes, auditions...'

'No time for homework, then?'

'Homework?' She makes a yuck face. 'The only thing I go to school for is drama — I love all that acting shit.' She taps the spliff. A clump of ash falls on the table beside the ashtray. 'Dad used to bang on about getting into uni 'n' all, getting a good career. But the only thing I really want is to be on the stage of a West End musical.'

A woman's head appears in the doorway. Jez raises her hand.

'Mum, didn't think you'd be up. This is Luke, a friend from school.'

A middle-aged woman in a quilted dressing gown and slippers lurches towards us. She's in a bad way. Eyes not focused.

'Luke?' She doesn't say hello, just stands there looking confused. Hair lank, sort of blonde, trickles down the back of her dressing gown. Her nose wrinkles and her hands flap the air. 'Jessamine, I told you before not to smoke those damned things in the house. Go out to the terrace if you must do that.'

'OK, OK, we're going. Keep your knickers on.'

We go upstairs to Jez's room. It's a tip. I thought mine was bad, but this is on another scale. Stuff is strewn over the floor — jeans, tights, a hairbrush, a fancy cotton face mask, unwashed mugs, teddy bears... The walls have an arty thing going on, painted in strips of turquoise and white.

'You can stay over if you like. Your place is a long way from here. We've got a guest room. Three, actually.'

'Thanks. What about your mum though?'

'She won't even know you're still here. She'll be on the vodka in a bit.' Jez sits on the double bed, takes off her trainers and chucks them towards the wardrobe, then takes off her clothes except her stretch shorts. She pulls a clingy black camisole over her breasts. Her nipples show through.

'Come and sit down.' She pats the bed. 'Back soon. Don't go anywhere.'

I hear water running in the bathroom. Curiosity gets the better of me. I get up and wander around, careful not to tread on anything. The wardrobe doors are open. Inside is packed full. A sequined, multi-coloured, patchwork-style jacket, a blue leather jacket covered in zips, a black top with a white furry collar. On the lowest shelf is a row of trainers, about eight pairs. They look brand new. I check out the dressing table. Stuff bursts out of bags and baskets and boxes. Girl's stuff – a tray of glittery powders, animal print notebooks, a tin of felt-tips. Jewellery too. Rings with big stones, a Rolex sprinkled with ice. A gold bracelet lies in a layer of chocolate crumbs and dust.

Footsteps. I sit back down.

'You've got some nice stuff.' I nod towards the jewellery.

'Thanks.'

'Where'd ya get it?'

She shrugs and sits on the bed beside me. 'My dad gave me the Rolex. And the bracelet.'

'What about those?' I point to the trainers. 'Did you nick 'em?'

'Course not. A friend gave them to me.'

I say nothing.

'It was someone I met a while ago.' She taps her fingers on her bare thigh. 'He's got money, he doesn't mind spending a bit here and there.'

'In a gang, is he?'

Her eyes narrow. 'I know some boys from a gang, yeah. You know, the ones that hang around after school. It's hard to avoid them.'

'I saw you on my local estate with some darkskin guys. In the summer holidays.'

Her face changes. 'What are you talking about?'

'I saw you on the Effra Lane estate.'

'What were you doing there?' A deep groove appears between her eyebrows.

'I pass through there sometimes. I live near the estate.'

'Why didn't you mention it before?'

I shrug. 'I was going to. I forgot.'

'You weren't spying on me, then?' She looks uncertain.

'Of course not. I just noticed you, that's all. I would've said hi but as we didn't know each other...'

'Whatever.' She looks like she's not sure whether to believe me.

I wait for her to say something about what she was doing there, but she doesn't.

'You should be careful,' I say. 'Getting involved with gangsters isn't the smartest move, y'know.'

Jez screws up her face. 'Give me a break. I don't need any lectures from a boy who's younger than me, even.'

'Just sayin'. How d'ya know I'm younger than you, anyway?'

'Lucky guess. Nearly everyone in our year is younger than me. When's your birthday?'

'October the fifth.'

'Told you. My birthday is this month. The twenty-second.'

She yawns and stretches. Her face is soft in the shadows. She pats the mattress, smiles.

'Are you getting in with me?'

'I'm zonked, to be honest. You said you have a spare room?' I feel uncomfortable turning her down. But she's sleeping with the guy who gave her the jewels, I'd bet on it.

'Don't go, please!' Her eyes plead with me. 'We don't have to do anything. I don't want to be on my own.'

'Why not?'

'You ask a lot of questions.' She slowly shakes her head. 'Just lie down here for a bit, will you?'

I take off my trainers, shirt and trousers and lay down beside her. The sheet feels smooth and cool, not like the polyester ones at home. It looks manky, though. No one's done the laundry in a while. I pull the duvet over us.

'I get bad dreams, that's why.' She says it like I've just asked.

'You've always had bad dreams?'

'From when I was small.' She turns off the lamp. A night light glows white in the corner. 'I hate the dark. Gotta have a light in my room at night.'

'I get bad dreams too. Since my mum got ill.' They're gruesome, so I don't say any more. The worst is where my mother is cut open and someone's about to take out her organs, but there's nothing I can do.

She lifts her arm. 'C'mon, snuggle up.'

I scoop my body around hers. Her skin smells of weed and jasmine and the Christmas puddings Mum used to make. I close my eyes, relax into the slow rhythm of her breathing.

———

When I wake, the sun's blasting in. I leave Jez sleeping and tiptoe downstairs. My head is fuzzy from dope. The bus comes quickly but it still takes forty minutes to get to school.

All morning I replay yesterday evening. I'm glad I didn't let Jez tempt me into anything beyond literally sleeping with her. At the end of English, Miss Collins catches my eye. I wasn't listening to what she was saying and I'm thinking she's gonna ask me why I wasn't paying attention.

'How's it going, Luke?' She's in a dress today, above the knee, and low-heeled ankle boots. Her braids twisted into a knot behind her head. She is always dressed smarter than the other teachers.

I say, 'OK.'

She glances around. We're alone. The classroom door is open.

'How's the counselling going?'

'I don't think there's much point carrying on, really.'

My counsellor is probably good at her job but I clam up whenever she asks me a question. She's got white hair and thick glasses with black frames that make her look scary.

'What about things at home?'

Her voice is gentle.

I shrug.

'It must be hard, with your mum not around anymore.' She looks sad.

'It's hard, yeah.' An ache comes into my throat. Suddenly I want to tell her everything, about Mum suddenly getting sick and Kevin not wanting me at home.

She touches my arm, on my shirt sleeve. 'Just get through one day at a time, that's all you can do.' She tells me how when her brother died, she felt like giving up with life.

'But you didn't?'

She looks down at the table. 'No, I didn't. I poured all my sad feelings into writing and whenever I did that, I started feeling better.' She leans forward, looks into my eyes. 'Maybe you can find something that makes you feel good about life again.' She glances at her watch. 'It's getting late, I'd better be going.'

———

Kevin comes up to me as I'm hanging my jacket. He's got a Heineken can in his hand.

'Where were you last night?'

'With a friend,' I say, turning to face him. I wait for a tirade. Get ready to run out of the house.

'Next time, just tell me where you're going, will ya? I was

worried.' He puts the can down on the staircase. 'Look, I'm sorry for what I did, Luke.' He coughs. 'I ain't much of a father to you, I know.'

I stare at him, too surprised to speak. He goes on, his feet shuffling.

'I wanna make it up to you, kid. We need to fix things between us. It ain't healthy how it's got.'

He's looking at me like he expects an answer.

'Sure.' Confusion chases away the rest of my words. This version of my stepfather is crazier than the last.

'Dinner's chicken noodles,' he says. 'I'm getting it done for six.'

I go into the front room. My sister is watching the latest episode of *Stranger Things* on Netflix. Her maths homework is on the sofa beside her.

'Hey, Kirst. You'll give yourself nightmares watching that stuff.'

'Luke!' She jumps up and throws her arms around me, hugs me so tight it takes the air out of me. 'We didn't know if you were coming back.'

'I texted.'

'I know. But Dad thought you might have gone for good. He was acting so weird last night.' Kirsty rolls her eyes. 'He even cooked dinner. He said he'll have to get used to it; cooking is a man thing now.'

We both laugh. That evening for about the first time since Mum died, my stepdad doesn't grumble or pick on me. He actually seems interested in me, rather than what I've done wrong.

'What's happening at school?'

He asks about my friends and what I'm up to. I don't say much. The shadows under his eyes are deeper than before.

Later, Kirsty comes into my room. 'Don't leave me here with him, will you?'

A hundred things run through my brain.

'He doesn't hit you, does he? Or anything else?'

'No, course he doesn't!' She pulls a crazy face. 'I feel lonely when you're not here, that's all. The house feels so empty. I miss Mum more than ever.'

'I know, Pixie, it's hard for you. You'll have to try and be brave.' I kiss her forehead and take her hand. Now Mum's gone, I'll have to take good care of my sister.

CALLUM

I STARED AGAIN AT THE PHOTO OF A WEED-INFESTED GRAVE, AS if it might tell me something that could help. Its sloping, moss-covered headstone bore the almost obliterated words DATE OF DEATH 1936. The date of birth wasn't visible, nor was the name of the deceased.

DS Rowan's unofficial search of a section of the sprawling Tottenham cemetery had yielded gruesome fruit. I swiped through the grisly photos on my screen: a singed fox's tail, a blackened foot of an unidentified small animal, and the like. The remains had been found within a pile of partially burnt material among a cluster of disintegrating graves on a bank of the River Moselle.

Unfortunately, nothing linked the grisly items to Solita's murder. Apart from the fox remains, the burnt material included other substances identified by Forensics as human: skin and hair. The DNA recovered from them was of poor quality and didn't match the DNA of any stored on the national database. There were partial sets of fingerprints on an iPhone cover found near the pile, but those didn't match any stored records, either.

Tottenham cemetery wasn't that far from the Effra Lane estate, though. Could Vincent Edwards have gone there with other members of the Skull Crew to perform some sort of ritual? We'd probably never find out, I thought gloomily. Despite five hours of poking about among neglected, waterlogged graves, Rowan's search squad hadn't found anything else. Given Detective Superintendent Bailey's reluctance to spend money on any line of enquiry unlikely to result in a suspect being charged, I didn't bother asking permission to extend the search.

Bailey had continued to downsize Operation Rye, no doubt with Pierce's backing. My core team now comprised only my four Sergeants – Harper, Rowan, Freeman and Hanna – plus Ferret and a handful of DCs. Rubbing salt into the wound, Smiley's pithy putdowns of late suggested he thought there was little hope of me bringing the operation to a successful conclusion.

No officer would risk doing anything outright to screw up an operation, but I did wonder what was going through Pierce's head. Did he see me as competing with him for the limelight, or the DCI's job, down the line? Andy was recovering slower than expected from his surgery and wouldn't be back at work until at least November, he'd recently informed us all.

I too was starting to feel despondent about Operation Rye. Eight weeks in, we'd had no breakthroughs. Every line of enquiry had either stalled or had reached a dead end.

Freeman and Hanna were sniffing around dozens of social platforms for a whiff of the suspects. We still didn't know the real names of Wolf or Muscleman, which didn't help matters. Vincent Edwards had no presence on social media. Rowan had dug up some interesting info on him, though. He'd been placed in a Catholic children's home for two years at the age of nine, after his mother was sectioned following the suicide of his father. Rowan was trying to contact the mother, who had apparently gone to live in Cuba, her country of origin.

The surveillance team hadn't any more sightings of the suspects, though they saw frequent signs of drug-selling activity on the estate; the gang's drug business appeared to be continuing unabated. Our undercover hadn't reported anything of note. According to DI Kenyon, he was popular with middle-aged women, who chatted to him about their gripes with the council along with more personal topics.

Short of a significant breakthrough, I estimated we hadn't long before Operation Rye was sent scuttling into the dark recesses of the HOLMES database.

———

Things weren't going well at home, either. Brendan had said little about his travels during the holidays and mostly shrugged me off whenever I tried to engage him in conversation.

'I care about you, Bren,' I told him over dinner. 'You know that, don't you?'

'Is that why you're always at work?'

Instantly feeling guilty, I put down my knife and fork and pushed my plate aside. Despite my good intentions, I was working late most evenings, whether on my laptop at home or in the office – and even when physically present, thoughts of the case often distracted me.

'I'm sorry about that, really I am. But it's hard, given what I have to do. I'm in charge of—'

'You're head honcho,' he interrupted, 'I get it.' He squashed an oven-ready chip with his knife.

'I'll ask your aunt to come over next week. She can cook

dinner and do a few things around the house, while she's here. Marcy would love to see a bit more of you—'

'I don't need anyone to look after me, Dad.' His tone was caustic. 'I'll be seventeen soon. I can cook better than you, anyhow.' He swallowed the mangled chip. 'How come you never talk about my granddad? Your dad, I mean.'

I looked at Brendan, unable to think of a reply. The question had taken me off guard. He was right. I never talked about Graham Waverley, unless I couldn't avoid it.

'I guess it's because we didn't get on very well,' I said lamely, aware of my son's scrutiny. 'He gave me a hard time when I was growing up. Well, both me and Marcy, but he put the boot in extra hard with me, dishing out punishments for every little thing he didn't like.'

'What sort of things?' Brendan leaned over his forearms. It felt like the first time for weeks he'd shown an interest in anything I'd said.

'If I was late home or I didn't clean my shoes properly, or talked back to him, or contradicted him – he was a control freak, basically.'

'What punishments did he give you?'

'He'd make me stay in my room for hours, that was one of his favourites, or stop me doing things I wanted to do. Sometimes he made me polish his shoes for hours, 'til my hands ached.' Just thinking about it, my muscles tensed and my heart began to thump. There were so many times he'd come down on me unnecessarily hard, most of the incidents had merged into one big festering blob of resentment. Apart from the last thing, the culmination of years of tyrannical rule. 'Once I went out to a mate's place when I was supposed to be doing my homework... When I got back, he flipped out. I told him I wasn't going to do what he said anymore. He didn't like that.'

'What did he do?'

'He stopped me going on a trip I was planning.' I felt my throat close. 'To Scotland, actually. I was the same age as you, roughly.' The two-week camping trip should have been the high-light of my summer; my mates and I had planned it for months. 'Count yourself lucky I'm so easy going.' I'd done my utmost to avoid being strict with my son.

'Why was he like that?'

'I've no idea. His father was strict with him, I think. Maybe he was just taking his anger out on me.'

Uneasy, I took our plates to the dishwasher. I badly wanted to change the subject. Brendan's first week in sixth form, his plans for the weekend – anything but this.

'I went to see the house where you used to live,' Brendan said when I returned to the table. 'The woman living there now showed me round.' The house, a few miles out of town, held few good memories. 'An old man in the garden next door came to the fence and started talking to me. He said my granddad used to make sculptures; he was always in his shed chipping away at bits of wood.'

'That's right. He used to carve small figures. Birds, wild animals—'

'Are any of them still around?'

'I think your gran kept some – your aunt's probably got them somewhere. The ones that weren't destroyed in the fire.'

'The fire he was killed in, you mean?'

'That's right.' My gut churned. Years ago, I'd told Brendan about the fire. But he'd want to know more, sooner or later. 'I'll ask Marcy what she's got of your granddad's, maybe she can bring them over.'

LUKE

I THOUGHT IT WOULD BE JUST ANOTHER DAY AT SCHOOL, trying to concentrate enough to take in the stuff we're learning, do all the things I'm supposed to.

I'm in the corridor on the way to the bench by the beech tree. I usually eat my sandwiches there. Sometimes Jez comes along and we share our lunches. When she's in school, that is.

'Yo, saddo!' Some boys come up behind me. 'Alone again?'

I look round. Four of them. Two black, two white. I know who they are. The two white boys are from my English class. One of them, Aden, has a rep for being aggy.

I walk faster, into the playground, trying to ignore them. No one has tried to bully me since Year 7, when everyone new was fair game. I've always hung out with other kids and been sociable, I guess that's why. Up 'til now, that is.

'Hey, pussy. I'm speaking to you.'

My heart starts pounding in my chest. I stop, turn to face them. It's Aden who spoke, the ringleader. He steps towards me. His mouth droops at the corners. I can't breathe for a moment. There's a roaring in my ears. I see my fist smashing into his jaw and blood pouring down his face. My foot strikes his solar plexus, toppling him.

'The cameras.' One of the darkskin boys jerks his head towards the playground entrance. 'Leave him.'

Aden gives me a screw look. 'We'll be back.'

My heart slows. CCTV cameras are planted all over the school so the teachers can see kids fighting.

When I get to the bench, Jez isn't there. I need her, suddenly. She would have made it better, taken away that boy's words. I sit staring into nothing, not bothering to eat. I know they'll come back, now they've started. I don't know what I'll do. Something's changed since Kevin hurt me. The old Luke would have just laughed or called those boys names back. It's like there's a fire smouldering deep inside me, waiting for a breeze.

JEZ

HAPPY BIRTHDAY TO ME

I PEEK AT MYSELF IN THE DRESSING TABLE MIRROR. MY NEW bra makes my boobs stick out and is so pretty under the sheer blouse, which is perfect on top of my skinny jeans with the leather jacket Zom gave me. I'm meeting Letty and Rowena at the pub to celebrate my sixteenth birthday. And Annabel, if she turns up. I'm hoping Zom might too.

I've been helping Zom out with a few things, and he pays me. Letty is going to ask Yasmin to get me work in her beauty salon too. Lately, I've had so much to do there's not much time left for school. Talking of which, Miss Jenkins has promised me a big part in *The Lion King* if they're allowed to put it on at the end of term, as long as I turn up to class regularly. She says I've got enough talent to get into West End musicals.

'Where are you going, love?'

Mum stumbles into my room, clinging to the door handle. I've asked her to knock before she comes in, in case I'm in the nud (aka, doing something I don't want her to see), but she always forgets. She's still in her dressing gown, which still has a big stain down the front from God knows what, and her hair is a mess. The sight of her makes me wither inside. I want to tell her how she looks, something that might jolt her out of this ghastly state. The sad truth is, nothing I say would make any difference.

'I'm going out to celebrate, Mum. It's my birthday, remember?'

She's been zonked out in her room since I got back from the shops this afternoon.

Mum smacks herself on the head.

'Oh, darling! I forgot it was today. And your sixteenth too.' She plonks herself down on my bed. 'I was going to make you chocolate brownies and a buy you a nice present... Can you forgive me?'

Chocolate brownies were the only things Mum ever baked. The last time was on my fourteenth birthday. Dad and Tara were still living at home then.

I had a card came from her this morning, a real one, not the Jackie Lawson ones she usually sends. Inside she wrote:

Have a lovely day!!! Lots of hugs, Tara

I nearly messaged her, since when have you given me lots of hugs? What a hypocrite. She's come to see me four times in the past two and a half years, though she knows I'm holed up here with Mum drinking herself into her grave, Dad never comes to see us anymore and we've got zero money left for anything after she's taken her booze money. I left the card face down in the kitchen.

Mum rambles on about being a bad mother, how she's going to rehab again just as soon as she's got the money. I get on with my makeup and try to look like I'm listening. She doesn't give me space to say anything anyways, just loops through exactly the same things as she's said twenty times before.

We live in this big detached house that cost a fortune, but there's sod all money coming in except a few quid from the government – plus handouts from my dad when he's feeling generous and the bits of cash I get from Zom. When Mum's buying five or six bottles of wine a week and nearly the same of vodka and gin, that's not enough to buy a packet of toilet roll after my dance classes, let alone something to eat or a month for her to dry out.

When she's gone from my room, I sigh in relief and get to work on the finishing touches of my outfit. Sixteen at long last. I can't wait for next summer, when I won't have to go to school. Then Gillian will finally have to stop threatening to put me in a children's home every time I bunk off school or Mum doesn't answer the phone.

I'm ready by six thirty. It's too early to leave, so I sit on the terrace with a chilled bottle of chardonnay from Mum's stash. The light is nearly gone but there's a good view from up here.

'Are you going out with those gang men again?'

She's dressed now, in a clean top and leggings. She's actually showered and washed her hair, I can smell the apple shampoo. That sour stink on her breath has gone too. That's one of the worst things about having a drunk for a mother, the hygiene things she forgets, that you take for granted a mother should do.

'No, just the girls.'

'How do you know these girls?' Mum sits down across the table, in caring parent mode.

'From Zom. He's got lots of friends. They're all right.'

She wrinkles her nose. Mum hasn't met Zom yet and won't if I have anything to do with it. She says I shouldn't be seeing older guys.

'What about your friends from Alexandra Park? Aren't any of them coming?

'I doubt it.' I'd better not see any of those cows who got me kicked out of Alexandra Park Girls. Good riddance to them.

'Not even Annabel?'

'Mum. Quit hassling me, will you?' My voice sounds a bit harsh so I put my hand on hers. 'I'll have my phone with me so you can ring to check I'm OK.'

'How will you get home? I don't like you being out late and coming home on your own.'

'I'll get an Uber, for God's sake! I'm not a little girl anymore.'

I drink my wine. Mum frowns.

'You shouldn't be drinking on your own, Jess.'

'What, I should be careful not to drink too much, like you do?'

She's hurt. 'I just don't want you to go down the same path as me.' Her voice is quiet. 'You have a future, you could be anyone you want to be.' She peers at the garden below, overgrown with weeds. 'Don't give up on your dreams, that's all I'm saying.'

I get up before Mum can start her tirade about me throwing away my life. Yeah, I'm in a strange place right now but no way am I going to turn into my mother. That's etched into my soul. There's nothing much to eat in the fridge so I spoon up half a can of baked beans, *au naturel*.

I arrive at the pub early and head to the table for four I've booked. Since I was last here it's been converted into an upmarket bar and restaurant with twenty varieties of gin and bar staff shaking ten quid cocktails.

Sure enough, Annabel doesn't show and there's no sign of Letty and Rowena. I wonder why I didn't invite Luke to come out with me for my birthday instead? I really like him and I think he likes me too. It would have been much better than sitting here like Billy No Mates. I have a sniffy moment, biting the inside of my mouth to hold back the tears. Thank God it passes before anyone notices. I scroll through hordes of birthday wishes on Insta, WhatsApp and Facebook. At least I have online friends who wish me a happy birthday, even if most are people I hardly know or I've never met. But at least they don't hassle you about your life choices or tell you you're rotten inside.

'Hey, birthday girl! Lovely to see you, darling! Shove over, let me get you a drink. What are you on?'

Letty is her usual exuberant self, throwing her arms round me. She's black, busty and beautiful. Never does much with her hair and hardly bothers with lipstick or mascara. But men would throw themselves at her even if she was wearing a nun's habit. Rowena, ghostly white beside her, looks me up and down with a smile that's more like a sneer.

'Hi, Jez. Many happy returns. How's things?' She turns to Letty before I've opened my mouth. 'A double G and T please, hun.'

Rowena's perfume catches at the back of my throat. A blast of envy hits as I take in her outfit – a plunge-back dress in a shimmery material. Definitely designer, it must have cost a few hundred. Her hair looks freshly balayaged and her nails are new. I rush to the loo and do what I can with my makeup.

Letty can tell I'm pissed off. She whispers to me it's bad for Row to try and outdo the birthday girl and I'm better looking than Row anyway. We bitch about Rowena while she swans off to this guy who's looking her over. Row went to a private school and has doting parents who took her skiing every year. Neither of us can understand why she's hanging around with gangsters.

Letty pats my arm. 'There's gonna be a party tonight, hun, at Yasmin's. Come with us, as it's your birthday.'

'Cool.'

As far as I've been able to make out, Yasmin is the gang's 'top girl' in their crew of groupies, girlfriends and baby mothers. She's the mother of Karim's three-year-old son. Karim is number two in the crew. The elders run things. They don't hang out with the others and have their own secret meetings. I've not met any of them. Zom isn't one but he says he'll be one soon. No one tells me much as I'm a girl – girls can't be proper members. But I find out bits and pieces. It's like the masons with all their special words, hand signs and whatnot.

Rowena sits swinging her leg, showing off four-inch stilettos.

Letty smiles at me. 'We'll introduce you to the top Gs, if you like.'

Letty is Spicer's girlfriend. Spicer is the crew's number three, I think. Since I started seeing Zom, she's been extra friendly to me. She says we girls should stick together. We've been out drinking five times now, usually with Rowena tagging along.

———

The bass is loud enough to crush anything small, like eardrums. There's an overpowering smell of skunk. I'm getting high just standing here. After the noise and the smell, I notice how rammed it is. No one is wearing a mask or trying to social distance, *quelle surprise*. I spot a woman who could be Yasmin. She's got a fur stole around her shoulders and is covered in ice.

I hurry to follow Row and Letty up the staircase. With all the chardonnay and the cocktails in the pub, I need to pee badly. When I come out of the bathroom, I can't find Letty. I start to panic, thinking she's left without me. The skunk must be making me paranoid. Maybe I shouldn't have had those puffs in my room first. I go back downstairs. I find Rowena on a sofa chatting to two guys.

Letty appears, shouting through the music. 'Jez, come and meet Spicer!'

Spicer has cornrows, three diamond studs in his ear and tattoos all over his hands and arms.

'Hey, Jez.' He waves at me.

I wave back.

Spicer starts nuzzling Letty's ear.

I see Zom. He's dancing with a girl, very close. Her boobs spill out of her dress. His hands are on her hips. He's crouching down so his lips are touching hers. They know each other, obv. I feel sick. He said I was special and I believed him.

I go where they won't see me. I tell myself so what, I knew from the start I was probably one of many. Zom's a gangster, after all. Half an hour later, I'm on a stool in the kitchen, knocking back another vodka tonic.

Letty finds me. I ask who the girl is.

'That's Jacy. His ex.' She lets me go on about how my birthday is ruined, then squeezes my hand. 'You should be careful with that one, hun. He won't treat you right. He only cares about number one. There's other boys who'll treat you like a queen. I'd be on the lookout for one of them, if I were you.'

She introduces me to more Gs. Then this guy comes up. He's not drinking or smoking anything. Letty introduces us. People are yelling in the background so I don't catch his name. I feel myself stand straighter. He looks different to the others, way more together. He's lean, not as well built as Zom. Without that odd dent in his cheek, he could be a male model or an actor, no question. He has a stillness about him, like he's keeping himself under control until he needs to unleash his inner cobra.

His necklace is made of what looks like dice, but when you look closer, they're actually miniature skulls.

'Ivory,' he says. He puts out his hand.

A buzz goes through me as I take it. No one my age shakes hands, especially since the pandemic.

'Pleased to meet you, Jez.' He's so chilled, so charming.

'Pleased to meet you... Sorry, I didn't get your name.' I feel a total dork. Thank goodness the music's loud so I have an excuse.

A guy comes up to him and starts talking, ignoring me. After a few minutes I get up and look for Letty.

'Who's that dude I was talking to?'

She grins, all her teeth showing. 'That's V.'

'V?'

'He's top G.'

'Really?' I'm starstruck.

———

I look around for Letty. I need to go home. No sign of her, but Zom sees me and comes over. He puts a hand on my shoulder.

'Hey, babe. Enjoying the party?'

I don't reply. He can fuck right off.

'Wanna go back to the den with me?'

I shake my head. He's been kissing someone else, of course I don't want to go with him. I look for Letty again, hoping she can call me a cab or whatever – I barely trust myself to stand up. Then I see her, miles away, kissing Spicer.

Zom says he'll get us an Uber back to the den.

'No thanks. I just want to go home. I'm wasted.'

He frowns. 'Don't be jealous, girl. She ain't nothin' to me, that bitch. Water under the bridge.'

I go with him because I'm too out of it to call an Uber or cab myself, and I don't want to have an argument with Zom in front of everyone.

As soon as we step through the doorway, he says he wants to fuck me.

'I can't now,' I say, taking off my jacket. 'I need to lie down.'

'You can lie down afterwards. I'm so hard for you, babe.'

Before I've even put my bag down, he grabs my arm, pulls me

to the sofa and starts taking off my top. I tell him to leave me alone but he doesn't. Suddenly, I'm scared. The room is moving in circles and my head feels so light I could pass out. I don't say anything else, there's no point.

Afterwards, I close my eyes. Tears dribble down my cheeks. I lie there not moving, don't even bother to wipe my eyes or put my clothes back on. Zom is talking to me. I don't answer.

'Shit, babe, you're scaring me! Sit up and drink.'

I sip from the glass of water. 'Why did you do that? What's wrong with you?'

'Don't get upset, babe. We've got a good thing going, you and me.'

He puts his hand on my arm. I want to push it off but I don't.

CALLUM

I WAS AT MY DESK WADING THROUGH THE EMAILS WHEN A CALL came in from the duty officer at Tottenham police station.

'DI Waverley? Someone in your team might want to talk to this woman that's just come in. Nora Symonds, she lives in the Effra Lane estate. She's asking to speak to the detective in charge of Operation Rye. She has information about two males behaving suspiciously on the afternoon of the murder.'

Another dead end most likely, I thought, putting down the phone. I told DS Harper to go over and try to find out whether this woman knew anything useful. Thirty minutes later Sam called, sounding unusually irritated.

'The woman knows something, but she's rambling. She'd obviously prefer to speak to you... I think you should come and talk to her, sir, before she has second thoughts.'

I grabbed my jacket and laptop bag and rushed downstairs, bypassing the lift. The building had been refurbished and kitted out with the latest technology – advanced security, state-of-the-art major incident rooms, auto-flush loos, you name it. For some reason though, the wheezy old lift was still in place. This was more than likely another false alarm. But I couldn't help hoping.

As soon as I arrived at the nick, DS Harper hurried off for a dental appointment. I made my way to interview room two.

'Mrs Symonds? Thank you for coming in. I'm DI Waverley, I'm in charge of the Solita Milton investigation.'

'Nora Symonds, that's right.' The woman stood as I entered, meeting my gaze with unwavering greyish-blue eyes. 'Pleased to meet you, Detective.'

My first impressions were of an intelligent, well-educated, self-possessed woman on the cusp of old age. Not well off and slightly eccentric. She wore cheap spectacles with a smudge on one lens, a cardigan and old-fashioned blouse over trousers. A floral scarf was tied around her neck and her shoulder-length grey hair looked freshly cut.

'Please, sit down.' I opened my notepad. 'You live on the Effra Lane estate, I understand?'

'That's right. I've lived in Delius Tower for nearly twenty years. Alone, except for the occasional cat – and the occasional friend who comes to stay.' She flashed a set of white, perfectly aligned teeth. I glanced at a black cotton face mask on the table in front of her. She looked at it too, with distaste.

'Do you need me to put that dreadful thing on?'

'No, don't worry about it, I'll do the same.' I slipped mine off, wary of making a false step in the minefield of Covid etiquette. If it helped the comfort of a potentially valuable witness... 'How can I help you, Mrs Symonds?'

'I've got to be honest with you, Inspector. I should have said something before. But every time I was about to pick up the phone and dial the police station, I thought better of it.' She shifted in her chair. 'These seats aren't the most comfortable, are they?' Another broad smile.

Despite my impatience, I smiled too. This woman wouldn't be hurried. She seemed to enjoy having an audience.

'I'll do my best to be brief. The afternoon that the girl was murdered, I was coming home from the library. I was about to shut my front door when I saw two young men coming along the corridor and go into the flat next door. They were talking and didn't see me. I recognised both of them – they used to be regular visitors.'

I asked if she could describe the men.

'The bigger one was white, very muscular – his shoulders in particular. Oh yes, and small ears. That's how I knew it was definitely him. 'The other one was black, about the same age but slighter in build. He had a thin face and a lot of facial hair... It gave me such a jolt to see them again.'

My heart rate increased. She was describing our two suspects, surely. I was about to ask what about the two men had seemed suspicious, when Mrs Symonds continued.

'I suppose I'd better tell you about the other matter as well. For the past few months there's been almost daily disturbances next door – loud arguments, bad language... I've reported it to the housing officer three times but nothing has changed.'

I sighed as quietly as possible, wishing she'd get to the point. Soon, Mrs Symonds would be off to sea and I'd be adrift, without any signposts to dry land.

'Did you report this to the police?'

'No, I didn't. I complained to one of the men next door a month or so ago, said I'd had it with their constant disturbances and if it didn't stop, I was going to the police.' She lowered her head, fingers playing with a loose button on her cardigan. 'I let myself get carried away.' Her Adam's apple shifted. 'I've had my suspicions for a while, you see.'

'Suspicions that...?'

'That something wasn't right with that flat.' She lowered her voice. 'My neighbour on the other side, Sophie, thinks I've got the headquarters of the local gang living next door.'

'That's the flat that the two men went into?'

'That's right.'

'Number?'

'814. Mine is 815.'

I noted down the number. This was getting interesting. Mrs Symonds took off her smudged glasses and gave them a wipe before continuing.

'There's been gangs around the estate for years, since I moved in. It's got worse lately, though. They think they can lord it over everyone else. Sophie warned me not to say anything about the noise. But I thought, Sod it, I've had enough. So, I had a word with one of the men in the flat – he's an Arab chap and always looks like he's having a bad day. He didn't say anything then but when I left my flat a few hours later to go for my afternoon walk, those two men I told you about were waiting for me.'

I waited for her to continue. I badly wanted to ask about the afternoon of the murder, so I'd know if all this was leading anywhere.

'The bigger one started walking beside me and talking to me in a hostile tone. He said some crude, horrible things. The other one laughed and said I shouldn't poke my nose into things that don't concern me.' She was visibly upset now, breathing hard. I moved her glass of water closer. 'I turned to go into the lift but they told me to come with them. I didn't know what to do. I was about to scream when the bigger one got out a huge knife – I'd never seen anything like it – and pointed it at my chest.' She closed her eyes for a moment. 'So, I went with them into the stairwell and did what they said. They put their hands all over me... I don't want to go into the details. It was horrendous.'

Mrs Symonds took a sip of water. The glass trembled and water splashed out as she returned it to the table.

'They said if I ever went to the police – if I grassed them up – I'd get worse. Then they left me sprawled on the floor. I must have been there for five minutes when the elderly man from the ninth floor came past and helped me back to my flat.'

I felt ashamed then for being impatient with this woman. Mrs Symonds had suffered so much, yet had been brave enough to come to the police, risking even worse.

'I'm sorry,' I said. 'It must have been very difficult for you to come here today, given what they did to you.' I wanted to squeeze her hand. Instead, I took a gulp of water to clear the lump in my throat.

Mrs Symonds rustled inside her handbag, produced a tissue, dabbed at her eyes then blew her nose. She put her handbag aside and looked at me. Her voice was stronger now, each syllable articulated with precision.

'What they did to me... I felt violated, it shocked me to the core. But what they did to that young girl was so much worse. When I heard on the news about her being stabbed, I felt sick to the stomach. I knew I had to tell someone about what I saw that afternoon. Every time I was going to, though, I changed my mind.'

'I'm very grateful that you've come in now, Mrs Symonds. Now, if you don't mind...' I asked if she would come with me to the interview suite, where we could video record the conversation.

'Of course. Lead the way.'

Opening formalities over, I posed the question I'd been waiting to ask.

'What *did* you see the afternoon of Solita Milton's murder, Mrs Symonds?'

'As I said, the two men who assaulted me were walking past my door as I was about to leave my flat. The smaller one had a rucksack over one shoulder. The bigger one had a red patch on the front of his sweatshirt. It was an irregular shape, as if blood had splashed onto him. I remember that clearly, because I wondered if they had a washing machine in that flat and who did their washing, and whether that stain would come out. Then the smaller one said something.'

She brought a floral-covered A5 notebook out of her bag and opened it at the bookmark.

'"She's history, fam. The blade went clean through her. She ain't gonna be telling no one you did it." The other one said, "V owes me for this. If he gives me any shit you gotta back me, man."' She grimaced. 'Those were the precise words they used. I wrote them down in my journal. I remember noticing the appalling grammar.'

Adrenalin pumped through me. Thank Christ. This was indisputable evidence – and it could be the breakthrough we needed. The words implied that the killing had been premeditated, and implicated the Skull Crew's leader in Solita's murder.

'Did you see or hear anything else?'

'No, nothing else.'

'Can I look at the journal?'

Reluctantly, she placed the opened notebook down on the table in front of me. The words were easily legible. 'This is important evidence. I'll have to keep it, I'm afraid.'

She seemed about to argue, then nodded. 'I'm sure you'll take good care of it, Inspector.'

I smiled. 'I certainly will. Going back to the conversation you overheard. What time was it?'

'A quarter past four – I checked my watch after I closed the front door. It showed twenty-five past but I always keep it ten minutes fast.'

'What did you do after that?'

She had sat down with a glass of water, 'quite shaken'.

'Have you told anyone else about what you witnessed?'

'I told my neighbour, Sophie. She promised to keep it to herself.'

My heart sank. If anyone in the gang ever found out what Nora Symonds had seen...

'What time did you talk to Sophie?'

'A little after seven that evening.'

'What did you tell her, exactly?'

'I said I'd seen two young men go to the flat next door, shortly after the young black girl was stabbed outside the estate – and one of them had what looked like blood on his top. She agreed that it was suspicious. I told her I was going to the police but she said not to, the gang might find out.'

Mrs Symonds rubbed at the worn strap of her bag. I asked if she would be willing to testify in court about what she had witnessed.

'Yes, I should think so.'

I breathed a sigh of relief.

'Thanks again for coming in, Mrs Symonds,' I said, closing my rough book. 'I can't tell you how important the information you've given us is.'

She nodded. 'I'm glad I've been of help. I only wish I'd had the courage to come in before.'

'What did make you come in, if you don't mind me asking?'

A few seconds passed. I've intruded too much on her privacy already, I thought.

'A few weeks ago, I was diagnosed with ovarian cancer.' Her eyes didn't waver from mine. 'The doctor says it could be terminal. I thought, why not do something useful in the time I've got left?'

I could have hugged her. 'I'm extremely glad you did, Mrs Symonds. I only wish more people had as much courage as you.'

'Is there anything else, Inspector?'

I asked about her plans for the next week or two. We needed

to think of the woman's safety, given the potential for retribution should the gang find out that she had spoken to us. *Snitches get stiches*, the saying used to be. *Ditches for snitches*, it went now.

'We need you away from the estate for a while. Is there a friend or relative you can stay with until I've arranged alternative accommodation for you?' If I had my way, I'd take this woman to a five-star hotel well away from that ghastly estate until she was found somewhere suitable. Unfortunately, the budget for such measures was limited.

'There's my goddaughter, I haven't seen her in ages. Or my sister. I'm sure I can arrange something with someone.' She blinked at me. 'Do you think I'm in danger, then?'

The short answer was yes. But there was no point putting the fear of god into the woman.

'By coming forward with information you are at a slightly increased risk of harm, it's fair to say. But I'll do everything I can to minimise that risk.'

'I see. Thanks for being straight with me.' She looked more resigned than upset or fearful.

'Do you have a mobile phone, Mrs Symonds?'

The woman picked up her bag and rested it on the table. 'Somewhere among this collection of bits and pieces, there should be.'

I suggested that she arrange somewhere to stay immediately, then waited while she phoned her sister in Horsham to explain she needed a bed for the next few nights, possibly longer. After a short break, I took Mrs Symonds through the arrangements I'd made.

'I've asked one of my officers to contact the council for you. They'll find you somewhere to live for a few months, out of harm's way, where no one will know you.'

Her eyes had become vacant, as if she hadn't heard. A plain-clothes officer would drive her back to her flat, I told her, and wait with her while she packed her things. Then they would drive her to her sister's. The crease on her brow deepened but she said nothing.

'If you're ever worried about your safety,' I went on, 'you can phone me, day or night.' I gave my number for her to write down. 'If there's an immediate threat though, dial 999.' We would set up a History Marker on her mobile and landline, I said, to save her from having to explain what had happened if she ever needed to call Emergency Services.

'You're going to a great deal of trouble.' She gave a dry titter. 'I feel like a VIP.'

'It's the least we can do.'

———

DI Kenyon agreed with me, that Nora Symonds's conclusion that the gang had made a base in that flat next door to her was credible.

A search of flat 814 might find evidence that linked one of the killers to the murder. But what I really wanted was the killers themselves. The surveillance team would keep a close eye on the flat in case Vincent Edwards, Muscleman or Wolf turned up.

LUKE

THEY TRIED IT ON AGAIN TODAY. THIS TIME, ONLY ADEN AND the other boy in my class.

I'm outside the classroom with some others, waiting to go in for the last period of the day – English with Miss Collins. I'm zoning out, not aware of anything much around me. Suddenly someone shoves into me hard from behind, making me stumble forward. I look up, see Aden standing behind me on the other side of the door, smirking at me.

I'm tense all through the lesson. When the bell goes, Miss Collins signals me to come over.

'Thanks for handing in your homework, Luke.'

'I tried my best with it, Miss,' I say. 'I know it's not up to the standard it used to be.' It only got a five – last year I used to get eights, nines and tens.

'That's OK. If you're doing your best, that's what matters. How are you getting on with the essay?'

'I've not started it yet. I find it hard to focus on things for long. Stuff gets in the way.'

She leans against the teacher's table, facing me, makes a *mmm* sound.

'That could be to do with losing your mum. Grief can affect people in all sorts of ways. Have you told the counsellor?'

'I'm not seeing her anymore.' That last session was bad. We sat in silence for most of it, then she said I don't need to come back.

'Is there anything else that might be affecting your work, Luke? Apart from your mum, I mean.'

'Not really.' I don't know what to say. I wish I could tell her about Kevin.

She rubs the back of her neck. Both her cheeks have a blotch of red. She knows I'm not being straight with her and I feel bad for that. She wants to help. She's the only teacher who's noticed I'm struggling.

There's a knock on the door, which is wide open. Both Miss Collins and I look up at the same time. It's Ruby, the girl who causes trouble in every class she's in.

'I thought I left my scarf here... Oh, sorry! Am I interrupting?' She backs away quickly.

'Wait, Ruby—'

Miss Collins looks at the doorway, shaking her head. Ruby's gone.

'I'll put you down for the extra tuition group in period six. It's for all of the core subjects. That will help you prepare for your GCSEs.' Her voice is crisper now. She picks up her bag of exercise books and goes ahead to the door. 'If there's anything you want help with, just ask. You have so much potential, I'd hate to see it wasted.'

———

Jez is hurrying along the corridor, head down. She doesn't see me.

'Hey, stranger.' I catch her up, walk alongside her. 'How did it go?'

A pack of kids emerge from a classroom ahead, crowding the corridor. She slows, looks at me. 'How did what go?'

'Your birthday. Didn't you say it was your birthday on the fourteenth? I thought I'd see you in school before then but you didn't turn up.'

'It was pretty crap, actually. One of my worst birthdays ever.' Her tone is weirdly upbeat. Is she upset with me?

'Only asking. I forgot to get your number, or I'd have called and wished you a happy birthday.'

She looks hard at me. Her cheeks are flushed, like she's been running. Her skirt is tight over her bum and her blouse is unbuttoned at the top, no tie. Her dark brown hair loops over her shoulder and down her back, a shiny snake.

'Sorry you didn't have a good time.' I look across the corridor to the school entrance. Kids are streaming out. 'Are you free now? We could go for a walk or something.'

'A walk? You know how to impress a girl, don't you?' Jez carries on along the corridor. Her legs are so long, I can barely keep up. 'Sorry, I can't talk now. I've got to see Miss Jenkins.' She rolls her eyes. 'She's probably going to give me another bollocking for missing yesterday's class.' She nods her head to the school entrance. 'Meet me outside the gates in twenty. I should be finished by then.'

———

'How did it go?' I ask. Jez leans against the wire fence, pulls a drink carton out of her bag, sucks up from the straw. 'Did she give you a hard time?'

She tosses the empty carton on the pavement and kicks it. Her eyes are glittery.

'Are you OK, Jez?' I stand in front of her, take hold of her arms so she has to look at me. 'What happened? Are you in trouble?'

She moves her head to one side, says nothing.

'Was it about you not going into school?'

She pulls away and starts walking. I catch up. Her head stays down. She presses a finger into the corner of her eye.

It's one of those days between summer and autumn. The leaves of smaller trees have turned yellow and gold. A bus goes by, rammed with school kids. We walk past the estate to the canal. Jez still doesn't talk.

'Let's sit down. Tell me what happened.' We sit on a bench inside the park.

'She's banned me.'

'From school?'

'No, the show. I can't be in *The Lion King*. I was going to be Nala. She's given my part to someone else.' Her chest heaves. 'It's the only frickin' thing I wanted to do in this school, and she's gone and taken it away.'

A tear drips down her cheek. Her desolation passes into me.

'Why? Because you didn't turn up to class?'

'I planned to come in yesterday but I couldn't, I had to do something outside school. I said I was really, really sorry. She goes, "Well it's not just this week is it, you've missed two periods since the start of term," blah blah. Then she goes on about me disrespecting some girl who's totally clueless and saying I'm not showing any commitment. I fucking hate her.' She digs in her bag, finds a tissue and wipes her face.

'That sucks,' I say. 'Why couldn't you go in to school?'

She shrugs. 'This guy I told you about. He asked me to do something for him. I didn't want to but I had no choice.'

'This guy from the gang?'

She nods.

'What did he want you to do?'

She frowns, shakes her head. 'It doesn't matter.'

'He told you not to tell anyone?'

'Yeah, that's right.'

It's chilly now. The bench is in shadow. 'Got a jumper?'

Jez doesn't answer. Her head is lowered, her elbows propped on her thighs.

I look in her bag, find her school jumper. 'Here, put this on.'

'Thanks.' She almost smiles. 'You're all right, you know.'

I ask if she wants to get something to eat. 'We could get a bus back to the estate. There's takeaways nearby.' I text Kirsty, say I won't be in for dinner.

We sit across the table from each other at the chicken shop. Out of the window, a line of traffic stops and starts.

Jez leaves most of her chicken and chips. I eat mine and wrap the rest for Kirsty.

''Scuse me a minute.'

A big bloke comes into the shop, orders in a loud voice. Pans clatter and frying smells fill the room. Jez comes back with more eye makeup on but it doesn't hide that she's been crying. Her eyes are extra sparkly.

'How's your stepfather been?' she says.

'Much nicer lately.'

'That's good.' She smiles teasingly. 'So, you won't need to stay at mine anymore?'

I smile back. 'I dunno 'bout that.'

He hasn't tried to hurt me again. But my heart starts racing whenever I hear his footsteps.

'He came into the kitchen the other day. I didn't see him 'til he was right behind me. My heart went crazy and my hand shot up like I was going to hit him. I didn't know what I was doing.'

She leans forward, takes my hand. Her skin is cool against mine.

'You shouldn't have to live with someone like that.'

'What can I do about it? I can't grass him up. He'd kill me. He used to be a pro boxer.'

Jez is winding her hair round her finger. Her eyes are fixed on mine. Today, they're a soft cloud-grey. 'You could come and stay at mine a while. 'Til you can earn your own money.'

'What about your mum?'

'She likes you. She told me after you'd gone.'

'Thanks for the offer. I'd rather not leave Kirsty alone with Kevin, though.'

'Does he hit her, too?'

'No, but he loses it sometimes. When you think he's OK, something sets him off.'

I look outside. Headlights pick out rushing figures. Jez takes out her phone.

'Give me your number,' she says. She taps it in, not looking at me.

I tell her I'll call a cab but she says she'll wait for the bus. Suddenly she leans forward and kisses me on the lips. A shiver goes down my spine and a smile passes between us. I don't say anything, nor does she.

JEZ

HOME COOKING

I couldn't tell Luke the reason I couldn't make drama.

Zom phoned me at seven fifteen in the morning while I was asleep. There was some fuck-up in the house where they cook up drugs and he needed my help. The gist was, they needed to get a large amount of 'hard food' out the door in a rush, but the boys already there were knackered after twenty-four hours non-stop and no one's youngers were answering their phones.

I told him I was knackered, too, after going to bed late and not sleeping well. Credit to Zom, he did sound apologetic for waking me up at such an unsocial time. He said he knew it was a lot to ask but he knew I wouldn't let him down.

'Spicer's over there. He asked if you'd be willing to step in. I said you'd be a safe pair of hands. You're smart, you've got gumption. It's a big deal, Jez. You'd be doin' me and the boys a big favour.'

Well, how could I refuse after that?

It wasn't what I expected, not that I'd thought much before

about what goes on in the drug dealing business. A minicab picked me up and took me to this scruffy house in south Tottenham. A boy in a hoodie answered the door. I'd done as Zom had said: not brought any cash and wore my raggiest clothes. My school uniform was in my tote bag – I had to be out of the place in time for drama at two o'clock.

The smell in the kitchen made me want to puke. I wondered if I'd be able to spend fifteen minutes there.

Spicer looked like he'd been up all night. He stood at the kitchen worktop poking a knife into a yellowish gunk in a big plastic beaker. Beside him, a boy about fourteen in a *South Park* T-shirt was pouring baking soda into a bowl. He had stains on his T-shirt and looked deeply miserable. The hoodie boy went back to stirring a bubbling pot on the cooker.

'Hi, Jez, meet the crack crew,' Spicer said. 'And this is Karim.'

It was the guy who'd interrupted me and V at the party. He was shorter and lighter-skinned than the others, with sullen eyes.

'You're Zom's girl?' He said it like I might have been a police spy and didn't speak to me again. He didn't do anything much except make phone calls and drink coffee.

Spicer set me to work in the next room helping to wrap up the rocks of crack they'd already made. *South Park* boy showed me how. Once I got the hang of it, I got bored and asked for some music. The boy insisted on loud grime, 'til I went to Spicer and told him to switch it off or I'd leave. Spicer laughed. He was chilled, the opposite of frosty Karim. He said he was glad Zom had thought to ask me to help.

After the wrapping was done, I helped clean up the kitchen. The mood was less frantic and everyone perked up. They were going to deliver the crack on time, Spicer told me.

It was three by the time we finished. I really didn't want to miss drama, not after the bollocking I got from Miss Jenkins in the last one, for telling someone that her acting was never going to set the West End ablaze. But I was done in by then, my throat was sore and I didn't want to do anything except go home and fall asleep.

Spicer told me what a big help I'd been, it was great to know that they could count on me to pitch in. He took my number and said he might have more work for me. I said no way am I doing that again and he laughed and gave me two fifties. Actually, that was more than I was expecting, so I was happy – until I was cut out of *The Lion King*, that is. Cut out of the biggest part I've ever had.

CALLUM

20TH SEPTEMBER

THE RESIDENTIAL STREET WAS QUIET, THE DARKNESS WAS broken only by the flickering light from a TV screen in the window of the house opposite. It was nearly eleven in the evening and I needed to be in bed. I tried Brendan's number once more then honked the horn. I was about to step out when my son hurried across the road towards the VW.

'Sorry, Dad, didn't hear my phone.'

'Never mind, you're here now.' I got back inside. 'How was the film?'

'Not bad.' Brendan got inside. I started the engine. 'It was an Almodovar—' He stopped, leaning forward into the footwell then sat upright holding something with both hands. The white, rounded object glistened faintly blue in the dashboard lights. A skull. A human skull? My pulse thudded in my ears.

'Christ.' Brendan held the skull higher, rotating it this way and that.

It was the right size and shape. I switched on the interior

light and checked off the key signs. Bulbous brain case, huge eye sockets above the nasal bone, a pointed chin bone at the lower front, small canines...

I tapped the frontal bone. It was plastic or resin, not bone. My breath surged out. It was one of those realistic, life-size skulls used in anatomy classes.

'It's not real,' I said, feeling like an idiot. 'It's made from a mould or 3D-printed, maybe.'

'It fooled me too.'

'Careful with it,' I said as Brendan held the object above his head and peered up into the base.

'Cool! It's even got a foramen magnum.'

'A what?'

'The hole for the spinal cord... The jaw doesn't move.'

'Can you put it down 'til we get home?'

'There was a blanket over it. I'll put it back where it was.' He set the skull down.

I drove towards the main road, my mind on high alert. When had that thing been put in my car? And how?

Brendan looked at me. 'Do you think someone got into the car while it was parked outside our house?'

I didn't reply. I'd locked it after I'd got home from work, I was ninety-nine per cent sure. Maybe someone had put the skull in my car while I was at work. I'd parked as usual that morning in my allocated space at the stalag. Could someone have taken my car key from my inside jacket pocket while I wasn't at my desk, hurried down to the car, planted the skull then put the key back? It was possible, at a stretch. The incident room had almost emptied out at lunchtime. Anyone in the murder team would have had an opportunity to grab that key, if they'd been quick – I'd gone for a twenty-minute jog around the park, leaving my jacket draped over the back of my chair.

———

I held an evidence bag open. 'Put it in,' I said to Brendan in the kitchen. He lowered the skull into it. I opened another bag. 'And the blanket in this one.' He squeezed in the small, rolled-up black blanket. I'd get the bags over to Professor Singh in the morning. I took out the bottle of Grappa from the cupboard; the Glenfiddich was nearly out.

'Is someone trying to scare you?' Brendan leaned against the door frame, watching me.

'It'll take more than some bloody idiot playing around with fake skulls to scare me.' I downed a small quantity of alcohol. 'Are you all right, kiddo? That was quite a shock.'

'Course I am.' He filled a beer glass with water and drank most of it. 'Who do you think it might be?'

I shook my head.

21ST SEPTEMBER

Next morning, I called Detective Superintendent Bailey at home and told him about the latest skull. There was a long pause then a throat-clearing noise.

'This is concerning, Callum. We'll see if Forensics comes up with anything. In the meantime, we'd better get you some extra security at home. This looks like a message from the skull gang.'

'With respect, sir, is that necessary? They're probably just trying to mess with my head. I doubt there's any intent to harm me.'

'It could be a warning. If they've found out where you live... I'm taking this seriously.'

I agreed to get a home security system installed pronto. The super offered to get it done through the Met but I insisted I'd organise it myself. Maybe I'd spent too long peering at footage from hidden cameras, but those security cameras would be operational twenty-four seven, recording me coming into my own house along with anyone who visited. I didn't want that data getting into the wrong hands.

That evening, Brendan helped me select a smart home security system featuring high-definition, wide-angle night vision video cameras and facial recognition software, which would send updates of any unusual activity outside the house to my PC and mobile phone. I also ordered a light- and motion-sensitive external light for the porch, and asked the electrician to install a timer so that the lights inside the house would come on after dark.

'Thanks for helping out,' I said. We'd been at the task for three hours. 'I don't like all this, but better safe...'

'No, it's cool.' Brendan yawned, grabbed his headset and got up from the sofa.

Though it seemed more likely that whoever had planted the skull was someone trying to mess with my mind rather than physically harm me, there was Brendan to consider. I would need to do everything I could to protect him.

JEZ

ZOMBIE

When the doorbell rings at eight in the evening, Mum's on it. I have to leap in front of her and coax her back into the living room where she was soaking her feet in a bowl of Epsom salts. The thought of Zom seeing Mum with her stained dressing gown and wet feet gives me the extra impetus I need.

'Who's that at the door?' Mum's voice comes through the living room door.

'A friend,' I call out. 'I'll be out for a while. Back later tonight, probably.'

'You didn't say you were expecting a friend! And I didn't say you could stay out late—'

I step outside, closing the door quickly behind me. Oh my godfathers, I hardly recognise him. Standing there in the front porch is my date, all six foot of him. He's dressed up. Suit, proper shoes, aftershave, the works.

He bends down to kiss my cheek, takes my hand and without a word ushers me into the BMW. Despite my intention to play it cool with him, I can't help smiling. Where has this Zom been hiding? He nearly always wears jeans and trainers when he takes me out – putting on a shirt is the closest he comes to dressing up.

I wonder what's brought all this on. Does he feel bad about forcing himself on me? Maybe he feels bad that the favour I did him made Miss Jenkins fall out with me. Maybe he's scared I'm going to tell him that it's all over.

We speed along, the speakers creating a concert hall inside the car. I steal a glance at Zom. Minus the stubble that usually furs his jaw, the planes of his face are to die for.

'How's my babe?'

'I'm good,' I say. 'And you don't look so bad either.'

He tilts his head back and smiles wide, his new gold tooth showing up top.

'I wanted to look my best for you, sweetheart.'

We stop outside an Italian restaurant in Primrose Hill. As I press the button on the door handle to get out, he reaches into his JD Sports bag on the back seat.

'One minute. Can you carry this for me, babe? Put it in your bag.'

It's a knife. The one he showed me before, with a bright green handle and a monster serrated blade. There's a leather cover over the blade now.

He laughs at my face. 'It won't bite. The blade is put to bed, no one's gonna be goin' near it.' He puts his hand on my leg. 'Someone might see me here, get uppity. I always carry my blade, just in case. Better safe than shanked.'

'So why do you want me to—'

'It's better this way. No one will think to look in a girl's bag, will they?'

I drop it in. My bag is big enough that it doesn't stick out.

The restaurant is lush. The most expensive place I've eaten

in for months – no, years; back when Dad used to take Mum, Tara and me out for dinner. By the time we've eaten and drunk our way through three courses, my head is nicely woozy and I've almost forgotten there's a massive knife lying inside my bag.

I scrape up the last of my creamy chocolate dessert. Yes, I know I'm messing everything up. I know that this guy is a dangerous man and no way is he good for me, and I know I care about Luke way more than I care about Zom.

Zom pays the bill. The waiter takes the wad of twenties and the two have a little banter. The waiter is kiss-arse polite. I watch my gangster boyfriend get treated like a slick businessman and have a silent laugh. Money makes the world go round, that's for sure.

We're sitting there, meal over, when I remember the knife in my bag. Something pops into my head.

'What happened with the old woman?'

'What old woman?'

'The one you told me about. You know, the one who was going to complain to the police.'

He's blinking and slowly shaking his head as if he can't remember.

'C'mon, tell me. What did you do to her?'

'We followed her when she was on the way out for her daily walk. Pulled a shank on her an' took her for a walk down the stairs instead. When we'd finished with her, she was ready to cack herself.'

My hand goes to my mouth.

Zom smiles. 'We didn't hurt her or nothing. Told her what will happen if she don't keep her mouth shut.'

'Oh my god.' I stare at him. I've been hanging round with these boys for a while, so I know they get up to some real bad-boy stuff. But the thought of Zom touching this woman chills me.

Zom yawns, stretching his arms above his head. His biceps show through his shirt.

'The bitch will keep her mouth shut now, if she's got any sense. Girl, you shoulda seen us afterwards, we was cackin' ourselves.'

I point to my bag, on the chair beside me. A horrible thought comes to me. 'You didn't use that knife on her, did you?'

'Don't worry, babe, we just gave her a whiff of it.'

His eyes are hard, sort of empty. Suddenly I wonder what I'm doing with this guy, listening to him brag about humiliating an old woman half his size.

MOVING OUT

Around three in the afternoon I'm sitting around the table with Karim and Spicer at HQ, surrounded by the remains of a Domino's pizza. Spicer has asked me to do some admin for them, sorting out phone numbers with Vodafone.

Karim's phone rings. He picks up, scowling.

'Fuck. Fuck. Fuck.' Karim glares at Spicer and throws the phone on the table. 'Listen up, man. Rasheed's younger saw some guy sniffing round outside just now. He was fingering the door frame like he was looking for a bug. The exact same guy was here two days ago, he looks like a fed.'

'Shit, bro. That's serious.' Spicer wipes cheese off his mouth. 'The five-o are watching this place, what did I say? They could be in here any minute.'

I look at Spicer, fascinated and horrified.

Karim snaps his laptop shut, goes into the corridor and comes back in. 'Nothing up there now. We gotta skeet. Get onto V.'

Spicer calls but there's no answer. The two rush about, rummaging under sofa cushions, removing Ziploc bags and pulling bags and boxes out from under cupboards and beds. They keep cash and drugs in them, I'm sure.

I try to be useful. They've almost forgotten I'm here. Spicer says to Karim that Yasmin put eight grand into the salon's bank account this morning.

'One good thing, blud,' Karim replies. 'One fuckin' good thing. We gotta stash the food at V's for now.'

Spicer checks his phone again. 'V still ain't answering.'

Karim licks his lower lip again, his brow rucked. 'What's that man doing?'

Spicer laughs, catching my eye. 'Down in the basement polishing his skulls, innit.'

I smile. Karim still looks mad. He tells Spicer to get everything into the boot of his car and drive it over to V's. I offer to help.

'What happens if the feds catch us with this?' I ask as we carry it into the lift.

'We'd get nicked for dealing class As and fuck knows what else, and banged up.'

'Right.' A frisson of excitement merges with my anxiety. I'm a proper bad girl now. I risk another question. 'Are the feds bugging the flat, then?'

Spicer half frowns, half grins. 'You're nosey, girl. You ain't no undy, are you?'

'Pardon me for breathing.' I pretend to be miffed.

We go into the basement car park. I help Spicer shove bags and boxes into his Alfa Romeo. Then I hurry back up to the flat and ring the latest code on the door: short long long short.

Karim lets me in. He says to go around the place with cleaning fluid and a cloth and wipe down every single surface as if my life depended on it. Though my domestic skills aren't the best, I apply myself with gusto to the task then get to work with the hoover underneath the sofa cushions.

Someone bangs on the door.

'Who is it?'

It's Zom. I let him in.

'What the fuck's goin' on here?' He sniffs and stares around at the unusually clean and tidy flat.

'The feds are onto us,' I say.

Zom screws up his eyes. 'What are you doin' here, anyhow?'

'Just helping out.' I stare back. 'Spicer asked me to.'

He glowers and goes into the main bedroom. He and Karim start shouting at each other. I go to the closed bedroom door and listen.

'How do you know what Fatboy says is true?' Zom sounds well pissed – and underneath, scared. 'He's off his face half the time.'

'Nah, he's all right, that kid.' Karim stays cool. 'Come on, man, help me out here.' The thump of furniture being moved. 'We've gotta move from this place in any case. Everyone on the endz knows SC is behind the girl getting shanked. The five-o have been sneaking about for weeks. There's rumours that someone saw you and Wolf coming back here after.'

'It's that fuckin' bitch next door. If she grassed us up...' Zom sounds like he's going to explode. 'She's been giving me the evil eye lately.' A horrible feeling comes over me. I know they're talking about the woman he and Wolf molested.

'You know what? You're the one who caused this problem. You must be losing your touch, man.'

Zom yells back. 'You're chattin' shit! If the feds come, I'm the one who's gonna be busted. Me an' Wolf.'

'Not just you and Wolf,' Karim says.

I go in to hoover. Zom rifles through shelves, pulling out clothes and stuffing them into a travel bag. Karim's phone rings. He walks away, holding it to his ear. 'V, we're on it. We're closing up shop—'

Spicer bursts through the front door, panting. Karim gestures at the phone.

'Tell him the feds are on their way! I just got a heads-up from Bluebird.'

I've not heard of Bluebird before, or met them. Anyways, in less than two minutes the four of us are running down the corridor. Karim's laptop bag is slung over his shoulder. He's carrying a box that was stashed under a bed. Spicer carries speakers, a computer screen and the skull poster. Zom is lugging his sports bag and a bin bag of clothes. I'm carrying my Balenciaga bag with my Grazia, my Paperwhite and mini umbrella in it, plus another bag with spare trainers and a big bottle of smoothie and two bags of computer bits.

'I wanna see the feds' faces when they break in an' see the place emptied out,' Zom says.

Karim presses the lift button, ignoring him. I have a fit of giggles.

'Ever had a taser fired at you, girl? It's like getting blasted by a cattle prod. All your bits start zinging.'

That makes me laugh even more. We all charge into the tiny lift, squashing a boy with glasses. Karim backs out, yelling he'll take the stairs. Spicer follows.

'How 'bout a quick one?' Without warning, Zom pushes his body against mine. 'I know how much you like an audience, babe.'

'Get off me.' For a moment I think he's actually crazy enough. The lift arrives at the ground floor and the kid hurries out. I stare back at Zom. His body blocks my way out.

'I know what you're thinkin', you don't need me now. But don't think you can get away from me, girl. I'll take whatever I want, whenever I want.'

That's when I know for sure. I've got to get away from Zom.

CALLUM

24TH SEPTEMBER

I SWORE UNDER MY BREATH AS WE HURRIED TOWARDS FLAT 814 of Delius Tower. There was no one inside now, we'd just been told.

DS Freeman and myself gloved up and went into the flat with the search team. Muscleman had been spotted by the surveillance boys entering the flat several hours earlier. I'd given the go-ahead for the immediate arrest of all those found on the premises. The warrant had turned up quickly but the tactical support team hadn't got there in time.

Inside, the place had been thoroughly cleaned and looked suspiciously empty. From the strong smell of lemon and bleach, it looked as if the occupants had scarpered only minutes earlier.

'Fucking great,' I said, heaving a sigh. 'They knew we were coming.'

'Looks like we missed the boat,' Freeman said. He sounded a bit too nonchalant about that. A whisker of unease stirred.

'Someone must have tipped them off.'

'Or they spotted the camera and got suspicious. The surveillance boys might have got sloppy.'

The search of the flat yielded a small package of cannabis underneath the sofa, but no knives, gloves, balaclavas or rucksacks were found, nor any items of clothing resembling those shown on the CCTV images. However, some fingerprints were found in various places and the dog sniffed out a tiny quantity of dried blood on the side of the bathroom sink.

Results on the fingerprints came in after we arrived back at the stalag. It was bad news – they didn't match any prints stored on the database. Not bothering to hide my disappointment, I told everyone on my dwindling team to go home early. The only ray of hope was the result of the DNA test on the blood.

On the way home, Professor Singh from Forensics called about the skull that Brendan had found. It had been 3D printed, like the paperweight skull. No fingerprints or DNA had been found on it.

'We've tested the hair we got from the blanket, though.'

My heart skipped a beat. 'Yes?'

'It's from a cat. A ragdoll or similar breed.'

My hopes of finding out the identity of the person who'd planted the damned thing vanished like chalk under a duster.

'Cheers, Suresh,' I replied. 'You've just ruined my evening.' Whatever breed it was, it made little difference. To my knowledge, the police didn't keep a database of feline DNA.

LUKE

THEY CAME FOR ME AGAIN TODAY.

It was lunch break. Jez had shared my lunch, then she went outside for a cigarette. I stayed on the bench, thinking I ought to look at my books if I'm gonna get any GCSEs.

'Yo, saddo. You don't only look like shit, you smell like shit.'

Aden stands with his legs apart, hands on hips. The other white boy, smaller and thinner, is with him. His chin is red with acne.

'Fuck off, both of you.'

Zitface smiles, curling his lip. 'Making out with the Jezzy, are we?'

Aden sniggers. 'Word is she's up for it.'

They're walking away from the bench. I follow. I know they're goading me.

They break into a run and disappear round the corner of the science block. I catch up. We're alone, the three of us. On one side is a fence and bushes, on the other is the football pitch. No cameras.

Aden moves to me, leering. 'Seen Miss Collins, lately?' Spit comes out with his words. 'Are you giving it to her, too?'

The fire takes over. When I was younger Kevin spent hours teaching me boxing, showing me videos of matches. He'd say, imagine you're dancing, every movement must be perfectly balanced and controlled. I thought he hadn't taught me anything. But as I start punching and kicking, something clicks into place.

I land another punch to Aden's face. He staggers back, moaning.

'Get him off me!'

Zitface kicks me in the knee, his heel striking hard, toppling me. I'm lying on the ground, defenceless. Aden comes over, snot and blood running down his face. He raises his foot, swings his leg back. The blow lands below my ribs. He kicks again into the small of my back. Again, into my balls.

The pain sucks away my breath. It shoots through my body to my fingers and toes, the worst pain I've ever had. I'm panicking, can't get enough air. Then something happens. Inside me, the flames leap. I'm on my feet.

Zitface yells at me to get off, then legs it. Kids and teachers arrive. They pull me off Aden.

'Fucking call an ambulance!'

'He's gone loco!'

'Shit, what have you done to him?'

Everything is muffled, unreal. The pain comes back, making me sway. Sweat or blood drips into my eye. I can't wipe it. Someone is holding my arms behind me.

'The show's over, kids.' Mr Lee. 'Go back to class.'

Mr Ryan, the PE teacher, crouches down beside Aden. Aden is on the grass, moaning. His face is a mess. Blood is smeared on his cheek.

Mr Lee tugs on my arm. 'Come with me.'

I dig my heels into the earth. I need to stay. I'm afraid of what I've done to Aden. Mr Lee makes me walk with him towards the school buildings. No one is around. We go to the first-aid room. A woman wipes blood off my face and asks where it hurts. My left hand is painful and I can't move my pinky. She presses my jaw, then my lower back and ribs where Aden kicked me. I don't say the other place where it hurts, cos I don't want her touching there.

'What's happening to Aden?' I ask. 'Is he going to hospital?'

She says I don't need to worry about that now and brings me a glass of water.

Mrs Singent, the head of year, takes me to sit in the waiting room next to the principal's office. No one comes for nearly an hour, then Mrs Singent brings me my bag and blazer and asks if I want a cup of tea. No one in school has asked me that before. I wonder if they've told my stepdad I've been in a fight.

A doctor prods my ribs and puts a splint on my fingers, then Mr Swinton asks me to come into his office. He says Aden is being examined in hospital. His voice is cold. He asks me what happened this afternoon, and I say Aden and Arron came up to me in the corridor and said things. They followed me out into the playground. I ran after them and we started fighting.

Mr Swinton throws questions at me.

'Who started the fight?'

I say I was the first one to hit.

'What did they say to you?'

'They said...' I dry up. I can't say what they said to me, or what they said about me and Jez, me and Miss Collins. I don't want either of them to be involved in this. And it would be snitching to tell.

'Have they said things before?'

I say nothing.

'Why did you carry on punching Aden when he wasn't fighting back?'

I can't say about the fire inside me, the red heat that took hold of me.

'Why did you carry on even when a teacher came and told you to stop?'

'I don't know.' I don't even remember doing it. I feel like a wriggling worm.

He screws up his face. 'You don't know?'

He writes something down then gives me a pen and paper and says to write down everything I remember about 'the incident'.

After that I'm back in the waiting room. The bell rings for end of day. There's a knock on the door.

It's Miss Collins. She's breathing heavily, like she's been running.

'I heard about what happened.' She bends down to me. Her hair swishes forwards. 'Why did you do it, Luke?' Her eyes dart around my face. 'I don't understand how you could do such a thing.'

'They were saying nasty things, Miss.'

'Who was saying things?'

'Aden Woods and Arron Tischler. They wouldn't leave me alone.'

'What did they say?'

I shake my head.

'Have they been bullying you?'

I don't speak.

'You know it isn't telling tales when bullying is involved, or they've been using racist language. If anyone's doing that, you must tell me.'

I look at my hands.

'Luke.' She steps back. 'You must tell the teachers everything.' She puts her hand on the door handle, looking uncertain. Then she reaches in her bag, brings out a pen and paper, writes something on it. 'This is my phone number. Call me if you ever need someone to talk to.'

I fold the paper and put in my pocket.

A few minutes later I have to go back into the principal's office. Mrs Singent comes in too, and sits down. Mr Swinton points to the other chair.

'You're in serious trouble, Luke. The school will be conducting an investigation into what happened. We may have to notify the police.'

'Aden will be OK, won't he?'

He gets out his phone.

I hardly recognise the face in the photo. Aden's top lip is cut and his face is swollen on one side, making his mouth lopsided. His nose is bent out of shape. One eye is nearly closed up.

'Aden's nose is broken and his cheekbone is fractured. He may need an operation once the swelling has gone down. Fortunately, there's no damage to the eye.'

Mrs Singent shakes her head. The principal leans forward in his chair, his hands pressed together like he's praying.

'Do you have anything else to say?'

'I — I didn't mean to do that.' My mouth is dry. I want to ask if someone can tell him I'm sorry, but I don't dare.

Mr Swinton's lips are a thin line. He says I'm excluded from school until the governors decide what action to take.

———

Kevin comes to pick me up. As usual I have to climb over the driver's seat because of the broken door handle on the passenger side. I wince in pain.

My stepdad doesn't speak all of the way home. I wish he'd say something.

I look at my face in the bathroom. There's a cut above my eyebrow and one eye is bruised and swollen. But I don't look anywhere near as bad as Aden.

Kevin brings dinner out of the oven. Kirsty helps to put it on the table, which is already set. No one speaks. I'm not hungry. I poke a few bits of carrot into my mouth, keeping my head down. I can't think of anything to say. Kevin puts down his knife and fork.

'Looks like you've turned into a fighter after all.' His voice has an edge. He slams his fist down the table. The table shakes, I almost jolt out of my seat. Kirsty stops eating, looks towards the door like she wants to run for it. 'Jesus, boy! What did you have to go and do that for? That boy's in the fuckin' hospital! You've broken his fuckin' cheekbone. Jesus!'

'I didn't mean to.'

Kevin scrapes his chair back. He stands there, red blotches forming on his cheeks. I look round for something I can use to defend myself with.

'For God's sake, Luke.' He pushes a hand against his brow. 'I know things have been tough since your mum died and I know we've had our issues. But why in Christ's name did you beat up that kid? Your mother always tried to keep you on the right path, even when you started mixing with fuckin' drug dealers.' He's working himself up. 'I told her I'd do my best to keep you on track, an' now you've gone and done this!'

Kirsty looks as scared as me.

'He insulted Jez. And Miss Collins.'

'That ain't good enough. People are gonna say things often enough. You can't fight 'em all. I'm goin' upstairs, I'll speak to you in the morning. Eat the rest of your dinner, Kirsty.'

JEZ

WHAT RUBY SAID

IT'S FIRST THING IN THE MORNING AND I'M AT SCHOOL ON time for once. I'm putting my lunch into my locker when Ruby comes over.

'There's something I think you should know.' Ruby's face is serious. 'Given you and Luke are friends,' she's waits for me to close my locker, 'have you noticed Miss Collins pays a lot of attention to him?'

I've seen them standing talking after class, that's all. But that isn't what she means.

Ruby checks both ways and quietens her voice. 'The other day at the end of English I went back into the classroom to collect my scarf, and I saw Miss Collins and Luke kissing.'

I go cold. 'Are you joking?'

'I'm really sorry, Jez. I know how much you like Luke.'

'Was he... Was he the one kissing her?'

'No, she was kissing him. I saw her pull him towards her. She looked like she wanted to rip his clothes off. She jumped away when she saw me. I just went home. I honestly didn't know what to do.'

A warbly sound fills my head. Luke and Miss Collins kissing. Is that even possible? I try to picture it. Ruby could be lying, couldn't she? But she looks like she's telling the truth.

Does Miss Collins fancy Luke? Does Luke fancy *her*? She's one of the youngest teachers and she always dresses nicely. She's pretty, in a low-key way.

A mad storm of jealousy hits.

'Jez, are you ok?'

I nod. 'Have you told anyone else?'

'No, only you. I thought you should know.' Ruby puts her arm around me. 'So sorry, hun. That Miss Collins is such a bitch. Going round hitting on boys in her class, it's appalling.'

All day, I can't stop thinking about it. By the time I leave school, I'm more or less sure that Luke isn't the one at fault. He isn't the sort of boy to get up to lord knows what with his teacher. That's why I like him. Miss Collins is taking advantage of him, she must be. I always thought Ruby was exaggerating about MC being a bitch. Now it looks like she's hit the nail on the head.

Something is tugging at me, though. What if I'm wrong and Luke really does like her, a lot? What if he likes her more than he likes me?

LUKE

I'm in my PJs, under the duvet, listening to Kevin's footsteps going around the house. He's always first up.

'Luke. Are you awake?'

I sit up. He pushes the door open before I can speak. I swing my legs out of bed, face him. He's not shaved today or combed his hair.

'I need to tell you something before I go into work.'

I wait, surprised at the calmness of his voice.

'I never told you I did time, did I?'

I shake my head. He stands at the door and talks at the curtains.

'I got out when you was two years old. A year later, I met your mother and we got married. She knew I'd been inside; I didn't hide nothin' from her. I didn't want you kids knowing what I'd done, though.' He looks at me. 'Do you know what I did?'

I shake my head again.

'I set to this bloke with a cricket bat. Could of killed him, easy.' He waits. 'I was a heavy for hire in them days. I knew people in the underworld, serious criminals. After my boxing days were over, that's how I made money. Anyone wanted someone roughing up, I did it. That and fencing stolen goods.'

My head feels like it will burst. My stepfather is an ex-con.

'Did you kill anyone?'

'No, thank Christ.'

Kevin wriggles his shoulder. He takes painkillers every day for his boxing injuries.

'If you go down the path I did...' He stops. His voice is thick. 'If you end up like me, I won't forgive myself.' He goes to the door. 'But I can't stop you from doing whatever you're gonna do. Maybe it's too late already.'

He goes downstairs. When I hear the front door slam, I pick up a textbook from the table and hurl it across the room.

———

I text Jez.

Are you around? Can I see you?

No reply. Maybe she's gone into school.

I can't settle to anything. There's my exams to revise for and an online tutorial to help me catch up with lessons I'm missing. But I have no heart for school work. What's the point, anyway? I think about how it might have been if Mum hadn't died. Studying every night like Manny does. Looking forward to going into six form college, uni even. Mum used to say, there's no one to stop you from doing anything if you put your mind to it. But she didn't know everything.

No matter what I do, I keep thinking of Aden lying on the ground, not moving. I think about Kevin doing time for beating up people. He was a thug, a man people were afraid of – and he thinks I'm going to follow in his footsteps. I feel sick.

At three o'clock I take the W3 to Muswell Hill. On the way, I get a text from Jez.

Everyone at school is talking about the fight, how you gave it to Aden. You're famous! See you when I get home.

Jez and I sit side by side on the terrace. Her mother has group counselling at Whittington Hospital. On the table are two glasses and a bottle of wine. It's half empty, Jez has drunk most of it. In the house at the end of garden, the blinds go down. I think of how Kevin used to be a criminal, and how he and Mum hid it from me and Kirsty for so long.

Jez crunches a handful of peanuts. Her hair is up. I've not seen it like that before. The setting sun catches the red and makes her beautiful.

'What did Aden say to you? Before you hit him.'

I think of what Aden said about Jez – and about me and Miss Collins. 'I can't remember.'

'Really?' Jez looks at me closely. 'You beat that boy unconscious, but you can't remember what he said to you?'

'Racist stuff. I don't want to repeat it.'

'There's rumours going around school, did you know?'

'What rumours?'

'That you're hot on Miss Collins.' Her eyes narrow. 'Is it true?'

'What the fuck are you saying?'

'Is it true?'

'They said some crazy thing about me and Miss Collins. I have no idea where they got it from. It's a total lie.'

'Have you ever kissed her?'

My stomach lurches. 'Of course not!'

'Did she try it on with you?'

'God's sake, Jez. No, she didn't.'

'Why are people saying there's something going on between you two, then?'

'Miss Collins used to talk to me after class because she wanted to help, to get me interested in school again.' I can see Jez almost believes me.

'Did they say anything about me?'

'No. Nothing about you.' I don't want her to be hurt.

She lowers her chin and gives me a look. 'So, why did you lose it like that?'

'I don't know. All the anger inside me came out at once, I couldn't take it anymore.' I look at my hands. 'It's the worst thing I've ever done.'

'Everyone does the wrong thing sometimes.'

She puts her arm round me, nestles her head on my shoulder. We haven't known each other long but it feels like we've been friends for ages. I can be myself with her, don't have to pretend.

We're silent a while. A Japanese maple blazes red at the end of next door's garden.

'I love sitting out here.' Jez sighs and picks up her glass. A horse chestnut leaf flutters to the ground. 'Sorry if I got a bit over the top about Miss Collins.' She smiles at me. 'It's only because I like you.'

I nod. 'What's happening with the crew?'

'Nothing much.' She doesn't meet my eyes. 'I'm helping them out with some things.'

'What things?'

'Things in the office. Sorting phone bills, phone numbers...'

'County lines stuff?'

'I don't know. They don't tell me much.'

'Are they paying you?'

'A bit. More than I'd get helping out in a shop.'

'What about Zom? Are you still seeing him?'

'No, that's all over. I can't be his girlfriend anymore now there's someone else in my life.'

'Who's that?'

'You, silly!'

I stare at her, don't know what to say. Don't know if I really believe she's not seeing Zom. He seems to have some sort of hold over her.

A shout from downstairs interrupts. 'Jessamine!'

Jez bounds away and comes back two minutes later.

'It's Mum.' Jez makes a gargoyle face. 'She's got something for dinner. I told her we don't want to eat with her but she's insisting.'

I follow Jez downstairs and into the kitchen. A woman is unpacking shopping from a wheelie trolley. Jez swipes a bar of Galaxy chocolate. No bottles of alcohol visible. She looks different to before, like anyone's mother round here might look. Lipstick on, hair combed. Black top, black jeans, turquoise necklace.

'Hello, Mrs...'

'Robbins,' Jez whispers in my ear. 'This is Luke, remember? He came over a little while ago but you were out of it.'

'Sorry if I made a bad impression, Luke. I'm definitely a work in progress.' She laughs and tells me to make myself at home. 'Would you like anything to drink?'

'Thanks, er—'

'Call me Mel.'

'Thanks, Mel. I'll have a glass of water.'

Jez looks annoyed. 'You can have wine if you like. Mum's got plenty.'

I offer to help set the table.

'No, love. Just sit down.'

I sit at the table, struck by the change in Mrs Robbins. She rushes about in the kitchen, putting things away, getting things out. Jez doesn't help much.

The three of us eat an awkward meal. Mel and I drink water, Jez pours herself a glass of wine from another bottle.

Mrs Robbins puts her fork down. 'You're in my daughter's year at school, aren't you?'

I nod.

'What subjects are you studying for your GCSEs?'

I tell her the list of subjects.

'It must be hard work.' I frown at Jez, who clearly hasn't told her mother I've been excluded from school. 'I wish Jess would make more of an effort and stop getting into trouble.'

I don't know what to say.

'Go back upstairs, you two. I'll clear up.'

Jez and I lie side by side on top of her bed. A stick of incense burns in a jar.

'Sorry about that. I didn't know Mum would want to make dinner for us. She never does normally.'

'It was good to meet her – properly, I mean. Does she know you skip school?'

'Yeah, the teachers have been on at her for months. Phoning, sending letters. I throw the letters away now if I spot them. Once, I happened to pick up the phone when Mrs Singent called to complain about me and Mum was crashed. She asked for Mrs Robbins and I went, "Yes, speaking," and pretended to be Mum, tutting about all the things the old cow said and saying, "Oh, dear!" like Mum does.' She snorts with delight. 'It was such a hoot!'

'You're a bad girl, Jez. I don't know why I like you so much.' Without thinking, I kiss her. Just a brush of my lips against hers.

She looks at me. I think she's going to make a joke but her voice is serious.

'I can't stop thinking about you, Luke.'

I wrap my arms around her, smell her. Peppermint. Cinnamon buns. I'm tempted to get under the covers with her. Her dark brown hair sprawls over my arms. I think about saying the stuff I should be telling her. That there's too much going on for me to get close to her – the trouble I'm in at school, the trouble with my stepdad. Mum dying.

It's cold when I wake. Moonlight seeps through the blinds. Jez is still nuzzled against me. I peel her fingers from my arm. She doesn't stir.

Woo-woo. Woo-woo.

An owl's lonely bleat. There's no owls on Effra Lane. I imagine it swooping from high branches, powerful and free.

———

When I get home next morning Kevin isn't in and Kirsty has left for school. I phone the academy. The receptionist takes pity on me and gives me Aden's home address. I cycle to his street and wheel the bike to the front door. Everything in me says this is a bad idea. I'm about to skeet when the door opens.

Though I've seen the photo already, his face shocks me. The damage I did is clearer. The eye is bloodshot, less closed up. A huge bluish black bruise stretches from below his eyebrow to the middle of his cheek.

'Shit.'

A muscle beside Aden's good eye twitches. 'What. The. Fuck.'

'I'm sorry,' I say quickly. 'I didn't mean to hurt you so bad.'

A woman shoves him aside. 'Are you the boy who did this to my son?' She starts shouting. 'What the fuck are you doing here? How could you hurt my son like this?'

I feel like the worst person who has ever walked the planet.

She goes inside, pulling on Aden's arm. He shrugs her off, steps to me. His chin almost touches mine.

'You have a fuckin' nerve coming here. You'd better watch yourself, we're gonna get you for what you done. We'll smash you into little pieces.'

———

I tell Kirsty about my visit to Aden, minus what he and his mum said.

'I think you're brave,' Kirsty says and crunches on a piece of toast. 'I couldn't have gone if it was me.'

Kevin clomps into the kitchen and tells Kirsty to go and watch TV. He waves a letter from school in my face.

'Do y'know what this means? You're up shit creek without a fuckin' paddle! I'm supposed to go in next week so those pricks in suits can tell me how you disgraced the school. I'm only glad your mother ain't here to see this.' He points to the stairs. 'Get to your room, before I lose it with you.'

I don't tell Kevin what Aden said. He wouldn't care if I got hurt, would he?

CALLUM

27TH SEPTEMBER

THE RUNNING MACHINE WHIRRED MALICIOUSLY AS THE muscles of my legs approached meltdown. I pressed on through the pain, thinking of the relief I'd feel when this torture was over.

My phone bleeped. I slowed the belt, hoping it would be the message I was waiting for.

'Hey, bro.' Marcia would be over for dinner tomorrow instead of tonight; she'd found some more of our father's carvings in her loft and wanted to sort through before she brought them over.

'Fine,' I said, 'see you then.' I could have done without any more carvings. Brendan's room was now home to a dozen of the damn things. It was natural for him to show interest in his grandfather. But it was troubling and a little spooky to see those creatures adorning our mantelpiece.

At last, the belt slowed. Six minutes of Medium, two of Very Fast and four of Fast was a personal best. I was towelling off when my phone bleeped again. It was Forensics – good news, this time. The DNA profile of the blood matched Solita Milton's DNA.

I fist-pumped the air. The search of flat 814 hadn't yielded the murder weapon, bloodstained clothing or other incriminating items – but at last we had a piece of evidence that linked flat 814 of Delius Tower to the crime scene. Combined with Nora Symonds's statement, the matching blood sample suggested the killers had used the place to clean themselves up after the murder. That evidence should help convince the jury to put away Solita's killers, if we ever found them.

I called Brendan from his studies and poured two glasses of Prosecco.

'Time for a little celebration,' I said. 'Operation Rye is still collapsed on the ground but we've just found a faint heartbeat.'

Brendan lifted his glass. 'Cheers, Dad. To the success of your investigation.'

Thank goodness, he had been more communicative lately. Marcia was now turning up for dinner once a week, which I guessed had something to do with it. He liked her being around, it seemed – and asking her questions about the grandfather he'd never met. Standing in the kitchen, we managed a proper conversation. Brendan was having trouble with mathematics and worried that he might be forced to drop the subject, which could hinder him getting onto a forensic science course at uni. I did my best to reassure him.

'You'll get there, Bren.' I yawned. 'I don't know about you, but I'm ready for bed.'

Brendan chewed his lower lip. 'Can I ask you something, Dad?'

'Go ahead.'

'What started the fire in the shed? The one that killed my granddad?'

That again. Why was he so interested? I gathered my thoughts.

'It was an accident. Your grandfather smoked... There was an inquest into it all. They thought he must have accidentally dropped a cigarette butt on the floor while he was in there. He sometimes left rags he used for cleaning on the floor, so plenty of fuel.'

'Did he go back to the shed, then? How did he actually die?'

'He smelt smoke and woke up, then went downstairs and found the shed on fire. My mother tried to stop him but he pushed past her. He wanted to get his carvings out.' An unsettled sensation grew in my gut. 'He got trapped by the fire.' I'd never forget those dreadful sounds.

'You were there, too?'

'Marcia and I heard Mum yelling and ran downstairs. I ran into the garden and saw him in the shed...' Remembering the smoke and the heat, I shivered. I had stood outside that burning shed, rooted to the spot.

'How long before the firemen came?'

'Nearly ten minutes.' An image flashed into my head – his body being carried out, his white dressing gown turned black.

'There was a post-mortem?'

'That's right. He died from smoke inhalation.'

Brendan looked uncomfortable. 'Sorry to bother you with all these questions, Dad. I didn't mean to upset you.'

'It's OK, Bren. You've a right to know. It's probably good for me to talk about it.'

That wasn't what I wanted to do, though. For twenty-five years, apart from conversations in the immediate aftermath of my father's death, I'd managed to avoid the topic almost entirely.

That night, I flitted in and out of sleep. If I slept, those terrible scenes would come back. Dawn arrived, my eyeballs grimy and heavy, before I nodded off.

———

The shed is burning. There's a figure inside, almost hidden in the smoke, rapping on the window, crying out.

Help me! Help!

I'm watching from the lawn. My legs won't move.

The raps and the cries fade. I fall onto the ground. I'm alone now, apart from... No. It can't be.

One by one, animals and birds flutter, creep and crawl out of the shed. They're life-size now. They form a circle around me, their eyes orange, gleaming, fixed on me...

I woke myself up with a scream. The nightmare was back.

JEZ

BIG DEAL

WE'RE IN WOLF'S FLAT. THE BOYS DO THEIR BUSINESS HERE now. It must be the scuzziest flat on the estate.

It's a weekday afternoon and I'm missing double English with Hotlips Collins, what a shame. I'm pretty sure now it was Miss Collins who ratted me out to the head of safeguarding the other week – I saw her looking at me weirdly the day before. (Mrs Singent gave me an inquisition about talking to suspected gang members outside school, and without a mask either.)

Five of us are sitting around the table. Zom is texting, Wolf is playing a game on his phone, Spicer is tapping his foot to beats on his headphones and Karim is doing drug deals on his phone. I pick up a cold slice of pizza from the box. Working here suits me way better than the beauty salon – I can't be arsed with constantly preening my hair and nails and having to be nice to gormless women. Spicer asked me to come in again to help sort out issues with the mobile numbers. I also help get the flat ready for meetings, and bring in extra chairs and coffees and muffins from Starbucks.

'Girl, come with me, will ya? We gotta meet someone.' Zom looks up from his phone.

I put down my Coke, surprised. I'm never asked to come out on gang business.

'What do you need me to come for?'

'In case the feds show.' He sucks his teeth. 'Girl, get a move on. Grab your bag, yeah?'

The others carry on with whatever they're doing. I pick up my leather jacket and bag, and hurry out after Zom. I've been trying to cool things off between us, slowly, so he won't notice.

'What's this meeting about?'

'This man, he's got some white for us.'

'You think the cops might turn up?'

He looks at me like I'm slow. 'They're on my tail.'

We get into the BMW. We're waiting at traffic lights when Zom says to me, 'I need you to put Sally in your bag.'

'What are you on about?'

'My piece, darling.' He sniggers.

'Your gun?' I'm not exactly on the ball, today. 'What do you want me to carry a gun for?'

'For protection. Just in case.'

I stare at him. 'I'm not carrying it unless I know what it's for.'

'This man might try to fuck with me, he ain't seen me before. I need my piece to hand, know what I mean?'

'Why can't *you* carry it?'

'You know why. The feds are stoppin' everyone now. They don't have to give no reason to search you. If they catch me with a gun, it's five years in the can.'

'What if the cops look in my bag and arrest *me*?'

'They won't, trust me. A white girl with a designer bag. The feds won't even see you, babe.'

'I'm not happy carrying a gun around.'

One hand on the wheel, he reaches into his inside pocket with the other and thrusts a wad of notes into my hand.

'Here's some p's. Buy yourself a nice dress.' He smiles. 'I don't want no scruffy chick hangin' off my arm.'

I flick through the notes, thinking I should give them back. Then I imagine coming out of Selfridges with a big yellow carrier bag. There's hardly one dress that's actually mine in my wardrobe. Most are hand-me-downs from my sister.

At the next lights he pulls a gun out of his waistband and holds it over my lap.

'Take it.'

'Is it loaded?'

'Uh? Course it is. Safety's on, don't worry.'

We move off from the lights.

'What if it goes off? I don't want to do this, Zom.'

He brakes suddenly. My head flops back onto the headrest. His reply explodes in the space between us.

'Bitch, just do it! I took you with me for you to make yourself useful. So fuckin' do what I say!'

Stunned, I open the Balenciaga bag by my feet and put the gun inside. There's plenty of room beside my make-up bag and bottle of coconut water. I push the bag as far from me as possible. For the rest of the way, I stare into my lap and think about that gun. Why did I agree to be part of this? I really don't want to see that gun in action. What if I get hurt – or someone else does? I'm not good with blood – seeing the slightest bit outside of where it should be makes me feel faint.

We're meeting the man in the parking area by the lock. Zom says we're early, we can sit in the café and relax. By the time we park up, the light is fading and my heart is bashing into my chest. My bag feels hugely heavy as we walk over to the café. A woman is sitting at a table outside feeding a sandwich to a slobbering boxer dog.

'Get me a coffee, will ya?'

Zom goes to sit down.

The man behind the counter is packing things away. He doesn't look pleased to see me. I order a tea and a coffee, glancing at the lineup of unhealthy-looking cakes. An old geezer is slurping tea.

'The scones are good, lass.'

The thought makes me queasy.

'Anything else?' Counter man rings up my purchase.

'Do you have a toilet, please?' I need to pee, badly.

'Not for customers.' I hand over all my small change and dump the tea bag on the counter.

The woman with the boxer has gone. Zom indicates for me to sit on the bench beside him. I leave as much space between us as possible.

'What do you want me to do when he comes?'

'Keep your mouth shut, that's all.'

'What if you need to use the gun? Will you give me a signal or something?'

'You'll know if I do, trust me. Relax, you're making me nervous.'

Before Zom can stop me, I excuse myself, rush behind the café and crouch over the weeds.

———

It's dark and I'm sitting in the front seat of Zom's BMW, shivering with cold and fear. We're parked in the middle of a big grassy area, empty except for us. Then it comes, the moment

I've been dreading. A silver Jaguar pulls up beside us, facing the other way so the driver's door is beside Zom.

A big white guy is at the wheel. He's a right old bruiser, as my dad would say. He says something I can't quite hear and reaches up to turn on the interior light. I try not to stare. A scar runs down past one eye that looks like it's been made with a nail. The skin is pinched tight around it, pulling the eye down. My heart starts racing but I play it cool, like I come on drug deals every day.

Scarface opens his window, so does Zom. He speaks like someone on *EastEnders*, in a low voice. He doesn't look at me. I take deep breaths, concentrate on holding in my pee. My bag is on my lap, opened just enough that Zom can grab the gun if he needs to.

Zom dips his head to the bulging Sainsbury's bag under my legs. I pass it to him. He hands it through the window to Scarface, who takes out a wad of fifties, inspects one and frowns. 'My boss ain't takin' no chances,' he mutters. Then he puts the money back in the bag, takes what looks like a bag of sugar wrapped in brown paper and passes it through to Zom. Zom places it by my foot.

Zom says something and Scarface says something back. It all sounds terse, verging on hostile. Scarface hands over two more bags.

'No sweat, man,' Zom says.

'Mind your fuckin' manners, arsehole,' Scarface replies.

Zom closes the window and revs the engine. I close my eyes and throttle my scream, waiting for Scarface to shoot us both in the head.

All the way back to the estate, Zom sucks his teeth and doesn't speak. I think about asking him to take the gun back but I don't dare.

We park in the usual spot in the tower car park. Before I get out, Zom takes the gun from my bag and tucks it into the waist-band of his jeans.

'You did good today, girl. Next time with Sally will be a piece of cake.'

I open my mouth to say what I've been working up to saying – I'm not carrying for you anymore and I'm not going to be your girlfriend anymore. But Zom gets there first.

'Wanna know what I been up to with this blade?'

Actually, I'd rather not.

'Remember the girl that got killed outside the estate back in July?' He smiles. 'I was the one that killed her.'

'What?' I can't make sense of his words.

'The boss asked for volunteers, so I put my hand up. He wanted a crew to take care of Doc's sister.'

'Doc?'

'The snake who stole our food. He ran off with four keys of white and went to ground. Planned to start his own line with it. So, we went after his sister. Me an' Wolf.' He smiles. 'I was just gonna carve up her face. But the boss didn't want her tellin' no tales, know what I mean?'

I dredge the article from my memory, the one in the *Evening Standard*.

Girl stabbed to death on way home from school

'The girl who was stabbed in the chest?'

He dips his head, eyebrows lifting. The back of my head tingles.

'You did that?'

'Told you I'm handy with a blade.'

I'm going to be sick, right now. 'You used that knife I've been carrying for you, didn't you?'

Zom smiles and talks into his phone.

'The food's here, man.'

We get out of the car. V walks over with Karim and Spicer. He's in jeans and a tracky top. He looks at me but doesn't speak. Zom releases the boot and goes with the others to peer at the goods. I heave a sigh. At last. Now we're not alone, I can relax.

Zom, Karim and Spicer drive off in the car. V is beside me. He asks if I'm ok.

'I'm fine now, thanks. It was a bit tense earlier. I've never been so close to a gun before.' You're talking to Top G, a voice in my head warns me. Don't say anything ridiculous. 'I'd better get home. My mum will be worried about me.'

'Let me call a cab for you.' V swipes a screen on his phone.

'All sorted,' he says seconds later. 'Wait here, it'll be here in two minutes. The driver is Hussain.'

'Thanks, V.' I smile my brightest smile.

As I lie in bed, I think about Zom's gifts to me and the cash he gave me for carrying 'Sally'. They're not enough, not anymore. A thought keeps coming.

Walk away from Zom, walk away from V. Walk away from them all, before it's too late.

BREAK-UP

Zom phoned while I was in the bath.

He asks what I'm doing Friday night, do I want to come over to watch movies? He's got some extra-strong weed. The sound of his voice sinks my spirits. Smoking extra-strong weed with Zom is the last thing I want to do.

'I'm sorry, I can't make it.' Frantic, I try to think of an excuse. Then I remember I've already got one. It's Luke's sixteenth this Friday and we're going out to celebrate. 'It's my friend's birthday, they're having a party.'

'We can go together. I'll pick you up at seven, yeah?'

'No, that wouldn't work. We've got a restaurant booked. It's only a small thing.'

'Are you ditchin' me, babe? Is that what you're tryna do?'

I know I've got to be brave. I'll have to tell him I don't want to be his girlfriend anymore. How can I be his girl when I'm in love with Luke? I know Luke isn't my usual type but he's real and honest. He cares too. He's everything that Zom isn't.

'I'm sorry to let you down Zom, but it's not working with us. I'm not the girl for you.'

It feels like a minute before he answers. I dig my salon nails into my palm.

'I've invested in you, big time.' His voice is a vicious growl. I pull my ear away from my phone. 'I hooked you up with my fam and helped you get a start in this game. You fuckin' owe me.'

'I don't owe you anything! I did whatever you wanted me to do, didn't I?'

A tap at the door. 'All right in there, Jess?'

I cover the phone with my hand. 'It's OK, Mum.' I wait 'til she's gone.

'If you want to take back all the stuff you gave me, you can bloody well have it!' I don't know where my courage comes from. Or is it stupidity?

'You're chattin' shit, bitch. I'm warnin' you, you're on dangerous ground. Next time you step out, you might be in for a surprise. Those youngers are gonna be free now to do whatever they like. You'd better watch out.'

He hangs up. I get out of the bath. I'm shivering. I can't stop even when I'm dry.

I go for a walk, think over my options.

I could cut my ties with the gang, start going to school regularly and try to get in with Miss Jenkins again... The thought is squashed before it's begun. Miss Jenkins isn't going to give me another chance. I'd never be good enough to get onto a West

End stage anyways, I've been kidding myself. Anyways, Zom will try to find me. He knows where I am. If I went to the cops, he might kill me like he killed that girl...

Besides, do I really want to leave my admin job now money is coming in regularly? Karim has put me on the payroll. Plus, there's my weekly salary from Yasmin for hanging out at the salon three afternoons a week. I'm safer staying where I am. Karim and Spicer will help protect me from Zom, won't they?

Our ex-dog-walker goes past, poodles sprayed out behind him. I wave back. It's so normal here. You wouldn't know someone's just slashed up my world.

CALLUM

4TH OCTOBER

THE INVESTIGATION HAD TURNED INTO A CUL-DE-SAC.

Briefings were now every four or five days. Despite Nora Symonds's information we were no closer to making any arrests. We'd added Vincent Edwards to our list of suspects but still hadn't got real names for Muscleman or Wolf. Nor did we have a clue as to where the killers were hiding out. Detective Superintendent Bailey phoned me weekly, conveying various shades of disappointment.

I'd not found any more fake skulls, at least.

Before going home that afternoon, I spent a few hours going through house-to-house reports and witness statements on the system. I'd had the team go through all of the information we'd accumulated since the start of the inquiry, desperate to find something we'd missed that could turn out to be the key to tracking down Solita's killers. This was the last possible avenue.

But I found nothing. I switched off the computer, defeated.

LUKE

I'VE BEEN EXCLUDED FROM SCHOOL UNTIL THE TWENTY-FIFTH of November. The governors decided it at the meeting yesterday. Kevin showed me the letter they sent. They accept I was provoked but they don't want me putting other pupils at risk.

'Two months isn't so long,' Jez says when I go over to hers. 'You'll be back in time for the mocks, won't you? They'll send you online lessons so you'll be able to keep up.'

For a moment I see myself working through the lessons at the old computer in my room.

Jez gives me a hug. We're in her living room. Her mother hasn't come downstairs yet.

'Don't forget, I'm taking you out for your birthday tomorrow. That'll cheer you up. Where do you fancy going?'

'I dunno. Wherever.'

'It'll be Nando's then, my favourite. There's one in Wood Green. Do you want to bring Kirsty?'

'Yeah, she'll like that.'

We agree to meet in the food court at Wood Green Cineworld.

———

'Here's to the birthday boy!' Jez raises her glass. 'Wishing you loads of amazing years ahead!'

Beside her, Kirsty holds up her glass of Coke. I raise my glass and try to look happy. I know I'm being a miserable pain in the arse.

'Luke?' Kirsty is pulling my sleeve. 'What's the matter?'

'Sorry.'

'Aren't you eating that? I'll have it.' Kirsty reaches over and scoops up a handful of my chips.

Jez winks at me. 'What about the three of us go round to watch a movie at your place?'

'Can we?' Kirsty looks at me, face questioning.

'Kevin might be watching telly.'

Jez pouts. 'He won't be up all night, will he?'

'He goes to bed about eleven,' Kirsty says hopefully.

I agree, so Jez can see our place. We can all have a Coke or something, Kevin can't object to that.

He's barely spoken to me lately. This morning I found a birthday card with a picture of a red Ferrari next to my cereal bowl. Inside it said 'To Luke' and below that 'Kevin'. No 'with love' and no present for the first time I can remember. Mum and Kevin used to give me a joint present, though I knew Mum always chose it.

The waitress leaves our bill. Nearly forty quid. Jez pays it all. She says it's her treat.

Kirsty and Jez carry on chattering away as they have all evening. Which cats are best for pets (Kirsty wants one), what's your fave show on TV (both say *Strictly*), Jez admires Kirsty's silver earrings that Mum gave her for her birthday last year and Kirsty loves Jez's trainers. I look down at our feet. I don't think I've seen Jez's silver and purple trainers before but she wears a different pair nearly every time we go out, it's hard to keep track. My trainers are faded, the same ones I always wear.

We get a bus halfway and walk the rest of the way home as we've just missed a bus. Kirsty holds one hand and Jez takes my other hand. I enjoy that more than anything else that evening. Crunching through the leaves on the pavement, feeling my hands in theirs, I don't feel so sad about Mum not being here for my birthday.

'The palace awaits.' I sweep my hand towards the house. Jez studies the patched-up little building. I wonder if she notices the peeling paint on the sills and the tape over the broken window beside the front door where someone once broke in.

Kirsty and I give Jez a guided tour of downstairs – hall, front room, junk room and kitchen. She looks around at everything with an excited face like a child at a sleepover. I take her up to my room. I wasn't going to ask her to stay the night, but now she's here I can't tell her to go all the way back to Muswell Hill.

'Got a spare toothbrush?' Jez comes out of the bathroom in my T-shirt.

I make a face. 'Shush!'

Thank God, Kevin is still snoring through his door. As I've only got a single bed, I tell Jez she can have it but she says no. I help get her mattress sorted, a cushion off the old velvet armchair and a folded blanket.

'Thanks for making my birthday special. Sorry I wasn't the best company.'

'No one can be chirpy all the time. What's on your mind?'

'What do you mean?'

'Don't give me that, Luke. I know something's up.'

I tell her about Aden threatening me. Jez brushes her hair with my brush, doesn't speak for a while.

'If you started hanging out with the crew, they would protect you.'

'I can look after myself.'

'Just saying. The boys look after each other. If you're not going to be working for your exams, you could earn some money—'

'From selling drugs, you mean? You really think I'd do something like that?'

'Don't bite my head off!'

'I'm not like you, Jez. I have principles.'

'And I don't? Fuck you too.'

'You might think there's nothing wrong with selling crack and whatever, but what about all the people who get hooked and end up dead?'

'And what about the shops that sell vodka and gin to my mother? She's going to die of liver disease probably, do you know that?'

Neither of us speaks. I turn off the light.

———

A noise wakes me up. It's getting light. I see Jez's silhouette against the curtains. She's putting on her clothes.

'Are you going?' I look up, still half in a dream.

'Go back to sleep. We'll wake your stepdad.'

'I'm sorry for what I said. I didn't mean it.'

She shrugs, hoists her bag over her shoulder. 'Maybe you're right.' Her voice is cold.

'Don't go.'

'I've got stuff to do. See ya.'

When she's gone, I can't go back to sleep. I want her here, with me. I wish I hadn't opened my stupid mouth.

CALLUM

5TH OCTOBER

'I'm going for a walk.'

'Where to? Wait a second—'

Brendan slammed the door behind him.

Another dinner conversation was over, without overt anger yet full of uneasy silences and sarcastic asides – not just from Brendan, sadly. Although I was old enough to know better, sometimes my son's sharp words made me fling back others, just as sharp.

I got up from the table and scanned the worktops – empty – and ran upstairs. Shit. His Nokia was there, on his bed. I kicked the sturdy metal bed frame with gusto, sending a stab of pain into my foot.

It was early, not even seven, and a mild night. Brendan was no longer a child – as he kept telling me. He was a generally sensible, capable lad. What was I worrying about? But it was dark outside and a host of fears niggled at me.

I called Marcy and asked her to let me know if Brendan came by.

'Of course,' she said. 'Why, have you two had another fight?'

'Just the usual,' I replied. My sister knew about the skull Brendan had found in my car. So did Kate. It was another reason for me to leave the force, in her view, the perfect illustration of the unacceptable nature of my job.

'Don't worry, he'll turn up in a while,' Marcy said in a gentler voice. 'He just needs his own space.'

An hour went by. An hour and a half.

What if they've taken him? What if the Skull Crew have got my son?

Unable to defend myself against my thoughts, I began phoning Brendan's friends.

Two hours later, he still wasn't back. I went back into his room and stood there, feeling a measure of comfort from being surrounded by his stuff. Then I sank onto his bed, my head in my hands.

———

The click of the front door closing. I ran downstairs.

Brendan stood in the hall. His nose and cheeks were pink, his eyes watery and his hair windblown. He wasn't hurt. Thank God.

'Where have you been?'

'I told you, I went for a walk.' He took off his jacket.

'You've been hours, I thought something had happened to you.'

He glanced at his watch. 'It's not even ten, what's the big deal?'

'You were walking in the dark for three hours?'

'I dropped in at Shelley's place on the way back.'

Shelley? My mind went blank.

'My friend, remember? I would have called but I forgot my phone.'

Relief turned to indignation.

'I've been calling your friends! I thought you might have been stabbed, or kidnapped—'

'Christ, Dad. What's the matter with you? You're acting ments lately. You need to do more yoga.'

He disappeared upstairs. Feeling foolish, I slumped into an armchair with a glass of Glenfiddich. Those skulls must be getting to me.

JEZ

PROTECTION

THE BUS IS EARLY FOR ONCE. I KILL TIME WONDERING AROUND the shops, looking out for things that'll be easy to nick. First is a pair of glitzy tights – I put them on under my jeans – then a bracelet. I can say I forgot to take them off if anyone finds out. I've been trying to turn over a new leaf and to pay for everything. But Luke's verdict on me has changed my mind. I may as well give in to temptation and be a proper bad girl.

I'm totally pissed with Luke, actually. I thought he really cared about me, then he goes and disses me like that, the prissy self-righteous arse. I never want to see him again.

McDonald's is busy. I find an empty table and order a coffee. This isn't a place I come if I can help it, but needs must.

Spicer gives a lacklustre wave. He doesn't look as cheery as usual.

Letty elbows me. 'Hey, Jez! How're you going, girl? We were worried about you.' I clock her Moschino jacket.

'Ups and downs, you know.'

I wait 'til we're tucking into our burgers to broach the subject of Zom.

'What I wanted to tell you guys...' Spicer looks up from his phone. I hope desperately that he and Zom haven't become besties overnight. 'Things have been a bit tricky with Zom lately.'

Letty's face goes mushy. Spicer's doesn't change. I wonder if I'm making a terrible mistake bringing up Zom in front of one of the crew's top boys.

'What is it, hun?'

'I... Well...' I go into stutter mode.

Letty lays her hand on my arm. 'Just tell it like it is, we're listening.'

I take a deep breath.

'Zom and I broke up last week. He didn't take it too well. He made out that some of the youngers might... You know, try it on with me.' I look around to check no one's listening. 'It freaked me out, to be honest. So, I was thinking... If there's any way you guys might be able to give me a bit of support, in case anyone thinks they can take advantage... I'd really appreciate it.' Letty's nodding along encouragingly. 'I'm really keen to do my bit for the fam, make myself useful 'n' all, know what I'm saying?'

Spicer is first to speak. 'No problem, Jez. You're safe with us.'

Letty leans over her orange juice, eyes shining and earnest.

'We get where you're coming from, hun. You want respect. You don't want no jumped-up bad boy giving you shit.'

I can't help laughing. Spicer laughs too. Letty winks at me.

'We girls gotta fight sometimes to get what we need. If anyone tries to bother you, hun, let me know and my man will sort it.'

LUKE

IT'S WEIRD HOW MUCH I TOOK SCHOOL FOR GRANTED. IT'S like a slab of my life is missing which I never noticed was there. I miss the way you knew exactly how the day would pan out, each divided up into fifty-minute chunks and every one having a purpose. I miss Miss Collins too.

I tried doing online lessons every morning and studying for an hour every afternoon. But my mind kept wandering onto other stuff. What Aden might do if he finds me. When Jez will reply to my messages. How I'm going to earn money.

Kevin doesn't know I've given up with school. He says I need to knuckle down and make an effort or I'll regret it later when I can't get a job. I asked for more money for doing repairs and painting jobs around the house. He said he's not giving me any more money and the standard of my work is rubbish. I slammed the door on him and went cycling.

Apart from writing things down here, cycling is the only thing that makes me feel better. When I'm on the bike I'm free of Kevin and my thoughts. My favourite route is east to the railway station, over the tracks and past the industrial area then along the canal into Walthamstow Marshes. Out there, you can see for miles, you can go in any direction you want. There's nature all around. Swans, geese, birds that swoop and glide and hover. That's when I feel most alive. I cycle 'til my legs ache and my lungs won't draw another breath.

———

Today I came home via the estate.

Outside the first tower there's a couple of kids on bikes not in school uniform, light-brown skinned like me. Their eyes track me as I cycle past. There's no sign of Minty.

I miss Minty, he was fun. I've hardly been back to the estate since school started cos of Kevin going on about it being a bad place and telling me not to come here. I spotted Minty a few days ago with another kid, hanging out at the back of the tower. I nearly went over but they're both in Skull Crew and I'm not.

The playground is empty. I carry on towards the towers. Glance up at the rows and rows of windows. In the concrete space between the towers, some Somali kids are playing football. Graffiti covers the No Ball Games sign.

I stop and watch. There's shouting, laughter and high fives as one scores a goal between two hoodies. Envy hits me. I want to be one of those kids. Not on the outside, on my own.

I'm about to make my way out when a darkskin guy shouts at me. New trainers, gold chain. I prepare to scarper.

'Oi, kid! Where you from?' He's older than me, has dreads down his back and a line shaved through his eyebrow.

'Just down the road.'

'What you doin' here?'

I shrug. 'Just looking round to see if my friend's here.'

'Who's that?'

'Minty. We played footy in the summer.'

'Not seen you before. Why ain't you in school?' He looks me up and down, eyes narrowed.

'Got excluded, di'n I?' I hold his stare.

'What'ya do?'

'Got into a fight. Bashed up this boy's face. He had to go to hospital.' I don't say it like I'm bragging. The man looks impressed, though.

'Shit man, is that right?' He looks around. The boys are still playing football. An old bloke hunched over a stick limps towards the block's entrance. 'What's your name, kid?'

'Luke.'

'Call me Angel. Good to meet you, Luke.'

'You in a gang?'

He makes a fist. The letters 'T, S, B' are inked into the first three fingers. I wonder if Jez knows him. Maybe she's here now somewhere, hanging out with her 'fam'.

'Wanna earn a few p's? I need something delivered.'

'Nah, sorry. I gotta go home.'

'I'll give you twenty. It's close.'

I start to cycle away. But something makes me turn back.

'OK, I'll do it.'

Angel tells me to wait at the back of Delius Tower, he'll be down in five.

He comes back and hands me a small package wrapped in a Tesco bag. It's heavy for the size. Not drugs, then.

'Give this to the kid who answers the door. Goes by name of Chills.'

I put it in my backpack. He holds up his phone screen.

'Here's the address. Remember it.' He writes a number in ballpoint on the back of my hand. 'Call this number when you're back an' I'll give you the cash.'

I pull out my phone from the inside pocket of my track pants and check the address on Google maps. It's a flat in a low-rise block on another estate. I ring the entrance buzzer three times before a crackly voice answers, then gallop up three flights of stairs and knock on the door.

A guy comes to the door in his boxers. He's skinny with slit eyes, smelling of TCP. I hold out the package.

'Chills?'

He grunts, grabs the bag and shuts the door in my face.

I cycle back fast as I can to the estate. Wait ten minutes for Angel to show. He ambles out of the tower, smiling.

'Good work, bruv. Got us out of a pickle.' He unrolls a twenty from a thick wad of notes. I thrust it into my pocket. 'Give us your number, yeah?'

———

On the way home, I know I've done a bad thing, taking money from Angel. It's probably come from selling smack and crack to desperate people. At the same time, I'm pleased to have earned twenty quid for twenty minutes work. That's way better than twenty for hours of sanding walls and getting shouted at by my stepdad.

Stepping into the hall, neither Kevin or Kirsty answer my hello. I'm glad. They would know I've done something bad, from my face.

I find the piece of paper Miss Collins wrote her number on in my chest of drawers and tap out a text.

Hi Miss Collins. Thanks for what you did to help me. I'm trying to keep up with lessons and study every day. Luke

I study for rest of the day and don't stop 'til it's late and my eyes ache and the words are blurred. When I'm getting ready for bed, there's a message back from Miss Collins.

So glad you got in touch Luke, I was worried about you. Look forward to seeing you back at school in November

JEZ

TOP BOY

V turned up for a meeting at our new base. I cleaned up the place beforehand, organised a whiteboard, seating and refreshments (beer, nachos and dips as it was the evening) and sat in the armchair in Wolf's old bedroom with my Kindle. The room smelled rank so I left the door open a little.

I caught snatches of the meeting. V talks in a quiet voice and I can't hear what he says. Then everyone talks at once. What I hear:

'The fuckin' bitch saw us and went to the feds!' (Zom)

'You're getting paranoid, bruv.' (Karim)

'Who else would it be, man? That's why they raided the flat. They're onto us!' (Zom)

Zom and Karim start shouting at each other.

Suddenly, V yells, 'Fuck the shut up!' and thumps on the table. The room goes quiet. I push the door open a bit more and go back to pretend-reading my Kindle.

'Could be someone else grassin' us up. That Sophie in 816,

she's got her snout in every trough. I seen 'em chattin' like they're like best buds.' (Angel)

'It's the Symonds bitch, I'm one hundred per cent. She's done a runner, fam. Ain't no one seen her for weeks.' (Zom)

'The council's probably got her another flat by now.' (Spicer)

'Ok, this is what we're gonna do.' (V) 'That photo of the Symonds woman. Everyone make sure you have it on your phones. We're gonna keep watch twenty-four seven in case she comes back. Soon as there's a sniff of her, we're gonna take her out.'

'What the—' Zom appears in the doorway. I have a mini heart attack. 'You been listenin' in on our business?'

I sit up, smiling sweetly to hide my fear. With the others here, I thought I was safe.

'Of course not. I left the door open to get rid of the smell of Wolf's socks, is all.'

Zom is looking like thunder. He comes toward me, his face screwed up.

'You're lyin', bitch.'

I get to my feet, back away. He pushes me. I'm knocked flat on the bed. He leans over, reaches under my T-shirt and grabs my breasts. I scream as loud as I can. He moves to slap me but I push myself up and bring my elbow down hard as I can into his chest. He swears, staggers back. I'm about to shit myself when the door flings open.

V and Karim run in.

'What the fuck is going on in here?'

Zom spits on the carpet. 'The bitch is a menace. I need to teach her a lesson.'

V speaks in a calm voice.

'Leave that girl alone, man or it's you that's gonna be taught a lesson. She ain't your private punch bag. Get outta here.'

Zom mutters and leaves the room. Karim thumps his fist into his palm.

'I swear, that man's gonna bring us all down.'

My relief at being rescued makes me dizzy. I try to stand and promptly fall back on the bed. V tells Karim to bring me a glass of water and asks how I'm getting home. I say by bus. I manage to guide the glass to my mouth without spilling any water. My hands are shaking so badly I probably couldn't even hold an umbrella.

V says he'll drive me home.

———

'Thanks for what you did back there.'

We're zooming around the North Circular in V's white Maserati. It's as stylish as any Italian handbag. God knows what Zom might have done otherwise, I think.

V keeps his eyes on the road. My eyes keep getting drawn to his cheek. Side on, up close, there's a triangular indentation. Someone's gauged out a piece of flesh with a fingernail, maybe.

V likes driving fast, obv. I try not to cling onto the door handle as we take off like Lewis Hamilton on steroids for another fast stretch between the traffic cameras. This isn't such a bad life, is it? I may have narrowly escaped being beaten up and raped by Psycho Killer, my mother is drinking herself to death and my father has forgotten I exist, but I'm riding in Top G's top-of-the-range Maserati and he's being nice to me.

We stop at the lights.

'I just wanted to say, V.' I lick the inside of my lips and do my best to sound casual. 'If you ever want me to do anything, please ask.' I laugh nervously. I sound like I'm coming on to him. 'I mean anything to help out the crew, you know?'

'You have something in mind?'

'I was thinking... My place is available if you need it. For meetings, for stashing drugs or whatever,' I quickly add, in case of misunderstanding.

'You're young to have your own place.' He sounds amused.

'My mum's place, technically. But she wouldn't mind. If she did, I'm sure I could persuade her. She's addicted to alcohol and prescription drugs, she's not really with it a lot of the time.' I pause, reminding myself not to oversell. It could be my passport to better things – and freedom from Zom.

He fingers his skull necklace.

'Left here, then first right.'

We're heading into Muswell Hill. I guide him home.

'How big?' V crouches over the wheel, looking up at the house.

'Six bedrooms. Proper ones, not cupboards that people pass off as bedrooms.'

'I'll come over sometime, take a look.'

'Great.'

I climb out carefully so's not to bang my head. The floor is hardly off the ground. Then I'm almost skipping down the path, as if Zom didn't exist.

CALLUM

I STUDIED THE PHOTO OF SOLITA PINNED TO THE INCIDENT board. She was holding up a tennis ball, a mischievous expression on her face.

'Such a waste,' DC Harper said, coming up beside me.

I caught a trace of her perfume or body lotion, faint yet distinctive. *Chloe*, I could have sworn.

'Going for a sandwich?' Sam's dark brown eyes examined my face. She was in a trouser suit, as usual.

We walked together in companionable silence. It felt good to be with Sam. I was falling into solitary habits of late, spending my breaks alone, thinking – and a good part of the evenings too.

'How are things with Brendan?'

'Still difficult,' I replied with a wry titter. 'He gets on better with my sister than me.'

We waited side by side in the queue.

'It must be hard for him, with his mum away. He's probably not very comfortable showing how things are affecting him, being a boy and everything.' She turned to me with a grin. 'Sorry, that was sexist.'

'We live in a sexist world.' I took my ciabatta and waited for Sam to get hers; I always ate mine back at my desk. She was right about Brendan. He was angry at his mother for leaving and at me for making her leave... And there was something else bothering him.

'It certainly is a sexist world,' Sam said as we headed back. 'You should see the messages I used to get on my dating apps. Some were horrendous.'

'You're staying away from dating, then?'

'For now. It's lonely, sometimes. But better to be lonely than stuck with the wrong guy.' There was an unusual note of sadness in her voice. Her voice lightened. 'Besides, I always seem to attract the wrong men. Women haters, scammers, criminals... I've dated them all.'

We arrived at the stalag.

'I'm off to the park,' Sam said. 'See you later.'

I headed back to my desk.

———

It was almost dark and the air was cool. Leaves mottled the lawn. I stood on the kitchen step looking into the back garden.

It had been another unremarkable day, full of activities that were likely leading nowhere. This evening, I needed to be away from the case in mind as well as body. Watching something on Netflix, maybe. As usual, on getting home I'd checked the not-so-smart security system. There'd been a host of false alerts, triggered by moving leaves and passersby. I'd made further adjustments to the settings, wishing I hadn't bothered to install the damn thing.

Smells of damp leaves and baking pizza wafted over, and

memories of long-ago autumn evenings. Playing conkers with Marcy in the back garden. The four of us eating hot dogs as we watched my father's firework display...

'He was a pretty good sculptor, wasn't he?'

I jolted from my reverie. Beside me, Brendan leaned on the wall of the house.

'Your grandfather? Yes, he was.'

Maybe it wasn't so surprising that my son was interested in his grandfather. Years ago, he'd admitted feeling sad at having no grandparents left. Brendan had never known his grandparents from the Waverley side of the family – my father had died at fifty-three, twenty-five years before Brendan was born, and my mother eight years later from pneumonia.

'He went to art school before he became an engineer, you know.'

'No, I didn't. But there's a lot I don't know, I guess.'

I frowned at the sour note in his voice. 'What do you want to know? I'll tell you if I can.'

'There is something... It's about the fire.'

'Go ahead.' A flutter in my chest. He was going to ask and I couldn't stop him.

'You said it took about ten minutes for the fire service to turn up.' He was wrestling with something; I saw on his face. 'Did you do anything to help my granddad before they came?'

'No, I didn't. The flames were too high by then. There was too much smoke.'

His face showed puzzlement, and something else.

'I was only a few feet away; I should have tried to save his life. I wish with all my heart that I'd done something. But my legs wouldn't move.' That was all perfectly true.

'You would have been risking your life, I guess.'

I said nothing. The shame flickered, deep down. I had let my own father die.

INSOR

'Where were you when the fire started?'

'Upstairs in bed. My mother, Marcy and I went to bed before my father did. He usually worked in the shed 'til after midnight.'

'What woke you up?'

'I heard my mother shouting downstairs. I looked out of my bedroom window and saw the shed on fire...' I frowned. This reminded me of how I questioned a suspect – only this time, it wasn't me asking the questions.

'So, your bedroom overlooked the garden?'

'Yes, it did. Why?'

'Nothing.'

Afterwards, as we ate pizza, I felt uneasy again – no, more than uneasy. It felt as if a scab, nearly healed, was being slowly ripped off. Maybe I shouldn't have encouraged my son's interest in policing and forensic science. If I wasn't careful, he was going to find out everything.

Before turning off my bedside light, I popped two Zopiclone pills from the packet. I avoided taking them when I had to work next day. But I couldn't face the nightmare again.

LUKE

A few days after the first delivery, I get a call from Angel.

He asks if I can deliver another package to a house on Green Lanes, about two miles away. I was going to say no, but Angel takes my silence for a yes.

'Good kid. Go fast as you can, we don't want him to score off no one else. He's a regular, always has p's. Be on your tippy toes, don't let him play no games.'

I take the package, a padded envelope, pop it in my backpack and race over there on my bike, nearly falling off when a lorry veers into the bike lane.

The house is run down. No one answers the door so I bang with the knocker. A skinny guy with big hollows where his eyes should be opens the door. As I ask for the sixty quid, he snatches the bag and tries to slam the door in my face. Just in time, I get my foot into the gap. Without thinking, I grab his hoody.

'If you don't give me the p's right now, I'm gonna mash you up.'

Even though the guy's tried to rip me off I feel bad saying it. He pulls on the waistband of his jeans and takes out a roll of notes. I've never seen anyone so skinny or smell as cruddy. I make him count out the tenners then I put them in my jeans front pocket.

After Angel's paid me, I spot Minty and another boy on the old sofa against the back wall of Delius Tower. The arms are slashed, the material is faded and stuffing's always dribbling out, but it's sort of comfy. Minty and I used to sit there.

'Yo, Luke! Come join us, bro.'

Minty waves at me. The other boy slugs from a can of Heineken.

'Long time no see.' Minty gets up and we spud. A top row tooth is missing from Minty's mouth that wasn't before. 'This is Raz.'

'Hey, Luke.' Raz gets up from the sofa and leans against the wall. He has light-brown skin and shiny black hair. He gestures at the space where he was sitting. I perch on the battered arm. Minty spreads himself along the length of the sofa.

'Any goss from Ginger?' Minty tosses a stone into the bushes.

'The Greens are itching for a showdown with us,' Raz says.

'What about?' I ask. I know the Greens are Skull Crew's main rival.

'Some bullshit. Payback for Ginger posting a video making one of them out to be a pussy.' He looks at me, his eyes thin. 'It goes way back. Ginger got shanked by a kid in their crew. You gotta blade, Luke?'

I show my knife to them. I've been carrying it in case I need to defend myself from Aden and his mates. Raz laughs, says I need something bigger. I say I don't have much cash.

'The last big fight with the Greens,' Minty says, 'twenty of us was fighting.'

'Man, that's scary.' I'm shocked, even though I know everyone bigs up what they do.

'Nah, you'd be fine,' Minty says. 'You should come with us for the next one. After what you did to that kid at school, you'd smash it.'

'What did he do?' Raz picks at a scab on his elbow.

'He gave it to this kid who gave him shit. Broke his jaw.' Minty looks at me proudly. 'This kid used to pick on me at school, you know. Ganged up on me with his racist mates. That's why I joined Skull Crew. My uncle said they'd protect me.'

Minty grins and offers me a piece chewing gum. I wave it away. The back of my eyes ache. Suddenly I want to cry like a fountain.

'Aden said his mates would have a go at me.'

'Don't you worry 'bout that, bruv. If those kids try anything, we'll give 'em summin they won't forget in a hurry.'

I wonder who he means by 'we'.

Raz gets up and kicks the base of the sofa. He looks impatient with us.

'The safehouse got raided, did you hear?'

'Yeah, man.' Minty tosses another stone into the bushes as he chews. 'That's old news.'

'Zom's after the woman who lives next door. She's done a runner. He's scared she's grassed him up for killing the girl and the feds will find him and put him away. He says she's dead meat if she shows up here.'

There's a whoosh in my ears and my heart starts to pound. I've sort of known it for a long time, but now I know for sure. Zom killed that darkskin girl who was stabbed here in the summer. And Jez is working for him.

———

We're hiding behind bushes by the path, looking out for someone to rob. Fishing, they call it. Minty reckons this is a good place – people get off at the station after work and walk this way home instead of along the main road. He scored a wallet off a bloke with earbuds in the other day. The bloke was so caught in his music he scarcely even noticed Minty step in front of him and slip a knife under his chin. His wallet had sixty quid in it.

'Got ya blade ready?'

I press the switch and the blade flicks out. It's an Italian stiletto switchblade with a titanium blade, razor sharp and pointed at the tip. The blade is six inches long. Small by crew standards.

Minty scans the path. It's getting dark. I'm at Tottenham Marshes.

'Remember, you gotta scare 'em into thinkin' you're gonna shank 'em if they don't cough up. Fear is everything, man.'

A shiver goes through me. The fear is all on my end so far. I've not yet used this knife on anyone, threatened anyone with it, even. I don't see how I'm ever gonna be able to dip this blade unless it's my life on the line. But Minty won't understand if I bottle it.

There's a rustle beside me. Minty crouches down, points to the path. Below his black hood, only the white of his eyes. I touch my own hood, checking it's up. He gives me the hand signal. I go cold.

It's a smallish white guy in jeans and trainers, a backpack hooked over his shoulder. Glasses, hair parted at the side. Works in IT, maybe. I wait 'til he's level and rush him from the side. He gasps and drops to the ground.

'Gimme your wallet!' I lean over him and shove the blade up close. 'Or I'll stab you.'

The guy gasps. Points to his backpack. Minty runs up, grabs the backpack, unzips the pocket. Tips out keys, a chocolate bar, a memory stick.

'Ain't no wallet here, man.'

'In the shoes,' he gasps.

Minty tips out the rest. A lemon, a pair of leather shoes. He pulls a wallet from one and gives me a thumbs up.

I put the knife away.

'Skeet!' Minty is running already.

I follow, glancing over my shoulder as we turn the corner. The guy is collecting his stuff, on hands and knees. A pang of remorse hits me. I hope he's got a good job.

'Four pinkies!' Minty holds up the loot when we're a safe distance. 'We hit the jackpot!' He hands me two notes. 'One hundred each.'

We walk back to the estate via the back streets, avoiding the railway station where there are cameras.

Angel lets us in. Minty says something to him and he holds up his hand to high five me.

'You done well, bruv! We're gonna celebrate.'

I follow Minty and Angel into the living room. There's bright colours everywhere, rugs, fabric hanging on walls. No sign of Angel's girlfriend. Some crew youngers I recognise are there – Raz and the guy with ginger hair. Elders too. I've seen some of them on the estate. One I don't know wears a singlet. He stands slightly apart from the others, not smoking, watching what's going on. His skin is tanned brown and he's more muscular than the others. His eyes say, Don't fuck with me.

'Hey, Zom,' Minty says to him. 'This is Luke.'

His eyes flicker. 'Hey, man. You're Jez's friend, yeah?'

I nod. I haven't seen Jez since she walked out of my room. Is she still working for Zom? Is she giving him what he wants?

'He's the one who mashed up the boy at school,' Minty says with pride.

'Is that right?' Zom smiles. His eyes stay cold as ice. One tooth at the front is gold.

A couple of elders congratulate me. I'll be 'rolling with the mandem soon', one says.

I know I've passed another test.

Since I've been hanging out with him again, Minty's let me join in with gang stuff like patrolling the estate with him, checking for enemies and police. We don't play footy anymore – Spurs must have turned him down, cos he's stopped talking about football.

Angel passes me a reefer. I take a puff, pass it on to Minty on the sofa beside me. For a short time, all my worries are washed away. What my stepdad might do next, where I'm gonna sleep if he kicks me out.

When I get up to go to the bathroom, Angel waves me over.

'Here, this is for you.'

He hands me a box. On the label it says 'Nike Air Max Plus. Size 43.' My size. I lift the lid. They're brand new, snuggled in tissue paper.

Without unlacing them, I drag off my mud-splashed old Nikes and press my feet into the perfect, untouched shoes. Suddenly, I remember the boxes of trainers piled up in Jez's room and how I slated her for having no principles. I'm no different to her really, am I?

'Kip here tonight if you want, bruv.' Angel gestures to the living room. 'The sofa folds out. My missus will make you oats in the morning.'

My phone pings. I'm lying in the dark in my new bed, trying to sleep.

Hello, my favourite young man 😊 *How's it going?*

It's Jez. I message her back.

Hey stranger. Missing you.

I can't keep the grin off my face. I was scared she might have gone for good.

————

'Hey,' I say, suddenly shy.

Jez throws her arms round me like we've not seen each other for years.

'Long time no see, kiddo. I missed you. I really wanted to see you but you know. I didn't think you wanted to see me.'

'Sorry about what I said last time. I didn't mean it.'

We get a table by the window. The waitress takes our order and lights a candle in a glass container.

'We're not on a date,' Jez says to her.

'Oh, I'm sorry.' The waitress is flustered. 'Shall I blow it out?' Jez laughs like it's the funniest thing.

'How have you been, anyways?' Her teeth gleam at me. It hits me again how beautiful she is and how mixed up I am about her. I told her I only want to be her friend but my eyes don't know that.

I tell her how I've been hanging out with Minty and others in the crew, the jobs I've been doing for Angel and the money I've earned. I don't mention I robbed someone.

'That's great you've been earning some p's. I said you should hang out with the boys, didn't I?'

The waitress comes with the order.

'Are you enjoying not going to school?'

'I miss it. That's weird, I know.'

'What do you miss?'

'I miss some of the lessons. Music, Spanish, football. The other kids. Some of the teachers too.'

'Miss Collins. Do you miss her?' Jez watches me closely. The corners of her mouth have slumped.

I shrug.

'Have you seen her since they kicked you out?' Her voice is suddenly high and jangly.

'Of course not.' I decide not to say I texted Miss Collins and she texted back. Jez would only get the wrong end of the stick.

'Are you going to do your exams?'

'I dunno. Mrs Singent sent an email to my stepdad saying unless I start sending in homework there's no point in me taking the exams.'

'Bet he liked that.'

'He went off on one, yeah. Said I'll end up on the dole or in the nick.'

'Don't listen to him, Luke. He's an angry old man who wants to take it out on someone else.'

I hear it again like he's just said it, with all the anger and disappointment in his voice. The other stuff too.

You're a bad influence on Kirsty. You're a total waste of space.

'Have you met any elders yet, apart from Angel?'

'A few.' Zom, I nearly say but I don't want to spoil the mood.

She looks into my eyes. 'Do you want to be one of the crew?'

'I don't know. I like the money. I like hanging out with Minty. But the rest...'

'Once they think they can trust you, they'll let you in. Then you'll have the chance to make real money. Some of the older Gs are raking it in, you know.'

'From selling crack?'

'From shotting, robbing, whatever. Zom makes a heap of money.'

'Do you see him still?' I can't help asking.

'Only for work. I've been doing deliveries for him. I stuff a couple of my bags with pebbles, and get the train out to St Albans or wherever. Drop them off to his punters.' She laughs. 'Once the transport police got on and I had to run into the loo and start shoving them up my you know what.'

'Shit, Jez.'

'It's just work.' Two patches of red appear on her cheeks. 'I don't sleep with him anymore. He's a basket case.' She holds her palm over the flame.

'Has he tried anything?'

She lowers her head, doesn't meet my eyes. 'He's not going to try anything, don't worry.'

'How do you know he won't?'

'Karim and Spicer are looking after me now.'

'You're not sleeping with them, are you?'

'What do you think I am, ho central? Spicer's girlfriend is my best friend and Karim's girlfriend runs the beauty salon where I work.'

I hope Jez knows what she's doing. I know she wants people to like her but these people are gangsters.

'Still going to school?'

She shrugs. 'Sometimes. If I'm not working.'

'What about drama? You want to get into the local theatre still, don't you?'

'There's an audition coming up. But the chances—'

'You should go for it. Don't give up before you've even started.'

'You're a fine one'. She pouts. 'You've given up on school, haven't you?'

I don't reply.

The bill comes. I pull out my twenties. As we leave the table, I pat my jeans pocket for my knife.

'Let me see,' Jez says when we're outside.

I give her the knife. She switches the blade open and stares at it. The fake pearl handle glistens. She closes the blade and hands it back. The light is gone from her face.

'See you then, Luke. Keep safe, won't you?'

We hug goodbye. I don't want to let her go.

JEZ

STASH QUEEN

I READ THE MESSAGE AS I WAS ABOUT TO GET ON THE W3 TO go to school.

We'll be over your place at 3

Figuring I should tidy the place so it isn't an utter tip when V arrives, I hurry home.

'What are you doing back?' Mum emerges in her dressing gown and socks, holding a burnt, half-eaten piece of toast.

'Got to tidy up the house. I've got an important visitor later.'

'Gillian? She's not due 'til Friday.'

'No, someone else. They're here to talk to me about work-from-home opportunities. Get a plate Mum, for goodness sake! You're making crumbs everywhere.'

'Work-from-home opportunities? What does that mean?'

'I'll tell you later, there's no time now. When are you going out to see Toni?'

At last Mum is out of the house. I offer to drive her to Toni's and pick her up later but she says at my age I can't drive without anyone in the car. Little does she know I've been making secret trips around Muswell Hill in the old Merc. Once I turn seventeen you'll never see me on a bus, I swear.

It took me a solid five hours to get the house ready to receive Vincent (Rowena let slip V's real name). The doorbell rings.

'Hi, guys! Thanks for coming over. Come in, make yourselves at home.' Politeness can't hurt, can it?

'Hey, Jez.' Spicer replies. 'How's it going?'

'I'm cool. Catching up on domestic tasks.' I indicate behind me with a smile.

'Nice place.' V's in a black tracky and black Nikes. He strides down the hall and inspects the alarm box.

'It works, yeah?'

'Of course.'

I pour three large glasses of chilled Chablis, taking a good swig of mine. V strides into the living room, peeking at photos I've plonked onto the mantelpiece to make the place look homely.

'Do you want me to show you around?'

'Lead the way.'

I climb the stairs, nervous now, like an estate agent who needs the next commission. Instead of pointing out the airy rooms, I focus on the alcoves and hiding places.

'So, here's the master bedroom. Lots of built-ins.' I gesture at the mirrored wall-length built-in wardrobe. 'Plenty of room for whatever you want to put there.'

V and Spicer exchange looks. They're impressed, defo. Spicer steps forward, his hand reaching to the door.

'OK to look inside?'

'Sure. It's only Mum's stuff.' It *was* her stuff. But I took the opportunity of clearing out some of her junk to make space.

Ditto for the bathroom and kitchen cupboards, which used to be groaning with meds/booze, and the chest in the landing, once crammed with old linen tablecloths, crocheted tea cosies, disintegrating photo albums and the family relics. (I moved the albums under the bed – I'm not totally heartless.)

'We've got a cellar too, I nearly forgot.'

V stops gazing at the view from my bedroom window and follows me downstairs. He peers around the cellar, goes to the rack of dusty wine bottles, picks up one of the few Mum hasn't drunk yet and brushes a label clean.

'I didn't know you were into wine.'

He looks up, raises an eyebrow.

'You know I'm not Zom's girl anymore.' I say it so Spicer won't hear, coming up beside V. He looks at me, not blinking. The man can hold a stare longer than anyone I've ever met. I feel my face warm.

'Glad to hear it, Jezebel.' He touches my cheek. 'You're a cutie, you know. But way too young to be chirpsing with me.'

'So what? I'm old enough to move drugs around, aren't I? Old enough to store your shit.'

'You've gotta mouth on you, girl.' He starts climbing the stairs.

Tour of the house complete, the boys go out for ten minutes and return with two large boxes, which they place in the bottom of my wardrobe underneath a pile of Tara's hand-me-downs I was going to chuck. They go back for more. This time they're lugging a crate covered in a blanket.

They get it into the cellar.

V fusses around the crate like he's tucking up a baby. Then he straightens up, brushing dust and grime off his tracky bottoms.

'What's in there, gold bullion?'

'Guns. Best not go peeping inside, or one might go bang in your face.'

I say nothing. Suddenly, this is serious.

'We're trusting you,' V says as he and Spicer head out. 'Keep this stash safe and don't let anyone go near it. And put the alarm on when you go out.'

When they've gone, I wait a few minutes and go up to my room. I pull the tape carefully off the lid of one cardboard box. Inside are clear plazzie bags of white powder. The other box has the same bags, but the powder inside is a dirty shade of white.

I run downstairs into the cellar and peep into the crate, under the layers of material and bubble wrap. Each gun is carefully wrapped in a duster or cloth. I put the lid back, stunned. There's enough guns in there to kill the entire street twice over.

Twenty minutes later, Mum's home. I bring her a cuppa and two digestive biscuits, and listen to her go on about Toni's troubles and other things. I feel guilty about turning the house into an armory-cum-drugs warehouse. Oh yes, and for getting rid of a large chunk of her booze and pills. She'll thank me for it in the end, though.

LUKE

'YOUNGERS, LISTEN UP!' SPICER'S VOICE CUTS THROUGH THE blur of noise behind Delius Tower. 'The Greens are on our ends. They're on the rec now, dissing us. Let's go get 'em.'

'This is war!' an older kid shouts, waving his knife. It has a curved blade, nearly a foot long. Ginger hair sticks up like a mop from his head.

A chorus of whoops and war cries.

'Dem youts gonna get fucked!'

Spicer finishes up. 'Look after each other and don't take no stupid risks. Don't be the fuckin' hero who ends up dead.'

'Ready, Luke?' Minty winks at me. I get a whiff of body odour. 'Ready, Raz?'

We make our way through the streets, soljas into battle.

I'm a Skull tonight, I'm part of the crew. Barely an hour ago Angel asked if I wanted to join the crew's youngers for a show-down with the Greens, if they come onto our territory again. I said yes before I could think.

The recreation ground is five minutes away. It's late, no one is around. There's twelve of us. None of us talk. Our job is to stand up to our opps, show them we're not pussies and come back with our rep restored. Raz showed me what started this feud, years ago – a grainy two-minute video clip on YouTube, of a boy getting mashed by five others in a car park and left with no boxers, arse-up in a puddle.

I'm chewing Minty's gum. It takes my mind off what's ahead. I touch my switchblade, tucked into the waist of my jeans. Raz showed me the bigger knife but I said no thanks. Also, I didn't tell him, but I've been taking kickboxing classes twice a week at the leisure centre. I practice every day now. My reactions are fast, the teacher says.

'Over there!'

I follow a pointed finger towards the end of the darkness. All I see is the lit shop windows along the road. Then I see a blackish blob moving towards us. There's not as many of them. But suddenly I'm stuck to the ground.

'OK, bruv?'

It's the ginger kid.

'I'm OK.'

He gives me a thumbs up, wraps a blue bandana round his neck and runs to the front of our group. I pull my skull balaclava down like the others are doing. Angel gave it to me. My fingers find the eye holes and adjust them so they don't go over my eyes. I feel a fake. Part of me wants to run home. I still haven't wet my blade even.

Some of the others hold their phones up above their heads. Someone lights a firework and lobs it into the empty space ahead. Red arcs across the sky. Suddenly everyone is running towards the small figures ahead. Minty and Raz have vanished. Someone tugs my arm.

'Move, man!'

I run.

It's chaos. Flashes of silver dip between grabbing, kicking

bodies. Panic rises in me. My mind freezes. There's lampposts along the path but everyone is in dark clothes and the light isn't enough to see anyone properly. I can't tell one kid from the other, though I tried to get a good look at everyone on our side before we set off, like Minty told me.

Duh. Of course, our balies have skulls on. Ahead, a Green slashes a Skull in the thigh with a blade the size of a machete. There's a grunt as he falls. Red streaks his leg. I touch the button and my blade flicks out of the handle. What am I doing here? What can I do with a knife this size?

The Green weaves among the crew's youngers and shanks another Skull in the leg. Then he moves towards a figure on all fours with a bandana tied round his neck, below his balaclava. White skin flashes above his glove.

Ginger. He's gonna get chopped. He's on one knee now, trying to stand. His knife gleams in the mud, too far away.

'Fuck, man. Help us!'

My body takes over. The Green's rambo lunges towards Ginger's head, my foot shoots out and knocks the knife from his hand. I nearly fall but get my balance back and launch myself at the opps. My right fist cracks into his temple. My left is ready, close behind. But the Green's legs are crumpling and he's falling like a brick, face into the ground.

'Behind you!' Someone shouts.

I duck the blade slicing towards my head and swing a foot into the enemy's gut. The knife falls. He totters back, gasping. I pick up his knife in my left hand as someone runs at me from the edge of my vision.

His blade catches the top of my arm. I put my hand to it, feel a warm, wet ooze. My palm comes away red. My heart beats fast, too fast. I want to lie down, get my breath. But the Green is coming at me again.

From behind, a small figure moves to my attacker and dips

him in the thigh. The Green is still holding the knife, trying to have another go. I pile in with my blade, pushing it into his bum cheek. He writhes on the ground, spittle on his lips, his blade slashing the air.

Sound of sirens. Flashing blue lights trace along the main road, twenty metres off.

'Luke! We gotta go!'

It's the one who fought off my opps. Minty. His bally is rolled up above his eyes. He's waving at me to follow. I look round the rec. The Greens have regrouped by a bench. Some are bent over their knees, panting. One is face down in the mud. Then I'm running like the wind.

———

Alcohol splashes onto the wet in my arm. I muffle my cry. The sting is way worse than the pain of the wound.

'It's gonna mend,' an elder says. He's looking after the wounded soljas. 'Go easy for a couple of weeks.'

We're inside Angel's flat on the estate. I can't see Zom. Two youngers have gone to ER to get treated for stab wounds. Both Raz and Minty are OK, except for Raz's twisted ankle. Everyone is drinking whisky out of mugs, telling stories about what happened. I stick to beer. I'm filled with post-fight glow, kitted out in Angel's joggers and hoody, both a size too big. On the way here we all went to the garages at the far end of the estate, took off our clothes. Someone poured petrol over them and we stood around coughing as they burned. Just in case, Minty said.

The ginger kid comes up to me, his leg bandaged in a cut up T-shirt.

'Thanks for saving my hide, man.'

I'm so chuffed I can hardly speak.

Another kid comes over. He asks is it really my first gang fight. I nod.

'He fought off three soljas in a row,' the kid tells everyone, jerking his head at me. 'He was all over the opps, kicking like a ninja!'

Minty joins in. 'Yeah, he saved Ginger from getting totally mashed.'

'Yo, Ninja!' someone else says. 'You're a star, man.'

Minty grins. 'We're calling you Ninja from now on, bruv.'

Angel high fives me. 'You proper smashed it, kid.'

———

I'm lying on a sheepskin rug beside Minty. I'm so tired I can't move. Around us, the sound of moans. I open my eyes. Four or five elders have turned up and are taking their places in chairs being emptied.

'Outta here, crew.' One of them pokes a sleeping body with his foot. 'Ain't you lot got no homes to go to?'

Before I get to the door, one of the elders lopes over. His skin is light-brown like mine. He's more lean than muscular. Moves like a big cat.

'Yo, Luke. I hear you earned your stripes out there.' His eyes are steady on my face.

'Cheers,' I say, grinning.

A group of us shuffle down the corridor. I find Minty. He looks smaller than ever in a too-big hoody.

'Was that—'

'Yeah, V. The main man. He don't usually give no attention to us.'

I remember what I want to tell Minty.

'I forgot to say... Thanks for what you did out there. You saved me from getting sliced into salami.'

'Any time, fam.'

I'm home in less than five minutes. The gate swings open with a creak. Kevin comes to the door as I'm struggling to find my key.

'What time do you call this? It's fuckin' three in the morning!'

I don't feel brave anymore, just small and scared. And tired, too tired to defend myself.

His jaw firms and his chin nudges up. He's not much taller than me anymore but inches bigger across the chest.

'What in God's name happened to you?' He stares at the scratches on my face. 'You've been in a fight, ain't ya? You've been in a fight with that gang of yours.'

His voice is loud enough to wake Kirsty. I nod, too scared to speak. I hate how he makes me feel, like a curled-up critter about to be trodden on.

'That's it.' He slams his fist into the wall beside me. 'As of tomorrow morning, you're outta here. I'm not havin' you in this house no more, cockin' your two fingers at me. Have you ever given a thought to your sister? What sort of example you're setting to her? You're a disgrace to your mother!'

Under the bedcover, I wrap myself into a tight ball. I'm shivering. My arm throbs. I wonder if I should put antiseptic on the wound.

Kevin's right about me not thinking about my sister. He's right about my mother too. If she was here now, she'd be ashamed of me. I'm ashamed of myself too. But I know that this is just the start.

CALLUM

18TH OCTOBER

It was one of my rare days off since Operation Rye began. Brendan wasn't yet home from school and the silence was starting to grate on my nerves. I looked again at the wooden fox sitting on the living room mantelpiece. In the half light, its eyes seemed to be watching me. As I stared, I could have sworn that one winked.

'God's sake,' I muttered, getting up and turning the object so its eyes faced the wall. I'm losing it, I thought with a stab of panic. 'It's only a sodding carving.'

Brendan seemed to have an affinity with the little figures – the only reason I tolerated them in the house at all. I pulled on my jacket and headed out. A short walk might clear my mind.

Along the road, trees stood bare-branched against the sky. Halloween was coming up. I passed a hollowed-out pumpkin skewered onto a gate post like a ghoulish head. The pressure of the investigation, the skulls and now Brendan's questions about the death of my father... I was close to the edge of the cliff, and it was a long way down. What if he found out the rest? How would I cope with that – and how would *he*?

Brendan had gone back to his withdrawn state, saying little. He was still talking to Marcy though, asking more questions about my father, so she told me. Her experience of our family had been rather different to my own.

I reached the woods. A subdued glow marked the remnants of sunset. This time last year, Kate and I had taken an impromptu break in Somerset, shortly before everything had slid downhill... Kate was meant to be coming home for Christmas – staying in the spare room, anyway. What sort of Christmas it would be, I couldn't imagine.

Arriving at the house, I peered through the living room window into what appeared to be a slice of cosy domesticity: flat-screen TV, framed sketches and photo-laden mantelpiece bathed in a cheery glow, courtesy of the lighting timer. I'd forgotten to close the curtains. For weeks I'd religiously checked them before leaving the house.

I set off a King Edward in the microwave and sat down at the table. My thoughts returned to the question that had pursued me all day. Was Operation Rye about to join the list of failed inquiries?

Despite all our efforts, we hadn't been able to locate Muscleman, Wolf or Vincent Edwards, let alone charge them. Yesterday, Detective Superintendent Bailey had summoned me to New Scotland Yard. He was pulling the plug on the undercover officer and was going to drastically reduce both the surveillance team and my core team. Funds were sparse and Pierce needed more resources for his Operation Hindhead. I'd not bothered to argue.

The microwave pinged. I rescued my potato, poured a glass of red and sat down at the table. Bailey's parting words came back.

'I'm afraid, Callum, that Operation Rye will have to be terminated too, very soon.' Unless there was an eleventh-hour development, I was going to fail Solita and her family – justice would not be done and her killers would go free.

Until the investigation was officially terminated, I'd keep going. But the voice in my head told me it was hopeless.

You've failed again, Callum. The girl's killers are long gone. You're never going to find them.

———

I woke at three thirty in the morning, shouting in panic. The nightmare again, worse than ever.

I'm in the garden. Behind me, the burning shed and a black sky tinged with orange. A circle of animals and birds is forming around me, my father's figurines magically come to life. Foxes, badgers, ducks... They come closer and closer. I put my hands over my eyes. Their eyes flicker with orange, accusing me.

LUKE

THE DAY STARTS LIKE ANY OTHER.

I'm on the sofa at the back of Delius Tower with Minty, laughing at videos on his phone. The day is damp, no one is about yet.

'Yo, Minty!' Ginger runs towards us. He stops, panting. 'I saw that woman that scarpered from flat 815.'

Minty rams his phone into his pocket and signals for me to come too. The three of us run to the front of the tower in time to see a grey-haired woman with misted glasses pulling a wheely suitcase to the block entrance. She taps the keypad and goes inside.

'I'm onto Karim.' Ginger hits a button on his phone. 'Shit, he's not picking up. You got Zom's number, bruv?'

'I'll follow her,' I say as Minty gets his phone out.

I want to do my bit to help. I pull up my hood, run to the tower entrance and punch in the code. The woman's getting into the lift with a man in a suit and a laden postman. She doesn't see me. I leg it up the stairs. If the lift stops on the way to the eighth floor, I'll get there before she does.

I wait in the stairwell 'til she gets out of the lift, then follow her down the corridor. The wheely trundles along the shiny floor. She stops at flat 815, slips a key into the lock and goes inside. I return to the wall beside the west stairwell.

'Yo, Minty. She's gone into 815.'

'Wait there, fam. I'm comin' up now. We gotta make sure she don't go nowhere. Zom's on his way. Ginger's tryna to get hold of Angel and Wolf.'

I slip my phone into my jeans pocket, feeling like a spy on a mission. Minty turns up a few minutes later, out of breath. He slumps against the wall beside me.

'This is big, Ninj. This could be the chance to make our reps.'

His phone brays like a donkey. I'm so keyed up, I laugh.

'Me an' Ninj are on it, Zom, no sweat. We'll wait for you by the eighth-floor lift. No, we won't let her get away.' He rolls his eyes as he tucks away the phone. 'That man needs to chill.'

'I'm not sure about this, Minty.' I feel uneasy. I don't want anything to do with Zom. His head has got something missing.

'Come on, Ninj, don't be a pussy.' Minty pulls a face. 'Turning things down ain't a good plan at our age.'

I say nothing. Two minutes later, Zom calls again.

'We're on it.' Minty looks at me. He's not excited anymore. 'Zom says get ready to jump her if she comes out. We gotta stop her screaming first – cover her mouth and stick a blade to her throat. Then we hold her down 'til he comes.'

A flutter in my stomach like I've eaten something bad.

'Chill, bruv.' Minty play-punches my arm. 'We're the backup, that's all. Zom will be here any minute.'

Twenty minutes later, Zom steps out of the stairwell, hoody up, holding a black JD Sports bag. Sweat shines on his brow. He scans our faces.

'You two part of this job, yes or no?'

Minty speaks first. 'I'm with you, Zom.'

'Yeah, me too.' I want to say no but I can't. 'What about Angel and Wolf? Ain't they in this too?'

'Angel can't make it, he's in Southend getting his car fixed. Wolfman is fuck knows where. So, it's just us three, innit?'

Minty bites his lip. I look at the floor.

'Right then.' Zom briefs us. 'We get her to open her door, then push her back inside and shank her.'

My heart thuds. No way can I do this.

'If that don't work, we switch to Plan B.'

'What's that?' Minty looks at Zom.

'We wait here 'til she comes out, all night if we have to, then we do it.' Zom puts his bag down. 'Phones on silent.' He brings out two pairs of disposable gloves, tosses one to Minty and puts on the other pair himself. 'There's no more,' he says to me. 'So, don't touch nothing in there.'

Zom pulls the green handled zombie out of his bag. It's not in a sheath. The jagged blade looks pure evil. My own knife is back at Angel's – I forgot to take it this morning.

'Take it, Minty,' Zom says. 'When the door opens, follow me inside and be ready to wet her. Aim for the throat, as deep as you can. Got it?'

Minty nods, chewing furiously, and takes the knife. His face is ash-grey.

Zom waves us forward. 'Let's do it, crew. Let's take out this fuckin' witch.'

Minty holds the knife inside his open hoody. We creep along the corridor: 812, 813, 814. Zom jerks his head at me: 815.

'Go ring the bell.'

I press once. My heart pounds so hard it hurts. There's a sound from inside. Feet moving. Then nothing.

Zom and Minty stare at me. Their backs are glued to the wall.

A small lightskin girl and her mum step out of the lift and

walk towards us. The woman's head is pointed down and the girl is chattering away. They go into a flat.

I let out my breath. I don't think they saw us.

Zom kisses his teeth. 'Do it again, man.'

I press the bell again, harder.

Zom gestures for me to stand beside Minty.

One minute passes. Two. The air is too thick to breathe. Faint sounds of children laughing and shrieking. Smell of piss and bleach from the stairwell. I check my phone: 12.02.

Footsteps inside, getting louder.

'Get ready to jump her. Soon as the door moves, we pile in. Me first, then Minty. Luke, bring the bag in with you an' close the door.'

I lower my head, lean my hands on my knees. I'm dizzy with fear.

'Don't fret, Ninj.'

The wheely pokes out the doorway. Then an ankle boot. A leg.

Zom springs onto the woman. She stumbles backwards, collapses against the wall. Zom crashes into a door frame. Minty steps over the wheely and holds the knife over the woman's chest. She's holding a can. Spray comes out in a hiss. Minty yells 'Fuck!' and drops the knife. The can rolls across the carpet.

The woman looks towards the door, and me. One leg is bent under her body. Her glasses are on the floor.

'Can't see! She's blinded me!' Minty is on his knees, rubbing his eyes.

I'm behind him, a foot inside the hall. Frozen.

Zom points to the knife. His head is cut above the eyebrow.

'Fuck's sake, Luke! Get the shank!'

I drop the bag and pick up the knife. The woman angles her head, looks into my eyes.

'Do it now, man! Shank her in the throat!'

I raise the knife above my head, aim the tip of the blade at her neck.

'No.' Her voice is quiet. 'Please don't.'

Her eyes are blue, the blue of a summer sky.

The hall crouches over me, dark, an endless cave. Sounds crash into my head. Time disappears.

PART TWO

LUKE

I OPEN MY EYES. I'M SITTING ON THE FLOOR. LIGHTS SWIRL across my vision. Carpet under my hands. The knife isn't in my hand anymore. How long have I been sitting here?

Minty is leaning against the wall, still rubbing his eyes.

Zom is crouched on the floor, bent over the woman. He's holding the knife. He's sawing something with it. There's a wet suck like a small animal claimed by bog. I can't see what he's doing. He moves and I can see blood spewing from a hole in her throat. Her head lolls to one side. A shudder goes through me.

'Get up, man.' Zom looms over me.

I see his hand at his side. The plastic glove on the hand that's holding the knife looks like it's been dipped in bright-red paint.

'Open the bag. Take out the sweatshirt and towels and give us one.'

Zom takes the blue towel I give him, wraps the knife in it and drops it into the bag. He takes off his gloves and drops them in on top. He takes the next towel from me, drags it over his face and neck, drops that in too. Then he takes the sweatshirt.

'Minty, your gloves. In here.'

A child's wailing starts, close by.

'Hoods up. Let's get the fuck out.'

I follow Minty and Zom out into the corridor, nearly tripping over the wheely. We hurry along the corridor and run down the stairs. Zom stops at the first-floor stairwell.

'Meet us round the back, yeah? Minty you follow me in one minute, got that? Luke you come one minute after.'

Zom leaves, then Minty. Then it's just me.

I pull my hoody down over my face as far as it'll go and head out into the drizzle. It's still daylight – seems like it should be night. I look around in surprise. Small kids carry on playing in the playground. Mums carry on talking. No one is coming after us. No one even sees us.

Zom is waiting at the back of the tower, under the community room porch. He's talking on his phone, fast harsh stubs of sound. Minty's eyes are red.

I lean over and throw up on the grass then raise my head to the sky. Rain wets my face. I want it to wash me clean.

'Give it here.' Zom takes the bag from me. He tells us to keep our mouths shut about what we've done. Then he tells Minty to go home, he wants to speak to me alone.

He doesn't touch me, doesn't hurt me at all. He doesn't need to. What he says makes me feel like he's pressing the cold tip of his blade against my throat.

I watch Zom head towards the basement car park. He's holding the black sports bag.

The camera. There's a camera on the wall above the car park exit. They put new lights in the car park a few days ago and another camera. Inside, up high, tucked into a corner. Not easy to spot. Ginger said someone should nobble it.

Does Zom know about the camera? Is it still working? Are we going to be caught?

I think about running after Zom to warn him. Instead, I wait for his black BMW to come out of the car park and turn onto the road leading out of the estate.

CALLUM

I WAS AT MY DESK, MAKING MY WAY THROUGH AN UNWIELDY chicken burger and trying not to let any more of its contents splatter over my keyboard, when my phone rang. DI Ellie Dalton flashed onto the screen, from the local CID.

'Callum? There's been a fatal stabbing on the Effra Lane estate. I'm at the scene. Have you been notified yet?'

I told her I hadn't.

'I thought you should know as you're investigating the Solita Milton murder.'

Even before Ellie told me what had happened at flat 815 of Delius Tower, cold dread settled over me.

'We're off to Effra Lane,' I said to DS Harper, leaving my half-eaten burger on the desk.

For the six minutes it took us to get to the estate, I prayed that the dead body wouldn't belong to Nora Symonds. Please, let it be a relative, a friend or a visitor.

Sam gave me a questioning look as I took another corner faster than the situation officially warranted.

'Hey, boss. I've just eaten a massive veggie burger.'

'It's her,' I replied. 'Our witness. I know it.'

I pulled up behind the SOCO van parked at the Delius Tower entrance. We suited up beside the van and ran into the tower. The lift didn't appear. I signalled for Sam to follow and started up the stairs.

Police tape cordoned off the eighth floor.

'I'll be dealing with this.' I showed my ID to the scene guard and gave him my credentials. Hands cold and clammy, I made my way over the stepping plates to flat 815.

A small wheeled suitcase lay on its side across the doorway, handle extended. A crime scene officer was bent down collecting samples from the bloody hall carpet surrounding a woman's body, which lay about six feet from the front door. I took two steps closer, close enough to be sure it was her. A gasp came out of my mouth, though I'd thought I was hardened to the most gruesome sights.

My shock wasn't only due to the gaping hole where her throat had been, though that was horrible enough. Her lips had been hacked off. Blood drenched the lower half of her face and dripped slowly onto the carpet.

I latched a hand onto the wall to steady myself. The mutilated body of Nora Symonds receded and sorrow swallowed me up. Then a blast of anger broke in. The very thing I'd been afraid of had happened. I had been well aware of the risk to Nora Symonds. But I had not kept her safe.

'Boss? Are you all right?' A hand brushed my arm.

'It's her. Those bastards...' My hands trembled as another wave of sorrow and anger engulfed me. Those bastards had wanted to make an example of her. The mutilation of the lips and the site of stabbing told me exactly what this crime was about. It was an act of revenge for the woman informing on them – and reminded everyone living on the estate what would happen to them too, if they talked to us.

'Why did she come back?' It was an effort to speak.

Sam shook her head. 'I don't know.'

I'd phoned Nora Symonds the week before to check how she was getting on in her new council flat. She told me she'd given it a go but it didn't get any sunshine, so she had moved back in with her sister in Horsham, indefinitely. I'd warned her not to return to her old flat – I could remember my exact words, near enough.

Don't go back to the Effra Lane flat, it could be dangerous. I thought I'd been clear. But why the fuck hadn't I said *Don't go back there under any circumstances, not even for ten minutes.*

One of the blue-suited SOCOs was examining the contents of the suitcase. He held up a labelled, tinted bottle in his gloved hand.

'Prescription medicine.' DS Harper nodded towards the bottle. 'Looks like she came back to collect a few things.'

'And they were waiting,' I replied. 'They must have seen her on her way in and jumped her as she was going back out.'

DI Dalton caught my eye and came over. I'd spoken with Ellie on several occasions recently; she'd been present at our briefings with local police teams to keep them in the loop, given our investigation was centred on their patch.

'Hello, Callum.' Efficient as usual, Ellie updated me on what had been done so far – photographs of the scene were almost complete, she'd talked to the crime scene manager about recovering items for forensic tests and had organised a post-mortem. Nora's sister had been informed and was on the way over to north London to identify the body.

Struggling to grasp the details, I thanked her and stepped

away from the activity to call Acting DCI Pierce. He was unavailable, a message stated.

'I'm at Effra Lane estate, at the scene,' I explained to his voicemail. 'The victim is Nora Symonds, our key witness. I'm SIO on this one, OK?'

It wasn't really a question. As the incident was clearly linked to Operation Rye, I would need to take on this murder as part of our investigation – though as acting DCI, Pierce would have to give it the nod.

Snapping into SIO mode, I went to speak with the crime scene manager. There was no sign of the murder weapon, nor had any other items been left by the killers. I got onto my phone and arranged the outstanding tasks.

On the way out of the estate, I noticed fresh graffiti on the wall beside the tower entrance. In large white capitals:

DEATH TO SNITCHS

Beside it, a picture of a skull.

———

DS Harper and I sat in the interview suite at Tottenham police station opposite Nora Symonds's neighbour, Sophie Ranelson. She was a white woman in her early thirties, her hair dyed blonde with dark roots. Her face, drawn and pale, bore a vacant expression – shock, presumably. This was the second time Sam had talked to her, my first.

'So, Sophie.' DS Harper looked at the notes that had been taken. 'You heard a disturbance in Nora Symonds's flat next door, then you went over to check on her and found her on the floor, apparently dead. Is that correct?'

'Yeah, that's right. There was the sound of men's voices

coming from next door. I knew something wasn't right as Nora wasn't living there no more... I went to have a look.'

'What did you see?'

'There was a suitcase sticking out of the door. I went in... I saw her lying on the floor, in that terrible state.' With a moan she lowered her head.

'I'm sorry if this is upsetting for you, Sophie. What did you do after you saw the body?'

'I came back into my flat, bolted the door and called 999.'

'You didn't check her pulse or check to see if she was breathing?'

She scowled. 'It was bleedin' obvious she was dead.'

Sam's eyebrows edged up. 'How long did the disturbance last, roughly?'

'Not long. A few minutes.'

'Do you know what time it was?'

'A bit after midday. The news had just come on the radio.'

'Would you mind taking us through what you heard before you went next door?'

'There was a loud thump like someone banging into something. Then men's voices. Young men, boys, I'm not sure. They sounded stressed. I couldn't hear the words. Then another thud... Must have been her, getting—'

I cut in. 'How many young men were there, would you say?'

'I dunno. Three or four.'

'While you were there, did you see any sign of these young men in the corridor?'

'No, no one.'

'When did you last have any communication with Nora Symonds?'

'Not for weeks. She never told me that she was gonna move out, what happened to her or nothing.'

'Have you ever seen anyone behaving suspiciously around Nora's flat – checking if she's in, that sort of thing?'

'I saw—' She stopped suddenly; her eyes wary. 'No, never.'

'What about before Mrs Symonds was attacked? This morning or yesterday?'

'No, nothing.' She picked at the ragged skin beside a finger-nail. Her fingers were in a dreadful state. 'I still can't believe that someone killed that lovely old lady. She was so kind, wouldn't hurt a fly.'

'Miss Ranelson, you were interviewed by us on the eighth of October, eighteen days ago, after Mrs Symonds made a state-ment to us. I've got your statement here.' I tapped into my laptop. 'You told us that shortly after Solita Milton was murdered, Nora Symonds told you about suspicious behavior she'd observed from two young men visiting flat 814. You admitted telling Mrs Symonds you thought she could be in danger from the young men who used to visit flat 814. You said you were worried in case those men might try to hurt her. You also said you warned her not to go to the police... What was it that made you think they might try to hurt her?'

Sophie Ranelson's eyes opened wide.

'Because she was living right next to those gangsters. I said so in the interview. Everyone knows what that Skull Crew get up to. It's common knowledge. Rape, torture, murder... They even printed leaflets and put them through letterboxes, did you know?'

I glanced at DS Harper. We hadn't known.

'I got one the day after they killed that young black girl outside the estate. *Don't say nothing or you're dead.* People got even more scared after that. Including me.' Miss Ranelson's expres-sion was fierce. 'I've seen what they did to that poor old woman. I have to bloody well live there with those murderers prowling about. They have eyes everywhere. They'll probably find out I'm here, talking to you lot.'

'Did you throw away the leaflet?'

'What do you think?'

'I understand how difficult it is, Miss Ranelson.' I gave her time to compose herself. 'Did you talk to anyone else about your fears for Mrs Symonds's safety, after she confided in you about what she'd seen?'

'No, I didn't.' In a moment, her anger vanished. Her manner became defensive.

'You talked to no one at all?'

She hesitated. 'I might have mentioned it to Leo, my boyfriend. He wouldn't have said nothing.'

'Do you know how gang members found out about Mrs Symonds talking to us?'

'I've no idea. After she left the flat there was a rumour going round that she'd said something.'

I gave her a questioning look. 'That rumour couldn't have come from you, could it?'

Sam glanced at me, surprise on her face.

Miss Ranelson fidgeted. 'No, it didn't come from me. Plenty of people knew Nora was having trouble with the gangsters next door. Months ago, before they killed that girl, Nora said she had a good mind to tell the police about them. It wasn't a secret. She chatted to people on the estate, she was that sort of woman. Word got round.'

'Thank you for being so helpful, Miss Ranelson,' I said, not bothering to keep the sarcasm from my voice. 'We'll be in touch.'

I stood up before I could say anything I might later regret. DS Harper swiftly put away her notebook and followed me out of the interview suite.

'I wouldn't want to get on your bad side, sir,' she said.

I didn't respond, still fuming. Whatever Sophie Ranelson might know about those responsible for this killing – and I'd bet all of my future pension there was something – she wasn't going to tell us.

'She's obviously scared stiff of the Skull gang,' Sam went on. 'Do you think she started a rumour about Nora Symonds going to the police?'

'Who knows. Maybe she told someone, or her boyfriend told someone, and word went around faster than fire in the Australian outback.'

We'd probably never know.

By the time we'd returned to Wood Green, the incident room was thrumming with activity. I was about to sit down at my desk with a coffee when Pierce frowned at me from the doorway of his office and beckoned me over.

'Close the door. Sit down.'

I stayed standing. Smiley leaned a buttock on his desk, facing me. Sweat glistened above his receding hairline. Another ticking off? He didn't like me putting myself in charge of this latest murder, of course he didn't. Even if it *was* a foregone conclusion.

'Why did you rush out of the office earlier like a bull in a china shop, without running it by me first?'

I blinked at him. 'It was urgent, and you looked busy—'

'Then you take over as SIO on the Symonds case without my say so—'

'I phoned you from the scene.'

'Callum, I'm the one running the murder team, not you. You're responsible for Operation Rye. I know we're rank equals. But since Andy asked me to step up, by default I run every new investigation.'

'God's sake, this isn't a new investigation. This murder is part of Operation Rye. Nora Symonds was our key witness.' I paused for breath, aware that my voice was too loud. Not only would the rest of MIT55 be hanging onto our every word, I'd bust a gasket if I carried on like this. 'I didn't know I needed to ask your permission before getting on with my job,' I continued in a calmer voice. 'I assumed it would be a formality, given—'

'Given you let your only witness get stabbed in the throat?' His eyes narrowed.

My gut twisted. That was uncalled for and Smiley knew it. I stepped forward; my fist ready at my side.

'Fuck you, Pierce.' I swung back my fist, longing to smash his face into a bloody pulp.

'Go on, do it! You know you want to.'

No, I was losing it. Letting out a long breath, I let him go.

Pierce mopped his brow with a tissue, glaring at me. 'You're going to regret that, Callum.'

'I don't know why Nora Symonds came back to the estate,' I said as calmly as I could. 'She had somewhere else to stay and I'd warned her not to go back. But I take full responsibility for any lapse on my part. I blame myself for not being clearer with her.'

I turned to the door.

'Before you go. As Operation Hindhead is ramping up, I've asked the super for extra resources. Your team on Operation Rye might not be expanded as much as you'd like.'

I pulled the door over-firmly behind me, glaring at the stealthy glances of those officers not fast enough to pretend to be hard at work.

Pierce was out to get me whatever way he could, the paranoid part of me insisted. The saner part knew very well he wouldn't do that by trying to throttle a significant, high-profile investigation – that would be far too likely to backfire, especially as everyone in the murder team knew there was no love lost between us.

On my desk I found photos of the contents of Mrs Symonds's

suitcase. I scanned the list of items. A Kate Morton paperback, a thick wool cardigan, a pair of knee-high socks, a photo album, a mug with a cartoon of a donkey's face, five boxes of prescription pain relief tablets, a bottle of asthma medicine and a large manilla envelope containing assorted postcards, birthday cards and letters.

Another wave of sadness and anger went through me, catching me by surprise. This wasn't the way I usually reacted after a murder – numbing myself from the pain, forcing myself to stay focused on bringing a killer to justice. But the more I fought to push the emotions down, they more they welled up. What had that poor, brave woman gone through in her final moments? I hadn't protected her, as I'd promised. She had died needlessly. It had happened again...

Another stone slipped out of position. Soon, the whole lot would fall.

My hands were shaking. Without warning, an image of the burning shed flashed before my eyes. I was back there, a sixteen-year-old boy looking on at his trapped, dying father. I heard the crackle of wood and the lick of flames, felt the acrid smoke clogging my throat...

'Are you all right, sir?' DS Harper's voice. Her touch on my shoulder felt like a caress.

I cleared my throat. 'I'll be fine. I felt a bit weird just now, that's all.'

'It could be a reaction to what we saw earlier. It was pretty horrible... You should take extra care of yourself from now on, sir.'

I gave her a grateful nod. 'Thanks, Sam.'

———

After some deep breathing, a mindful walk to Lorenzo's and a strong coffee, I was able to focus on my holding statement for the media.

Driving down to the mortuary, I wondered what the hell could I say to Nora's sister. How could I explain what had happened?

I met Alice Symonds before taking her to identify Nora Symonds's body. A no-nonsense blonde in low heels and a trouser suit, she'd taken time off from her work as a criminal barrister. Nora had possessed 'a stubborn streak', she stressed.

'She wasn't one to be told what to do, Callum. You shouldn't blame yourself for what happened. Nora obviously decided she was going back to get her things, and that was that. She told me she was going to London to have lunch with two friends – she never mentioned returning to her flat on the estate. If she had, I'd have told her not to be so bloody stupid.'

I appreciated the sentiment behind the words, but it didn't erase my sense of guilt.

On the way back to the stalag, I phoned Bev Milton, mindful of the potential danger to her and her daughter, even if – so far – she wasn't fully cooperating. When I told her of Nora Symonds's killing, she inhaled sharply.

'Oh no.'

'It's being treated as murder,' I explained. 'My gut feeling is that the Skull Crew are involved.'

She didn't reply. I'd talked to her several more times over the weeks to try to elicit useful information on V and other gang members her son had associated with. Mrs Milton's silences and hesitations had convinced me she was either lying, or holding back information that could help us find the killers.

'You need to consider moving into alternative accommodation with Leonie, for your safety and hers.'

'I'm not sure, Callum,' she said eventually.

I urged her to think carefully about her situation and promised to be in touch shortly.

Before getting out of the car, I phoned Sophie Ranelson. She and the other residents on the eighth floor of Delius Tower were being given alternative accommodation by the council while the crime scene was active. I told her I would ask for a further period of accommodation in her case as a precautionary measure, until we had Mrs Symonds's killers safely in custody.

In the incident room, detectives were viewing the latest CCTV footage received from the council. I joined the huddle of officers around DS Rowan's computer screen. The CCTV camera positioned outside the Delius Tower exit, now repaired, showed three males arriving at various times in the twenty-eight minutes before 12.04pm, the estimated time of death. It also showed what appeared to be the same three young men leaving separately, several minutes after the time of death. Though their hoodies were up in all the images and it was raining, their faces were visible.

One looked older than the other two. He was white, dark-haired, heavily built and muscular.

The other males looked between fifteen and seventeen. The black kid was slim and shorter than average; the other had lighter skin, white or mixed race, and was average height and build. Neither had any facial hair.

'We're pretty sure that's Muscleman,' DS Rowan said, pointing to the older male. He selected the image of our power-fully built suspect in Solita Milton's murder and brought it side by side with the latest image.

'Yep, I agree,' I said. 'That's the same guy.'

By early evening, more results came in.

'Look at this, boss! It's definitely Muscleman.' DS Rowan jumped out of his chair in his excitement, spilling coffee from the plastic cup held by Pierce who happened to be passing by.

'Careful,' Pierce growled.

Rowan explained the footage was from the two recently installed cameras inside Delius Tower's basement car park. These images were higher quality than the others, crisp and well lit. The cameras had caught a heavily built man leaving the garage on foot twenty minutes before Mrs Symonds's estimated time of death, returning on foot seven minutes after it. His face was visible as he left the garage. Further footage showed what appeared to be the same man driving a black saloon car into and out of the garage. Both the face and the registration number were caught clearly.

A check of the PNC database found the car registered to a Dritan Deda, born 6th May 1999. The photograph on the registration record matched the face on the CCTV image – the driver was the registered owner of the car. The same Dritan Deda had, at aged eighteen, served three years for GBH. Relief filled me, as warm and sweet as a Mars Bar on a summer's day. At last, we had identified Muscleman.

'We're getting closer, guys,' I told the small group of detectives left on Operation Rye. 'Very well done, all of you. It's only a matter of time before we can bring in Mr Deda.'

Ferret gave a 'yay!', DS Freeman fist-pumped as if watching Arsenal score and DS Harper grinned, her dimples showing. Even DS Hanna looked pleased. DS Rowan tugged on his trendy sweater.

By the end of the evening, we'd begun a search for Deda and his car – neither had been found at the registered keeper's address, that of an estranged girlfriend who denied any knowledge of his whereabouts. We were waiting on results from a so far unidentified palm print in the hall beside the front door, and DNA tests on skin and blood fragments obtained from the frame of the living room door. The incident room was buzzing with activity and high spirits. After so many weeks of following a road to nowhere, I welcomed the change in mood more than anyone. I left for home in a determined mood, my wobble that afternoon almost forgotten.

———

When I finally made it home, Brendan's unwashed mug lay in the kitchen sink. After checking my son was definitely in his room – he was in bed, sound asleep – I lay down on my bed, wishing Kate could be with me for one minute.

That night, I couldn't sleep. My brain kept coming back to the sight of Nora Symonds lying dead on the floor of her flat. I imagined Sophie Ranelson waiting for her boyfriend to return, starting at every sound outside her front door. Why had I been so quick to judge her? Most people in her situation wouldn't risk bringing the wrath of a violent gang on themselves, would they? I probably wouldn't have been any braver than Sophie Ranelson – and certainly not as brave as Nora Symonds.

The mutilated face returned. The red mess where her lips had been.

I groaned. A long night stretched ahead. I went downstairs and drank a generous measure of Glenlivet. My thoughts darkened. Not only was Nora Symonds needlessly dead, we had lost our key witness. The woman would never have the chance to testify and be cross-examined in front of a jury.

I glugged more whisky into the tumbler, my anger returning. The bravest woman I had ever met had been slaughtered because she'd tried to help us bring a young girl's killers to justice... I crashed the tumbler down onto the granite worktop. It shattered on impact. A shard of glass lodged in the delicate flesh between my finger and thumb. Blood poured out.

As I went about cleaning and bandaging the wound, and then cleaning up the mess I'd created – fortified by another swig of whisky – my resolve strengthened. There was only one thing I needed to do now: bring in the killers of Nora Symonds and Solita Milton, every single one of them, including the man ultimately responsible. One way or another, I vowed, I was going to do that.

LUKE

THE FIRST THING I DO WHEN I GET TO ANGEL'S IS STRIP OFF my clothes and trainers and dump them in the washing machine. There was blood on my hoody, I didn't notice before. Angel's girlfriend set up the hottest wash on the machine and added stain remover. She told me to have a bath, that would make me feel better.

I scrub 'til my skin is cleaner than clean and there's nothing of that old lady left on me. The only part of her I can't get rid of is the memory of her face. Her eyes looking at me as I held the knife over her. They were so calm, so still. Like she knew I wouldn't do it – or she knew this was going to be her end and she couldn't do anything.

I start to cry. I hate myself for what we did to Mrs Symonds. She never did anything to hurt me. I never even met her before today. Why did I follow her to her flat? Why did I stay and help to kill her? I wish I'd never gone near her, more than anything in the world. I want to go back to being who I was. I want to go back to school and tell Miss Collins I've made a mistake, I'm ready to work hard now.

My tears roll down my cheeks and disappear into the water. I think of what Zom said after Minty left the two of us at the back of the tower. He told me he was going to watch me like a hawk from now on. Then he smiled and told me what he'd do if I ever tell anyone what the three of us did today.

'I'll cut off your lips like I did to that fuckin' bitch. Then I'll cut out your tongue and carve it into pieces. And I swear, man, I'll do it all while you're still alive. And if that don't put you off goin' to the feds, I'll make sure you go down for her murder.'

I try to steady my breath, stop the panic that's slipping over me.

———

'Zom and me go back a long ways,' Angel says when he gets back. 'So's you must respect what Zom says. He's worried you're gonna tell the feds tings to get him put away. So, if you're ever not here no more, if you're not rollin' with the crew no more cos you don't like how I'm talkin' to you or what I'm tellin' you to do or whatever, he'll know you went to the feds and told 'em porkies.'

A horrible feeling comes over me. But I say yes, like this is all right with me.

Outside, it's getting dark. Kids swarm round the bus stop. Ten minutes later I'm on the W3 heading towards Jez's place.

The journey is surreal. Nothing feels the same. A girl in uniform sitting opposite looks at me. She wears a cotton face mask over her nose and mouth. There's a question in her eyes. *What have you done?*

Am I a murderer because I helped Zom kill that woman? Would Mrs Symonds forgive me? Would my mother forgive me?

I phone Jez. She's the only person I can talk to. She doesn't pick up so I text.

I need to see you. I'm on the way over.

The bus climbs the hill and stops at the top outside Alexandra Palace ice rink. The sun's just set. Down below, London spreads out. Glittery towers rise from a distant orange rim. I wonder what they're doing in those towers.

Jez's stop is next. She still hasn't replied. Is she in St Albans delivering drugs for Zom? I get off the bus, scared at the thought she might not be at home. What if she's staying with Zom tonight? She's too scared of him to say no and too pretty for him to leave her alone. But whatever she's up to, it doesn't change how I feel about her. I run out of the park into the wide street, not caring about anything except that Jez will be there.

The house peers down. There's no lights on in the front. I ring and ring at the door. No one comes. I phone Jez again, get voicemail. I'm about to give up when Jez's mother comes to the door in her dressing gown, her eyes not focused.

'Hi, Mrs Robbins. Sorry to wake you up. Is Jez in?'

'Oh, it's you. Come in, love. Sorry I'm in such a state, I wasn't expecting a visitor. Jez is back later, I think. She sent me a message. Hold on, let me check.' I follow her into the kitchen. She reads out the message. 'Back by nine. Late shift at work.'

I could have kissed her, almost. The high of relief fills me. She leaves me in the kitchen with a cup of tea and comes back smelling of apples, dressed like any other mother from round here.

'Are you hungry?' I say no but my stomach growls.

Mrs Robbins chats to me while she cooks, about a relative who caught Covid and nearly died. Then she changes the subject.

'You seem to know Jessamine quite well... You're the only friend who's come over in over a year. There was a girl at her old school she was close to but that ended when she had to move on, you know?' She wipes the table where I'm sitting with sanitiser. 'I know something's going on. She says she has a part time job so she can't go to school so much, but she won't tell me anything about it. She's coming home at all hours... Do you know anything?'

I don't know what to say. Should I tell her Jez is with a gang that sells crack and heroin, and is being exploited by dangerous men who don't care what happens to her, as long as she's useful to them? And that the same goes for me too, probably?

'I don't know what to do, Luke. The social worker says they might have to take Jessamine into care.' She gulps a colourless liquid from a tall glass. 'They don't think I'm a fit mother, you see.' Her voice leaks sorrow and embarrassment. Now I really don't know what to say. Mrs Robbins doesn't seem to mind this one-sided conversation, though.

We eat dinner. It's full of silences and long stretches of Mrs Robbins talking. I barely notice what I'm eating. What would Jez's mother say if she knew what I'd done a few hours ago?

My phone pings.

On my way. See you soon. J

Jez arrives while I'm helping Mel load the dishwasher. She gives me a funny look, grabs a couple of beers from the fridge and thuds up the stairs. I thank Mrs Robbins and escape.

Jez and I stand in her room looking at each other, two awkward teenagers. I reach out and touch her shiny brown hair. Her face is pale. Her lips are bare of lipstick. I'm about to kiss her when she moves. She takes a box of matches and lights a red candle on the mantelpiece. The air smells of mulled wine.

'I've had a shitty day.' She sits at her dressing table.

'What happened?'

'The guy who was meant to be there to protect me, wasn't.

One of the crackheads went ments and tried to steal all my pebbles. I scratched him on the face and he got angry and tried to stab me.'

'Did you get hurt?'

'One of the crackheads staved him off. I'm shocked, is all. It's never happened before. Thank God he didn't get any pebbles or Zom would've gone nuts.' She looks like she's going to cry. I take her hand, squeeze it.

'Don't do that job anymore, please. You could be killed.'

'I know. I'm going to tell Zom I don't want to do it anymore.'

I think how we're both owned by Zom and can't do anything about it. I think again about the dead woman. They'll have found her, hours ago. I see her blue eyes looking at me.

An owl calls, pulling me back to now. Jez stretches out her long legs and looks at me carefully.

'Has something happened?'

I don't reply.

'Something's happened, hasn't it?' Her cheeks flush. 'That woman was killed today, did you know? Nora someone. The one who suddenly disappeared, who Zom thought might go to the cops.'

'How do you know she was killed?' I want to tell her everything. But now I'm not sure. Would Zom hurt me if he finds out I've told Jez? What if she tells someone what I tell her?

'I heard it from Spicer. Plus, it's in the *Standard*.' She taps her phone and reads out the article. 'Mrs Nora Symonds, 72, was stabbed to death in her flat on Effra Lane council estate near Tottenham, north London early this afternoon, after intruders forced their way inside her property. Senior Investigating Officer, Detective Inspector Callum Waverley, said: "At this stage we believe three males were involved in the attack on this woman which led to her death. We believe they left the scene on foot shortly afterwards. We urgently need to identify them and find them."

'Mrs Symonds had lived on the estate for twenty years. Neighbours told us she was a kindly, thoughtful woman. Mr George Wallis, 82, told us: "She was always happy to put on the kettle and have a chat. I think she was lonely – she didn't have much family. But she brightened up my day often enough. It's a real tragedy, what's happened."

'It says at the end that anyone with information can anonymously call Crimestoppers.'

She passes over the phone. There's a photo of me, taken from above. You can see my face. It's smudgy and grey though. So is the one of Minty. The one of Zom is crystal clear.

'You were one of the ones that did it, weren't you?' Jez is staring at me. She looks at the CCTV picture and back to me. 'That's you, isn't it?' She grabs the phone back. 'Christ, Luke. What happened?'

I choke up, can't speak.

'Who did it? Zom did it, didn't he? I know it wasn't you. You'd never do a thing like that.'

'I can't tell you. Zom said he'd—'

'Please. I'm on your side.'

'He told me to stab her. But I couldn't.'

It all comes out. How I went to the flat with Minty. How Minty dropped the knife and I picked it up, intending to kill her.

'Zom stabbed her in the throat,' I say. It's true, I know it is. 'Then he cut up her face.'

'Shhh, shhh. It's OK now. Breathe. You'll get through this.' She's stroking my head, rubbing my shoulders. I try to breathe. Panic fills me, robbing my air.

'The police will be after me. What if they find the knife and think I killed her?'

Jez doesn't reply. I think of the girl on the bus looking at me. Did she recognise me from the photo in the *Evening Standard*?

'Was it on the news? Did they put my photo on TV?'

'Calm down, for God's sake! Jesus.' She shakes her head at me. 'I don't know if it was on TV. But no one could tell it's you in that picture. There's no hair showing and your skin is so pale, you could be white. I saw it and I didn't clock it was you.'

I go to the window. Trees tower above the garden. The sky has cleared. I wonder if I'll ever see the owl flying, hear the beat of his powerful wings.

'I don't want to do this anymore.'

'Do what?'

'I don't want to be in Skull Crew. I don't want to be part of it anymore.'

I turn to Jez. Her face is shocked.

'But you can't leave. Zom will kill you.'

I tell her what Zom threatened me with if I told anyone or went to the police. She doesn't speak for a long time.

'Are you staying with me tonight?'

'If you want me to.'

'Don't be stupid.'

I sleep in Jez's bed. She kisses me and I would have carried on, only she pulls away.

'I thought you wanted to.'

'You deserve someone better than me, Luke. I can't make you happy. It's better if we're just friends.' Her voice is sadder than I've ever heard it.

I hold her tight. My shoulder is wet where her face rests.

Her voice is a whisper. 'Can we stay friends forever?'

CALLUM

Next day, I woke two minutes before my alarm went off, my mind a blissful blank. For a moment I had no idea what had happened the day before. Then I felt the soreness in my hand and remembered the obscene horror of yesterday's discovery at the Effra Lane estate. Fuck this sodding world. Groggy, head throbbing from alcohol and lack of sleep, I forced myself out of bed.

Arriving at the stalag, I ignored the curious stares at my bandaged hand. DS Harper greeted me with, 'You look rough today, sir,' and offered to get me a coffee from the machine.

'I can manage, thanks,' I barked, hurrying to the safety of my desk.

There was an email waiting from Detective Superintendent Bailey announcing that he'd returned two DCs to my team and was letting the surveillance team continue. It was significantly less than I'd asked Bailey for.

I steeled myself to read the forensic pathologist's initial

report on Nora Symonds's death. Thank God, the mutilation of the victim's face had occurred after death. The cause of death was blood loss. The wound, nine inches deep, had been inflicted by a blade with a serrated edge inserted into her larynx. Nora Symonds had most likely died within a minute or two. The wound was similar in some ways to that found on the first victim. Both had been made by a large zombie knife with an upper serrated edge; it was likely that the same knife had been used to kill both females. Also, both victims had died from a single stab wound.

After a dose of caffeine, I felt ready to conduct the morning briefing.

The news wasn't good. Our search hadn't found Deda's car; a trawl of ANPR cameras had picked up his BMW turning into a street a mile south of the estate, where the trail ended. Near neighbours of Nora Symonds hadn't witnessed anything suspicious in the days before her death and no one in Delius Tower had seen any of the three suspects around the time of the killing. The palm print obtained from beside the front door hadn't matched any prints on the database.

'We urgently need to ID the two younger males caught on CCTV,' I impressed on the team. I was becoming increasingly concerned about them. Both looked under eighteen, so by law, still children.

DS Hanna raised her hand. 'It's likely they are being controlled by the older gang members – and they could become highly vulnerable as the net closes in.'

'Any results from the media appeals?'

Since the report on Nora Symonds's killing came out in yesterday's *Evening Standard*, thirty-seven phone calls had been made to Crimestoppers, the search officer told me.

'A lot seem to be from the usual sprinkling of tossers – I mean deliberately unhelpful callers. But we have some repeated names that seem credible. Looks like the black kid is Tyler Cosgrove. He used to go to St Thomas More before he was excluded. He is known as 'Minty' and he 'rolls with' the Skull Crew.'

'What about the mixed-race boy?'

'Two callers identified him as Luke Delaney. He's also been kicked out of school, it looks like. He's in Year 11 of John Berriman Academy, not far from the estate.'

'Brilliant, we're getting somewhere. DC Perry, what have you got?'

Ferret was jabbing his hand in the air.

'An English teacher phoned in at seven this morning, sir. Isobel Collins. She was concerned about changes in Luke this term. She disagreed with the principal about him being excluded. She saw the *Evening Standard* report with his photo, mentioning that he's a suspect in the murder and she's now freaking out, in a nutshell. Oh yes, she said she hoped we would handle him carefully if we find him.'

'Did she now?' I made a note to visit Isobel Collins.

After the briefing, I leafed through transcriptions of the Crimestoppers calls. One referred to Dritan Deda's street name.

The henched one is Zom. He's a killing machine, a fucking cold-hearted psycho who preys on lost kids. The sooner you get him banged up the better.

———

I made sure to get home at a reasonable hour so I could grab a few fresh ingredients and cook dinner – it was going to be a stir fry again.

'You don't have to go to all this trouble for me, you know.' Brendan slouched against the kitchen door.

I looked up from the hissing wok. 'It's no trouble. Drain the rice, will you?'

Sulkily, he picked up the saucepan. I brought the wok over to the table and started serving.

'What's up? Had a tough day?'

A shrug. 'Not really.'

I waited; Brendan began to eat without enthusiasm. I persisted. I'd not spoken to him since Sunday afternoon, when he'd appeared briefly before going back to his room. He'd been worried about a maths test.

'Were your maths results OK?'

'Yeah, fine. Shelley's been helping me.'

'You two seem to be getting on well.'

Another shrug.

I gave up and started eating. My appetite was fading fast. But after half an hour preparing dinner, I wasn't going to let the food go uneaten.

'You've got another murder, then.' His tone was flat.

'Yes, a woman from the estate. It's been pretty full-on since.'

He kept on eating and didn't look up. I let silence settle over us. What was the point in pushing things? But the silence got to me. When I put down my cutlery and Brendan made to leave the table, my pent-up frustration poured out.

'Brendan, don't go. Talk to me, damn it!'

He sat back down.

'What's upsetting you? Is this about your mother leaving, or us splitting up? Is it something I've done, or not done?'

He shook his head, his expression resigned. I threw up my hands.

'It's my fault Kate left, OK? I admit it, I've been a piss-poor father – and I still am, probably. But I'm trying my best.'

'Oh yeah?' He stood suddenly. 'Is that right, Dad?'

'Please, don't keep running away. I want us to be close again, like we used to be.'

'Why are you lying to me then?' His face contorted, reminding me of his tearful rages, years before. But I'd never seen him so hostile as right now.

'What are you talking about?'

'Oh, forget it.'

He ran upstairs, slamming the door to his bedroom. Ten minutes later as I was stacking the dishwasher, I heard his feet on the stairs and rushed into the hall.

'Where are you—' The front door slammed.

'Fuck's sake.' I let out a long breath. I couldn't take much more of this.

I did some yoga postures on the living room floor. My frustration ebbed, replaced by a gnawing guilt. I was to blame for what was going on with my son, wasn't I? Brendan had guessed I wasn't telling him the truth about the death of my father.

JEZ

JUNKIE

Mᴜᴍ ꜰᴏᴜɴᴅ ᴏᴜᴛ ᴀʙᴏᴜᴛ ᴛʜᴇ ᴅʀᴜɢꜱ ꜱᴛᴀꜱʜᴇᴅ ɪɴ ᴍʏ ᴡᴀʀᴅʀᴏʙᴇ today.

I came into my room after my shower and found her kneeling on the floor with the two boxes.

'This is cocaine, isn't it?' She looks at the white powder on her finger like it's plutonium.

'What are you doing going through my things?'

'I was worried. You don't answer my questions. What am I supposed to do?'

'So that makes it OK for you to go snooping around my stuff?'

Since I got home at one thirty in the morning the other day, Mum has been asking me questions all the time. She said she's never heard of a beauty salon that's open at midnight.

'What the hell...' She starts rummaging through the other box. She takes out one of the clear plazzie bags of grungy looking powder and prods it accusingly. 'What the hell is this, Jessamine?'

'Heroin.'

'Heroin? What the bloody hell are you doing with heroin?'

'It's not mine,' I say. 'I'm not a junkie. I'm looking after them for someone, that's all.'

She drops the bag on the floor. 'What do you mean, that's all? Who gave you these? Why are they in my house?'

Her face turns the colour of strawberry ice-cream. It surprises me how angry she is. How can she be so hypocritical? In the months she's been hitting the bottle and the tranquilisers, she's stopped noticing things. I'm scarcely there for her most of the time, unless she needs something. The only thing she cares about is if her vodka and gin supplies are running low. I'll have to play it carefully, though.

'For goodness sake, Mum, keep your hair on. There's no need to make a scene. I'm doing this as a favour for someone. He's a musician, he sells a bit of this and that on the side to help keep himself afloat, that's all.'

She stands up with a big huff.

'I'm going to call the police right now and report you for having illegal drugs, unless you give me a good reason not to.'

I huff back.

'Do you want me to have a criminal record? I'd never get another job! I'd end up being a junkie on benefits.' Mum's mouth pops open. 'It's only for a short time. Dave is coming back to pick them up soon.' I don't know where Dave the musician came from, but it seems to do the trick.

She looks suspiciously at the two boxes.

'That's not "a bit of this and that on the side". That's enough to supply bloody Brighton for a month!'

She's cracking jokes now, that's a good sign.

'He used to be an addict, that's how he knows people to sell to. He has to earn money for more drugs.'

'This is crazy!' She throws up her hands. 'Heroin is danger-ous, Jess. It ruins people's lives. I'm not having it in my house.'

'It's only dangerous because it's illegal.' I've been reading up on this stuff.

'I'm not having a debate with you about this, Jessamine! There's no way you should be storing drugs for someone at your age. At any age. How old is this guy?'

I shrug. 'Twenty-five.' Letty told me that V, Karim and Spicer were best mates at school, and Row used to be V's girlfriend.

'He's exploiting you. A man of that age with a child of sixteen—'

'I'm not a child.'

'Yes, you are! Under the law you are until your eighteenth birthday. How did you meet him, anyway?'

'At a pub.' She frowns. 'I wasn't drinking,' I add quickly. 'Only Diet Coke.'

'Are you sleeping with him?'

'Of course not!' I think of the times I've slept with Zom. Mum would probably think that was exploitative too.

'How did it come to this?' Tears come into Mum's eyes and her voice goes squeaky. 'I did my best to raise you to be a good girl, and...' She moves her head from side to side.

'You aren't going to go to the police, are you, Mum? I'd get into big trouble with Dave.' My heart patters away. What if the police come and confiscate the drugs? They might find the weapons. I'd be totally in the shit and V would be out of his skull, haha. Christ knows what he'd do to me.

'I won't go to the police if you promise you'll get rid of these boxes as soon as humanly possible – and not to have any more contact with this man.'

'I promise.' I go to hug her. 'Thanks, Mum. I'm sorry I worried you.'

She bats me off. 'I'll have to tell your father, you know.'

'Please don't tell him! He'd just shout and get into a state. Please.' He'd tell the police, too, I bet.

'If those boxes aren't gone from here soon, I'll have to.' She picks up the packet of brown again and stares at it.

'Try some, if you like. It's good for relaxation.'

Mum looks at me, then back at the packet. Once an addict, always an addict.

'You can smoke it; you don't have to inject. You know, chasing the dragon.'

'For God's sake, Jess.'

She puts it back in the box. But I know she's tempted.

LUKE

THE FOLLOWING DAY, MINTY AND I MEET AT OUR USUAL SPOT.
He said that when the woman sprayed pepper into his face, he
thought it was acid and he would go blind.

'I was praying, man. Praying for salvation. I ain't never prayed
before.'

'Yeah, I know. What we did yesterday was the scariest thing
I've ever done in my life.'

I don't say that I feel bad about my part in the killing and I
don't want to be with the crew anymore. I don't want him to call
me a pussy.

Minty pops gum into his mouth. 'You won't tell no one I
dropped the shank, will ya?'

''Course I won't.'

'And I won't tell no one you shanked her.'

'What are you on about?' I can't believe Minty's said that.
'Zom killed her, not me.'

'Zom says it was you. He said you're gonna be pointing the
finger at him.'

'That's not true! Minty, you gotta believe me.'

'I dunno what you did, Luke, I couldn't see nothing, my eyes were on fire. First I saw was that woman lying on the floor, blood spurting out of her neck like a waterfall.'

I go cold. I know it was Zom who killed Mrs Symonds, not me. Only I still can't remember him doing it. I remember the blood on her afterwards and the *glug suck* noise from her throat, I wish I could unhear it. But the bit when he stabs her isn't there.

I gotta hold it together. My mind isn't working like it should. Maybe it would be too horrible to remember everything.

We walk to the chicken shop and get two bags of chips. As we're walking into the estate, acrid brown fumes waft up from the line of garages at the far end. Minty sniffs the air.

'Someone's burning their car.'

We go sit on the roof. Zom turns up, smelling of smoke. My heart begins to hammer. I put down the remains of my chips. I've not seen him since yesterday after we left the old lady's flat. He shouldn't be here. This is where youngers hang out.

'Yo, crew. Anyone know about the new cameras in the car park?'

Everyone looks at Zom.

Ginger says he spotted cameras there three days ago. 'I said let's go nobble 'em. But everyone was like, let's get this video done, innit.'

'So, you left 'em there to pick up anyone that goes into the car park?'

Ginger frowns.

'Karim knew about it too, y'know? He said for us to be careful down there with them new lights and cameras, don't try to tief no one. I thought he was on it.'

Zom stares at Ginger like he's gonna explode. Then he turns to me and Minty.

'I don't know nuttin,' Minty says. 'Nor does Ninj.'

Zom snarls and heads to the steps. I let out my breath.

'Yo, Ginger!' A kid yells. 'Check this out.'

The others crowd round someone's phone. Minty frowns at me. Neither of us move.

'You was there, wasn't you?' Minty says. 'When Ginger said about the new cameras. You heard?'

'I heard, yeah. Then I forgot.'

He keeps chewing, his eyes slits. I hold his gaze.

'You knew too. Didn't you?'

'Nah, I didn't. I ain't no snitch, man.'

Minty spits out the gum. It lands by my foot. Then he goes over to the others.

Kirsty's steam train *choof choof* startles me. I switch my phone to silent. She's left five messages asking why I've not called, what's going on. I don't know what to say to her.

The chips lie heavy in my stomach. I go back to Angel's flat, let myself in with my key. It's only one thirty. I don't know what to do. I lean on the balcony rail and look out. Behind the estate is the railway line and the main road, and behind that is the industrial estate and the flat grey of the reservoir, and behind that are Walthamstow Marshes and more towers on other estates, little wispy grey fingers.

I hear Angel talking in the kitchen.

'He's a natural fighter an' he's got real heart an' guts. I don't wanna lose him, fam. No way.'

I freeze. Is it me he's talking about? Who is he talking to?

'We gotta treat him careful, that's what I'm sayin',' Angel says. 'You pushed him too fast, he wasn't ready. Yeah, right. We'll see what V thinks.'

He goes quiet. After a bit I go into the kitchen. Angel looks surprised.

'You OK, kid?'

'I s'pose.' I don't think I will ever feel OK again.

'Give it a few days an' you'll feel better, yeah?'

I nod and stare at the floor.

'You're a good kid, I know you are. You wanna stand up for your crew. You won't go mouthin' off to no one.'

He takes a couple of lagers out from the fridge, offers me one. I shake my head.

'Go and rest up on my bed, kid. There's someone comin' to see you later.'

———

I barely hear the tap on the door.

'Hey.'

I open my eyes to a tall lightskin man. He's got that kind of face you want to keep looking at. I know it from somewhere.

Sleep pulls me back down.

I wake to voices. A fug of weed creeps in. I check the time. Hours have gone by. I stumble into the bathroom. Pee, splash water on my face. Angel is talking to the man.

It's V. He waves me over, side hugs me. He smells of cloves and old leather. Angel goes away.

'Luke. Good to see you again. You were out for the count back there.'

V's smile takes away my awkwardness. He checks his watch. It's an IWC, big bucks.

'I gotta go. Wanna come for a drive?'

Come for a drive. No one ever asks me that.

'I'll get my stuff.'

I put on my trainers, T-shirt and hoody, grab my phone.

His car is long and low like a crouching animal. It gleams white and starts with a growl like the yawn of a lion.

I don't ask where we're going and he doesn't say. Electric

guitar from a classic rock station pumps out of the speakers. Houses speed past. He turns up the heater and opens the roof. I don't need to talk. I don't know what this is about but right now it doesn't matter. My head is still in that weird state you get from sleeping in the daytime.

We're heading north, out of London. Things are further apart, cleaner. I spot cows and a horse.

We're driving down a lane. Woods one side, fields on the other. A house in the distance, the daylight fading. V stops the car.

'Wanna have a go?'

'Drive, you mean?' Unlike most boys I know, I'm not a car geek. But I know this car is special and I'd be crazy to turn down the chance to drive it. 'You'll have to tell me what to do.'

We swap places. V helps me adjust the seat so my feet reach the pedals and I can see in the mirror.

'You've not driven before?' He sounds incredulous.

I shake my head. 'I wanted to learn but my stepdad hasn't got a car.'

'A boy your age should be driving. Abso. Fucking. Lutely.'

He shows me the basic stuff. He sets it to automatic. The lane is empty and wide enough not to worry about driving off the road.

In five minutes, I'm driving. The speedo shows thirty miles per hour. I pump the gas pedal, feel the car respond. My smile gets bigger.

'Shit! This is fantastic!' I don't care if I sound like an eleven-year-old at Thorpe Park.

'You're doing great.' We veer left. 'Keep it in the middle of the road, I don't want to end up in the ditch.'

I adjust course, still smiling like a crazy man. When I tell Jez I drove V's Maserati Granturismo today, she'll go totally green.

'This is amazing.'

'Hit the gas if you want. Ain't no one to run over out here.'

Fifty miles per hour... Sixty... Seventy. Ahead the road bends and I have to swing the wheel suddenly, oversteering and nearly crashing us.

'Shit! This is proper fast.'

'It's got a V8 engine.' V leans over and turns on the head-lights. 'Slow down before you get to the bends, not while you're turning or you'll skid.'

We're zooming down the hill with views left and right and a bowl of sky above. I feel like I'm flying. The speedo hits one-hundred-and-five miles per hour as we hit the bottom. I get that hollow rollercoaster sensation as the wheels lift off the ground. I've forgotten everything that's not inside this car, I don't care what's going to happen to me. I could do this forever.

I carry on at the wheel 'til it's properly dark. I don't want to stop. V grins like he's enjoying it as much as me.

'You're a natural,' he says as we swap seats. 'A proper speed freak.'

I'm puffed with pride.

'I'm serious. I've never known a kid to learn so fast. You should try motor racing sometime. You might give Lewis Hamilton a scare, one day.'

I don't reply. Lewis Hamilton is one of my heroes. I've never told anyone, in case they laugh at me for thinking a poor kid from the Nizz could ever end up like him.

We turn back. I daydream that I'm overtaking Hamilton at Brands Hatch.

'My place is near here.' V turns the music off. 'Wanna take a look?'

'Yeah, sure. I don't have to be anywhere.'

Where else would I have to be? I'm with the leader of Skull Crew. The man.

The headlights are on full beam. We pass big houses with driveways, a war memorial, a church. There's no shops, hardly anyone about.

We stop at a house with a tall sloping roof and fields opposite.

'My hideaway.'

I follow him inside. The rooms are huge. V leads me into the kitchen, pours me a glass of wine.

'It's from the cellar.'

The wine isn't vinegary like the other wines I've tried. It bathes my mouth with blackberries. I understand now why people drink wine.

'Do you live here on your own?'

He laughs. 'When my women aren't over.'

He tells me to chill while he tends to business. I look round the house while V checks his messages. Most rooms have paintings on the walls. Some are weird. In the biggest room, there's a naked girl bound by her hair to a cross.

'What do you think of the house?' V comes up from behind and takes me by surprise.

'I've never seen a house like this, except in films.' V laughs again. 'I grew up in a two-bed flat on the estate. Hated it. From when I was a small kid I dreamed of living in a proper house.'

'What happened to your parents?'

'Dad killed himself when I was nine. Mum lost it, got sectioned.' He sloshes his wine in the glass.

'What happened to you?'

'I got put into care, ended up in this Catholic place. They were fucking sadists.'

A weird feeling goes through me. Why has he brought me here? Does he want to do something bad to me? I don't get those vibes from him though.

We eat in the big room. My wine glass is full again. We sit at one end. Three candles burn at the other.

The cutlery is heavy. I wait for V to start before I tuck in, remembering it's good manners. It seems ages since I ate at a table. At Angel's we eat standing up in the kitchen, or on our laps watching true crime documentaries.

'What happened to your parents?' V says when we've finished. 'Angel told me your stepdad was looking after you.'

'Yeah, Kevin. My real dad left my mum years ago. I never knew him. My mum died in July. She had cancer.'

'How do you get on with Kevin?'

'Not very well. He used to get angry with me all the time. Then he kicked me out.'

'So, you're on your own now. That's a tough place to be – unless you can find your own family.'

I don't know what to say.

'One thing I tell boys like you, who are trying to find their place in the world – find what makes you feel good and do it. That might sound stupid but trust me, life can be short. You don't get many rolls of the dice. You've gotta take your chances while you can.'

'I guess.' I don't know anything that makes me feel good. Well, not stuff I could get paid for. 'I like being with animals, I like cycling.'

'And driving fast, right?'

'Yeah, definitely.' We both laugh.

'I'll take you out again in the car, how about that?'

'Wicked.'

'What about girls? You're a fine-looking guy. You have girls around, yeah?'

'Only Jez.'

'Ah, the one and only Jez. She's your girlfriend?'

'Not exactly. I like her a lot, though.' I feel bad talking about Jez to V.

V's forehead puckers. 'I heard you helped Zom deal with the Symonds woman.'

A knot forms in my stomach. I wait for what's coming next. He's going to ask why I didn't kill her, like Zom told me to.

'That was good work, Luke.' I breathe again. 'That shows me you have potential to go a long way in this crew. You can think on your feet, you can work with others and I know you can handle yourself in a fight. You have guts and a fire in your belly.' He presses the scar on his cheek. His voice quietens. 'But to become one of us, truly one of us, you need to be able to follow orders. If someone higher up than you tells you to do something, you have to do it straight away.' His eyes fix on mine. 'You know why we had to kill her?'

I blink, swallow. My palms are wet.

'Because she went to the police?'

V waits, his eyebrows raised. 'She went to the police about what?'

My heart is racing as fast as my mind.

'About the girl being killed outside the estate. She told them it was Zom who did it. And you – we – we need to show people what happens to snakes.'

'Very good.' V leans forward again. There's a glint in his eyes. If I ordered you to do something, would you do it?'

'Yeah, of course I would. Definitely.'

'What if I said go and stab a kid you know? A friend of yours?'

Fuck.

'I'd still do it.'

I wait for him to order me to stab Minty or Jez, but he only gets up from the table. I breathe again.

'I'll drive you back to Angel's soon. First, I want to show you something.'

We go down a steep flight of stairs to a long, cool room, high enough to stand without bending my head. Fixed on the walls are swords, a scythe and old objects. We go past cupboards and shelves holding glass bottles with stoppers. One is labelled hydrochloric acid.

'This is where I store my traditional remedies. They're useful for times when you don't want to see a doctor.' And this is where I keep my other collections.' It's something like an altar, decorated with candles and wooden crosses. Two high African drums stand on either side. 'Most of it came from my mother, she was from Cuba. They use it in rituals for their traditional religions.'

I try not to smile. On top is a statue of a bearded man. He has a wooden cross in one hand and a skull in the other. Around him are dolls and smaller statues.

'Wow.' I step up and touch a statue of a man with a gold crown and a gold pendant round his neck.

'That's one of the gods they worship in Santeria. It's big in Cuba. People think gods will give them protection from evil spirits and help them get what they want.'

We walk to a sideboard next to the end wall. Six skulls are lined up on top.

'This is my skull collection.' V smiles. 'Don't ask where these come from.'

They're human skulls. Two are slightly smaller than the others. One is broken at the top like it was bashed in with something hard. I shiver. What the fuck is next?

'People say I put my enemies' skulls here when I've finished with them.' V rotates one of the skulls a fraction so the eye sockets are facing out.

I'm quite keen to leave the cellar by now. I follow V up the steps, along the hall into the living room.

'Chilly in here, innit? I'll put the fire on.'

We sit watching the flames. The armchair is black leather and super comfy. I sip my glass of brandy. It burns my throat and I don't like the taste but I try to swallow some to be sociable.

'You started Skull Crew, didn't you?'

V yawns and clicks his knuckles loudly. 'Me and three mates started it, yeah. Karim and Spicer, plus Doc. We were all in this other gang. I was bored. I wanted to do something else, that would make us good money.'

'What's the skull thing about?' I'm fearless now.

'Me and Spicer, we saw a program about a drug lord in America who put skulls outside people's doors to scare them into paying up what they owed. I thought, yeah, that's it! We're gonna do that too.' His face goes serious. 'The skull thing. It's not only about scaring the shit outta people. It's about how to live in the time we have. You can drag out your days doing shit that pleases other people, the safe path, the path that keeps you in poverty, ashamed of who you are. Or you can take your chances and live big. Live for now.' He stares into the fire. 'Us road men have chosen that last path, Luke. You've got to choose which one you're gonna take.'

———

We drive home in the early hours. V looks at me.

'You'll have to do the ritual soon. All new members have to do it. It'll make you one of us.'

I don't reply.

Back at Angel's, I unfold the sofa bed carefully, so as not to wake anyone. Which path am I going to follow?

As I'm drifting off to sleep, I think of the skulls lined up in V's cellar and what he said about people thinking they were the heads of his enemies. Why did he show me them? To show off? To make me afraid of him?

The words I overheard on the balcony come back.

I don't wanna lose him.

I thought Angel meant he didn't want me to leave Skull Crew. But maybe he meant something else.

CALLUM

28TH OCTOBER

FORENSICS PHONED EARLY IN THE AFTERNOON WITH RESULTS of the tests on skin and blood fragments found at the crime scene. I braced myself for bad news. It wasn't. The DNA profile matched that stored on the database for Dritan Deda.

As I put down the phone, adrenalin surged. We now had enough evidence to charge Deda for Nora Symonds's murder, once we found him. We'd checked utility companies and service providers for anything registered in the name Dritan Deda, but drawn a blank.

The man seemed to have no friends or associates outside the gang world and no relatives that he wasn't estranged from, and no social media profile to speak of; DS Freeman's hunt for Deda on social media had come up with nothing. We got nothing from a former girlfriend and his mother hadn't seen him for seven years, so she claimed.

Dritan 'Zom' Deda was our main suspect, wanted for the both murders. But we also had to find our other suspects,

Vincent Edwards, 'Wolf' and Deda's two young accomplices, 'Minty' Cosgrove and Luke Delaney, before anyone else got killed. I believed that Edwards had ordered both murders; if we were lucky, one or the other of the suspects would lead us to him. If any of them visited Effra Lane estate, our surveillance team would be ready. In the meantime, I would doggedly pursue anyone who might have knowledge of Deda's or Edwards's whereabouts.

First on my list was Solita's mother.

DS Harper had visited Bev Milton yesterday. Mrs Milton was still maintaining that she knew nothing about Jayden's friends and associates. However, she now admitted that she might have heard Jayden mention the Skull Crew. I needed to talk to her myself.

'Jon, fancy a trip to the estate?' DS Rowan was a fresh face to Mrs Milton, and harder headed than Sam.

We parked beside Luther Tower and walked up. This time, I locked the car myself.

'We have to find a way to get her to talk,' I said. 'Her son was one of the inner circle – he'd have known Edwards for years. She must know something.'

———

I introduced Rowan to Bev Milton. She reached out to shake his hand. Leonie waved at us from the kitchen, where her homework was spread out on the table. Bev went to put the kettle on.

I sat down in my usual seat. Rowan plumped himself on the sofa. There were a few more greys in Bev Milton's hair this time. She was neatly dressed in a skirt and a high-necked jumper embellished with discreet gold jewellery.

'How are you, Bev?'

'I'm doing my best. Trying to keep going for Leonie's sake.'

'It'll take time,' I said.

She took a sip of tea. Her eyes slipped away again. I scanned the spines in the floor-to-ceiling bookshelves. Dickens, Bronte, Jamie Oliver, *The Times Atlas of the World*... Mrs Milton was a well-educated professional who had probably got all three of her children to do their homework. How had her son ended up in a violent drugs gang?

'As I said on the phone, we're following up leads in our inquiry into Nora Symonds's murder. We think the man responsible is also responsible for Solita's death.' I paused. This was where it could get tricky. 'The man's name is Vincent Edwards – also known as V.'

She looked at me steadily, mouth firmly shut.

'You've heard that name before, haven't you?'

'I told you before, I can't help you there.' A small area on the side of Bev Milton's face made an odd involuntary movement, like a grimace.

'I know you know who Vincent Edwards is. Your son knew him, didn't he, when he was part of the Skull Crew?'

I waited. Mrs Milton's eyes skittered from mine. She ducked her head. The sound of her breathing filled the room.

'We urgently need to find him and stop him hurting anyone else. I need your help, Bev.'

She looked up. Her words were almost too quiet to hear.

'Yes, Jayden knew him.'

I nodded. 'Go on. Tell me the rest. How did they know each other?' I gestured to Rowan to take notes.

'Jayden was friends with Vincent at secondary school. They were in the same year. Vincent and some other boys started to get into trouble with the police, and Jayden got caught up in it. I don't know why he went that way. He was easily influenced, I suppose. He was getting up to lots of bad things – muggings, burglaries – but he kept it all hidden from me and Lou. Things came to a head and he was sent to prison.' Her voice wavered. 'Lou was never the same after that. He refused to visit Jayden. He passed before Jayden came out.' She wiped her eye with a sleeve.

'I'm sorry, Bev.'

She took a sip of water.

'When was the last time you saw Jayden?'

'It was about a month before Solita was killed. He came here to see me.'

Rowan looked up from taking notes. 'For any particular reason?'

'He came to borrow money. Five thousand pounds.'

'What was the money for, did he say?'

'He said he needed it for a deal. I assumed he meant to buy drugs.'

I took over. 'Why would you assume that?'

'That's what he does to make money.' Her voice went quiet again. The pain she felt showed in her eyes. 'He buys and sells drugs.'

'How much did he ask for?'

'He wanted five thousand pounds.'

'Did you give him the money?'

'I didn't, no. He knows I don't approve of how he lives, and I don't have that kind of money to spare, in any case. I'm a teacher, not a lawyer.'

'And you've had no contact with him since?'

A moment's pause. 'That's right.'

'He didn't contact you before or after Solita's funeral?'

'No, he didn't.'

'Do you have any information about Vincent Edwards that could help us find him? Any other names he might be using?'

She shook her head.

'Do you have any idea at all where Vincent Edwards might be

living? Is there anything your son might have said, anything you've come across – anything at all?'

She stared into her lap with a resigned expression. Rowan and I looked at each other. My frustration bubbled to the surface like lava spilling from a volcano.

'I'm sorry to have to say this, but quite honestly, I can't ever remember seeing a mother less interested in catching the killer of her child.'

Rowan's jaw slackened. Bev Milton jerked upright. I shouldn't have said it, I knew as soon as the words came out. This was definitely not the correct way to go about talking to an intimidated witness grieving for her slain daughter. I'd stepped over the mark this time.

'I want to help, I really do. But Vincent...' Her voice was loud, unsteady. She looked over to DS Rowan who sat mesmerised, pen poised, and back to me. 'He threatened me. He came over the day after Solita was killed and sat down where you are now, polite as anything and said he was very sorry for my loss, I must be stricken to lose Solita. Then he told me if I said anything about him or his gang to the police, he'd have someone cut out my tongue – and if he couldn't find me, he'd look for Leonie.' She shut her eyes for a few moments. 'I believed him. I absolutely believed him. No matter what you say to me, that you can protect me and what's left of my family, I know that doesn't count for anything. He got to that poor woman who tried to help you. How can you protect us from someone like him?'

For a few seconds I was struck dumb.

'I understand, Mrs Milton. I know this is an impossible ask. But it's like this. If you don't help us, we're not going to catch the man responsible for your daughter's death. He's going to keep on peddling drugs and ordering innocent people to be maimed or killed.'

'What if I'm the one who's maimed or killed?' A fleck of spittle shot from her mouth. 'Or Leonie?'

I'd tried my best. Now I had to admit defeat. I gestured to Rowan and prepared to haul myself off the sofa.

'Wait a minute.' She held up a palm. 'I've got something that might help.'

Bev Milton went out of the room and came back a minute later with a tablet computer. Rowan and I gathered in silence around the coffee table while Mrs Milton navigated to a folder. She swiped past the first six photographs, then stopped.

'This is from Karim's birthday last year. Jayden WhatsApped this to me.'

It was a selfie. Four young men were posing for the camera, their arms wrapped around each other. Behind them, part of a house was visible and beside it, a brick wall and a tree.

'When was it taken?'

'It must have been August, soon after Vincent moved in. All four of them were there.'

'All of them?' DS Rowan asked.

'The ones who started Skull Crew. They all went to St Thomas More. They used to do everything together.' Her eyes were moist.

'Did Jayden say where this house was?' DS Rowan continued.

'I think he said it was in Barnet.'

'Barnet in north London?' Barnet was on the edge of London, miles from the estate.

'In north London, yes.'

'Could he have said High Barnet, or East Barnet?'

'I think he just said "Barnet". Jayden was interested to see what the house was like.'

'Was the house rented or did it belong to Vincent, do you know?'

'I don't know. Someone could have been letting him use it – maybe one of his woman friends. Jayden told me there were several, each trying to outdo the other to please Vincent. The man had no scruples, he'd let them suck up to him then toss them away.'

I brought the photo closer. 'Can you show us which one is which, Mrs Milton?'

She pointed to each young man. Jayden Milton – almond-shaped eyes, a shy smile on his small, lean face; Karim Ali – unsmiling, in a baseball cap and sunglasses; Dale Newton, aka Spicer – hair in cornrows, deliberately pulling a cross-eyed expression; Vincent Edwards – caught mid-laugh, gleaming teeth on show, an indentation clearly visible on his left cheek. He looked nothing like the man in his solemn mug shot, the only other photo I'd seen of him.

'This is very helpful, Bev, thank you,' DS Rowan said. 'We'll need to take the tablet away to the inspect the photograph. There might be some useful information we can extract.'

'You said your son was interested to see what the house was like?' I asked as Bev Milton closed the tablet. 'Why was that?'

'There had always been friction between them. Jayden thought Vincent was greedy, he took more of the profits than he should.'

'Did something happen between Jayden and Vincent the last time they saw each other?'

She rubbed the top of her hand, avoiding my eyes. I knew we were close to home.

'You know what happened, don't you, Bev? Did your son quarrel with Vincent?' I nodded to DS Rowan to restart his notes. 'Was that why he ran away?'

She kept her eyes on her hands.

'Jayden left a note in the kitchen after he came back from meeting Vincent. He said Vincent was after him. Those were the words he used. He said he didn't want to leave us but he had to.' Mrs Milton wiped her eyes again.

'Why would Vincent be after him?'

A slight movement of the head, which I took for a 'no'.

'Please, Bev. Is there anything else you know that might help us?'

She took out a tissue and blew her nose.

'I think the four of them were meeting to divide up the drugs. If Jayden couldn't stump up the cash... Maybe Jayden and Vincent got into an argument. Jayden often used to say that Vincent was ripping him off. Jayden was a hot head... If he lost his temper, there's no telling what he might have done.' She sat back; her eyes unfocused. 'Whatever happened between them – that's why Vincent had Solita killed. My son is the reason my daughter was murdered. I'll have to live with it for the rest of my life. If Jayden hadn't run away, Solita would still be here now. They would have killed him instead of her.'

She began to cry. Deep, wrenching sobs. I got up, resting my hand briefly on her back. 'I'll make you another cuppa, love.'

A few minutes later I found Bev Milton drying her face and DS Rowan clutching his knees, staring at the floor.

'I'm sorry you've had to go through all this, Mrs Milton. Truly sorry.' I put the fresh cup of tea on the table by her armchair. 'Two more questions and we're done.'

She nodded.

'Did Jayden say where he was going?'

'He said he was going to lie low a while. He didn't say where.'

'You've no idea where he might have gone? Did he have friends in any particular town or city?'

'No. He could be anywhere. I don't think he had many friends.'

Her use of the past tense struck me.

'If you talk to him again, would you ask him something for me?'

'You want me to get the address of Vincent's house?'

'Yes, I do. Or any detail that might help us locate it. Tiles on the roof missing, beside a Tesco, that sort of thing.'

She nodded.

I hesitated. It felt like prying but I had to ask.

'Would you mind showing us the note that Jayden left? You've kept it, I presume?'

'Of course I did.'

Her lips a stiff line, Mrs Milton left the room. She returned and thrust a small notepad sheet in front of me.

'Thank you, Bev.'

A quick read of the note confirmed what she had told us; there was nothing else that Jayden had written which offered us anything useful.

Dear Mum,

This is the hardest thing I've ever had to write.

Vincent is after me, I can't come over anymore. I'm sorry, I never wanted this. I don't want to leave you and Sol and Leonie but I have to. I know you won't understand what I've done so I won't try to explain.
You are the best mum ever and I love you more than I can say.

Jayden

We waited for Mrs Milton to arrange for a neighbour to take care of Leonie, then took her to the video interview suite at Tottenham police station to formalise what she'd told us. Afterwards, I told her that she and Leonie should consider moving into a hotel room outside of the area until the council could provide them alternative accommodation. Given what had happened to Nora Symonds, we should take every possible precaution. I would pay for the rooms myself, if necessary.

'For how long?'

'Until we get these men into custody. Another week or two I expect. I can't give you a guarantee.'

'What about the impact on Leonie? She's already had her life turned upside down. Besides, anyone who wanted to find us would still be able to. Unless I stop teaching and take Leonie out of her school, what's the point in us moving out?'

'I take your point, Bev. But I strongly advise you to put your safety first. Even if it means stopping work for now and taking your daughter out of school.'

'All right then.'

I phoned DS Harper and told her to make sure that Bev Milton and her daughter had somewhere suitable to stay, and to take her home to collect some things.

Jayden had vanished for good, as far as I could see, and was unlikely to pass on Vincent's address to his mother. But now we could add Karim Ali and Dale 'Spicer' Newton to our murder suspects. The photograph of the four most senior gang members wasn't only evidence of their close association – it could help us find them.

Analysis of the image showed no recorded location information. But there was potentially useful information in the photograph itself. The gabled roof caught my eye – and the monkey puzzle tree in the garden. I asked DC Perry to team up with another detective and find all properties, within five miles of High Barnet underground station, with such a tree using Google

Maps and any other means they could think of, and start visiting them.

'What do you want us to say we're there for?'

I tried not to roll my eyes. Ferret had that week lost one of his beloved pets and was in the throes of grief, which seemed to be affecting his capabilities.

'Say you're investigating a serious crime. Whatever you think will get you in the door. Check out who lives there, see if anything seems off.'

'I'll help out, sir,' DS Hanna cut in. 'I've got spreadsheet experience that might be useful.'

'Right you are, Sandra. Let's get back to work.'

I took out a granola bar from my desk, mulling over Bev Milton's revelation. It fitted with what we'd been told and gave Vincent Edwards a motive for ordering the murder of Jayden's sister. The man deserved to get sent down for a long time, as far as I was concerned. But catching him wouldn't be easy. The money this guy was making would be way more than what most people earned. He would be doing everything he possibly could to keep from being caught and to keep that money flowing in.

JEZ

ACCIDENT

Everything's gone wrong. I can't believe what's happened. Mum was going on about Gillian coming over tomorrow and what Gillian was going to think about me skipping school and being friends with drug dealers and how she would definitely put me into care if she finds out I've a megaton of cocaine and heroin stashed in my wardrobe. It was stressing me out big time.

Having all that brown tucked away in my wardrobe got me thinking. What if I tried a tiny bit before Spicer and V come to collect the boxes? Spicer told me it's stock that came direct from the supplier, so it won't have any of the disgusting things they add to it. You'd never catch me shooting up from one of those pebbles. Anyway, I'd probably faint if one came anywhere near my arm. But that's not the only way, is it?

While Mum was ranting, I slipped upstairs taking Mum's lighter, a bowl and some aluminium foil from the kitchen cupboard with me. I opened one of the packets of brown, took out a few teaspoonfuls and put them into the bowl – I didn't have a clue about how much. It's the colour of oatmeal, not really brown.

I tore off a piece of foil and folded it in four and rolled up a thin tube from a page out of a magazine. Then I sprinkled a bit of the powder onto the foil and heated it gently from underneath (I got all that from the internet). The stuff quickly turned to liquid and began to give off fumes. I grabbed my tube and started inhaling.

Instantly, I felt floaty and calm. All my worries about Mum being an alcoholic and Zom threatening to shank me and rape me if I don't do what he wants and what if Gillian decides to put me into care, left without even a wave goodbye.

I heard Mum go into her room, crying. She often gets teary when she drinks, but I'd never heard anything as sorrowful as this. I went in. She had a vodka bottle by the bed. I tried to comfort her but she kept crying and swigging from the bottle in between sobs. It was horrible.

I'm not sure why I did it. I wanted to stop her feeling so fucking sad. I went into my room, put another few spoonfuls of powder on the foil and took it to Mum.

'Try a bit of this,' I said. 'It'll make you feel better.'

I sat down on the bed beside her and held the flame under the foil, which was a bit tricky. Mum put down the bottle like I told her and started inhaling. I didn't have to convince her.

'Is it working?' I said a few times, but she ignored me. Then she put down the tube with a big smile and leaned her head back on the pillow.

10.30PM

It's not the first time Mum's passed out. She does all the time when she's drinking heavily. I called an emergency drugs helpline the first few times it happened. They said I didn't have to call 999, I just had to make sure she was comfortable and sitting upright in case she vomited and stopped breathing.

So, at first, I wasn't alarmed. I checked she was upright, went downstairs and ate a sandwich and listened to music on my iPod. But I'm freaking out now. She hasn't come out of it yet. Her breathing is really shallow and I can hardly feel her pulse.

This is what I found on the web:

Warning signs of heroin overdose include:
Bluish nails or lips
Depressed breathing
Weak pulse
Pinpoint pupils
Disorientation or delirium
Extreme drowsiness
Repeated episodes of loss of consciousness
Coma

I think I should call 999. Maybe the drugs have messed with the alcohol.

I've phoned Luke five times but he's not answering. Rowena said don't let anyone find out I've been giving Mum illegal drugs, and make sure I hide the smack before I call 999.

10.45PM

The ambulance is coming.

I've just got a WhatsApp from V. Row must have told on me. I can't stop looking at it.

Be careful what you say to the feds, pretty girl. You don't want to lose those lovely lips of yours.

LUKE

'He's a fed, man! Look at him.' Ginger points to a window in the tower opposite. We're on the outside walkway on the fourth floor of Delius Tower.

'Yeah, bruv.' Minty rushes to reply. 'He's defo undy. There's a fuckin' huge mike under his batties.'

Everyone laughs.

There's been more talk of cops hanging around the estate. Ginger reckons he saw the sun catch on a whopper of a lens. Karim sent everyone another WhatsApp to be careful in public areas cos the cops have microphones that can hear someone whispering a mile off. I reckon it's only a matter of time before someone recognises me from the *Standard* photo. Maybe the cops have found me already.

'Anyone heard from Zom?'

It's me who asks. Each day, the thought of him coming for me preys on my mind. It's like Zom knows what I'm thinking of doing.

'He's gone, bruv' Ginger says. 'Don't reckon he'll show his face for a while, with the feds all over the shop.'

Angel told me my ceremony is going to be on Halloween night, the day after tomorrow. It's a special thing for new members, though this time it's only me. I'll have a test to show my loyalty. V decides what everyone's test is. Then I'll get a blood baptism from V in front of the elders and I'll be a real member of Skull Crew.

I haven't got long to decide what to do. If I leave, I'll miss hanging out with these kids that no one else cares about.

———

I go for a walk. I need to get away from the estate for a bit, so I can remember who I am.

Spits of wet land on my face. Buses go by, full of schoolkids. I pass the house where I used to live, wonder if Kirsty is home.

It's quiet by the canal. The River Lea it's really called. It's not wide or pretty like the Thames. No one would make a special trip to come here. It's just a long strip of water, home to birds and boats. But it's special to me. You can follow the towpath without thinking where you're going and it'll take you somewhere.

The rhythm of my legs moving under my jacket makes a swishing sound. A goose skims dark green water. The light is murky. I pass the park where I went with Jez. It seems like years ago.

I sit down on a bench. I hardly notice a man stopping to sit down at the other end. He's dark-skinned, has kind eyes. He gets out a packet of cigarettes. Lights one, takes a long inhale.

'Not the best of days.' The man glances at me. 'But there's nothing like sitting out in the rain and watching nature.'

He's wearing a rain jacket and hiking boots. Doesn't seem like a dealer or an undercover cop.

'Yeah, it's peaceful here.'

A flock of birds with pale pink patches cross the water. The man offers me a cigarette.

'No thanks.'

I go back to staring at the water. The rain has stopped, the sky is greyish yellow. The churn in my head gets worse. I wish I could keep walking along the canal forever.

'You all right, fella? You look like you have troubles.'

'I do, I guess.'

'Do you have anyone to talk to?'

I think about Kirsty and how I can't go into the house to say hello in case her father's there. I don't talk to Minty anymore. He's always watching me, we're all watching each other. There's only Jez. And maybe Miss Collins, somewhere.

The guy puffs on his cigarette. Smoke melts into wet air.

'Do you want to talk about it?'

'It's just... I've got to decide something. Something big.'

He stubs out his ciggie, keeps looking at the water. I wonder if he's heard.

'Decisions are hard,' he says suddenly. 'The best thing is not to think about them too much. Do what your gut says. Then everything might turn out OK.'

'Thanks,' I say.

'Good luck, fella.' He gets up from the bench.

————

It's dark and I'm still sat here. I pick up my phone and dial her number. It rings three times. A voice says, 'Hello, Izzy here.'

'Miss Collins?'

'Luke.' She doesn't speak for ages. 'What's happening? Are you OK?'

'I'm in trouble,' I say.

'What sort of trouble?'

Her voice is kind. I feel tears welling up.

'I need to get away from here. Far away. I don't know where I'm going to go.'

'I'll help you, don't worry. Listen, give me your number in case I need to call you back. It's not coming up on my phone.'

I give her the number.

'Now, tell me what's happened.'

'My stepdad told me to move out. I've been hanging out with the gang on the estate. I did something really bad.' I don't know how to say the rest. 'I can't do this anymore. But if I run away, they're gonna find me. They'll cut out my tongue and—' My throat closes up. I can't speak. I can't breathe.

'What's happening? Luke, are you OK?' She sounds panicked too.

'I'm OK now.' I take little sips of air.

'Listen, Luke. These men sound really dangerous. I think you should go to the police straight away.'

'I can't. They'll put me in prison.'

'Where are you staying now?'

'I'm staying with one of the elders on the estate.'

'Do you need somewhere safe to go tonight?'

'I'm OK for tonight.'

'I might be able to help you find a place to stay for a bit. There's somewhere I'm thinking of... It's out of London. I'll need time to sort out a few things.'

'OK. Thanks.'

'I'll be in touch soon.'

I sit there, breathing in the quiet. I'm relieved and confused and scared. When I'm too cold to sit, I walk some more.

JEZ

SUSPECTED OD

MUM'S CHEST ISN'T MOVING. I PULL ON HER ARM, SHOUT AT her, put ice cubes on her face. She stays the same.

'I'm sorry, Mum. I'm sorry.'

I whisper it over and over.

I try the kiss of life, what I remember from school first aid sessions. I take away her pillows, then pinch her nostrils shut, breathe into her mouth twice then let go of her nose.

Nothing happens. I do it again.

Her lips are slightly blue now. Oh my god, oh my god, oh my god.

I press down on her chest with both hands, hard and fast. After a minute of pumping, I stop. My arms are exhausted and her chest still isn't moving.

A siren blares outside. I open the door. Two paramedics run upstairs. I watch from behind. One is hitting her chest like it's made of concrete. I hold my breath and wait for her to come to life.

They stop what they're doing and look at me. Their faces tell me everything.

———

I'm on Mum's bed, holding onto Mum's hand. Mum's hand feels cold now. I feel her cold going into me. I'm frozen. The woman takes my hand. She wants me to leave Mum and go with her. I hear someone on a radio, saying, 'Suspected OD'.

The police officer takes me downstairs. She asks if there's another adult around, a family member who can be with me. I give her my sister's number. I don't want to tell her my dad's but she says he needs to be told.

She makes tea and asks me what happened. A switch goes on in my brain. I remember what I decided to say.

'Mum was drinking heavily in the afternoon. She was upset about my father never visiting and not bothering to help look after me. I didn't pay too much attention as she's often like that. She went upstairs to her room. I stayed downstairs watching TV.

'Later, when I was going to bed, I called out goodnight but she didn't answer. I went into her room and saw her in bed, passed out, with a piece of foil with a lighter beside her. There was a strange smell.'

The police officer looks sympathetic. She asks if I ever saw Mum take illegal drugs. I say no. She says she understands how hard this is for me.

My hands are shaking as I pick up my tea. I'm not putting it on. What will I say if they ask about the heroin and where Mum got it from? They won't be able to tell that I gave some to her, will they? I cleared up some specks left on the table and I made sure the packet was put back in the box at the bottom of my wardrobe.

The questions aren't too bad, though. I say I live alone with my mum and a social worker comes over every so often to check how I'm doing, and how Mum is coping with being an alcoholic and looking after me. The officer nods. She says they'll bring my statement for me to sign once it's on the system.

The floor above creaks. The other police officer is walking about in my room. My mind races. Will he look inside the wardrobe? Will he search the house and find the stash in the cellar? What if they arrest me and take everything and V thinks I've grassed him up and tells Zom to kill me?

I rest my head on the chair.

The police officer comes down. He hasn't found anything I don't think. He tells me and that he's notified my sister and she will be here soon.

The woman officer says about how I can't be living here on my own and what happens next.

I can't take it all in. All I know is, they mustn't find out what really happened.

———

They take Mum away in a white body bag. They try to keep me from seeing her but I've got to see, so I know for sure that this is real.

Brenda, the emergency social worker, has already turned up. She's calm and serious, and gives me long looks over the top of her reading glasses. I don't think she believes what I've told her. Brenda is more on top of her game than Gillian. I tell her I'll be all right on my own, my sister will be here any minute. She says she'll wait.

My phone buzzes. It's Luke. He says he wants to see me. I tell him this isn't a good time; my mother has just died. He wants to know about Mum. I say I can't talk now.

I lay on the sofa like a zombie. This is the worst thing that's happened in my whole life.

CALLUM

29TH OCTOBER

AT THE MORNING BRIEFING, I SUMMARISED WHAT WE KNEW about our two youngest suspects.

'First, 'Minty' – real name Tyler Cosgrove, fifteen years old. He lives on Effra Lane estate with his mother, uncle and two siblings. It seems he's had contact with Skull gang members over a long period. We believe he was recruited by an older gang member about a year ago, soon after he was expelled from St Thomas More Catholic School, for persistent aggressive and violent behaviour. At fifteen he was sentenced to a twelve-month Youth Rehabilitation Order for shoplifting and car theft offences.' I paused. 'The other boy is Luke Delaney, we believe.'

This boy interested me more.

'Sam has spoken to the headteacher at the John Berriman Academy, Luke's school, and some of his teachers. I've also spoken to his stepfather, Kevin Delaney. Luke was well behaved, but his behavior deteriorated after his mother's death. Luke was temporarily excluded from school last month after he injured a boy in a fight – it was reported to the school's liaison officer but no further action was taken. A few weeks ago, Kevin Delaney asked Luke to leave home. He was worried about Luke's influence on his half-sister, Kirsty – Luke had been hanging out with hoodies on the Effra Lane estate. Mr Delaney hasn't heard from Luke since he left home and doesn't know where he's staying.'

'Great parenting skills,' Ferret muttered. 'Some people shouldn't be allowed to have kids.'

I let that go.

'I've alerted Social Services to the situation with Luke,' DS Rowan said. 'They didn't have any information on him, and weren't aware he'd left home.'

'Sam, did you get anything from Luke's teachers?' I turned to DS Harper.

'His English teacher has been helpful, Isobel Collins. She said Luke was a clever, hardworking boy with a lot of potential but things went downhill after his mother died. She is angry about him being excluded... She thinks Luke might have got involved in a gang through a girl he knew at school, a sixteen-year-old Jessamine Robbins. Isobel teaches her too. I've not yet been able to speak to the girl, but she may be able to help us find out more about the Skull Crew and how we can get to Luke.'

'Thanks Sam, good work.'

'Now, PS Jacob's surveillance report. Luke Delaney has been spotted at the estate recently. The team has also sighted Deda and two of the top three in the Skull Crew, Karim Ali and 'Spicer' Newton. We also now have an address for Minty on the estate and one for Wolf in Southend – and his real name, Damon Banefield. However, gang members are now aware and have started to taking measures to avoid being followed.' Bailey had wanted to axe the surveillance op to prevent possible embarrassment on our end. But I'd pressed for a little longer in case Deda showed again. 'We'll have to decide very soon whether to go in and nick the suspects we've located – Wolf, Minty and possibly Luke – or to hold off 'til we have Deda and the higher-ups too, with the risk that we might lose the suspects we already have.'

DS Rowan's hand shot up. 'I say go in now, boss. It'll put pressure on the others.'

'I don't agree.' DS Hanna got to her feet, surprising me. The gang specialist was thorough in her work but reserved, and rarely spoke up in briefings. 'What's the point of nicking Wolf and two kids without the man who did both these murders, or the men at the top of Skull Crew? Minty and Luke are just wayward kids.'

'Those kids could get crucified if we have to let them go and they're suspected of blabbing,' DC Perry added. 'I think Sandra's right, we should wait 'til we can get them all.'

It would be my decision. But I agreed with Sandra and Ferret. If we arrested Minty and Luke now, without Deda et al., and without enough evidence to charge them, they might well be viewed as grasses when they were released. Then there was a risk those kids would come to serious harm.

———

It was nearly four when DS Harper and I arrived at the John Berriman Academy. My aim was to find out the extent of Isobel Collins's contact with Luke and whether she could help us find him.

I swigged from my bottle of water. The gleaming corridor and the scattered easy chairs transported me back to my grammar school days, those hours spent sitting outside the head-master's office following whatever trouble I'd got into.

'I'm Miss Collins,' a young black woman said as we intro-duced ourselves. Her braids fell past her shoulders. 'Isobel Collins, I mean.' She smiled with her eyes. 'You get so used to being called Miss around here.'

As she answered my opening questions, I curated my first impressions of Isobel Collins. Attractive, yes. Younger than I'd expected. Engaging, I should imagine; the sort of teacher that pupils would take to. I wondered how Luke had reacted to her.

'It's completely out of character for him to become involved in anything like this,' Miss Collins was saying. She sounded upset. 'Any crimes he may have committed must have been under coercion.' I nodded. 'I imagine he's terrified of what will happen to him if he's caught.' She placed a palm on the table between us. 'You need to be careful not to provoke him into doing something desperate.'

'We're doing our best to manage the situation, Miss Collins,' I replied curtly. 'Have you been in contact with Luke since his exclusion?'

'I've emailed him about his online lessons and his revision plan.'

'Anything else?'

'I had a text from him a few weeks ago, saying he was doing his best to study.' She fingered a strand of hair.

I felt a swell of impatience and irritation. She definitely wasn't telling me the whole story.

'So, Luke has your mobile phone number?'

'Yes, I gave it to him the day he was excluded. It's not what I'd normally do, but I was worried about him.'

'Please contact me immediately if you have any contact whatsoever with Luke.' I gave her my work mobile number. 'I can't stress how important this is. We need to make sure he's safe.'

'I agree with Isobel Collins,' I said to DC Harper as we drove back to the office. Sam was driving, which was just as well as I could barely keep my eyes open. 'The boy may be getting desperate. We need to be very careful how we approach him. He knows we're closing in. The gang knows it too. They've probably threatened to disembowel him if he so much as glances in our direction.'

'Couldn't we bring him in for questioning? If we can't charge him yet we could at least keep him in custody for thirty-six hours, and hope that we track down V in the meantime.'

Now everyone is calling the Skull Crew's leader 'V', I thought grimly.

'That's what I'm struggling with, Sam.' I lowered my window to let in a blast of cool air. 'But if we bring in Luke and have to release him, they might think he's talked. He'll be even more vulnerable.' I grimaced at another twinge in my gut. 'Deda and Edwards are the real criminals. Not these two frightened kids they've coerced into doing their dirty work.'

'So, we have to wait until we can get them all?'

'I know waiting is hard, especially when there are kids involved. But we're close, really close. All we need is another break or someone put a step wrong, and we'll be able to track down Deda and Edwards. Then we'll nick them all.'

As I spoke, I wondered if I was kidding myself. What if we couldn't find Deda and Edwards, and, in the meantime, something happened to Luke or Minty?

'What if Luke or Minty stabbed Nora Symonds, not Deda?'

'That would be difficult. But whatever crimes they may have committed, they're still children who are being exploited by adult gang members.' The car was slowing, yet again. 'What did you think about Isobel Collins? I had a strong feeling that she was lying, she's been in contact with the boy. Or is it me?'

'No, I felt that too. She might think she ought to help protect him.'

I groaned and let my eyes close.

I'd not slept through the night for goodness knows how long. The pressure of the investigation wasn't helping. Since the murder of Nora Symonds, Detective Superintendent Bailey was asking for daily updates on the operation.

As I was dozing off, my phone vibrated. PS Jacobs's name flashed up.

'Sorry to disturb you, Callum. I thought you should know right away. One of boys heard something interesting from the estate just now.'

'Go on, I'm listening.'

'It was a conversation between some younger gang members. There were several references to 'the Halloween thing' and 'Luke's big day'. Most of the words were garbled but the gist is that something seems to be in the offing for tomorrow night. No intel as to where.'

'Keep an ear out for anything else, and keep a close watch on the estate exits for the suspects entering or leaving. I want to be updated as soon as there's any news.'

Sleep banished, I chewed over the new intel. The connection with Halloween didn't bode well. What did they mean, *Luke's big day*? Was it a celebration of Luke joining the Skull Crew? Or an initiation ritual, perhaps?

———

After a blissfully uneventful evening – Brendan and I cooked a stew together without any harsh words between us – I went to bed early. The suggestion of a possible incident on Halloween night circled my mind as I fell asleep.

Hours later, I stirred to a series of taps, irregularly spaced. I was beyond tired, and really didn't want to wake up. But the sounds persisted, raising me into a state of alertness. It was someone tapping their knuckles against glass. Each was smudged somehow like a sound effect in a horror film. Someone was tapping at my window.

With a groan, I pushed myself upright. No one would be tapping on a window that was fifteen feet up from the pavement. I drew back the curtain and checked, anyway. My VW was parked as usual outside. I switched the hall lights on and made my way downstairs. No sign of anyone through the glass panels in the front door. I went into the living room. The fox carving on the mantlepiece stared back at me. I opened the front door and stepped outside. No one.

Before going back to bed, I checked the security system. No one had come through the front gate since the postman the morning before. Fear prickled at the back of my scalp. Those sounds must have been more auditory flashbacks – without the smell of burning, this time...

It was time to face the truth. I could no longer tell the difference between what was real, and what wasn't.

LUKE

It's Halloween. My ceremony is tonight. I've decided what I'm going to do, but there's somewhere I need to go first.

By the time I get to Jez's, it's nearly two in the afternoon. She hasn't answered any of my calls and messages. Someone who looks like Jez opens the door, only she's older and not beautiful. There's an unusually clean smell of lemon and bleach. Usually, this place has a musty smell, like a bat cave.

'She's in her room.'

I take it as an invite to go up.

'Jez, it's Luke.' The door's shut. I knock, wait for a reply then go in. I can't see Jez at first. The blinds are shut. Then I see a bulge under the duvet.

'Jez? What happened to your mum?'

I pull back the duvet. She's wearing her Paddington Bear PJs. I help her sit up. Her eyes are red rimmed and her breath smells. Her mouth twists.

'She's dead, Luke.'

'How did she die?'

She moans.

'She was drinking, in her room. She passed out. There was drug stuff by her bed. Bits of brown on some foil.'

What the fuck? Dread fills me. 'The heroin V put in your wardrobe?'

Jez nods. Her eyes are so big and her face is so pale, she looks like an elf.

'I couldn't wake her up. Then the ambulance came and the police. They took her body out in a bag.'

Tears glide down her cheek. A sound like hiccups, her chest moving up and down. I stare at her. I can't believe this.

'What did she die of?'

'They think it was an overdose, or a reaction from the alcohol.' The sobs ebb away. I pull out some tissues from a box on the chest of drawers, pass them to her.

'How did she get the brown?'

'I found the box opened on the floor. She must have taken some.' Jez looks away from me, fiddles with her nail. 'I told you, I was storing some boxes for V in my wardrobe.'

Something about this feels wrong.

'You didn't give it to her?'

She shakes her head. 'No, of course I didn't.' The sound of vacuuming downstairs. She scowls. 'I thought you'd take my side, at least.'

'What do you mean?'

'The social worker doesn't believe me. She thinks I did this to Mum on purpose.'

'Why would she think that?'

'I don't know. She must have found something in my file.'

Jez pulls her hair away from her face and drinks the rest of the water in the glass. The dread inside me gets worse. I'm almost too scared to ask.

'Like what?'

'Some girls thing, that's all.'

'That thing you got expelled for? Just tell me, will you?'

'This cow pretended all along she was my friend, then landed me in it. I got the blame for all the things we'd done together. So, I gave her what she had coming for fucking me over like that. I locked her into the toilet with me after school and gave her a haircut. Had some scissors in my bag, coincidentally. She had this real peachy hair, blonde and wavy.' Jez looks uncertainly at me. 'I just meant to teach her a lesson. But she was like, 'What are you doing bitch?' and started scratching and biting me to get hold of the scissors. They were sharp, she got some cuts. I got cuts from her too, though.' She gives me a defiant stare.

'Didn't the school call the police?'

'Her parents didn't want them to. The head expelled me instead. My dad wouldn't talk to me afterwards. He went to live full time with his other family in Jersey.' She reaches for her glass of water, finds it empty.

I take the glass into the bathroom. In a horrible way, all this makes sense. Maybe I knew all along that there was something wrong with Jez. But how can I judge her, with all the bad things I've done?

I wait 'til she's sipped more water.

'When is her funeral?'

'They have to do a post-mortem first, get a coroner's report or something.'

'Your sister's going to stay with you for a while? That's her downstairs, is it?'

'Yeah, Tara.' Jez pushes back the duvet, swings her legs over the edge of the bed. She stands, wobbles. 'Come here, Luke. What's the matter?'

'Tell me the truth about your mum. What really happened?'

Silence. She's gonna block me again. I'm ready to walk.

'Wait.' Jez picks up a one-armed teddy bear from her chest of drawers and runs her finger along its nose. 'I brought her some of the brown to try. I'd just had some and it made me feel so good. I put it on some foil so she could inhale it like I'd done. She was really upset, I thought it would help. I didn't think anything bad would happen. Honestly, I didn't. Then I went back later and she was...' She steadies herself against the chest of drawers. 'She was...'

Her face has gone chalk white. A churning in my ears.

'Why did you really give it to her?'

'I told you.' She glares at me, still holding on to the chest of drawers.

'You really didn't think that heroin might harm her, when she'd been drinking?'

'No, stop grilling me! You're worse than my father. What about what you've done, anyway? You helped to stab a poor defenceless woman to death. How can you point the finger at me when you've done something like that?'

There's tears in her eyes.

'I came to say goodbye.'

'What?'

'I'm leaving the crew.'

She frowns. 'But the ceremony is tonight.'

'I'll go away before then.'

'Where are you going?'

'I don't know. Somewhere out of London.'

'They'll come after you. They won't let you get away.'

My phone buzzes. I check the screen. It's Miss Collins. I let the phone switch to voicemail.

'Who's that?'

'Someone who's offered to help.'

'What, that Miss Collins from school? The English teacher?'

'Yes, her.' I've had enough of lying.

She blows through her lips. 'Are you sleeping with her? You are, aren't you?'

'How could you even ask me that?' I want to punch her. It's true, what I thought just now. I don't know this girl at all.

Jez looks scared.

'Why is she calling you then? What's going on?'

'She's offered to help—'

'How come she's got your number?'

'She gave me her number at school after the fight, said I could call her if I needed to talk. What's your problem?'

'I'm sorry, Luke.' She touches my arm. 'I've never liked any boy as much as I like you.' She licks her bottom lip. 'You're really leaving?'

I nod.

'Will I see you again?'

'I don't know.'

'I need you, Luke. Don't go.'

'Come with me then. We'll leave all this shit behind.'

She looks shocked.

'We can't. Zom would kill us both and V would put our skulls in the basement.'

'You've been watching too many horror films.'

She shakes her head. 'They have the power, we don't.'

'That's not why you won't leave, is it?' I understand how it is, suddenly. 'You like doing things for them, sucking up to them.' I can't hush my mouth. 'If V came in right now and told you to kill your sister, you'd say yes, wouldn't you? It would be as easy as killing your mother was. I was right about you all along.'

'No, that's not true! Luke, please, don't go!'

I run downstairs and slam the front door behind me.

JEZ

THREE INTO TWO

THE DOORBELL WAKES ME UP. TWICE. THREE TIMES. WHY doesn't my sister answer the door? I pull off the duvet and pad downstairs in bare feet and pyjamas. I've no idea what day it is, what time it is. If it's the police or a social worker, I don't care.

Outside is grey and blowy. It's Spicer and V. Spicer smiles.

'Hey, Miss Sleepyhead. You look rough.'

'We haven't got all day. We've come to get the stash.' V walks past me into the hall.

'My sister's here. She doesn't know about it.' The door into the kitchen is shut. The radio's booming away, she must be in there dancing to Tina Turner or something. My heart pitter-patters.

V and Spicer are heading upstairs. Spicer turns to me.

'Tell her we moved house and you stored some of our shit for us. Don't tell her what it is.'

I wonder if she'll notice they're here. I could let her stay in the kitchen, but she might come out and see two big guys with tatts carrying boxes out of the house and think we're being burgled.

'Jess, you look terrible!'

My sister stares at me when I go into the kitchen. She puts toast on and starts to chop cheddar for cheese on toast. I tell her a couple of my friends have turned up to take their possessions back, they won't be long. She stops chopping and gives me a doubtful look.

'Friends? Who are they?'

'Just friends. They won't be long.'

Her eyebrows come together. 'Are they gang members?'

'So what if they are?'

My sister runs out of the kitchen. V and Spicer are coming downstairs carrying the drug boxes.

V smiles. 'So sorry, miss, we'll be out of your hair soon.'

'Thanks, doll.' Spicer calls out, winking at her. 'The weather sucks, innit?'

'Dreadful.' Tara looks marginally less worried.

I chivvy her back into the kitchen. 'The toast's burning. Are you making me cheese on toast, or what?'

'For God's sake, Jessie. Those two are gang members, aren't they? I'll have to tell the social worker about this.'

I can only manage one slice. Tara nibbles at the other. There's a loud bump from the front door.

'You'd better go and see they're OK. Haven't you got any slippers?'

The front door's open. I stand on the mat and try to see over the bush. The van is parked up. V comes back, head down, jaw clenched. He gives me a nasty stare and says to come with him. I follow, skipping over puddles. He opens the boot and pulls off the lid of the top box. 'What the fuck is this?' He holds up the packet with a slit across the top, rolled over and stuck down with sellotape.

It's the one I opened. Why didn't I hide it somewhere instead of putting it back? What a doof.

V puts the bag back, closes the boot and turns to me.

'I'm asking you nicely, girl. Don't mess with our shit.'

'I'm sorry. It was only a bit I took.'

He looks around quickly. 'I trusted you with our food.' His face freezes. The weird scar on his cheek catches my eye; a small, silvery pit. 'And you go and give it to your mother.' His hand moves. I flinch, thinking he's going to hit me. 'You stink, girl. Go inside and take a shower. Gotta go, your friend's at the graveyard. Don't want to keep him waiting. We're having a little ceremony for him.'

'Is he—' I stop myself. Is he going ahead with it? I was going to ask.

V gets into the driver's seat and winds down the window an inch.

'Take care, Jezebel.'

Ignoring my sister's calls, I run upstairs. I feel sick. Why is Luke in a graveyard? He should be away from them all by now. Did he change his mind about leaving? I rub myself dry. Slowly, I get angry.

Who the fuck is Luke to tell me anything? He thinks I'm not worthy of him, I'm a sleazeball incarnate. But he's the one who went with Zom to shank an innocent woman. He's the one going ahead with this stupid ceremony when he says he wanted to leave the gang. He's the one without principles, isn't he?

And I don't believe there's nothing going on between him and Miss Collins.

I pick up the glass of water and hurl it across the room. It smashes against the fireplace with a tinkling sound. I hate Luke Delaney.

LUKE

Angel isn't at the flat when I arrive. I take out the rucksack and start to pack.

Inside it, I put my last birthday card from Mum, my phone charger and the envelope with my earnings in, except for sixty quid. I add my warm jumper. I put my phone and the three folded twenties into my jeans front pocket. All the rest I leave behind.

I leave my door key on the table and haul the rucksack onto my back.

Voices. Men's voices, echoing along the corridor. Zom and Angel. I go cold. What are they doing here so early?

The lock turns. I hide the key under a coaster, pull off the rucksack. Their footsteps go past into the kitchen. I'm about to make a run for it when the door opens.

'Hey, bro.' Angel fist bumps me. 'Ready to go?'

'I thought the ceremony was later.'

'Change of plan. We gotta stop off at the church on the way to V's.'

'The church?'

Angel says nothing. Zom comes into the lounge. He spots my rucksack on the floor.

'It's for staying over at V's,' I blurt out. 'He said I can stay over after the ceremony.' I get ready for Zom to narrow his eyes. But he nods.

'I'll head to the toilet then,' I say. My back is damp with sweat.

'Don't be long. Minty's at the church already.'

Taking my backpack with me will look odd, so I leave it on the floor. I pray neither of them will look inside or ask why I'm taking so much for one night. I'm trapped.

It's nearly dark outside. I put my Puffa jacket on over my hoody so I've extra pockets for carrying stuff. There's a cab waiting.

Zom gets in front beside the driver. I'm in the back with Angel.

We drive in silence. Zom glares at me over his shoulder.

'You're quiet back there, man. Gettin' shook 'bout what's comin'?' I say nothing. 'You gonna have a surprise soon.' Zom laughs. 'Can't wait to see your face when you find out what it is. When you see Mr Sardine.'

'Mr Sardine?'

Zom laughs harder. Angel shakes his head.

'Don't mind him, fella. He's off his meds.'

The driver pulls up in front of a church near the entrance to the cemetery. I get out first, ready to make a run for it. I'm a fast runner... But they're out of the car too.

Raindrops spatter on us. I follow Angel and Zom through the gate in the low wall, wondering what the hell we're gonna do. We walk over to Minty, leaning against the church. There's a laundry bag at his feet. Something is moving inside.

It's a ginger cat. It hisses and claws at Minty as he tries to get it out.

'Fuck you, cat!' He closes the bag, examines his arm. 'It scratched me!'

'Maybe you'll die of rabies,' sneers Zom.

'Don't fuck about.' Minty scowls. 'Hey, Luke.' He says it in a strange voice.

'This is your next test, bro,' Angel says to me. 'The big one. V needs you to kill this. He needs its blood for your ceremony.'

'You want me to kill the cat?' I wait for him to laugh and say, Got ya.

'You'll do it easy, no worries.'

'Where's the cat from?'

'It's my sister's,' Minty says. 'I grabbed it when she went out to Tesco.'

'You're joking.' I've a lead weight in my stomach.

'Got a blade on you?' Zom steps to me, serious.

The ground wobbles. I look at Zom then at Angel and Minty, still waiting for one to break out laughing and say they're having me on.

'Here.'

Zom lays down a knife. It's a zombie. Its blade is massive and has a jagged top edge, like the one he killed Mrs Symonds with. But the handle is orange.

'You gotta slit its throat an' pour its blood into the jar... Easy-peasy.' Sick seeps over the back of my throat. I can't do this. 'Got the jar, Minty?'

Minty opens a Sainsbury's bag and produces a big glass jar with a lid.

'It's OK, Ninj,' he says. 'It's only a cat. My sister don't look after it no more.'

'Just a sec,' I say. 'I need to pee.'

I jog behind a yew tree. The trunk is centuries thick. I let my piss stream arc so they can see I'm not faking. In one moment a hundred things go through my head. How long will it take to reach the gate? How fast can Zom run?

My rucksack. I've left my rucksack with the others. Nearly all of my money is in it. But I've got my phone and my Oyster and the twenties...

Next, I'm running for my life. I leap over the churchyard wall and leg it along the street. My long thin shadow stretches ahead.

'Get back here now or you're dead!'

Zom's yell powers me on. I imagine his thick quads closing the space between us, his zombie blade gripped tight.

CALLUM

31ST OCTOBER: 5.30PM

AFTER HOURS OF WAITING FOR ANY FURTHER INTEL ABOUT THE Halloween event, and with no sign of Luke or the other suspects, surveillance team leader PS Jacobs radioed in.

'We've spotted Luke Delaney. He's with "Angel" Gabriel and Deda.'

The three had hopped into a car outside the estate, a dirty white Vauxhall saloon. The surveillance team were now in pursuit. I felt a jolt of adrenalin. For the first time, we had both 'Zom' Deda and Luke in our sights. My gut told me to act now, with or without V.

The sighting triggered a coordinated response between the Rye team and the Met's operations room at Hendon. Twenty minutes later, a tactical firearms commander arrived in Major Incident Room One. She was a few years older than me, I guessed. Her manner was crisp, matching her superintendent's uniform. Side by side, we watched a monitor showing real-time positions of the armed surveillance vehicles following the Vauxhall. She appeared unfazed by the prospect of commanding an operation to apprehend three fugitives including a double murder suspect armed with a dangerous weapon.

'Don't let them get away, will you?' I urged her. She looked at me stonily, then back to the monitor.

I was in no position to give orders; I knew very well. What happened next would be largely out of my hands. A team in SO19, the Met's firearms unit, had been deployed; all going well, as soon as 'Zom' Deda, 'Angel' Gabriel and Luke Delaney were nicked, another armed unit would simultaneously arrest 'Wolf' Banefield in Southend.

Further updates came over the radio in the clipped tones of the operational firearms commander on the ground.

'Target is static in traffic, over.' A series of crackles. 'Now west, west, west on Church Road... Target now outside the cemetery entrance. Target is static outside All Hallows Church on Church Lane next to Bruce Castle Park. Standby, three targets exiting the Vauxhall. Standby for directions.'

A gravelly bass came over the radio. 'PS Black, TST. ETA six minutes for last location, over.'

With Tactical Support on the case as well as Jacobs's boys and the firearms team, luck was on our side...

'PS Jacobs.' The nasal London twang of the surveillance team leader. 'We've got eyeball on the target vehicle. Confirmed Zom, Angel and Luke are on foot towards the church. Standby. They've stopped by an IC3 male aged fourteen to sixteen, five feet seven inches, close cropped hair, wearing grey hoody and black tracksuit bottoms, holding a large shopping bag. Standby, confirmed the male they've met is Minty and there is an object in the bag, over.'

What the fuck were they doing in the churchyard? I met the tactical commander's eye. She frowned.

'Keep the commentary coming, PS Jacobs. Further update on what they are doing please, over'.

'Minty's taken a cat out of the bag, literally. Zom's produced a knife. Twelve-inch blade, easy. Stand by.'

A cat? The tactical commander and I looked at each other.

The tactical support team broke in. 'PS Black, TST. ETA three minutes, over.'

'All TST units standby,' barked the tactical commander. 'SO19 prepare for State Amber but do not, repeat do not, move forward until we have further update on the knife, over.'

I exhaled in frustration. Fuck this delay. If the tactical commander didn't call the firearms team forward soon, we could lose our chance to make the arrests.

'Luke's having a pee,' came PS Jacobs's nasal voice. The sound of rustling undergrowth. 'He's making off! Zom's in pursuit with the knife. We need urgent armed back up, over.'

A flurry of snapped commands was matched by racing images on the monitor as the firearms team scrambled forward. Then everything dropped into a black hole.

LUKE

I DART THROUGH HIGH GATES INTO A VAST SPACE. IT'S DARK. I veer off the path towards a row of upright oblong stones. Headstones. They're all around me, poking out of the earth. I twist and turn, leaping over them. Stumble, bang my knee and stifle my cry.

The noise of Zom's footsteps has gone. But I know he's still behind from the occasional grunts.

The headstones get bigger. Some are closed in on top like small houses. Angels crawl over their corners. My trainers sink into soft earth. I stay low, keeping to the bigger stones for cover, darting from one stone to the next, leaping over soggy graves. My breath comes hoarser, louder. My lungs are going to explode. I need to stop.

I crouch behind a stone. It's darker here, in the shadow of the wind. I pray I've given Zom the slip. Ahead, the rush of the Moselle. I hope it masks the noise of my panting. I don't dare look behind to check in case he sees me move.

I squeeze my eyes shut, try to keep as still as this stone. Ready myself for the clutch of Zom's hand on my shoulder... He can't be far off. He'll be creeping over graves, marking the spot where he'll dig mine.

Then I see his jacket, the glimmer of reflective strips. He's a bus length away, walking towards me, phone held out, scanning the ground on either side with the torch beam. He's gonna see me.

I run for it. Towards the sound of the river, over the narrow bridge and along the path to the other side of the cemetery. I sprint faster than I've ever done in my life. The ground is firm here, there's no barriers or obstacles. On the other side of the wall, I can hear the road.

The gates are shut.

No.

A burst of panic hits me. I run at the wall beside the gate. I could scramble up, maybe... My hands and feet struggle to find a grip. Then my fingers find a small hole in the wall and my foot finds another small hole. I gather all my energy and haul myself up and over.

Cars rush past both ways. On the other side of the road, people cluster beside a red bus stopped there. The straggly queue slowly disappears into the bus. I run across the road, swerving out of the way of a bonnet just in time, and leap up through the middle doors as they close.

CALLUM

IF ONLY I HAD A CIGARETTE ON ME, I THOUGHT AS THE seconds turned into minutes. The tactical commander didn't meet my eye. She seemed impervious to the tenseness of the situation.

The radio crackled into life; PS Jacobs.

'We've lost Luke,' he panted. 'Zom's still somewhere in the cemetery. I don't think they saw us looking. We need SO19 to remain close but revert to being covert. Angel and Minty are still at the churchyard. We have eyeball, over.'

The tactical commander responded.

'Any of them armed or carrying a weapon apart from Zom, over?'

'Negative.' The swish of moving legs. 'No sign of Luke. Stand by. Angel and Minty on foot towards Church Road. Angel and Minty are right, right, right into Church Road. Standby... Now eyeball on Zom. He's running towards Church Lane from the church gate towards the target vehicle, still in situ. He's going to get in, over.'

'TFC to OFC, State Amber.' The pitch of the tactical commander's voice went up a notch.

'PS Black, TST.' The gravelly bass came over the radio. 'We're at the scene, twenty metres from the church. Awaiting instructions, over.'

The tactical commander shot a warning glance at me.

'PS Black from TFC. Stand by and do not approach! We are at State Amber, about to go to State Red on OFC's call, over.'

I held my breath. Once the operational firearms commander on the ground called State Red, all hell would break loose by the church.

'OFC to all SO19. State Red, State Red.'

Through the open microphones all I could hear was the operational commander's gruff bellows amid a cacophony of 'Stop! Armed Police!'

'Target one in the Vauxhall,' a voice cut in. 'I'm trying Hatton rounds on the tyres but ARV to respond in case, over.'

Two gunshots reverberated across the airwaves.

'Missed the tyres. Vauxhall making off north towards Church Road, weaving across the road. The target is beside the driver. ARV unit to respond urgently, over.'

What I took to be an Armed Response Unit call sign came up on the air.

'We are behind the target vehicle. Do I have authority to pursue, over?'

I dug my fingernails into my palms. The tactical commander eyeballed me warily.

'The initial phase only. We'll confirm if and when you can move to the tactical phase once I've consulted with the pursuit tacad.'

'We can't let Deda get away,' I said, boiling over with frustration. The pursuits tactical advisor in Hendon would be wary about instigating a high-speed chase by armed police through north London traffic.

'Remember who you're talking to.' She tapped her superintendent epaulettes, then ordered the tactical support units with taser to close in on the other two targets, Angel and Minty.

I stayed quiet as further updates came in. Armed police were on Deda's tail. We needed to apprehend the others too, before they could be alerted.

Minutes went by with no further updates. Unable to keep quiet any longer, I grabbed a radio.

'DI Waverley to PS Jacobs, update please?'

'Minty and Angel still in range, boss. We're on foot about twenty metres behind.'

'Don't lose them. We'll get you back up, over.'

If Minty and Angel were alerted before we could arrest them, we might never see them again. The same went for Wolf.

'You need to get ARVs to arrest Wolf,' I insisted.

The tactical commander glared at me, then issued the arrest order.

Seconds went by, a minute. I clenched and unclenched my fists. How long would it take to secure Angel and Minty? What was happening with Wolf? But I dared not break the silence in case it alerted the fugitives.

A relieved-sounding PS Jacobs panted over the radio.

'Two in custody, boss.'

'Well done. Take one to Tottenham and one to Enfield.'

Confirmation came of Wolf's arrest in Southend. Thank God for that, I muttered. But Deda was still on the loose. I turned to the tactical commander.

'Where the fuck is Deda?'

With a half-smile, she picked up her radio. 'ARV with eyeball on target vehicle. Update please, over.'

'He's trying to lose us. Taking all the back streets. Currently heading east on Whitehall Street towards Love Lane, over.'

The tactical commander's face remained impassive. I popped a Murray Mint into my mouth. A minute went by. An excited voice came on the radio.

'Stand by, target vehicle pulling up on White Hart Lane. Target is off, off, off on foot onto the High Road towards the stadium. We're pursuing on foot.'

Unable to keep still, I got up and paced up and down. From their desks, DS Freeman and DS Rowan were surreptitiously following the proceedings. The breathless commentary kept coming. Then a final dejected update.

'We've got a total loss somewhere in the vicinity of Sainsbury's. He could have gone anywhere... We'll do an area search but I think he's gone, over.'

I ordered the other units to join in the search, but deep down I knew it was hopeless. Deda had given us the slip. I headed out of the incident room, felled by bitter disappointment.

Returning a few minutes later, I met the tactical commander on her way out of the building. She nodded to me, sour-faced.

'Sorry it didn't go as you hoped.'

I bit back my instinctive reply. 'That's how it goes sometimes.'

Three out of five wasn't so bad, I told myself. But I'd have swapped them for Deda and Luke in an instant.

————

DS Freeman came over to my desk as I munched on a therapeutic granola bar.

'Bloody bad luck, boss.'

'We were so close.' DS Rowan hovered behind him. 'We would have had them all, if Luke hadn't scarpered.'

'We'll get another chance.' DS Harper touched my shoulder sympathetically.

'What were they doing with a cat, anyway?' Freeman went back to swivelling his chair. 'Were they going to slit its throat, do you think?'

Harper made an appalled face at Freeman. 'Do you have to be so gruesome?'

'Poor cat, it's going to be a life down—'

'Whatever they were doing,' I interrupted, 'it looks like it was the final straw for Luke.'

'They'll be pissed with him for running away,' Rowan replied. 'Especially when they find out the others have been arrested.'

'Exactly. We need to find Luke before they do.' I asked my three sergeants and our level-five-qualified DC to get started on a questioning strategy. The custody sergeants would keep our three detainees stewing while we got our act together. 'I'm off to grab a coffee, I'll go over it with you later.'

I set off towards Lorenzo's. Yes, we'd been close. But close wasn't what counted.

LUKE

EACH TIME THE BUS STOPS, I CHECK TO MAKE SURE ZOM ISN'T getting on. What if he's found some sneaky way to get ahead of the bus? But I know that's just me being paranoid.

I take out the contents of my jacket, hoody and jeans pockets. Apart from my phone and Oyster, there's a wrinkled satsuma and three pounds eighty pence in coins, an ibuprofen packet and the three folded twenties.

I read my messages. Nothing from Jez.

A text from Izzy: *Are you all right Luke? Please let me know how you are.*

A WhatsApp from Angel. *Get your ass back here man or you'll be in deep shit.*

Minty: *WTF are you up to? Zom's going loco here*

Zom: *Your dead meat. When i catch you im gonna skin you alive*

I shiver and put the phone away.

The bus is headed for Finsbury Park station. I could get a train out of London, or... Where am I going? Train fares are expensive. Where will I stay tonight? Can I trust Miss Collins or should I find somewhere else to stay? An Airbnb will cost at least thirty quid. I can't go back to Kevin's. They'll be sure to look there.

The hairs on my neck stir. Kirsty. How could I have forgotten Kirsty? What if they come for her like they came for Doc's sister? I phone the house landline. It rings out. I phone Kirsty's mobile, get voicemail. I leave a voice message.

'Kirst, don't go home this evening. If you are home, get out right now and go to over to Vicky's. I'm not kidding. Call me asap, I'll explain.'

I can't think of anything except what might happen if Kirsty doesn't do what I say, or doesn't pick up the message. Zom and the others could be at the house now, waiting for her to show. I can't risk them hurting my sister. I know she's not my real sister but she's the most important person in the world to me.

My phone rings.

'Hey, bro.' I breathe again. 'What's going on? I just got your message. It freaked me out.'

'Where are you?'

'At Vicky's.'

'This will sound weird, but there's a good reason, I swear. You've got to go and stay with Aunt Jemma for a few days. Right away.'

'What are you talking about? You're scaring me, Luke. What about school?'

'Don't go to school, not until I tell you it's OK.'

'I'll have to ask Dad—'

'No. Don't talk to him, don't go home. Get on a train as soon as you can, don't wait for morning. Once you've arrived, call home to say you're safe. I don't want him to know where you are. I'll call Aunt Jemma and Kevin to explain.'

She doesn't speak for ages.

'I don't understand.' She sounds like the little girl I knew for so long. 'What about clothes? I'm still in my school uniform. And I've no money on me.'

'Borrow some clothes from Vicky, can't you? You shouldn't need to pay for anything. Aunt Jemma's in zone six, you can use your Oyster.' No reply, only the background sounds of TV. 'It's only for a little while, Kirst.'

'OK then.' Her voice is small. 'I'll get the tube to Loughton.'

A picture comes into my head of my sister high up in Aunt Jemma's tree, scrabbling for apples. I can't imagine being without her.

'One more thing. Don't give anyone this number, will you? Your dad or Aunt Jemma, or anyone in the police.'

'No, of course not.'

'I'll explain everything soon, I promise.'

CALLUM

7.10PM

My phone rang as I was doing some shoulder rotations at my desk.

DI Ellie Dalton.

'Hi, Callum. Got a minute?'

'Sure.'

'I've got something you might find interesting.' She paused. 'It's to do with a sixteen-year-old girl who might be mixed up with a local gang.'

'Go on.'

'Two nights ago, emergency services were called to the home of a Melanie Robbins in Muswell Hill. She died from a suspected heroin overdose. The post-mortem showed large amounts of alcohol and heroin in her blood. My sergeant talked to Mrs Robbins's daughter Jessamine, who was in the house at the time.'

I pricked up my ears.

'Jessamine said she didn't know her mother had been taking drugs – illegal ones, anyway. Anyhow, we did a bit of digging.

Apparently, Mrs Robbins and her daughter are known to Social Services, who were considering whether to place the girl into care due her mother's alcohol issues, and suspected grooming by gangs outside her school, the—'

'John Berriman Academy?'

'That's right. You've already come across her?'

'She's linked to a suspect in our inquiry.'

Ellie coughed.

'The thing is, the traces of heroin found in Mrs Robbins's bedroom were tested – she'd smoked it, apparently – and they came up as over ninety-five per cent pure.'

'It raises alarm bells, definitely.' Something more akin to a shriek. 'Is there anything else?'

'I talked to Brenda Lawson, the duty social worker who was with Jessamine after Mrs Robbins died. She had suspicions that Jessamine might have been involved in her mother's death somehow.'

'Based on what?'

'Nothing concrete. The girl's manner, I think.'

'Thanks for sharing this, Ellie.'

I interrupted the interview preparations.

'Sam, come with me. We need to talk to Jessamine Robbins.'

I took the passenger seat. It was well past sunset. As we headed west towards Muswell Hill the streets began to sprout trees and expensive cars.

Sam glanced at me as she tackled another roundabout. 'Shouldn't we be getting this girl into the station so we can video her?'

'My gut tells me she'd freeze up as soon as we mentioned taking her to the nick. If she's involved with this gang, she's going to be reluctant to tell us anything anyway. Let's play it by ear.'

The young woman who opened the door to us was definitely

older than sixteen. She had similarities to the photo of Jessamine; the same intense grey eyes and broad, low-set mouth.

'Are you the detectives? I'm Tara Robbins. Jessie's sister.'

'Our condolences, Tara.' DC Harper stepped ahead of me into the hall. 'How is Jessamine?'

'Same as when I arrived, really. Not talking, in bed all the time.'

The house was old with high corniced ceilings, original fire-places and period features. I followed Tara Robbins and Sam into the living room.

A tall, slim, ultra-pale girl was slumped on the sofa in a dressing gown and flip-flops. The proportions of her face seemed a little off, somehow. Eyes too far apart, nose too far above her mouth.

'I'm DS Harper and this is DI Waverley.' I raised a hand.

The girl looked in our direction. A slight movement of the eyes; her brain was far away.

'We appreciate this is a difficult time for you, Jess,' Sam continued. 'But we'd like to speak to you about some matters relating to our investigation.' The smallest change in the set of the girl's mouth was her only acknowledgement. 'As you're under eighteen,' Sam went on, 'would you mind if your sister stays in the room, as the appropriate adult?'

'Um, no, I'd rather she didn't. I'm fine by myself.'

Tara, clearly annoyed, left the room. Sam and I sat down on two uncomfortable wooden chairs opposite the sofa.

'We're investigating the murders of Solita Milton and Nora Symonds at a nearby council estate,' Sam said as we took out our notebooks.

The girl's eyes widened. She sat up straighter and crossed one leg over the other.

'Don't worry,' I cut in, 'you're not a suspect.'

'Jessamine.' Sam smiled. 'We'd like to ask you a few questions about the night your mother died. I understand you told police officers that on the night she died, the twenty-ninth of October, you were with your mother all afternoon and evening?'

'That's right.' Her eyes were focused now.

'You took a day off school?'

'I didn't have much to do in school that day, my mum was getting really stressed about the social worker coming to visit. I thought I'd stay home and try to help her calm down.'

'How was your mum that evening?'

'She was quite gloomy. She'd been drinking.'

'Do you know what drugs your mum took the day she died?'

'She took tranquillisers every day. I don't know about any illegal drugs.'

'Did you see her take any illegal drugs before that evening?'

Jessamine rubbed her jaw, looking thoughtful. 'She mentioned she had a friend who took heroin occasionally.'

'Your mother wasn't in the habit of using heroin, then?' I asked.

The girl's eyes flicked to me. Her face was hostile.

'No, she wasn't. But when I saw that stuff by her bed...'

'Have you ever come across heroin?'

'Only in films.' She smiled. 'That totally put me off. I don't know why people do that to themselves.'

Something about her casual reply disturbed me.

'Any reason why you're away from school so often?'

'I get bored with it. I'm sixteen. I've got a part-time job at a beauty salon and I'm training to be a beautician.'

'What's the name the salon?

'Beauty Box, on the High Road.' I wrote down the address to check later. It could be the place that the undercover mentioned, where the gang laundered their drug profits.

'Have you ever been approached by gang members, Jessamine? Or anyone you thought could be in a gang? We've heard that gang members often try to talk to pupils at your school.'

'They've never talked to me.'

'Has anyone ever bought you clothes or handbags or shoes, and later asked you to do something for them in return?'

'Only my mum. When we had some money, she used to bribe me to do housework.'

The inappropriate mention of her mother struck me.

'Have you ever been asked to do anything for someone older, like carrying drugs or weapons?'

Her foot jerked, as if she'd been given an electric shock. 'No, nothing like that.'

'Have you ever been pressured to have sex with someone older, or do something you didn't really want to?'

She shook her head vigorously. 'No, never.'

'Your friend, Luke Delaney. Do you know where he is?'

'He's not my friend anymore. I've no idea where he is.' She frowned. 'Why are you asking about him?'

'You're not in any trouble, Jessamine. But we're concerned for Luke's safety, as well as yours. You may know that in July a girl your age was brutally murdered outside the Effra Lane estate, close to your school. Also a seventy-two-year-old woman was killed on the twenty-sixth of October by the same man, we believe. We urgently need to find Luke so we can protect him – and we need your help.'

'I would if I could. But like I said...' She looked down at her foot, jiggling a flip-flop.

DS Harper caught my eye.

'When did you last have contact with Luke, Jess?'

The girl hesitated. 'A week ago, I think.'

'In person or on the phone?'

Again, a hesitation. 'On the phone. We messaged each other sometimes.'

'What about?'

'What we were up to, films we watched – you know, like friends do.'

'Why aren't you two friends anymore?'

'He got upset about something.'

'What was that?'

'I can't remember.'

'You two were quite close, then?'

Sadness lingered on her face. It felt like her most honest response so far.

'We used to be.'

'Did he ever mention that he was involved in a gang?'

'No.'

'Did you ever get the impression he might be?'

'He hung out with some dodgy kids sometimes, but you know. What teenager doesn't?'

This was going nowhere, I thought.

'I'm going to show you some photographs,' I said. 'Do you know any of these people, or have you seen them?' One by one, I laid down photographs of 'Angel' Gabriel, 'Wolf' Banefield, 'Minty' Cosgrove, 'Zom' Deda and 'V' Edwards. At each one, she said 'no' without hesitation. I gave it one last shot.

'Have you ever heard of the Skull Crew, Jessamine?'

'No.'

'Do you know anyone called Zom?'

'No, sorry.'

'What about someone who calls himself V?'

'I really wish I could help you. What have they done?'

I glanced at Sam, my patience exhausted, and handed

Jessamine Robbins my business card. 'That's my direct line. If you have anything you want to tell me, please give me a call.'

She looked at the card as if it might be laced with poison, and put it into her dressing gown pocket.

DS Harper leaned forwards.

'Could we take your mobile number please, Jessamine, in case we need to update you with anything?'

Reluctantly, she gave out a number.

'Thanks very much for your help, Jess.'

I got to my feet. 'Thank you, Jessamine.'

———

On the way back to Wood Green, I vented my frustration.

'That girl wouldn't know the truth if it bit her on the backside.'

Sam looked over from the wheel with a grin. 'I thought she was lying too... about nearly everything. Any of your granola bars left, sir? I'm bloody starving.'

'In the glovebox. Go on, have a couple. Do you think she could have given her mother smack?' I wouldn't have put it past her, somehow, though the inquiry into the mother's death was more likely to see it as an accidental overdose than a suspicious homicide.

'I suppose it's possible. But why?'

'She was angry with her mother for not looking after her? Because she wanted to keep her quiet about something?'

'Hmm.' Sam chewed off a piece of granola bar. 'Maybe.' Her face was lit by a succession of streetlamps. Even under their unkind rays, her face was striking. 'She's definitely a troubled young woman.'

We pulled up at a set of traffic lights.

'Do you think she's involved with the Skull Crew?' I ask.

'I'd say so, from how she reacted to our questions.' Sam tapped the wheel. 'She was too quick to deny everything.'

'She's involved, I'm sure of it. The way she reacted when you mentioned the murders... Not asking a thing about them. She's definitely involved with Luke.'

'Absolutely,' Sam shot back. 'And did you see how she reacted when you put down the photo of Deda? She looked away really quickly, like she couldn't bear to look at him. I think something's going on between them – or was.'

'That would account for her being less than open with us. Having a guy like him watching your every move would scare the shit out of anyone.'

'Solita was her age too. If she knows he killed that girl...'

'I hope Jessamine isn't sleeping with him, for her sake.'

9.15PM

I watched the interviews with the three gang members on the remote monitor. As expected, both 'Wolf' Banefield and Minty were both no commenting.

Banefield's close-set eyes and small face reminded me more of a rat than a wolf, though 'Rat' might not go down as well in gang circles. He grunted another 'No comment', taking obvious satisfaction from the hints of frustration in DS Rowan's voice.

Minty, by contrast, was a likeable character. DS Harper was doing her best to draw him out; several times he smiled at a question she'd put to him. It was difficult to imagine him stabbing anyone in the throat.

'Angel' Gabriel was also being interviewed under caution. Hopefully, the possibility of being charged with murder might loosen his tongue. I'd assigned him to DS Freeman, whose interview skills could do with honing. To my surprise though, Gabriel looked as if he might be responding to Freeman's typically robust approach.

'What sort of friends were you and Luke?' DS Freeman raised his eyebrows. 'He must be a good six years younger than you.'

'Fuck off, man!' Gabriel slapped the table, showing his tattooed fingers. His brief signalled for 'No comment' but Gabriel hadn't noticed. 'We were buddies, that's all. He was staying at my place for a bit. He said he'd got into some trouble with his stepdad. He wasn't going to school no more.'

'What did he do all day?'

'How do I know? I wasn't his boss.'

'Did you get him selling drugs for you?'

'Course I didn't. It wasn't like that.'

'You've got quite a nice little business going off of that estate, haven't you?'

The brief asked what evidence there was for this. DS Freeman gave him a withering look and turned back to Gabriel.

'What were you doing outside the church this afternoon with Luke Delaney, Tyler Cosgrove and Dritan Deda?'

'I told you, we met there to have a chat.'

'Funny place to have a chat, isn't it? Outside a church, in the dark on a miserable evening?'

Gabriel glared at DS Freeman.

'Fuck's sake, man, I'm telling you. I was never anywhere near that old woman that got stabbed up. This is harassment.'

Leaving Freeman to get on with it, I phoned DS Harper at Enfield station. She and DC Perry were on a short break from their interview with Tyler, aka Minty. For the past hour and a half, the boy had answered 'No comment'.

Sod that, I thought.

'I'll be over in ten. Tell Ferret he can go home. I'm sure he could do with catching up on his sleep.'

As I entered the interview room with Sam, Minty glanced up at me, yawned and pointedly looked at his brief's watch.

'Is it ten thirty already? My mum will kill me if I'm not back soon.' He was a scrawny slip of a lad.

'We're going for as long as it takes,' I said after Sam restarted the recording and did the formalities. 'If it takes all night.' Minty's brief frowned at me but said nothing.

'She's a strict mum, is she?' Sam asked.

'You bet.' Minty gave an amused titter. 'She likes to think she is, anyhow. But she knows I'm a lost cause. Reckon she's given up on me.'

'What about your uncle, is he strict with you?'

'Nah, not really. He can't stop me neither. I stay out late, do whatever I want. He's like, "Go and do whatever, we've got two more kids to look after, we're washing our hands of you, rah rah."'

'It's late and we all want to go home.' I leaned forward. 'We can end this soon if you start talking, son.' I reminded Minty that we had CCTV of him going into the Effra Lane estate block shortly before the murder of Nora Symonds, and leaving a few minutes later. His bravado vanished. Conflict played out on his face.

'I didn't do it! I swear on my mum's life! It was Luke. Luke merked her. He did the murder.' His eyes implored me.

'Ask to take a break,' the brief told Minty.

Minty ignored him.

Riled at the interruption, I carried on with my questions. I didn't believe the boy; he was lying about Luke to protect himself.

'Luke killed Nora Symonds? How did he do it, exactly?'

'The woman pepper-sprayed me and the knife fell on the floor. Luke picked it up and shanked her in the neck.'

'Were you carrying the knife when the woman sprayed you?'

Minty looked confused. He glanced at his brief, who shook his head.

'No comment.'

'Were you there with Nora Symonds when she was killed?'

'Yeah, I was there with Luke.'

'Minty, tell me. Who else was there with you?'

Minty glanced at his brief, who'd put his finger to his lips.

'I can't say.'

It was back to 'No comment'.

At ten in the evening I called time on the sessions. 'Wolf' Banefield was already back in his cell; he'd not answered any of our questions. I released Gabriel without charge, with a pair of surveillance officers following him, and sought permission to charge Minty and Banefield. No murder weapon had been found but the evidence against the pair was strong enough, so I hoped.

At eleven thirty, a CPS lawyer gave us the go-ahead. Banefield was charged jointly with the murder of Solita Milton 'together with one other' – Dritan Deda, once we got him into custody. 'Minty' Cosgrove was charged jointly with the murder of Nora Symonds 'together with two others' – Deda and Luke. It should have been a moment to celebrate but it was late, I was dog tired and the twinges in my gut were getting worse. Kate would have insisted I go to the doctor, if she were still around.

As I was walking to the VW, Detective Superintendent Bailey called. God's sake, what did he want now?

'Good to hear about the charging of your two suspects. It's about time we had some good news. Now, about tomorrow... Pierce has offered to do the media briefing in the morning, instead of you. I think that's a good idea—'

'I'm OK to do it,' I protested. Pierce wanted to take credit for the latest progress, did he?

'Callum, I'm concerned about the impact all of this is having on you. You've seemed very stressed lately – understandably – and with the review ongoing...'

IOPC investigators, as I well knew, were looking into the death of our key witness – the matter had been routinely referred to the Independent Office for Police Conduct given Nora Symonds had died following police contact. They would then decide whether or not we – I – had made the right decisions leading up to her death.

'Sorry, sir. What's your point?'

'To be frank, I'm not just concerned about your stress levels. Your anger issues are hindering your ability to do the job. I've noticed and so have others.'

Had Pierce told Bailey about the incident in his office? I'd bet he hadn't mentioned how he'd provoked me.

'Right, sir,' I said through clenched teeth. 'Pierce can do the briefing, I don't care. If that's all, I've had a long day. I need to go home and get some kip.'

'Be careful, Callum. None of us are invincible.'

I climbed in the car, fuming. On top of my own misgivings about not having done enough to protect our witness, the criticism stung. Bailey was right, though. My anger was getting in the way of the job.

As I waited at the lights, my phone warbled gently from its dashboard holder. An alert from the home security system flashed onto the screen: PACKAGE DETECTION ALERT. There'd been a spate of alerts recently from various deliveries – the smart home security system didn't recognise delivery drivers, who always had different faces, and had only recently managed to recognise the postman. At the next set of traffic lights, I played the three-second video that the system had sent. It was only my neighbour setting a package onto the doorstep.

A loud *honk* from the van behind made me start. I called Brendan via the car speaker.

'Are you all right?'

A yawn down the line. 'Yeah, I'm fine. Fell asleep revising chemistry. What is it?'

'Nothing, just checking. Go back to sleep, I'll see you in the morning.'

The package was the book on meditation and relaxation practices I'd ordered.

As had happened the night before, a noise woke me up a few hours after I'd got off to sleep. This time it wasn't a tapping, more of a scraping. My senses went on alert. The sound was coming from downstairs. After a minute or so, the noise stopped.

As I was drifting back off, a small thud. My heart thudded in response. A few seconds later came another thud, hardly audible. Those sounds were from inside, I was certain, and I bloody well wasn't imagining them.

I glanced at the alarm clock: 2.47am. Fuck it. I went downstairs, putting my dressing gown on as I walked. The hall and landing lights now stayed on throughout the night, courtesy of the timer I'd had installed.

The smell hit me first. A metallic smell mingling with something slightly rotten.

Something lay on the hall floor – several things. On the doormat was an animal's paw. It had been neatly severed about an inch up the leg. A mass of sticky blood surrounded it. I nearly vomited on the spot. I went closer. A cat's paw, maybe? I wasn't great at identifying animals but this wasn't very catlike.

There was something else. A few inches away on the rug lay what looked like a large dark brown leaf. I bent down and peered at the object.

Shit. It was an ear – the ear of a fox. A slim, upside-down 'V', the outer fur black-fringed at the tip, the inside fur soft and white... No way could I fail to recognise that. I ran into the kitchen, tore off a piece of kitchen roll, went back and scooped up the ear. Then I put the ear on the worktop, bent over the sink and dry-heaved.

Stepping around the patches of blood, I strode to the front door, opened the gate and looked up and down the street. No one on the street, no passing cars. No sign of anything unusual. Back inside, I picked up the severed paw with another paper towel and placed it next to the ear. I cleaned a red streak off the light switch then looked down at a red smear on the sleeve of my white dressing gown, and cleaned that up too. Finally, I poured hot water and bleach into a bucket and mopped up the bloody residue from the hall floorboards.

Brendan didn't stir.

It was evidence, I thought, looking at the two furry lumps wrapped in paper, now spotted red. I'd bag them and get Forensics to check them out. They were unlikely to contain anything useful. The security system might, though.

I hurried up to my office and checked the security system. It showed a view from above the porch of someone jogging up to the front gate, opening it and jogging to the front door. A slim figure in jeans and trainers carrying a plastic bag, face swallowed by a hoody. It looked like a kid. A boy about five feet four inches. The figure stepped briefly onto the doorstep, then jogged back through the gate.

His face wasn't visible. I stopped the video as the figure was about to step onto the porch. Under the hoody, he was wearing a balaclava. I stared at it. A skull's jaw showed in white over the black fabric, like a ghostly grimace.

I replayed the video several times. The kid's clothes were like any other kid's, nothing distinctive. I could bring the micro-SD card into work, get the image enhanced. But the face wasn't visible; no amount of enhancement would change that.

I poured myself a whisky to calm my jitters. Had someone paid that kid to drop off the fox parts? Was this a gift from the Skull Crew? Were they taunting me, showing me they still had the upper hand despite the arrests yesterday? My thoughts sped on, out of control. What if this was all down to Pierce? What if he was trying to derail me by making me so paranoid, I'd have to step down from the murder team? It would suit him to have me out of the way so I didn't detract from his chances of promotion.

No. Not even Pierce would pull something like this.

And how the hell had whoever it was found out my address? There had been data breaches over the years; hackers into the Met's server could have sold personal information to criminals, perhaps. Or had someone had followed me home from work, or someone at work had found out my address? Pierce would probably have access to it. Also, several MIT55 colleagues had been to the house, over the years. DS Harper had picked me up once about a year ago, when my car was being serviced. DC Freeman had done the same. And hadn't DS Rowan been in the incident room the other evening when I'd ordered some workout gear? He could have glimpsed my address...

When I went back to bed, I couldn't sleep. My private space had been invaded. The thought of someone I didn't know – or someone I did, even worse – shoving hacked-off animal pieces through my letterbox... What's more, whoever it was knew where I – and Brendan – lived, and could come back at any time.

My mind kept coming back to one thing. Was it only coincidence that they'd picked on a fox to mutilate, or did they know I hated foxes?

I dug into my memory. What had I said to DS Rowan in the incident room about foxes after he'd found those remains in

Tottenham cemetery? *I hate the things, personally*. DS Harper had been there too, and several others.

Could someone in MIT55 be working for the gang? If so, could one of the skull gang be paying them to help bring me down, and to attempt to sabotage Operation Rye?

Surely not. Exhaustion was playing tricks on my mind. But in a way, it made perfect sense.

By dawn, I felt wretched. If someone really did want to unhinge me, they were already halfway there.

JEZ

RAT HUNT

AFTER THE POLICE LEAVE, I GO OUT ON THE TERRACE AND drink a glass of wine from the bottle under my bed.

Am I turning into my mother? Then I feel bad for even thinking that, when she's only just died and even worse because she would still be here if it wasn't for me. I imagine Mum watching me right now. A shiver goes through me like someone's walked over my grave.

I can't believe what the police were asking. Jessamine, what do you talk about with Luke? Jessamine, are you banging all of Skull Crew? And all those questions about my mum. What the actual fuck? I'm surprised they didn't ask if I was peddling drugs too. That DI Waverley was too much.

There's no way I'm going to be calling him. No fucking way.

Rowena phones. Have I heard, the cops have arrested half of the crew?

'What?' I've no idea what she's talking about.

'They were at the church by Tottenham cemetery this

evening for Luke's initiation thing. The feds were waiting. Angel, Minty and Wolf are in the slammer and Zom got chased by cops in body armour who tried to shoot him! He had to hide in a kebab shop. V thinks someone tipped them off.'

'Oh, my lord. What about Luke, is he all right?'

'He's run off. No one knows where he is. V and Zom are going nuts.' Her voice goes quiet. 'He hasn't called you, has he?'

Fuck, is she V's spy or something? Maybe he's asked her to see what she can find out.

'No, I haven't heard from him. I've been a bit out of it actually, with my mum dying 'n' all...'

'Oh, you poor thing, I'm so sorry.' Rowena puts on her sympathetic voice. 'I shouldn't have bothered you with all this. You have other stuff on your mind right now, of course you do. When is the funeral, hun?'

After I manage to get rid of her, my brain goes into overdrive.

What if V finds out I've been talking to the cops? What if he thinks *I'm* the rat?

No, no, no. Why would I want to snitch on them? And how would I have known that Luke was going to be at the church?

Duh. V told me that Luke was going to be there, that's how. And now Luke's scarpered and the police almost caught Zom. V will be even more paranoid now. What would he think if he found out that this afternoon Luke told me he was going to run away, and I'd never said anything? He'd think I was on Luke's side, not his. He might think I gave the police information because I was scared of Zom hurting me and wanted him to be put in prison...

I finish the bottle of wine.

———

It's nearly midnight. I'm in bed, half dozing, when I get a WhatsApp call. I grab my phone thinking it might be Luke. But it's V.

'I know you're close to Luke,' he says. 'Did he tell you anything before he fucked off?'

'No.'

'You didn't know Luke was planning to take off?'

'No, I didn't. I know he was in touch with a teacher from school a few days ago. His English teacher, Miss Collins. She might have persuaded him to leave.' Hotlips Collins had better watch out.

'You think Luke might blab to the feds?'

'No, of course not.' I still hate Luke but I can't land him in the shit.

'What about you, missy?'

I get immediate palpitations. 'What about me?'

'What if the feds came looking for class As and asking questions about murders, what would you tell them?'

I clench my pelvic floor muscles. He knows about DI Waverley coming to question me.

'I wouldn't tell them anything. You know I wouldn't.'

He says he'll WhatsApp me soon. I hardly sleep that night thinking about Luke and DI Waverley and what V might do to me if he finds out I've been lying to him.

LUKE

A blast of noise wakes me. I sit upright. It's only another announcement, a list of names that mean nothing, each merging into the next like one long name.

We're stopping again, another place I've never heard of. I can't see anyone get off or on. It's dark outside. There's not enough light to read the station sign.

The train moves away, rattling and swaying. I check my phone – twenty minutes to go. It was meant to take an hour and a half from Stevenage where I changed trains, but there was a delay at Peterborough.

Miss Collins called earlier and left a message for me to call her back and let her know when I'll be arriving in Lincoln. She will drive up and meet me in the city and take me to the house where I can stay for a while.

I'm not sure I can trust Miss Collins – what if she says something to the police? Maybe she's said something already. But my return ticket to Lincoln cost twenty-two quid. I haven't got enough cash left to get somewhere else to stay.

Kirsty calls again. Aunt Jemma was pleased to have her visit, says she can stay as long as she wants. Kirsty sounds happier now. Her bedroom has a TV and there's fields and a lake outside instead of tower blocks. But Kevin was angry when she told him she wasn't coming home tonight. He said he'd tell the police if she isn't home tomorrow.

'Luke?' She says after I say goodbye.

'What?'

'Are you in trouble?'

I want to reassure her but I know she'll see through that.

'Yeah, Kirst, I am. But don't worry. I'll be all right once I've figured out what to do.'

'Be careful, won't you?' Her voice sounds small and frightened. A rush of love comes over me.

'I will. Be nice to Aunt Jemma and don't stay up too late.'

It's twenty past nine when we arrive at Lincoln. The platform is empty. It's weird to have no bags. I wish once more I'd not left my rucksack behind. At least that cat isn't lying on the ground with its throat slit. Then I remember Mrs Symonds lying on the floor and the blood seeping out of her throat, and go cold.

———

I wake up with a start. An orange light shines through dirty windows. I can't remember where I am. My body is stiff with cold and cramp. I'm lying on the floor. Then I remember a homeless guy pointing to a withered building saying I won't get a hostel now, so try in there.

The building is derelict. The ground floor is one big space and smells shitty. No sign of anyone else.

My phone lights with another WhatsApp notification. I'm going to ignore it and go back to sleep. Then I think it might be Miss Collins or Kirsty. But it's not.

Hey kid. I hope your enjoying your little holiday cos it's the last one you're going to get. You know what happens to slimy little worms?

I'm not going to forget how you fucked me over by running off like that, just as I was getting ready to welcome you in. Just so you know, Minty, Angel & Wolf got picked up yesterday after you fucked off. They're not happy, you can imagine. Especially as it looks like it was you who grassed us up.

If that's true, Luke, you'd better get ready to run faster than a rat out of its hole. Zom is itching to carve up your cute little face and ass, just as soon as I give him the say so. After he's finished, I guarantee all you'll want to do is crawl into your grave.

Sweet dreams,

V

I lie down and close my eyes but all I see is an oblong hole cut deep in the earth, waiting for me. I can't get rid of the picture in my head. I'm proper shook, like I've smoked too much skunk. My breathing is weird and I'm trembling. My blood rushes through my veins like a waterfall. I could die here and no one would know. Maybe that would be the best thing.

———

Next time I wake, a grimy light is making its way through cracked windows. Across the room, a sound like someone calling out in their sleep. I start. As my eyes get used to the gloom, what I thought was a pile of logs turns into the curled-up bodies of two men. I can't stay here.

No one's about. The day is chill and grey. I follow the road towards the city centre.

The first café is closed. The sign says it's open in thirty minutes. The next is closed too. I sit on the step and wait, shivering. I need a hot cup of tea. Mum would have made me one. She would have put her arms round me and told me everything would be all right.

Then I'm crying like a lost little boy. I try to hold back the tears but they won't stop.

———

I stare at my phone on the table. The battery is on eight per cent charge. If I'm going to call, it'll have to be now.

'Miss Collins? It's me, Luke.'

A long silence.

'Are you OK? I thought something had happened to you when you didn't call back.'

'I'm OK. Sorry, I didn't know what to do. Can you still help me?'

'Yes, I'll help you. Where are you?'

'Lincoln. In a café.'

'What's it called?'

I check the menu. 'The Blue Dolphin,' I reply, and give out the address.

'I'm still in London. It'll take me about three hours to get there. Can you stay where you are 'til then?'

I say yes.

'I'll see you about eleven, eleven thirty then.'

'OK.' I swallow the lump in my throat. 'Thanks, Miss Collins.'

I drink the rest of my tea. It's wonderfully hot.

Calm comes over me. No one's gonna rush me with a knife in here. Suddenly, I remember I haven't eaten since a packet of peanuts on the train yesterday evening. I order a scone and a bowl of porridge, then rest my head on my arms and close my eyes. She's coming. Miss Collins is coming.

CALLUM

1ST NOVEMBER: 8AM

'MORNING EVERYONE. OUR PRIORITY TODAY IS TO FIND AND arrest Luke, Deda and Edwards – Luke being top priority. We know he's vulnerable and quite likely shit scared at the moment.'

I took a sip of water. My mouth was dry. After about two hours sleep, I'd woken on edge, fractious and close to exhaustion, convinced that something horrible was going to happen to Luke before we could bring him in. Or to my son, perhaps. Before leaving for work I'd woken Brendan and instructed him to throw some things in a bag and get the next train to Wales. He was to stay there for however long it took us to catch the remaining fugitives. He'd been unhappy, to say the least.

'We've had no further CCTV sightings of Luke since yesterday evening when he passed through Finsbury Park and King's Cross/St Pancras stations. He could well be in eastern England by now.'

I took another sip of water, fighting to focus on what I was saying. An image of Luke's dead, mutilated body floated into my head. Just as well Pierce was taking the sodding media briefing.

'Anything from the search of Wolf's mother's house in Southend?'

'We found an item of clothing containing specks of blood,' DS Freeman replied. 'No results yet from Forensics.'

'Sandra, Ferret... How's it going with the search for Edwards's hideaway?'

'We're still plugging away,' DS Hanna replied, pushing up her glasses. She sounded a tad defensive. 'We've visited all the properties on our list centred on Barnet. We're about to start on another set of properties, further east.'

'We're throwing everything at it, sir,' DC Perry added. He wore jeans and trainers, and looked more unkempt than usual, his eyes shadowed and his jaw invisible under what looked like several days' growth. 'It was nearly midnight when we finished yesterday.'

'Keep up the good work, you two.'

I hurried through allocating the day's tasks. It was time to get on with finding the kid and the men he was running from.

'Thanks everyone for all your hard work. I know how disappointing it was to have Luke and Deda slip through our fingers yesterday... Let's pull out all the stops now to finish the job and bring these criminals to justice.'

'Are you all right, boss?' DC Harper cautiously approached my desk. 'You don't look so good.'

I hesitated. The stress must be getting to me – I'd even started to suspect Sam last night. Suddenly that seemed laughable.

'Something came through the letterbox last night. It was pretty nasty.'

DS Harper's eyed widened.

'No need for alarm, I'm quite OK.'

'I'll keep this under wraps, sir.'

'That would be a good idea, Sam, thank you.'

Word got around faster than lightning in this place. The less I said the better, until I found out who was responsible.

Sam scrutinised my face. 'Are you OK? I'd have been freaked out, if it was me.'

'It was pretty horrible, to be honest.'

I attempted a reassuring smile. Sam's hair was a less bright shade of auburn than it had been, I noticed. More natural-looking – and quite stunning. The colour wasn't at all natural though, I mused as I chugged down a coffee beside the machine. Just as she called herself Sam not Samaira, her Asian name. The 'Harper' was the result of a marriage gone wrong, I vaguely recalled. Maybe away from work, she was someone else entirely...

I thumped the wall.

God's sake, Callum, you're losing it.

No way was Sam behind this. I needed to keep my faculties so I could find evidence of who really was behind this attempt to intimidate me. The alternative was a path to madness.

My phone rang. It was Bailey, calling me back. From the end of the corridor, I outlined my grotesque discovery the night before.

'Jesus, that's all we need. Are you all right?'

'I'll survive.'

'Given what happened to Nora Symonds, I'd be happier if you and your son stayed somewhere else for a while. At least until we've rounded up the remaining offenders.'

'I've already sent my son away – I'm not letting them drive *me* out too.'

'It's your choice, Callum,' he said gruffly.

'They're just toying with me, trying to mess with my mind. If it *is* the gang that's responsible, that is.'

'Who else would it be?'

I didn't reply.

LUKE

I JOLT UPRIGHT. MISS COLLINS IS STARING AT ME.

'Luke? I'm sorry, I didn't mean to startle you.' She keeps her distance, not moving, like she doesn't know what to do. Before, we'd been teacher and pupil – what are we now? I get to my feet, wipe sleep from my eyes. She doesn't look like a teacher anymore. Her eyebrows are straggly, her lipstick has come off and there's a spot on her chin.

'Hi, Miss Collins. You look different.'

'It's the jeans, maybe.' She smiles, looks down by my feet. 'No bags?'

'Had to leave my backpack behind when I ran away.'

'Do you need to get some T-shirts and a toothbrush while we're in town? The cottage is in the middle of nowhere.'

Miss Collins takes me to M&S and helps me stock up. Socks, boxers, Ts, tracksuit bottoms and a beany. I also buy a phone charger. Enough to last a few days – a few weeks, probably.

———

'Where's the cottage?'

'It's in the Lincolnshire Wolds. My parents rent it out during the summer.'

Miss Collins switches the radio on, hops from one station to the next and turns it off again. We don't talk much. She says she hasn't told anyone that she's helping me.

A glimmer of sun comes through the clouds, making the wet roads glisten. The road gets twisty and narrow. We climb hills, pass through woods. I put the window down and listen to birds chirping. The air smells nice. We turn into a bumpy track just wider than the car.

'This is it.' She gestures at a small house with rose pink walls. 'The view isn't bad, is it?'

I get out of the car. The house is on the edge of a huge field. Above it, the sky stretches out for miles and miles.

'I've never seen anything like it.'

She joins me with the bags and a big smile. A sign on the wall says 'Rose Cottage'.

'Let's go inside, shall we?'

———

I race around the house, peering into rooms and leaning out of windows. From the top rooms there are views for miles. I feel like an excited kid on holiday.

My bedroom has a sloping ceiling. I love that I have to bend my head when I stand on the lower side. There's a big window facing west. From the smaller window I can see a thin glistening road and the chimneys of another house poking through trees. It's the only other house I can see.

I flop onto the bed. From here I can see fields and hedgerows, and in the distance a huge oak tree. The sun is getting low, making everything golden. I've never been anywhere so peaceful. This is nothing like London, nothing like Angel's cramped noisy flat on the estate or the falling-apart house that used to be home. I'm safe here. I never want to leave.

'Luke! Are you coming down?'

Miss Collins is rushing about dusting ledges and opening curtains. Her blue jeans and furry ankle boots make her look like a teenager. I get the feeling she likes looking after me. I plonk myself into an armchair and press the button to tilt it backwards.

'I'm going to cook supper. Do you like shepherd's pie?'

We eat at an old wooden table in the kitchen. Miss Collins hasn't said anything for a while. She looks serious, like she did in English class when no one answered her question properly. She's stopped eating her shepherd's pie.

'Are you going to tell me what's going on? The police are after you. They think you helped to murder that woman, Nora Symonds, on the estate. Did you hurt her, Luke?'

The sick feeling comes back. I knew this couldn't last, this little piece of happiness.

'What happened that day, Luke? I need to know everything.'

I tell her about Ginger spotting the woman and how I followed her up to her flat, then rang on the door and went inside with Minty and Zom.

'I didn't want to go in with them. But...' Why hadn't I run away? 'I had to do what Zom said. He had a knife. Me and Minty, we did what he said.'

I can't look up. I'm scared of what might show in her face. I tell her the rest. How Zom gave his knife to Minty and rushed at Mrs Symonds. Minty dropping the knife when she pepper-sprays him and me picking it up when Zom tells me to.

A gasp.

'You stabbed her?'

'No.' My voice wobbles. 'I couldn't do it.'

'Who killed her?'

I try to summon up images of Zom stabbing Mrs Symonds in the throat. I can't. But I saw what he did afterwards.

'Zom did,' I say. 'He cut off her lips too.'

'Oh my god.'

'He told me that if I ever tell anyone what happened, he'd cut off mine too.'

'Oh my god,' she says again and puts her hand on mine. Suddenly she gets up and so do I. I feel her arms tight around me and her breasts pressing into me. Then she pulls away.

'I'm sorry.' I don't know if she means she's sorry for what happened in that flat or for hugging me.

She takes the plates out with the remains of the shepherd's pie and comes back with two bowls of salted caramel ice cream. We eat it in silence.

'I shouldn't be doing this.' Miss Collins looks at me and away. 'I could get into trouble.'

'Do you want me to go?' I put down my spoon.

'Of course I don't.'

I help clear the dishes then we watch a film. This is the first normal thing I've done for ages. The most normal thing, anyway.

———

'You need to go to bed, young man.' Miss Collins sounds like a teacher again.

'Do I have to?' I pretend scowl.

'You've been yawning for the past hour. Go on, upstairs. Sleep tight, see you in the morning. No more looking at your phone.'

'See you in the morning, Miss—'

I stop. She says I can call her Izzy but I've got so used to calling her Miss Collins.

Halfway upstairs, I remember my phone. I've been keeping it turned off in case the police are tracking it.

Leaving the front door on the nib, I run down the road for a few minutes until I get to another house and stand outside. Then I turn on my phone. There's a text from Kirsty.

You need to call my dad. He's called 3 times this evening asking if I've heard from you. He's going ments.

I call Kevin. He answers at the first ring.

'What the fuck's goin' on, Luke? I've been worried sick. The cops have been asking where you are an' if I've heard from you. Kirsty's at her aunt's, she refuses to go to school or come home, says it's what you told her to do.' His voice bellows into my ear so I have to move the phone away. 'What the fuck is goin' on?'

'She'll be safe at Aunt Jemma's,' I say. 'If she comes home, or starts going to school something bad might happen.'

'What do you mean?'

'I don't think they'll try to hurt her, but—'

'Who are "they" for crise-sake?'

I can't say their names, can't even say Skull Crew.

'I'm scared, Dad. They'll kill me if they find me.'

TV in the background.

'Luke, whatever you've done... I promise I won't be angry. I know I've not been much of a father to you but please, listen. You have to turn yourself in to the cops. You've no right to put your sister in danger. And you'll be safer in the nick than are you hidin' out from those bloody gangsters.'

I want to shout at him. I can't go to the police! They'd lock me up in a cell and I'd shrivel up and die.

'Please, Luke. Just turn yourself in.'

He's gone. I check my messages again. Thank God, there's nothing else from V. I start typing a message to Jez, and change my mind. I think of what Kevin said about giving myself up. It comes back suddenly – I didn't call him Kevin, I called him Dad.

I look up at the sky. The stars are crazy bright. A fuzzy band crosses the blackness – the Milky Way. I haven't seen it for real before.

I stay there for ages, trying to take in the whole night sky so wherever I am I'll be able to see it.

CALLUM

As soon as I got home, I phoned Brendan in Wales. He was in better spirits and understood that I wanted him to be safe.

'How long?'

'I don't know. We're in the final stages.'

'OK, then.' A pause. 'What was it that came through the front door?'

'Something very unpleasant.'

'What?'

'Please, Brendan. It's not important.'

'All right then. Good luck catching the villains.'

I took my plate of baked beans on toast to the living room and ate it on my lap in front of the TV. My thoughts veered back to Luke and his possible whereabouts. Something was going on with Isobel Collins... She'd told me she was taking the day off to go to a funeral. When I'd phoned to tell her that Luke had run away from the gang, I'd sensed something slightly off.

I rang her landline at home – it switched to voicemail – then her mobile.

'Isobel Collins? It's DI Callum Waverley.'

'Oh, hello.' She sounded flustered and less than pleased to hear my voice.

'I wanted to check in with you again about Luke Delaney. Have you had any contact with him since I spoke to you earlier?'

No reply.

'Isobel?'

'Sorry, I'm a bit tired. No, I haven't. Why, has anything happened?'

'I'm worried about Luke. If we don't find him soon, he's liable to be in serious danger. Do you have any idea where he might have gone? Any idea at all?'

Another hesitation. I could almost hear the cogs turning in her brain.

'I don't, I'm sorry. I'll let you know if he gets in touch.'

'Miss Collins. Helping a person who's wanted by the police is a serious offence. If that's what you're doing, you could be charged with assisting an offender and sent to prison. It could mean the end of your teaching career.'

'I understand. I promise I'll let you know if I hear from him.'

'Where are you?'

'I'm at a friend's place... She's looking after me for a couple of days.'

I ended the call. I suspected Isobel Collins was lying. Her phone's location hadn't shown up on the call details, annoyingly. But the super wasn't likely to authorise the tracking of her phone without something stronger to go on than my hunch.

I stayed on the sofa with the TV off and the lights dimmed, listening. Without the usual sounds of Brendan helping himself to snacks in the kitchen and thuds of bass from his room, it felt deathly quiet. Once in a while a tube train rumbled past on the way to East Finchley station and the house creaked as it settled for the night.

LUKE

I GET UP AT DAWN, SHOVE AN APPLE INTO MY JACKET POCKET for breakfast and leave a note for Miss Collins saying I've gone out for a walk.

It's cold and blowy. I start walking uphill. After a while I'm standing on the top of a rounded ridge, looking down on Rose Cottage. I can see for miles and miles in every direction. In the distance, looking east, I make out a band of pale blue. Happiness rushes through me, mixed with sadness. The sea has always been a special thing. I wanted to see it one last time.

On the way back to Rose Cottage I have tears in my eyes. I want to keep walking and walking and see everything there is to see.

———

Miss Collins runs out of the cottage when I walk through the gate.

'You didn't answer your phone!'

'I didn't take it.' I drink a glass of water in the kitchen.

'We have to talk, Luke.' Miss Collins leans against the tall cupboard. 'When you phoned me the other day you were so scared and upset... I wanted to help you. I thought you could stay here for a while, that it might help you work out what you want to happen next.' She bites her lip. 'But I wasn't thinking properly. I've been an idiot, a total idiot.'

'You aren't an idiot. And I know I can't stay here anymore.'

She comes closer. 'I don't want to send you away. But a detective phoned me last night. He asked if I knew where you were. He told me I'd be in trouble for helping you.'

My heart stops. 'Did you tell him I'm with you?'

'No, I didn't tell him anything.'

'How did he know your number? Did you talk to him before?'

'He came to the school last week with another detective. He wanted to speak to everyone who knew you.'

'What's his name?'

'DI Waverley.' She puts her hand on my arm. 'Luke—'

I shrug it off.

'Luke, you need to turn yourself in. If this goes on any longer... Let me drive you to the local police station.'

Images flash through my head. Me in handcuffs, being led to a cell. Inside, trapped, unable to breathe.

'I'll turn myself in soon,' I say. 'I have to go to London first. I need to see someone.'

———

Miss Collins drives me to Lincoln. She asks who I'm going to meet but I don't say. I feel bad though, for not trusting her when she's done so much to help me.

We walk together into the station. I've got my return ticket and phone in my pocket, and in the backpack I got with Miss Collins are the clothes we bought together and a ton of food –

sandwiches, apples, peanuts and a tub of flapjacks. I feel like a
kid leaving for his first day at school.

We stop at the ticket barrier. My train leaves at 3.27pm – ten
minutes. I shuffle my feet. There's a big lump in my throat.

'Bye, Miss Collins – Izzy. Thanks for everything.'

'Look after yourself.'

Her eyes are damp. She touches my arm.

The train comes on time. Once we've been going half an
hour, I unwrap my phone. I've covered it in foil, which is meant
to stop it transmitting GPS signals. I check my messages.
Nothing new, only the one I found from Jez first thing this
morning. I read it once more.

Come to Ferry Boat Inn at 6 this evening. I need to see you I'm in trouble

CALLUM

THE MORNING BRIEFING WAS BRIEF. THERE HAD BEEN NO further sightings of Luke Delaney. Forensics had matched the blood on the clothing in 'Wolf' Banefield's mother's house with that of Solita Milton; Banefield was going to need a good lawyer. But the palmprint found on the hall of Mrs Symonds's flat wasn't a match to Minty.

'We already know it's not Deda's – which leaves Luke Delaney as a possible match.' I rubbed my eyes, trying to focus. Last night, I'd dreamed I was trapped in a dark pit full of skulls. 'OK, everyone, let's get on with the search. We need to do our utmost to find Luke before Edwards and Deda do.'

While I was on my second coffee, Kevin Delaney phoned.

'I spoke to Luke last night. I thought you should know.'

'He called you?'

'He called me back.'

'What time?'

'About eleven. I asked him to give himself up.'

Kevin Delaney didn't have any idea where Luke was staying or who might be helping him. We'd checked that he wasn't at his aunt Jemma's along with Kirsty; Kevin had already told me that his daughter was staying with her, as Luke was concerned that she might be hurt by the gang.

'Can you give me the number Luke called you from?' When he'd been asked for Luke's number earlier, Mr Delaney had insisted he didn't have Luke's most recent number.

'I don't know. It didn't show up on my phone.'

'Mr Delaney, Luke's life is in danger.'

A sigh down the line. 'I'll ask my daughter again.'

He called back ten minutes later and gave me a mobile number. I thanked him and told him that the number could help us trace Luke.

'Let me know immediately you have any further contact with your stepson, and tell him he needs to turn himself in right away. We'll treat him fairly. We know he's in danger from older gang members and we want him to be safe.'

At the end of the morning there still had been no further sightings of Luke, and no further leads as to his whereabouts.

Instead of going out for lunch, I did a few shoulder rolls at my desk.

4.15PM

My mobile rang. My heart jolted when I saw it was Isobel Collins.

'I lied to you last night.' She sounded upset. 'I'm really sorry. Luke has been staying with me.'

I grabbed a pen. 'Where is he?'

'He's on his way to London. I dropped him at Lincoln station an hour ago. He's been with me in the Lincolnshire Wolds since yesterday lunchtime.'

Frustration surged through me. What was this woman playing at? If only she'd told me the truth last night, a team could have gone to the property and arrested Luke. As it was, he was still in danger and I'd have to arrest Isobel Collins for assisting an offender.

'What train did he get?'

'The 3.27pm to King's Cross.'

'Where was he headed, exactly?'

'He wouldn't say. He said he was going to see someone in London, that's all. I don't know who or where.'

Kirsty? No. Something told me it was Jessamine.

'What was he wearing when he got on the train?'

'Jeans, hoody and trainers. He was carrying his jacket and a blue rucksack.'

'Thank you for that, Miss Collins.' I promised I'd be in touch.

I checked my watch. 4.22pm. The 3.27pm to King's Cross was due in at 5.23pm. I asked DC Perry to contact the transport police and alert them to Luke's expected arrival at the terminus. I arranged for a plain-clothes Tactical Support Group team and gave instructions for them to arrest Luke Delaney, should he be spotted. He was unarmed, I stressed, though likely to attempt to evade arrest.

Still no pings from Luke's phone. We had received authorisation to track it; a telecoms tech had set up a laptop in the incident room which would show any communications between the phone and nearby mobile towers. It was likely the phone was either turned off or had been abandoned.

5.33PM

The TSG leader radioed in to the incident room. His voice was despondent.

'No sign of a boy of Luke's description getting off the 5.23 train.' I went over and grabbed the radio.

'What, he got off the train and vanished? He must be on it still.'

'We're searching the train right now.'

Damn it, we were going to lose him. There were six underground lines leading out of King's Cross. I alerted PS Jacobs to the possibility of Luke Delaney arriving at Effra Lane estate and spoke to DC Perry.

'Right, Ferret. See if we can we get any more TSGs to cover the exits of the local tube stations – say Tottenham Hale, Wood Green and Finsbury Park.'

I called everyone over for a brainstorming session. We needed to be in Luke's head to have any chance of finding him.

'Where's Luke going for this meeting and who is he seeing? Any thoughts?'

'His stepdad?' DS Harper replied. She had dark circles under her eyes.

DS Hanna shook her head. 'Why would Luke go to see his stepdad?'

'He could be meeting his half-sister,' DS Rowan offered. 'He's hardly likely to be heading to the estate, with cops and gangsters crawling all over it. Or the family home for that matter.'

'Kirsty says he's not arranged to meet her,' DS Harper replied. 'I believe her. She told me just now that Luke hasn't been in contact since yesterday.'

'That leaves Jessamine,' I said. 'We know they fell out. My hunch is he wants to make up with her. Or her with him.'

Rowan looked up from his laptop. 'The nearest tube to her house is Wood Green. Or there's Alexandra Park railway station.'

DS Freeman swivelled his bulk to and fro.

'Would he really risk coming back to London just to see her?'

'He would if he cares about her.' Sam rolled her eyes. 'Love, ever heard of it?'

'I don't think Luke would risk going to her house,' I said. 'It's more likely to be somewhere they both know, where we wouldn't think to look.'

Freeman smiled. 'What, like a pub or something?'

'They're underage, Rob,' Sam shot back. 'They're not meant to be hanging out in pubs.'

'Haha.'

'It could be a pub, or maybe a park,' Rowan said. 'But we can't go to them all.'

'No more TSGs available, sir,' Ferret called out.

I exhaled in frustration. 'What about uniforms?'

'There's none to spare. I've already asked.'

I banged my fist onto the desk harder than I meant to, garnering raised eyebrows.

'OK, we'll have to leave the tube stations unmanned.'

I called Isobel Collins.

'Isobel? Can you do something for me? It's urgent.'

I ran through what I needed her to do. I didn't expect Luke to answer Isobel Collins's call. He may have switched off his phone to avoid being tracked, and in any case the phone might not be getting a signal if he was on the underground. But if he did pick up, there was a chance he might listen to Isobel and turn himself in before all this ended with something terrible happening. If Luke was planning to return to anywhere near his old stomping ground, sooner or later the Skull Crew would find out.

'He picked up,' Miss Collins told me a few minutes later. 'But he put the phone down as soon as I said my name.'

Fifteen minutes later I took a deep breath and dialled Luke's number. It was worth a try. The phone at the other end rang four times then picked up. At the other end, the sound of breathing overlaid with traffic.

'Hello, Luke. It's me, Callum. I need to talk to you. Please, hear me out.'

No response.

'Luke, we need to get you to a safe place—'

The line went dead.

JEZ

A PART I CAN'T REFUSE

I CHECK MY WATCH FOR THE THIRTIETH TIME. WHERE THE hell is Luke? He was meant to be here at six and it's nearly half past. I wish I hadn't suggested this place to meet.

I take a few deep breaths, feeling another panic attack coming on. On the bus yesterday coming back from meeting V, I suddenly felt faint and nearly keeled over onto the woman sitting next to me. She said it was probably a panic attack and if it happened again, I should put a paper bag over my head – or breathe into a paper bag, that was it.

The shaggy-bearded bloke behind the bar is staring at me like I've got chickenpox all over my face. I turn away from him and check my bag again for the letter.

'You're still here,' Luke says.

'Duh. Ten out of ten for observation skills.'

He pulls off his backpack, takes off his jacket and whips off his beany. He's wearing clear glasses with thick black frames.

'Did you miss your train or something? I've made my way through a glass of wine already.'

He doesn't reply. He glances around, pulling at his T-shirt like he's too hot.

'I didn't know you wore glasses. They kinda suit you.'

'They're a disguise.' He takes off the glasses. 'I thought I saw a bunch of cops on the platform pulling into King's Cross, so I nicked them from a guy on the train – and the beany.'

I smile. 'You're getting good at this.'

He looks at me like I'm talking nonsense. I know I shouldn't make light of the situation but it's my way of dealing with it. If I didn't laugh, I'd cry and cry and never stop.

'Where did you stay last night?' I ask, trying to sound casual.

'Does it matter?'

I'm pretty sure now that I know who he's been staying with. I try not to care. We're not sleeping together, are we? He's not made any promises to me. I must stop being a jealous bitch.

'What did you want to see me about?' Luke looks cross. He digs the heel of his hand into the table. 'I came cos I thought you were in trouble.'

'I am in trouble.'

'What is it?'

'It's Zom. He threatened to hurt me.'

'What?' I see the concern in his face and know for sure he cares about me.

'It was yesterday evening. He took out his knife and...'

Luke's face has gone almost white.

'Let's go outside,' I say, getting up from my stool and hooking my bag over my shoulder. 'People might hear us in here.'

He doesn't want to go outside. He wants to get a glass of water and have a pee.

'I'll see you outside in a minute, then.'

I pace up and down the parking area. I feel sick. What's

wrong with me? I need to tell Luke – we'll hide out somewhere, together. I'll tell him right now.

I turn to run inside the pub and stop. Luke is coming through the door and walking towards me.

There's a screech of brakes and smell of burning rubber. A white van pulls up. Luke sees the four men in balaclavas piling out of the van and looks at me. I'll never forget that look as long as I live.

CALLUM

I FORCED MYSELF TO TAKE LONG, STEADY BREATHS. THE slender thread of hope inside me was almost broken. Since I'd made that call to Luke, I'd been cursing myself. He'd have bolted by now. At least no one apart from Luke and the officers around me would know I'd made that call; the caller ID is always withheld.

'We've got him, guv! Data's coming in.' The telecoms guy pointed to the laptop screen, showing a bleeping dot at the centre of a shaded circle superimposed on a map of north London streets. 'The phone is in the vicinity of Jarrow Road in Tottenham Hale.'

'Hallelujah! DC Perry, get on the radio and wake up Sergeant Jacobs. Alert Tactical Support too. I want Luke brought in, first chance we get.'

It would take five to ten minutes minimum, I estimated, for a TSG team to get to Tottenham Hale, and the same for the surveillance team. No one would be within reach of Luke yet.

'Looks like he could be heading towards Ferry Lane,' DS Rowan said.

'There's a pub there,' DS Freeman said. 'Uh oh, the signal's gone.'

I peered at the laptop screen. The dot showing Luke's phone's estimated location had disappeared. We waited in silence for the phone signal to come back.

'I'm off for a pee,' I said when I couldn't hold it in any longer, jogging into the corridor towards the men's room. Something would kick off now, no doubt.

'Boss!' Ferret shouted as I ran into the incident room. 'Suspected kidnap of Luke Delaney. One of the bar staff at the Ferry Boat Inn called 999 just now and reported seeing someone being kidnapped. A mixed-race youth, sixteen to seventeen years old, five feet ten inches, buzz cut in a Puffa jacket, jeans and trainers. The youth had just walked outside the pub when a white Ford Transit van pulled up. Four men in balaclavas got out and shoved the youth into the van. A girl got in too, it appears without being forced. White female, sixteen to seventeen years old, five feet nine inches, long brown hair. The two had been talking in the pub five minutes beforehand. Before that the girl had been on her own and looking agitated like she was waiting for someone. The van sped off down Ferry Lane towards Walthamstow.'

'Did they get the reg?'

''Fraid not. There's a long scratch or mark across the left rear door, though.'

What were the chances of finding a white Transit van in the dark without the registration number? I told DC Perry to get hold of the commander of the kidnap response operation, then I briefed them on the situation. Everyone in that van was to be arrested as soon as it was safe to do so. One or more of the kidnappers were likely to be carrying a dangerous weapon.

I leaned on my desk and gulped down the rest of my Coke,

caught between shock and despondency. My worst fear had come true.

'Looks like Luke's been abducted by Zom and the Skull Crew,' I said, 'with the help of the lovely Jessamine.'

Freeman didn't hold back. 'The kid's in the shit. Down the crapper.'

DS Harper stretched out her fingers and glared at Freeman as if she'd like to rake her nails across his cheek.

'It's a classic honeytrap,' Rowan said. 'Jessamine Robbins lures Luke Delaney back to gang territory, and now...'

'They're gonna make mincemeat of him.' Freeman finished the sentence with a belch.

Rowan sucked his teeth. 'What a bitch.'

'She's a nasty piece of work.' Even Sam couldn't disagree.

What was wrong with Jessamine Robbins, I wondered. How could anyone be so entirely lacking in any moral compass?

'Any thoughts on where they're taking him?'

'The nearest ditch?' Freeman offered. 'Sorry, boss.'

'They have to be off to V's hideout,' Rowan said.

'Exactly,' I said. 'They're taking him to the big boss so he can dish out whatever punishment he sees fit.'

And we were powerless to stop them. We could do little except watch and wait. A dedicated ops room would be set up elsewhere to handle the deployment of covert response and firearms teams, and hostage negotiators. Not that I expected much in the way of negotiation. I kicked the waste-bin in frustration, sending it scudding across the floor. Empty cans and Mars Bar wrappers tumbled out. No, it wasn't very professional. But if Pierce or Bailey had walked in at that moment, I couldn't have cared less.

'OK, everyone. Off your phones, listen up.'

The few officers still in the incident room looked at me expectantly. DS Hanna stopped her phone conversation and looked away from the spreadsheet on her monitor. She was coordinating the search for Edwards's house; all the DCs were out visiting the remaining properties in London with a monkey puzzle tree in their gardens.

'We're not going to give up on finding Luke. Our number one priority is to work out where they're taking that kid and stop him getting delivered to Edwards on a plate.'

My stomach churned at the thought of what the gang might do to him. I'd seen enough mobile phone videos of teenagers being tortured by gang members intent on revenge, to know what could happen to Luke. We had to get to him before Vincent Edwards did.

LUKE

I'm alone in the dark, sitting on the floor of V's cellar. My arms ache from being behind my back and my wrists hurt. I heard the key turn in the lock when they left. There's no way I can get out of here.

They took my phone and backpack, and all my clothes apart from my T-shirt and boxers. Then Zom, Spicer, Karim and Angel took turns to spit in my face.

I can't stop thinking about Jez and how she turned on me. I never once thought that she might betray me. Turns out I was wrong. That hurts more than anything. It's worse even than wondering what they're going to do to me.

Now my eyes are used to the dark, the chink of light under the door is enough to see by. The altar with the weird statues has fresh candles in the candlesticks. There's a narrow table a few feet away from it, like the one you lie on at the doctor's. Stacked up against the walls are packing crates with red numbers stamped on the side. I can't see the skulls from where I am, that's the only good thing.

A sound up above. My heart thuds. Lights flash on, the door

opens and V appears at the top of the staircase. He's dressed in a black sweater and black jeans.

'Long time no see.' He looks totally calm. That scares me all the more.

He comes down the steps, bends down to me, takes hold of my jaw and looks into my eyes. His eyes don't blink. They draw me in like wells that go down forever. I can't turn my head away.

'Aren't you going to say hello, young man?' He kisses his teeth. 'Manners aren't what they used to be.'

'What do you want?' It bursts out of me. 'Why can't you leave me alone? I haven't done anything to hurt you!'

V stands up straight. I have to tilt my head up to look at him.

'Someone's been calling you, I see.' He takes a phone out of his pocket and holds it up. It's mine. The screen shows my incoming calls. He points to a withheld number. 'It's the DI who went to see your friend Jez, a little bluebird told me. I know all about DI Waverley.'

'No, it's not him!' How does he know that the DI called me? Maybe he has black magic powers after all.

'You know him, don't you? You called him from outside the church. That's why he came running over to hoover up my boys just as you bolted.'

His eyes gleam. My mouth is frozen in horror. Then words burst out.

'No, I didn't. I swear I didn't!'

'Jez told me everything. How you had your escape all planned out. How you mouthed off to your English teacher.'

'I told Miss Collins I wanted to get away. But I never went to the police. I swear I didn't.' My teeth are clacking against each other. With fear, not cold.

'I know what you've done, Luke. What hurts me the most isn't that you fucked us over by spilling to the feds. What really hurts is that at the very moment I put my trust in you, you run away like a fucking cat with a dog up its arse.'

He dips his head all of a sudden like he's going to headbutt me. When I flinch, he smiles.

'Luke, Luke. Why did you do it? I was touched when you said you wanted to be a racing driver. You had me in your palm, kid. I was ready to help you reach for your dreams.'

'I'm sorry. I-I didn't mean to hurt you.'

'Don't worry. I'll make it up to you, I promise.'

V walks to the altar. He lights three tall candles, then some more. Soon the whole thing is a shimmer of light.

'What are you gonna do?' My heart is beating too fast. I'm sweating though I'm icy cold.

He points to a large glass jug below the narrow table. I didn't see it before.

'That's to hold your blood, Luke. We're going to take over from where we left off. Only this time, the cat is you.'

He lopes away. The door snaps shut.

I remember that poor creature struggling to escape Minty's bag, and beat my knuckles into my brow. No way can I get out of this. I think of the first time I saw V, after the fight on the rec. How impressed I was and how much I wanted to impress him. What was I thinking? How I hate that stupid kid.

CALLUM

'SANDRA, FERRET – WHAT'S THE LATEST ON THE SEARCH FOR Edwards?'

While sporadic updates on the search for Luke's abductors came in from the control room, I focused my efforts on locating where Vincent Edwards was holed up. It felt as if we were looking for a pin in a hundred haystacks.

'We've visited nine out of the twenty-four properties on our second list,' DS Hanna replied. 'All north of the river.'

'Keep going, guys. We'll search for Edwards's hideout all night, if we have to.'

'What if Bev Milton's leading us up the garden path?' DS Rowan shook his head. 'Mr Big might live in Brighton, for all we know.'

'This is all we've got to go on, right now. If you've got a better idea, let's have it.' Glaring at him, I took a slurp of Coke Zero. Rowan had voiced my own misgivings, though. Quite possibly the house wasn't in north London at all.

I called Bev Milton once more and asked if she'd had any contact with her son.

'I'm sorry, Callum. Jayden isn't answering his phone.'

The latest unintelligible update on the kidnap response operation came over the radio.

'They've spotted a white Transit van with a mark on a rear door,' Ferret called out. 'Near Barnet Hospital, heading north. 'TSG and SO19 are standing by.'

I waited, my frustration mounting, trying not to think about what Luke Delaney's abductors could be doing to him. My request to get a chopper out looking had been turned down. I turned to the detectives gathered around the desk.

'Where the hell are they?'

DS Freeman stopped gnawing his finger.

'They have to be in Barnet by now. If that's where they were headed.'

'They could be in Glasgow by now too. Let's face it, we have no fucking idea where they've gone.' By the time we found out, Luke could be lying on the ground with a bullet through his head.

'Still nothing from Luke's phone?'

The telecoms guy shook his head.

'It's either turned off, destroyed or is somewhere where there's no signal.'

'What about Jessamine's?'

'Not a peep.'

Another smidgeon of hope vanished. By now, Luke had to be with the gang leader, wherever that was. We'd not had a peep out of Jessamine's mobile phone, either – most likely she'd abandoned it after our visit and was using another.

'Uh oh, wrong van,' DC Perry called out. 'The Transit van turned into a McDonald's and a white man in his sixties got out.'

I scrunched the Coke can and grabbed my phone. This was

intolerable. I had to do something; however unlikely it was to yield a result.

'I'm going to join in the search. Ferret, call me at once if there's anything significant. Sandra, send that second list of addresses to my phone. Rowan, Freeman, Harper... Brainstorm to see if you can come up with any fresh ideas and do whatever you can do to help Sandra.'

'Shall I come with you, boss?' DS Harper was out of her chair already.

I hesitated. I ought to have another officer as back up. Although Sam was as capable as a bloke in many ways – I suspected she was a faster runner than Freeman – I didn't want to risk her being hurt. The other thing was difficult to admit to myself. Since those fox parts had come through my letterbox, I no longer trusted any of my officers one hundred per cent. Not even Sam.

JEZ

ONE LAST THING

I'M WRITING THIS SITTING ON THE TOILET SEAT IN THE bathroom. No one downstairs is missing me yet, hopefully. After throwing up, I feel slightly better – and as my notebook is in my bag with me...

It all kicked off half an hour ago. V came into the room where we were all sitting and told us to 'Come down and watch the show'.

Since they picked up me and Luke, I've pretended I'm going along with them. I said I was glad they're holding Ratboy, as V calls Luke now.

'Come on babe, get your ass over here,' Zom said. 'You gonna be part of this too.'

I knew if I didn't do what Zom said, he'd make me, so I went with him and the others down the cellar steps. I don't care anymore what happens to me, but I care about Luke and what happens to him.

It was like Las Vegas down there, every single candle on the altar lit. A tall man in a black tracksuit with skull mask stood in front of a long table. I didn't realise it was V at first – it looked like someone in a horror movie. When I saw Luke, I shoved my hand over my mouth to stop my scream. He was lying flat on the table in his underwear, tied by the wrists and ankles.

V reached for a knife. The blade reflected dozens of tiny flames. Luke made a sound that made the back of my neck tingle. His head moved towards the row of chairs. His face was grey. I don't know if he saw me. My hands started to shake. I wanted to tell V to let Luke go, I wanted to claw at his face. But I said nothing, did nothing.

Spicer leaned across me to Zom.

'This is gonna be better than the fuckin' Superbowl.'

'You see OK, girl?'

V moved the tip of the blade down Luke's left arm. A line of red beads appeared on his skin. Luke's leg juddered and V smiled. My stomach flipped.

'Excuse me, I need the loo. Must've had too much to drink.' I grabbed my bag, smiling at Zom. 'Back in a jiffy.'

I hurried into the kitchen and searched for my phone – Zom took it away from me when we were on the way here. Eventually I found it, turned off, beside the toaster. Thank god.

———

The phone still has a thin slice of battery left and two bars of signal.

So, this is it. I'm done with writing now. I'm done with everything, except for one last thing.

LUKE

Someone is cutting me. I know blood is coming out because my arms are wet. It doesn't hurt anymore. But each cut is a shock, makes my heart batter my chest. The cords around my wrists and ankles keep me in place, though I keep tugging at them. I wonder how long it will take for him to kill me.

I can't see his face. There's only a skull staring at me, a death mask. I wonder if his face is a mask too.

Everyone is far away; they can't help me. I turn my head and look at their faces, but they're blurred like I'm underwater.

Please. Stop.

The words come into my head but I don't know if I'm saying them. V pulls off the mask. His mouth curls up like a smile and he puts the knife on the altar.

I'm cold. The room is fading, I haven't long left. I close my eyes, feel myself leaving.

'Stop! Leave him alone!'

Jez is running towards me. She stops, looks at me. Her long

dark hair drapes over her shoulders. Her face is flushed and tears are running down her cheeks. She's the most beautiful girl I've ever seen.

V steps away from me.

'He didn't snitch, he didn't!' Jez yells. She picks up the knife from the altar. Blood drips off the blade. 'He never called the police. He would never betray you.'

'You did though, didn't you?' V's smiling.

She tries to cut the cord at my wrist but V grabs her hair and yanks it, pulling Jez along. She screams. V lets go, she loses her balance and smashes into the altar. The knife falls. Candles topple. Flames eat up the black cloth.

Jez looks straight into my eyes. She opens her mouth like she wants to tell me something. Then V turns to Jez with a snarl. He's holding the knife. The blade flashes and her body goes still.

Something explodes by the wall. I strain my neck to see what's going on. Sparks and smoke are shooting out of one of the crates. I tug at my bindings.

Let me go, I try to shout. But my voice won't come out. No one takes any notice.

A noise from the top of the stairs like wood splitting. The lights go off. Everyone is running.

Then nothing.

CALLUM

'HOW MANY MORE TO GO?'

Sam consulted her phone and looked up at me from the passenger seat.

'Six.'

'Plug in the coordinates.'

Wearily, I started the car. I had reached the end of my tether. This was a fool's errand, surely. Nearly every detached or semi-detached house in north London with a monkey puzzle tree, or any vaguely spiky looking shrub close by, had been visited. So far, none had raised the slightest suspicion that they were sheltering the leader of a violent drugs gang.

Ahead, the Mondeo's headlights carved out two bores in the mist. Street lamps were fewer and the roads emptier, here on the northern fringes of London, a few miles from the M25. Teams from SO19 and TSG were ready, in case of a miracle. Luke's phone was still dead – Luke could be too, for all we knew.

This would certainly be a good time for some divine intervention, I thought, as we passed a church. Seeing the small thin slabs of stone sticking up, I had an impulse to stop. Did Edwards live near a graveyard? That would suit his proclivities. Maybe we should have focused on church conversions...

The futility of it all hit me. I pulled up by the side of the road and lowered my head onto the wheel. We'd wasted hours, days, in this pointless search. We'd never find Luke.

'Don't give up, boss.' Sam put her hand on my arm. 'We'll find him.'

The softness of her voice brought tears to my eyes. Suddenly I wanted to weep, for all the effort that had led nowhere.

Sam was leaning towards me. I raised my head, smelling almond oil and dark chocolate waft over. I let her hold me, as much as was possible given the separation of our seats. Her hand gently moved on my back. I couldn't help but respond. I needed to kiss her, to feel her skin under my lips.

The ring of my phone over the console's loudspeaker made me start. We pulled away from each other. Talk about bad timing.

Any news? I was about to ask, expecting it to be DC Perry with another update. But no name or number showed on the display. Could it be Luke? Hope surged through me. I pushed the call connect button and waited for the caller to speak.

'Hello?'

But the small, desperate voice seeping through the speaker wasn't Luke's. It was a female voice, young. I tried to decipher her words. They sounded muffled, as if she was talking through a cloth.

'I can't hear you, speak louder.'

'I said V's going to kill him. He's got Luke tied up in the cellar...' The rest of her words disappeared.

'Jessamine? Where are you?'

'It's a house in a lane off Clay Hill. It looks a bit like a church from the outside.'

'Clay Hill in Enfield?'

'That's it.'

'What's the lane called?'

'Flask Lane? There's one of those monkey trees in the garden. Hurry up.'

Jessamine Robbins ended the call.

I turned to Sam. 'Find Flask Lane.'

'There isn't a Flask Lane in Enfield,' Sam replied, frowning over the GPS. 'But there's a Flash Lane, off Clay Hill... It's six miles away.'

I called the incident room.

'We've got the address where Luke is being held. Get onto control, I need armed backup asap.'

———

The road twisted and turned as I drove east, as fast as I could without risking lives. I parked outside our destination, a large house set back from the road. One section had tall eaves, resembling a church. Several police vehicles were already pulled up in the gravel driveway, beside a Maserati and a Saab.

I jumped out of the Mondeo and ran towards the house. A fine mist of smoke hung in the air. Officers in caps and bullet-proof vests were running in and out of the house.

At the front door an SO19 officer blocked my path. I shoved my warrant card in his face.

'Where's the boy? Is he alive?'

I looked past him into the house. Smoke curled up from a set of stairs off the hall, clouds of grey rolling towards us. In the hall, an officer was struggling to handcuff a man with Arabic features – Karim. Two others lay on the floor, already handcuffed. I recognised Angel's cornrows and Spicer's dreadlocks. A heavily muscled white man was pinned against the ground, about to be handcuffed – Deda. Where was Edwards?

'The boy's still down there, tied up. He's unconscious. One of the targets has been shot. He's alive and a threat.'

A chill went through me. 'You can't just leave them there.'

'We can't get to them, the fire's out of control. Leave now, sir. Fire and ambulance are on the way.'

For a split second I saw my father's figure through the window of the burning shed. Heard his desperate banging and his slowly fading calls for help. It might be too late by the time they arrived. I couldn't leave Luke to die, not like this... I pushed past the firearms officer and ran into the dim interior. The stench of burning hit me – a fireworks smell of potassium nitrate, mingled with ammonia and other chemicals.

'Stay where you are! Stop!'

I scarcely heard the warning. I ran down a steep flight of steps into the source of the smoke, pausing to peel off my jacket and shove a handkerchief over my nose and mouth. Then I made my way through the swirling smoke towards the far end of the cellar.

It was fiercely hot. Smoke partially hid the floor and walls. I couldn't see Luke or Edwards. An altar of some kind was burning furiously. On it lay dolls and figurines, toppled over.

'Luke! Where are you?'

I stood still, listening for any signs of life. Nothing except the crackle of flames and the thud of things falling. Along the wall, flames were consuming a stack of wooden crates. Dark, acrid smoke coiled up from them. A body lay on the floor. I could just make out a girl, on her side. I peered down. Blood pooled at her chest.

I groped my way towards a narrow table. A boy lay on top, on his back, eyes shut. His ankles and wrists were fastened to the table legs. Blood dripped from a half dozen wounds on his upper arms.

My legs felt weak. I stumbled towards him, put my head on his chest. A faint rhythm. I had to do something. Luke would die soon, surely if he stayed here.

'You're too late.'

I spun around to face a figure clothed in black, partly hidden by the smoke. Vincent Edwards, it had to be. I could only see the white of his teeth and a smudge of red on his abdomen. The smoke shifted. I saw his arm held out in front of him, his fingers curled around the handle of a long, sharp blade.

Edwards lurched towards me; knife wielded. I had no chance, unless... With all the force I could muster, I thrust my foot into his knee. He buckled and collapsed to the floor, moaning. Blood seeped into the fabric over his midriff.

Coughing, I pulled the knife out of the gang leader's hand and slit the ties that secured Luke.

'Luke, wake up! Wake up!'

The boy didn't stir. I put the knife down, I summoned all my strength, picked him up and carried him towards the dull patch of light from the top of the staircase.

Behind me, a few feet away, the sound of something heavy being dragged. Edwards. Did he have the knife? I'd left it in there... I took another step, and another. Halfway up I stopped and leaned against the wall, hacking out the crap in my airways. The heat of the flames had penetrated my shirt. I was struggling to breathe and had no energy left. The smoke was overwhelming me. With Luke in my arms, I couldn't keep going.

A chill seeped through me. My life was going to end, just as my father's had. It was payback time. Unless I put the boy down and left him here.

I looked down at Luke's face. A muscle twitched at the side of his mouth, as if he was smiling at my predicament.

No. I couldn't leave him.

And I couldn't give up. It wasn't much further, hardly any distance now...

A brawny officer ran towards me as I emerged from the cellar. He took Luke from me; carried him along the hall. I staggered behind them, my eyes streaming, my lungs desperate for air. Outside, as Luke was lowered to the ground, I doubled over, gasping, hacking out dark phlegm. Then I knelt on the gravel beside the boy. His brow was smudged with soot. I took hold of his hand.

'He's still with us.' The SO19 officer looked up from checking Luke's vital signs.

'Luke,' I said. 'Listen to me. You've got to wake up.'

His eyelashes flickered, that was all. I squeezed his hand.

'Please, Luke. Come back.'

Minutes passed. My hope teetered. Then distant sirens, slowly growing louder.

Two fire engines pulled up in the driveway then an ambulance close behind. Shouts, the crackle of radios. Two paramedics ran towards us. I let go of Luke's hand and watched as they tried to resuscitate him.

LUKE

IT'S NOT LIKE THEY SAY, YOUR LAST MOMENTS. YOUR LIFE flashing before your eyes. Maybe mine hasn't been all that special. All I see is a photo of Mum from before she got ill, the one on my phone that I took when she was dancing to the TV and didn't know I was there.

My body feels light. I'm floating, a leaf on an ocean.

A voice comes and goes. I wonder if Mum has come to say goodbye. I try to remember her voice. How light it was, the warmth of it.

This is a man's voice though. I try to come back but I can't open my eyes. I'm going far away, where no one can get me.

CALLUM

STANDING IN THE HOSPITAL CORRIDOR, PEERING IN THROUGH a glass panel in the door, I felt a jolt of emotion. Luke was wired up to monitors and attached to a saline drip, both arms heavily bandaged. His face was strangely calm given the wounds inflicted on him and what he must have thought would be certain death. He looked so innocent, so peaceful.

Finally, heeding the doctor's request, I left the ward, leaving instructions for her to contact me if Luke's condition changed. He was slipping in and out of consciousness and very weak from blood loss. She wasn't certain he would survive.

DS Harper was waiting at the hospital entrance to drive me home. She'd driven me from Edwards's house to the hospital, telling me I looked a fright and insisting I get myself checked out. I'd glimpsed my reflection in a glass door, and had done a double-take – my face, neck, arms and chest had been black with soot.

'Are you going to be OK?' Sam gave me a probing look.

'Hopefully. The doctor says there shouldn't be any lasting damage to my lungs.' I'd been treated for smoke inhalation and minor burns on my face and neck, and told to go home and get plenty of rest.

We cruised down the Great Cambridge Road, radio on low. Sinking into the passenger seat, I closed my eyes. The events of that night had taken their toll. My neck and shoulders ached, my cheeks and jaw were slightly burned, my eyes were gritty and sore, and my tissues filled with black bits every time I blew my nose. But at least I'd stopped coughing and no longer felt like throwing up.

'It'll be on this one,' Sam said as the hourly news bulletin came on. She reached to turn up the volume.

Last night police arrested five members of a north London gang. The men are believed to have abducted and tortured a sixteen-year-old boy, who is now in hospital in a critical condition. They are also being held in relation to two murders at a north London council estate earlier this year—

I switched off the radio. That was all I'd needed to hear.

'We did it, sir.' Sam had tears in her eyes.

I couldn't reply, emotion closing my throat. At long last, all the Skull Crew we had been hunting were in custody. Dritan Deda, Michael Gabriel and Vincent Edwards's right-hand men Karim Ali and Dale Newton, were spending a night behind bars at various north London police stations. Edwards was in North Middlesex Hospital under armed guard being treated for a gunshot wound to his abdomen. If justice prevailed, they were all likely to be off the streets for a very long time.

As we waited at traffic lights, my stomach rumbled loudly. I'd not eaten for hours, apart from a flimsy hospital sandwich while waiting to see Luke. I retrieved a squashed Mars Bar from the glove box. The burst of elation that had hit me earlier, had vanished. What was there to feel good about? Jessamine Robbins was dead and it was touch and go whether Luke would pull through.

A call came through the speakers. DS Rowan's voice.

'Boss. We found something in the house.'

'Are you going to tell me or what?' I'd left Edwards's hideout as the search was getting underway.

'A big haul of class As and a chest of firearms. They were in one of the downstairs rooms.'

'Good result.' I was too weary to feel any satisfaction.

'Something else... There was a handwritten note in the bag belonging to the girl, addressed to Luke. I've emailed you a photograph.'

'Thanks, Jon.'

'How are you holding up, boss? You were in a bad way when you left the scene.'

'He still is,' Sam cut in, winking at me. 'He looks like death warmed up.'

'I don't feel too good, to be honest,' I said. 'The doctor told me to go home and rest. You guys might have to get on with the interviews without me tomorrow morning.'

'We'll be fine. Go and get some kip, sir. You're a hero now, you know. Everyone is saying you saved that boy's life.'

Maybe I had misjudged Rowan. Underneath the smarty-pants swagger, he was a good sort after all.

'I don't know about that. Let's just hope he pulls through.' If anyone had saved Luke, it was Jessamine Robbins. In the space of a few hours, my view of her had changed.

She was no angel, granted. She had lured her friend to his captivity. But without her phone call to tell us where he was being held, Luke would almost certainly be dead by now and his kidnappers long gone, having done their utmost to remove any evidence linking them to their crimes. What's more, it looked as if Edwards had stabbed the girl as she'd intervened, trying to help Luke – had Jessamine given up her life for this boy?

'Wood Lane, isn't it?' Sam's voice broke into my reverie. 'Nice part of London. Wish I could afford to live around here.'

Lost in a haze of near sleep, I didn't reply. My colleague lived in a flat close to Wood Green shopping centre, I recalled. Sam pulled up outside the house, squeezed my hand and told me to get a good night's sleep.

It was only later, while I lay in bed, that I realised she'd known the street I lived in, despite her only other visit being over a year earlier – and she'd pulled up outside the right house without asking for the street number. Wasn't that odd?

But maybe her memory was better than mine... The note of unease submerged under the first waves of oblivion.

LUKE

A WHITE ROOM, THE SMELL OF DISINFECTANT. I'M IN A BED high above the floor. Wires and tubes hang off me, leading into machines. My arms are swathed in bandages. I wiggle my fingers and toes. My right arm is heavy and the top of my left arm hurts.

How did I get here? I try to think back. Before I can remember anything, I start shaking. I touch the red marks on each wrist. It's where the ties cut in.

Things come back. A blade gleaming with the light of a dozen candles. Whiffs of incense, skunk and sweat. Jez.

I lurch upright. Where is Jez?

A man dressed in white comes in and asks how I'm feeling.

'Where's Jez?' My voice comes out in a little croak.

He looks at me like he's calculating something.

'Someone will come soon and talk to you about what's happened.' He starts checking me, takes readings.

'What's happened to Jez?' My mouth is dry. I have to know.

'You've been through a lot, young man. You need to rest.'

As the man goes out, I catch sight of a cop in uniform sitting behind the door. Is it so I can't get out, or so no one can get in?

———

A doctor comes to look at me. She says I'm lucky I'm young, my injuries will heal. I ask when I'll be able to leave. She raises her eyebrows and says, I don't know about that, in a different voice. I want to ask more questions but she's gone and I'm falling asleep again.

CALLUM

'THREE CHEERS FOR THE DI! HIP HIP...'

As I walked into Major Incident Room One at midday, the Operation Rye team got to their feet, everyone competing to make as much noise as possible. I tried to look gracious rather than embarrassed. They congratulated me on the arrests the night before and for carrying Luke Delaney to safety; he had made good progress overnight, the doctor had told me. Murder team officers on other inquiries poured into the room. If I'd not acted, another DI pointed out, Luke might have died in the extra ten minutes it took for the fire and ambulance teams to arrive. DC Perry patted me on the back and DS Hanna managed a smile. Rowan pumped my hand and Freeman high fived me.

'You're a star, sir,' Sam said. 'But shouldn't you still be at home in bed?'

I'd already received hearty congratulations over the phone from DCI Andy Coleman, now recuperating from his operation

on a St Lucia resort, and an email from Detective Superintendent Bailey, saying he had 'looked forward to this day for a long
time'. The only person who had said nothing was Pierce, who
stayed in his office with his door closed, holding a phone to
his ear.

'OK, everyone, back to work.' I headed to the sanctuary of
my desk. 'We've got to press on with getting our evidence
together. I'd like to send it to the CPS by the end of the evening,
so we can charge the bastards.'

The four gang members in our custody – Dritan 'Zom' Deda,
Dale 'Spicer' Newton, Karim Ali and Michael 'Angel' Gabriel –
would need to be charged before nine forty-five the following
morning, when the extended custody period was up. But this
evening would be even better.

A team would start questioning Vincent Edwards as soon as
he was discharged from hospital. The bullet in his abdomen
hadn't caused serious injury, missing his key organs. Apart from a
conspiracy to murder charge for the two council estate killings, I
wanted to charge him with the murder of Jessamine Robbins and
the attempted murder of Luke Delaney. Luke would be arrested
as soon as he was fully conscious, and would also be interviewed
once discharged from hospital.

As I was reviving myself with a coffee, Pierce gestured at me
from behind the glass partition of the DCI's office. Rude
bugger... I couldn't wait for Andy to be back in that office.

Pierce pointed at a chair on the other side of the desk. I
ignored him, shutting the door. In the months he'd been
installed at that desk, his eyes had sunk further into their
sockets.

'Well done for the arrests, Callum.' His tone was lukewarm
verging on icy. He wore a crisp cotton shirt, this time white with
cufflinks and a Tag Heuer watch. His attire had gone upmarket

lately. 'I'm glad you've suffered no lasting damage after your adventures last night.' He frowned. 'From what I've heard, you could easily have been killed down there.'

He paused for my reply. I said nothing.

'I talked to the SO19 team leader about what happened. He said you went into the cellar without authorisation, despite being told it was unsafe to enter. You disobeyed two direct orders to stop.'

I shrugged. I'd acted on instinct. I was beyond caring what this obnoxious man thought of me.

He raised his eyebrows. 'Well?'

We glared at each other. I felt an urge to get my recent suspicions off my chest.

You were behind those skulls and that crap coming through my door, weren't you? Sorry it didn't do what you were hoping.

But it couldn't be Pierce... Surely, he wouldn't risk losing his career and going to prison. And even if it was him, I wasn't going to give him the satisfaction of knowing he'd got under my skin.

'It was my decision, and I stand by it. I judged that it was more important to try to save the boy's life than sit around waiting for him to die.' I glanced at the door. 'Is that all?'

'No, it's not all. I'll expect to see the justifications for your actions yesterday written up in full today, while they're still fresh in your mind. I've mentioned your questionable conduct recently to the IOPC officers.'

'I thought they'd finished with us.' Two officers from the Independent Office for Police Conduct had been sniffing around Operation Rye in the days following Nora Symonds's death. I clamped my hand to my brow. 'Shit, Jessamine Robbins. They'll have to look into her death too.'

'I thought that might bring you down to earth. I'll expect your full cooperation.'

I stomped out, slamming the door. I could do without the

IOPC on my back, as well as Pierce. As for Pierce... Was he just a mean-spirited, self-serving git – or was he out to crucify me?

Back at my desk, I found an email from Professor Singh. Nothing useful had been found on the fox remains pushed through my letterbox. No fingerprints, no fibres, no seeds, no chemical traces, no foreign DNA.

I dabbed some Biafine lotion on my jaw, thick with singed stubble, which helped the pain.

No murder weapons had been found for either Solita's or Nora's murder, an unwelcome hole in our evidence. A specialist team had searched everywhere obvious, including Edwards's spacious house and garden. We already had evidence for Vincent Edwards's role in the murder of Jessamine Robbins. So far though, we had no solid evidence that Edwards had ordered the deaths of Solita Milton and Nora Symonds. It seemed unlikely that anyone in his outfit would intentionally kill without V's go-ahead. But that wasn't enough to charge him with conspiracy to murder.

Then, a breakthrough.

'Got him!' DS Freeman yelled from his desk, almost giving me heart failure. For hours, he and DC Perry had been trawling through the several gigabytes of data that the telecoms tech had unearthed from Edwards's mobile phone.

Freeman pointed to his computer screen.

'All three messages were sent from V's phone to Zom's within an hour of Solita's estimated time of death.'

Wolf is coming over to give you a hand

Shes leaving school now. Shes alone. Get ready

Make sure you get the right one. She's small & has a blue backpack

'Fucking brilliant!' I said. 'Well done, both of you.'

Freeman went to high five Ferret.

5.15PM

Edwards was released into our custody with his bevy of antibiotics. I watched the proceedings on a remote monitor as Freeman and Ferret questioned him.

It was 'No comment' all the way. The gang leader's voice was level and cool, his face a mask. The only sign he gave that he was human came when he grimaced from time to time; his wound was obviously causing him discomfort.

I wondered again what would have happened if Jessamine hadn't phoned me when she did. Had he thought he'd get away with his depraved crimes, that he'd be able to scarper to an island in the sun? He had very nearly gotten away with it – and there was still a chance he might manage to wriggle free over some technicality or problem with our evidence. He had made enough money out of illegal drugs and extortion to hire a fancy lawyer.

10PM

Seriously flagging, I gave up waiting for Edwards to cooperate, polished off a Red Bull and set off to Wood Green police station. I watched the video feed in a nearby room, waiting for DS Freeman and DC Perry to take a break. As soon as DC Perry mumbled the time and switched off the recording equipment, I ran over.

'I've got something else to ask Mr Edwards – in private and off the record.' I smiled at Vincent Edwards and his brief, beside him, a dapper dark-skinned man in a perfectly fitting suit and yellow silk tie. 'You don't mind, do you?'

The two exchanged words. The brief didn't look happy, but Edwards gestured for me to go ahead.

I turned to the interviewers, waiting for me at the door.

'Give me five minutes, will you guys?'

Freeman nodded. 'Sure, boss.' Ferret cocked his head, his expression quizzical.

I settled into the empty seat opposite the gang leader.

He was observing me with a slight sneer, his handcuffed wrists resting on the table. I made little effort to contain my anger. I hadn't activated the recorder, so there would be no remote monitoring of the proceedings.

'It's you who's been threatening me, isn't it? You got someone to put a fake skull in my car and shove fox paws through my letterbox, didn't you?'

His expression shifted. The sneer was gone and his eyes were vacant again.

'Admit it, you bastard. You got one of your crew to come to my house to try to freak me out, didn't you?'

He smiled with his mouth only, the top lip thinning and the scar on his cheek distorting.

'How did you find out where I live?'

'It's not hard to find out an address. There's plenty of people who hate you pigs and what you get up to.'

'Is that right?' I stood and leaned over the table between us, breathing hard. 'What people are you taking about?'

Edwards smiled again. He seemed to be enjoying himself.

'Maybe you should look closer to home.'

'What the fuck do you mean by that?' A fleck of spittle shot from my mouth.

'What I said. There's plenty of people hating you boys in blue, you can find them everywhere.' A sneer twisted his face. 'Could be one of them working for you even, this very minute, who knows?'

My heartbeat was uncomfortably fast. I pushed my hands down onto the table to stop myself from doing anything I would later regret. Much as I longed to land a punch right between his eyes, that wasn't going to help the prosecution case.

Edwards sat watching me, his face immobile.

This was as far as I was going to get, I knew. But it was enough. Whether or not it could be proved, I was as certain as I could be that the intimidation and threats against me had been carried out on the say-so of this vile man – and that someone on my team had helped him. I called for a PC to deal with him, headed back to the incident room and asked the CPS for the go-ahead to charge Edwards and his gang. Two Red Bulls later, the CPS lawyer called. We had enough evidence to charge all of them.

11.30PM

We charged all of the detained gangsters with Luke's kidnap and attempted murder.

Spicer and Karim were also charged with conspiracy to murder Solita Milton and Nora Symonds.

Deda was charged with the joint murder of Nora Symonds, together with Minty and Luke, once we'd charged him, and the joint murder of Solita Milton, together with Wolf.

Vincent Edwards was charged with conspiracy to murder Solita Milton and Nora Symonds, the murder of Jessamine Robbins and the attempted murder of Luke Delaney, as well as firearms offences and possession with intent to supply class A drugs.

It was a moment to savour. I shook hands with everyone still standing on Operation Rye – Pierce had disappeared, surprise, surprise – and bought them all a beer at the Green Man. By

then, I was practically dead on my feet. But no way could I miss
this.

LUKE

A MAN IS IN THE HOSPITAL ROOM WITH ME. HE'S IN A JACKET and jeans. Not old, not young. His eyes are sunshine on granite. Grooves cut his forehead like fork lines in mashed potato. He moves towards me with a slow tread like he's trying not to disturb the slightest speck of dust.

'Hello, Luke.' I recognise his voice. It's the DI, Callum someone. He tells me his name and sits down on the chair beside my bed. His jaw is red, dabbed with white lotion.

'What happened to Jez?' I can't wait any more.

He looks tired but his eyes are alert, like a string of supercomputers is connected to them. He waits the longest time then clears his throat. I know what he's going to say.

'She's dead, Luke.'

I want to ask if he's sure.

'I'm sorry. I know she meant a lot to you.' He looks at his shoes. 'Jessamine saved your life, did you know? She phoned me and told us where you were.'

I can't speak. He hands me a photograph of a page with writing on.

'We found this in Jessamine's bag. It's addressed to you. I thought you should have it.' He gets up, rubbing his knee and coughing. He's hurt too. 'I'll be back shortly, when you're properly awake.'

When he's gone, I read the note. It's in Jez's loopy writing.

Hi Luke

I've just called the DI and told him where we are. I hope I didn't leave it too late. But if you're reading this it must mean the police have come and you're still alive. (my logic isn't too good, haha)

I couldn't bear to watch what they were doing to you. I know it's my fault and I shouldn't have gone through with it. What I texted you about being in trouble was true. I couldn't tell you the rest though. V asked me to be the bait to lure you back. I said no I wasn't going to betray you, I wasn't going to do anything for him or Zom ever again. He phoned Zom to come and Zom put the tip of his blade to my cheek. V said if I wanted to keep my face I would have to do what he said.

I know that's no excuse for what I did. Maybe you can't forgive me but please, don't hate me.

Look after yourself and think of me sometimes. Love you always, Jez

I put the note down. Tears are flowing down my cheeks.

———

DI Waverley comes back. He says he's sorry, he's going to have to arrest me. He dips his head at the younger cop who steps closer to the bed.

'Luke Delaney, I'm arresting you on suspicion of the murder

of Nora Symonds at 815 Delius Tower, Effra Lane Estate, Effra Lane in Tottenham on the twenty-sixth of October this year.'

The words loop in my mind. Shock collects in my belly. I didn't think they'd arrest me. I thought they'd give me a chance to explain things first.

The younger cop tells me I have the right to remain silent but anything I say may be used as evidence in court. He says I've been seen on CCTV going into the block where the woman was stabbed to death.

They look through my stuff in the cupboard by the bed and take away everything, even the cash in my jacket pocket. They take my phone too and say the contents will be checked and may be used as evidence. The DI says I'll be interviewed at a police station once the doctor has discharged me. He asks if I have any questions.

I shake my head.

The young cop heads to the door. The DI hangs back and asks if my wounds are painful. I gesture to my left arm, above the elbow.

'It hurts here the most.'

He nods.

'Hang on in there, kid,' he says.

———

The nurse says, 'You've got visitors,' and winks at me.

It's Kevin and Kirsty.

My sister cries out as she sees me, leans down and kisses my brow like Mum used to. She's wearing black pumps and her hair is in another style that makes her look older. She asks what's under the bandages and if my arms hurt and how long it'll be before I'm better.

My stepfather looks paler and thinner. He stands close to the bed without touching me then sits down in the chair and speaks quietly, pausing a lot like he's uncertain what to say. I think he wants to say something but not with my sister here.

Kirsty fills the gaps between Kevin's sentences.

'We're going to be moving to a bigger house soon, away from the estate.'

'You want me to move back in?' I say to Kevin. Doesn't he know I've been arrested?

'If you'd like to. If you're...' Kevin glances at Kirsty and back to me. 'I've put the house on the market. You'll want a bit of space now you're nearly grown – and I always hated the place, in the shadow of that estate. It'll be a fresh start.'

'Who's that man sitting outside?' Kirsty peers towards the open door. Kevin and I look at each other. He knows I'm in trouble.

'The police have to keep him safe,' he says to Kirsty. 'In case any of those bad men who hurt him turn up.' Her eyes go big and round.

The nurse knocks and says we have to keep conversation short, I'm still weak and he has to change my bandages. Kirsty squeezes my hand.

'I can't wait for you to come home, Beamer. It's not the same without you.'

'Chin up, sis. See you soon, OK?' I give her the biggest smile I can find.

'Bye, Luke.'

Kevin leans in and puts an arm round my shoulders. My throat blocks. He hasn't done that for the longest time.

CALLUM

Mr Swinton dragged his fingertips over his cheeks.

'I'm at a loss as to what to say, Detective Inspector. Miss Collins and I have had our differences, but my opinion of her has changed over the course of the term. She's proved herself to be a capable teacher – a highly capable teacher. I had high hopes for her.'

'I'm sorry, Mr Swinton.'

'I'm sorry too.' Mr Swinton's back straightened. He picked up the phone on his desk.

I waited for the English teacher in a small room beside the principal's office that I suspected was used to store badly behaved pupils.

'DI Waverley? You wanted to speak to me?'

I signalled for Isobel Collins to sit down.

'Miss Collins,' I began. 'You've admitted to me that you helped Luke Delaney by giving him shelter, knowing that he was wanted by police for a serious offence.'

Her mouth fell open. She slumped over the table. Had she hoped I might overlook what she'd told me? From her shudders, it was clear she was crying. I found an opened packet of tissues in my jacket pocket and offered it to her.

'Isobel?'

'I'm sorry,' she said between wipes of her face. 'I made a terrible mistake. I allowed my judgement to be swayed. Please, Callum, is this really necessary? If I have to go to prison, I'll lose my job.'

I steeled myself against the desperation in her voice.

'I know this is difficult for you. But this is *my* job, I'm afraid.' I got to my feet, distinctly uncomfortable. 'Isobel Collins, I'm arresting you for assisting an offender, Luke Delaney, on November the first...'

I explained I would take her to Tottenham police station where she would be questioned about the matter. She looked at me with eyes glazed. Her head was somewhere else – with Luke, perhaps.

EARLY AFTERNOON

After a couple of hours in the incident room preparing Luke's interview strategy, I was knackered. My head ached and my legs felt as if I'd run a marathon.

'You're no use to anyone in this state, sir,' Sam said crossly. 'Go home and rest up.'

'Better do what the woman says, boss,' Freeman smirked, 'or you'll be toast.'

I drove home. I didn't want to leave the Rye team at this crucial stage but there was no choice. My body knew what it needed.

Brendan put his head around my bedroom door. He'd returned from Wales last night. I'd relented and decided it would be safe enough for him to move back home instead, given that the top echelon of the Skull Crew were now locked away.

'Dad? You're home early.' He was in his boxers, exposing a toned stomach and sculpted pecs. 'Jesus! You look awful.'

'I'm not feeling so good, either'.

'The fire got your beard.'

Brendan's face steeped in concern.

'Are you going to be OK, Dad?'

'I need to take it easy for a while, that's all.'

'Call out if you want anything. I'll keep my music down.'

EVENING

Brendan put a mug down beside me.

'Thought you might want to wake up before the evening, or you won't sleep later.'

Bleary, I propped myself up on my pillows.

'Are you hungry? I could cook something if you like?'

'Maybe something light.' I smiled to myself. This was a first.

Brendan opened the curtains a few inches and perched on the laundry basket. The dregs of daylight revealed his mop of brown hair, delicately boned face and soft blue eyes. I could have been looking at myself at his age.

'What happened the other day? Did the men you were after start the fire?'

I explained what the fire investigator had said. Fallen candles had probably accidentally set off the fire, then stored guns and ammunition had exploded, sending the whole cellar up in flames.

'How did you get hurt, though?'

'There was a boy trapped in the cellar. He'd been kidnapped and tortured. The man who'd hurt him was down there with him.'

'You went into the fire to get the boy?' Brendan looked at me, wide-eyed.

I nodded.

'You could have been killed, couldn't you?'

'Maybe if I'd thought about it longer, I wouldn't have gone in.'

———

Later I went downstairs and found Brendan lying on the sofa, staring into the wall, his headphones abandoned on the floor.

'Everything OK?' I switched a lamp on.

'Did you do it because I asked you why you didn't try to save Granddad?'

'Did I do what because of what?' I lowered myself carefully into an armchair. Various parts of my body had minor burns, or other minor injuries resulting from my exertions in the cellar.

'Rescue that boy. Because I asked why you didn't try to save my granddad.'

'No, it wasn't because of that. It was just something I had to do. We'd been hunting the boy for weeks... He's almost your age. I didn't want his life to end like that.' The sound of Brendan's breathing. 'But maybe at the back of my mind... Maybe I wanted to make amends to your grandfather, somehow.'

'For not trying to rescue him, you mean?'

'Something like that.'

Could I tell my son now? That he was right, there was something I'd lied about, something that I should have told him years ago – and my wife, my mother, my sister, the police and everyone at the inquest?

Brendan hunched over, forearms on his thighs. I had to strain to hear him.

'I'm sorry I said that thing about you not saving my grand-dad's life.'

'It's OK, Bren. I know you've been angry at me.' I leaned over and ruffled his hair like I used to when he was small. 'What you said about me lying to you...'

I need to tell you something.

'I didn't mean it, OK? I was pissed off with you, that's all.' Brendan yawned and collected his headphones. 'Better go, I promised to call Shelley.'

I knew if I wanted a close, lasting relationship with my son I needed to tell him everything, and soon. But what if he couldn't cope with the truth?

LUKE

I'M SITTING IN A SMALL ROOM WITH A YELLOW AND BLACK striped carpet. It smells of fag ends. The DI is across the table from me, asking me questions about what happened in the cellar. Next to me is a solicitor and another woman to help me answer the questions. I didn't want my stepfather here.

Earlier the police searched me, took my photograph and fingerprints and made me put on their clothes. I feel like a real criminal now.

'Where's V?' I ask when I've answered everything. 'Is he dead?'

'No, he's locked up. You're safe from him, don't worry.'

'What about Zom? Where's he?'

'He's locked up too, he won't be going anywhere for a long time. No one can hurt you anymore.' He writes something in his notebook. 'Now, there's one more thing I need to ask you.' He doodles on the bottom of the page. 'It's about the woman who was stabbed to death inside her flat in Delius Tower a few weeks ago. Nora Symonds.'

I focus on the waspy carpet. I need him to know I didn't kill Mrs Symonds.

'It wasn't me.'

'We know you were there at the time she was killed, Luke. We've got you on CCTV.'

'I didn't kill her.' I say it louder.

The DI closes his notebook. He says he'll continue with the questions tomorrow.

———

The door slams. I'm in a tiny room with a tiny window. Bed, toilet, basin. The walls are made of bricks. Echoes down the long corridor; metal clinking, voices, footsteps.

I lie down on the bed, close my eyes. The room goes dark. I'm tired but I can't sleep. The police know I helped to murder Mrs Symonds. They think I might have stabbed her too. But I didn't, I know I didn't.

When I next open my eyes, it's dark still but the ceiling is rounded like I'm inside a cave. I look around. Why has the ceiling changed shape?

I'm back in the old lady's flat. She's on the floor, looking up at me. Her face is chalk white and there's a whisker on her top lip. I look down at my hand. I'm holding Zom's knife, the zombie with the zigzag blade and green handle. Zom's yelling at me.

Shank the bitch!

My hand grips the knife harder and I feel my arm muscles tense as my arm bends, and my hand moves higher...

'No!'

I wake myself up. I'm filled with the worst, most horrible feeling. I can't believe what I dreamed.

Is that what really happened? What if I stabbed Mrs Symonds and I've forgotten?

I start to shiver.

CALLUM

6TH NOVEMBER

I squashed my empty Diet Coke can and aimed it at the bin. It clanged, bounced off and scuttled across the floor. I was alone in the incident room, watching the recording of Luke Delaney's interviews.

I fast forwarded the interview to the moments before the murder.

'What happened after Minty dropped the knife?' I heard DS Harper ask the question.

Luke hesitated, frowning. 'Zom picked it up... He stabbed her.'

'Did you touch the knife at any time?'

'No, I didn't.' He lowered his head. There was a wobble in his voice that I hadn't noticed during the interview itself.

'What happened after Zom stabbed Mrs Symonds?'

'Zom was crouched beside her. He was cutting her face. I felt faint so I sat down against the wall.'

I shuddered and stopped the tape. What had this boy felt,

witnessing such a depraved act? Though it wasn't yet clear who had stabbed Nora, my money was on Deda. I had no doubt that the mutilation was his work. Minty had claimed in his statement that he had been temporarily blinded by pepper spray and hadn't seen anything.

On the way to the machine for another Diet Coke, I collected my thoughts.

We had enough evidence now to charge Luke with the joint murder of Nora Symonds. He'd admitted intent to harm her on entering the flat. What's more, we had proof that he'd been in her flat. An hour earlier, Luke Delaney's prints had been found to match the palmprint discovered on the wall of Nora Symonds's flat. I hadn't yet asked the CPS for the go-ahead to charge him. First, I wanted to slot another piece of the jigsaw into place.

Legally, for the joint murder charge to be proved against Luke, it was enough to show that he and the other two defendants had acted together, intending to cause significant harm to the victim – we didn't need to provide evidence showing which of the three had inflicted the fatal wound. Both Deda and Minty had claimed in their statements that Luke had stabbed Nora. Either Zom and Minty were lying, or Luke was. Unfortunately, we had no evidence to decide between the two versions.

My job now was to look coolly at the evidence and avoid becoming entangled with my emotions. Despite what he may have done, Luke was also a victim, one who had nearly been murdered by members of the gang he'd been helping. And I couldn't help wanting to believe Luke. He was clearly intelligent and seemed a decent kid, at heart. He'd answered the many questions put to him thoughtfully and truthfully – as far as I could tell – without one 'No comment'.

Enough for today, I told myself, closing my laptop. Time to get some rest.

7TH NOVEMBER

After some reluctance, Luke told the interview team more about Zom's threats to him and Jessamine Robbins, and how he had been fooled by V. It was understandable, given his near death and the horrific violence inflicted on him – his arms would be permanently scarred – that the boy might be frightened of the repercussions of talking. However, watching the recordings, I couldn't shake the feeling that something was off, something I couldn't put my finger on. There was something he wasn't telling us. What it was, I had no idea.

I sat in with DS Harper for Luke's final interview, saying little until the end.

'Is there anything else you haven't told us, Luke?' I leaned forwards. 'This is the time to tell us, if there is.'

The boy's gaze roamed the room. Apart from a slight sideways movement of his head, he gave no reply.

'You need to speak for the videorecorder,' his appropriate adult said.

'There's nothing else,' Luke added in a quiet voice.

There was nothing to be gained by questioning the boy further, I decided. Two hours later, we charged Luke Delaney with the murder of Nora Symonds jointly with Dritan 'Zom' Deda and Tyler 'Minty' Cosgrove.

8TH NOVEMBER

That morning, Luke appeared at the local magistrates' court. I watched the dejected, perplexed look on his face as the charges were read out and he was led away to Feltham Young Offenders Institution, where he was due to remain until his plea was heard at Inner London Crown Court.

For the rest of the day, the mood back in the incident room

was upbeat. The wheels of justice were turning; the Rye team joined in bursts of impromptu singing led by DS Freeman. My own mood alternated between relief that we'd finally got to this point, and sadness. It had jolted me to see Luke in court earlier. Whatever he had done or not done, I felt intensely sorry for him.

Since the night of the fire, my body had been recovering. Psychologically, I wasn't doing so well. My thoughts returned obsessively to who might have been behind that gruesome delivery through my letterbox. I didn't care so much about myself. But Brendan being in danger was another matter. At my insistence, he had gone to stay with a friend temporarily. Bailey had suggested I stay on my guard until the Skull Crew trial was over.

My suspicions of Sam had been playing on my mind all week – and so had my attraction to her. Since my small epiphany when she'd driven me home from hospital, I'd remembered other things. Weeks ago, she'd said something about criminals being attracted to her. What was that about? Could she have been dating a gang member, and somehow been persuaded to betray me and the Rye team?

It was almost impossible to believe. But strolling towards the drinks machine, I felt more and more uneasy. Someone on the team had to be working against me. It wasn't just the attempts to rattle me, it was our lack of progress for so long. Could someone be helping the gang by trying to obfuscate the inquiry? If that was true, they were still trying to undermine the team's efforts to gather the evidence needed for the gang to be brought to justice.

As the afternoon drew to a close, yells and hoots of laughter made work impossible. I ordered the team to join me for a few bevvies at the Green Man.

———

I'd intended to go home after the first drink. But the warm fuzziness in my head turned to a glow, which turned to determination. If there was a bent copper inside MIT55, I was going to find them before Operation Rye could be further compromised.

Most of the team had dispersed, leaving me alone, nursing the dregs of my shandy. Snatches of conversation dragged me from my thoughts.

'Look at Waverley, sitting there on his own like an alchie.'

'What a tosser.' Pierce's derisory laugh. 'Probably stewing up another plot against me, mate.'

I looked up. Acting DCI Pierce was chewing the cud with his crony, DI Jim Crane. Crane's reply wasn't audible.

'He's losing his marbles, accusing everyone of Christ knows what.' Pierce tapped his temple, looking straight at me. 'Needs his head examined, if you ask me.'

I'd not intended to confront Pierce with my suspicions – quite the reverse. However, in that moment all remnants of reason vanished. I put down my glass and went up to Pierce.

'It was you, wasn't it? You're the one who's been threatening me. You got someone to put those fucking fox parts through my front door!'

Shock froze his features before a contemptuous smile spread over his face.

'You've done it now, Waverley.' He got to his feet. Crane snatched up his glass and backed away. 'You need your fucking head seen to.'

My punch sent Pierce sprawling backwards. Fortunately, Crane and a drinker at an adjacent table pulled me away before I could do any serious damage. I strode out of the premises, took a cab home and drank a bottle of wine. It took the rest of the evening for the satisfaction of that punch to wear off.

9TH NOVEMBER

'Fancy a sandwich?'

I wanted a chat with DS Harper, alone.

'So, sir,' Sam began as we walked towards Lorenzo's, 'I heard you took a swipe at the acting DCI after everyone left the pub.'

I must have looked startled. Sam laughed.

'Everyone knows how you floored him. Looks like DI Crane said something.'

'Fuck it,' I muttered. I'd hoped Pierce wouldn't report the incident, given it had happened off duty and we'd both been drinking. But if everyone knew, he might have to say something.

'What made you do it, sir?'

I made sure no one was in hearing distance.

'The man provoked me. I shouldn't have risen to it.'

Given the stirrings of doubt I now held about DS Harper, I didn't want to get into detail. Especially as since my confrontation with Pierce, I'd become almost certain that he wasn't my target, after all.

'You're not his biggest fan, are you, sir?'

'He's a...' I bit back more apt words, 'a total arse. His views are a long way from mine, put it like that.'

'His views on...?'

'The usual: immigration, racism in the Force...'

'He's a right-wing bigot, is he?'

'You're not far off the mark. Strictly between ourselves, of course.'

'Officers like him make me want to puke. No wonder so many of the public hate us.' I looked at DS Harper, surprised at her vehemence.

'You've had some racist shit to deal with, in your time?'

'For sure. My first boss was a right one, over in Enfield. Never stopped asking me to make the coffee. I overheard him calling me "the Paki chick" to someone, can you believe? I got a transfer; I couldn't take it. Got my own back though. On my last day I brought him coffee and dumped half a packet of Sudafed into it.'

I chuckled. 'Remind me never to ask you to make me a coffee.'

We walked back from the café in silence. The air seemed crisper today, the branches sparser.

'How are your injuries, sir? Healing up, I hope.'

'Much better, thanks. I'm still sore in places but my lungs feel normal again – and my energy's coming back.'

'I wanted to say... I'm sorry if I embarrassed you last week. When I kissed you in the car, I mean. I suddenly felt so emotional.'

'There's nothing to be sorry about, Sam. I didn't hold back, if I remember correctly.'

It was the first time either of us had mentioned the incident. I stopped walking, turning to face her, aware of her eyes on me, the long lashes casting a faint shadow on her skin. A flush spread over her face, warming its walnut tones. I had an urge to take her hand and grip it tight.

As we arrived back at the building, I remembered what I'd meant to ask.

'Are you still having a break from dating?'

'Are you hitting on me, sir?' The mischievous grin broke out. 'I don't spend much time looking, no. But I've kept my eHarmony subscription going, just in case.'

'I hope you're being careful. You don't want to meet any more dodgy types.'

She frowned.

'You said before you'd dated some dodgy characters in the past? Chancers and criminals...'

'Oh, right.' The brightness left her face. 'Yes, I'm ultra-cautious now. No one gets past stage one unless they fill in my ten-page questionnaire.' Her voice was flat. 'I'm off to the park. See you in a bit.'

I watched her striding purposefully in her low-heeled boots, hands thrust inside her jacket. Had she thought I was going to ask her out on a date, then realised I was digging for something else? Had she realised that I had doubts about her?

Damn, blast, bollocks. I should have kept my mouth shut. Sam was sensitive, as well as astute. If there was anyone I needed to be careful with, it was her.

23RD NOVEMBER

First thing in the morning, I was at Inner London Crown Court to hear the gang members give their pleas. Luke Delaney pleaded not guilty to the joint murder of Nora Symonds. Minty and Zom did the same. The other gang members pleaded not guilty to the charges against them too. All were scheduled to stand trial at Inner London Crown Court on the tenth of February.

I set off for Wood Green. The last stage of Operation Rye was keeping me busy; we were helping the prosecution build a case against the gangsters and working with local teams to bring in the rest of the Skull Crew. Six gang members had been charged and further arrests were planned. All going well, we would break up the gang for good.

As I headed into the tube station, Bailey phoned.

'My office.' It was something bad, I didn't need a crystal ball to work that out.

The detective superintendent nodded curtly at the empty chair opposite his own. I gazed at the fortress of his desk and waited for him to speak.

'You've made a huge effort to get these thugs off the streets,

Callum. Thank you for sticking with it, despite the pressure. I know you're still working hard to get the rest of the bastards.'

He regarded me from the canopy of his bushy ginger eyebrows. I tensed. There was a 'but' coming.

'However, I need to raise a rather disturbing matter. Martin has told me about the incident between the pair of you in his office last month. He said you showed physical aggression towards him. He also claimed you attacked him in the pub recently, in front of a witness. He was reluctant to say anything, but word has got around...' Bailey's eyebrows merged into one, reminding me of a hairy caterpillar. 'I'm afraid Callum, I can't let this go.'

He raised his voice to its full, unnerving capacity.

'Whatever is going on between you and Acting DCI Pierce, I want it to stop now. Attacking a fellow officer is absolutely unacceptable behaviour, whether on duty or off. If anything similar happens again, I'll see that you're out of MIT55 immediately, do you understand?'

'Yes, sir.'

'The other thing. I understand you accused Martin of being involved in the threats against you, despite my express instruction to not accuse anyone without coming to me first. Is that correct?'

'That's correct, sir.' I shifted in my seat, withering in his glare. 'I didn't mean to. But in the heat of the moment—'

'That isn't good enough, Callum. As I said, I very much doubt that anyone on the murder team is involved. I suggest you put this idea behind you and stop making these unfounded allegations.' Bailey began beating out a rhythm with his foot. His shoe gleamed a rich shade of chestnut. 'You've not received anything else untoward, I take it, since those animal remains?'

'No, sir, I haven't.'

'The most likely source was the skull gang, in my view. Until the trial is over, we need to assume that a threat still exists.'

'Yes, sir.' I didn't disagree. Myself and other officers from the Rye team would constitute the majority of the witnesses giving evidence against the Skull Crew.

'If you accuse anyone else without solid evidence to back you up and without going through the proper channels, I'll have Pierce take over your operation. Is that understood?'

'Understood, sir.'

Bailey stroked his ginger moustache, not speaking. *Here it comes*, I thought.

'You came up with the goods in the end, Callum – and you've proved yourself to be an exceptionally brave, dedicated officer. But I'm concerned about the strain such a prolonged operation has placed on you, on top of pressure from this skull business. Your recent behaviour – the violence, these wild accusations, the anger you've displayed on other occasions – it suggests signs of mental instability, frankly. You should know that I've been in touch with Occupational Health. They will be contacting you to arrange a psychological assessment to ensure your fitness for duty.'

I went cold. 'With respect, sir, that's not necessary.'

'I'm afraid you've got no say in the matter, Callum.' Bailey let out a heavy sigh. 'I want this process underway before the Christmas break and I expect you to cooperate fully.'

While the day carried on for everyone else, I stood outside the New Scotland Yard building reeling. Bailey clearly thought I was deluded in thinking that an internal threat existed. With both him and Pierce against me, what chance did I have of being vindicated? Now my fitness for duty was in doubt, I might not even see the trial.

A bitter wind gusted. I hugged my arms around my body, trying to process this blow.

The thing was, Bailey was right about one thing – mentally, I was struggling. The threats, the nightmares, my role in Nora's murder, the fire in the cellar; all of it was pushing me closer to the edge. I needed help. At long last, I was ready to admit it. That, and a long break from the Met doing sod all.

But I was going to hang on a little longer. I'd be damned if I was going to be shoved aside before I'd seen Nora's and Solita's killers convicted of their crimes and put away – and before I'd found out the identity of the bent cop in the murder team. No one was going to threaten me and my son, and get away with it.

26TH NOVEMBER

'Heading to the pub, sir?'

'Is the pope Catholic?'

I smiled at DS Harper, relieved at her overture. She'd been cool towards me since I'd put my foot in it with my question about her dating practices. In silent consent, we headed to the pub beyond the Green Man, where we'd be less likely to meet people from work who might overhear our conversation. I found us a couple of stools at a corner table and Sam ordered the drinks – she insisted on buying.

After a large gulp of red wine, Sam pulled a strand of auburn hair back from her face.

'Did you ever find who was behind that nasty incident at your house?'

I shook my head. 'There's a few names on my list.'

She kept her eyes on my face. When she hadn't spoken for an age, I knew something was wrong.

'What's the matter, Sam?'

'You think it's me, don't you? The person who put that skull in your car and those remains through your letterbox... You think it's me.' She spoke quietly, yet her eyes blazed.

'That's not true—'

'Please don't lie to me, sir, or take me for an idiot. I know you suspect me, I've seen how you've started looking at me lately, like you're wondering what the hell I'm up to. It's so fucking obvious.' Her eyes narrowed. 'You think I planted those skulls and tried to freak you out because I'm in the gang's pocket, don't you?' She didn't wait for my answer. 'Well, fuck you too, Callum! You don't know me one bit.'

I had to put my cards on the table.

'I admit I've had occasional thoughts as to whether you could possibly be involved in that business, along with several others. But I've never accused you, Sam. I'm sorry if I've been clumsy about things.'

'When you were asking personal questions, when you were letting me get close to you, did you suspect me then?' Her eyes flashed. She drank more wine. Some spilled as she put down the glass. 'Were you thinking of ways you could get me to trip myself up, so I'd show you my secret life as a gangster's moll, or whatever it is you think I am—'

'Stop it, Sam! That's not what I think. I haven't been trying to trip you up, or trying to take advantage. I was – I am – genuinely fond of you.' Tears clouded her eyes. 'I was wrong, OK? I made a big mistake and I'm sorry. For what it's worth, I know you have integrity. You're one of my best officers, without a doubt.'

It was the truth; I was at last certain. Sam wiped the corner of her eyes, staring at me, mute.

'I'm so sorry if I hurt you, Sam. This whole skull business has been tough. I've had to get extra security at my home, I'm worried about my son...'

Still no response. Finally, Sam snatched up her coat and bag, and got to her feet.

'Sod off, Callum and leave me alone! I don't want to talk to you anymore unless we're on duty.'

She strode out of sight, knocking her stool over in her haste to get away from me. Desolate, I gazed at DS Harper's wine glass on the table. A smudge of colour on the rim was the only trace left of her.

I drove home and drank too much red wine.

I'd been a total clod. How could I have suspected her? I'd destroyed the goodwill between us in one fell swoop. The only good thing to come out of this – I was certain now that the person I was after wasn't Sam.

––––––

For a couple of weeks after that, I fell into a quagmire, wondering if I was finally becoming unhinged. I had no idea who I was after anymore – if there was anyone at all. On bad days, I started to believe that my suspicions were unfounded, as Bailey had tried to tell me all along. No one on my team was trying to unbalance me – I'd done that to myself. Edwards and his gang were responsible for the intimidation, end of.

15TH DECEMBER

Around eight thirty that evening, as I was tackling some long-delayed admin, I noticed DS Hanna at the other end of the inci-dent room talking on her mobile.

It would be a private call, I guessed. Apart from me, she was the only officer still at work. She spoke quietly and kept glancing around the room. Something about her manner struck me. I got the impression she was trying to get rid of whoever it was, without result. Catching my eye on her, she walked quickly out the room with the phone clamped to her ear. Five minutes later she returned, her eyes red-rimmed and watery.

I went over. 'Are you all right, Sandra?'

'I'm fine, sir.'

'Another late one? You always seem to be beavering away.'

'I've always got plenty to do, which suits me.' A quick smile.

'Got much more to do? I don't want you to conk out from overwork.' I smiled.

She gave a miniscule nod.

'I'll call it a day, sir. I can get on with this tomorrow.'

I caught sight of the phone on her desk, partly hidden under a tissue – one of those basic, clunky pay as you go phones that don't do much beside make calls and take photos. Most of the murder team sported advanced smartphones stuffed with apps.

'Whereabouts do you live, Sandra?'

She hesitated. 'Edmonton, sir.'

'You've got a car?'

'No, I get the bus. Or I get a cab home if it's late.'

'Edmonton probably isn't the safest place to be walking at night.' The suburb had a reputation for gang violence – as Sandra would know.

'It's OK, actually. People think Edmonton is a bad area, but when you know somewhere well, you know?' She sounded defensive.

'Have you always lived there?'

Her brow furrowed. 'My parents were from Lebanon and Algeria but I'm Edmonton born and bred. I was brought up on a council estate.'

'That must have been tough at times.'

She shrugged in reply.

I looked at my watch. 'I'm finishing up now, I'll give you a lift home, if you like.'

'No need, sir.' She sounded alarmed at the prospect. 'I'm meeting someone in Wood Green later.'

'No problem.' She had just lied to me; I was ninety-nine per cent sure. She didn't want me to see where she lived. Or maybe she didn't want to face any more of my questions. 'Have a good evening, Sandra, what's left of it.'

Relief crossed her face. 'Thank you, sir, you too.'

As I went to my desk to finish up, I reflected on how little I knew DS Hanna. Months ago, Freeman had mentioned she did more overtime than most. While apparently a hard worker, she had remained aloof, not mixing or joining in social events. But not everyone was outgoing. I, myself, had been more inward than usual, now my job was on the line...

With a sensation akin to dread, I thought of my first appointment with the psychologist, a Ms Karina Jenssen. It was set for next week. A second session was scheduled two weeks later. Occupational Health had explained that the assessment usually required two or three sessions, at which point I would either be allowed to continue in my job subject to any conditions – such as regular counselling – or she'd recommend that I be suspended from duty until I could be reassessed.

Reading between the lines, if Ms Jenssen gave me the thumbs down after the second session, it might be only a matter of days before I'd be forced into sick leave. If I didn't find out what was going on in this place soon, it would be too late.

16TH DECEMBER

I arrived at the stalag at seven twenty that morning. For weeks, something had been trying to surface from a murky part of my mind.

DC Perry had been responsible for drawing up lists of properties to visit, with features similar to the house in the background of the photo we'd received of the four Skull Crew members. The day after the arrests at Vincent Edwards's house, I'd overheard a fragment of Ferret and Combover's conversation as they walked towards the incident room, coffee cups in hand.

'Pity about that report,' Combover had said. 'We should have checked it.'

'Yeah, big pity,' Ferret had replied.

Amid the drama of those days, I'd forgotten about it. Now, I wondered what exactly about that report was 'a big pity'.

Ferret looked surprised to see me already at my desk when he arrived at seven thirty. I went over to him as he took off his scarf and beany.

'You're in early, sir. The yoga's working, is it?'

I ignored the quip.

'Dylan, was Vincent Edwards's address on your spreadsheet all along?'

Ferret looked uncomfortable. He rubbed his scalp, studying his trainer on the floor. The rule was no trainers but I'd never bothered to enforce it.

'I'm afraid it was, sir.'

'What?'

'I was going to tell you, but—'

'Can you explain, please?' A thousand thoughts whirled through my head. 'How far down was it on the list of properties? I don't remember seeing it.'

He pursed his lips, hesitated again. 'The address was on the spreadsheet, not on the list given out.'

I frowned, trying to get it straight. 'How could that be?'

'The list we used was from a report run off the spreadsheet. When I checked it the day after the arrests, there was an address missing. I asked the officer who ran the report and they said they'd deleted the address by mistake.'

'Who was the officer who ran the report?'

'Er – DS Hanna, sir. We were struggling to get everything done in the time and we were rushing...'

'How exactly did she come to delete the address?'

Ferret glanced towards the door as two detectives came in.

'She said she'd had to delete some addresses that came up which we'd already been to, and in the process she must have accidentally deleted the first new address: Edwards's address, unfortunately.'

'So, Edwards's address should have shown up at the top of the second list, is that what you're saying? We would have visited his house the day before Luke was kidnapped, if that data hadn't been deleted?'

'That's right, sir. Spire House, 313 Flash Lane.' Ferret's face flushed. 'It was bloody frustrating after all the trouble we went to getting those addresses and prioritising them. I'd been getting double vision staring at trees on Google Maps. I should have checked the report off against the spreadsheet but given the rush...'

'I understand, Dylan. Don't worry, neither of you are in any trouble. To get this clear, was this address the one most likely to be Edwards's address?'

'Yes, sir. That address had the best match of the search terms in the second area we looked at. Definite monkey puzzle tree and gabled roof. I'm so sorry we fucked up, sir, I know how crucial it was.' I'd never heard him sound so crestfallen. 'Shall I tell Sandra you want to talk to her when she comes in?'

'No, please keep this conversation to yourself. I'll bring it up with her at an appropriate time. I'm sure you're right, it was a genuine mistake under pressure.'

Ferret turned to switch on his computer.

'One more thing, Dylan. Is there any chance someone else, apart from Sandra, could have deleted that address from the report?'

He raked his fingers through his hair. 'I had access myself...'

'Send me that report and the spreadsheet, will you? Don't worry, you're not in any trouble.'

The deleted address strongly suggested that Sandra was up to something. But the evidence wasn't watertight. I needed to find something else, something that would prove or disprove DS Hanna's involvement with the Skull Crew – without making her suspect that I was on to her. What that could be, I had no idea.

———

I left work early. Monday was roast chicken, Brendan's favourite meal. He was staying at a friend's house but with frequent visits home to collect whatever he'd forgotten.

After putting the chicken in the oven, I wondered if DS Hanna's former colleagues might be able to help me. I would need to be careful what I said though, in case word got back to her.

Andy Coleman had picked Sandra for the Rye team before going off sick; she'd recently transferred to MIT55. I'd OK'd the others soon after my arrival from Wales. I wondered who he had spoken to about Sandra. Fortunately, I knew Sandra's former boss in the Walthamstow gangs team. I explained to him that I needed an unofficial heads-up from someone who had worked closely with Sandra, as a matter had cropped up that involved her.

'Did you ever notice anything unusual about her? Or something that struck you about her behaviour, for whatever reason?'

He hesitated. 'She was always diligent, hardworking. But I often felt like she was holding something back... That's all, really.'

I thanked him and was about to end the call.

'There's something else. After she left, one of my DCs

mentioned he was glad she'd gone. He didn't explain further. You'd better ask him about it yourself.'

I asked for the DC's number and left a message on his voice-mail, then started preparing the vegetables.

My phone rang five minutes later. A shot of adrenalin went through me. But it was Kate.

'Hello, Callum. Do you have a few minutes?'

Given she was planning to spend a week at the house over Christmas with me and Brendan – Lucy would be in LA with her girlfriend's family – I assumed she wanted to discuss the arrangements.

'Hi, how are you doing?'

'I've met someone,' she said. 'I'm sorry, Callum. I want a divorce.'

She explained while I listened, too stunned to say much.

Her new 'partner' lived in Dublin. She wasn't sure yet but she might stay on there indefinitely. Also, she wanted Brendan to come and see her over the Christmas holiday.

I put the phone down half shocked, half relieved. So, my marriage was over... The new guy would no doubt want to meet Brendan, I thought with more than a hint of jealousy. It would be the start of a new family for him, perfectly timed for the Christmas celebrations.

Picking up a bottle of Glenfiddich, I had an urge to down several glasses and get fiendishly drunk. I put it back down and began setting the table. While Brendan was living with me – as he would be again full-time, once the trial was over – I had to think of what was best for him.

'Kate just called,' I said when Brendan arrived. 'Did you know about—'

'Liam? Yes, she told me. She asked me about Christmas too, what I wanted to do.'

He looked uncomfortable.

'How do you feel about going over there for Christmas?'

'It would be cool to see her new place and everything. I don't want to mess up your plans though. You were expecting me and Mum to be around.'

'It's your choice. Of course, I'd love you around, but with just the two of us...' There was also the potential threat from those members of the Skull Crew not yet apprehended. Maybe this was for the best. 'Why don't you check out the flights to Dublin?'

By the time I'd gone to bed, Brendan had booked a flight departing at midday on the twenty-sixth of December and returning to London two weeks later.

LUKE

Kevin and Kirsty come to visit on Christmas Day. Kevin has a better lawyer for me. The lawyer says he may be able to get me off the murder charge. He thinks accusing people of joint murder is wrong cos it's a way to lock up more non-white kids.

When they've gone, I think of this day last year, us all dancing to *Strictly*.

I didn't tell them about my bad dream. I've not told anyone.

It came again last night. I'm in the woman's flat again, holding Zom's knife. My heart thuds like a giant hammer. This time, I plunge the knife into her throat.

I woke up trying to scream. But the scream got stuck in my throat.

I'm more scared than I've ever been in my life. Once, I thought I knew above anything I didn't kill Mrs Symonds. Now I don't know for sure. Is the dream trying to tell me something? Could I really have stabbed her and forgotten? What if I had an epileptic fit or something when I was doing it, and some circuit in my brain tripped out?

Zom never actually told me that he killed her, and Minty never saw who it was. I thought Zom was trying to shift the blame onto me, telling the police I did it. But maybe it *was* me.

Just writing it down makes me want to die. I wish with all my heart that I'd never gone inside that flat, and I'd never started hanging out with the Skull Crew.

CALLUM

25TH DECEMBER

I watched Brendan open his present, some noise-cancelling headphones I'd chosen from Amazon and wanted him to be delighted with. His reaction was muted. I prepared a free-range chicken for lunch, which ended up dry and overcooked. We pulled crackers and ate my burnt offerings without jollity, the table seeming far too big.

Clearing up done, I sat alone in the winter gloom with the carved figure on the living room mantelpiece, testing my resolve not to succumb to irrational fears.

The fox was sitting on its haunches, its teeth exposed. Every time I went into the room, I became more aware of its presence. Now, as I looked at the small wooden fox, I had a bizarre sense that there was something malevolent about it – the same feeling I'd had as a small boy, banished to sit in the shed alone as a punishment.

Memories rushed back. How I'd sat in there for hours, surrounded by carvings my father hadn't yet finished – foxes, badgers and the like. It wasn't physically uncomfortable – there was a powerful light bulb hanging from the ceiling, an oil heater and my father's chair to sit on. But being so close to those carvings, lined up on the shelf, had unnerved me. My overactive imagination imbued them with some undefined power over me. I'd sit in the shed desperate to run but knowing I'd have to go back and stay there even longer if I defied my father.

The fox's teeth bared even further. I jolted upright.

Fuck's sake, Callum! You're a sane, rational man, a police officer.

I shut my eyes, opened them. Fuck it, I'd had enough. I got up from the armchair, grabbed the small wooden fox and threw it with all my might against the fireplace. With a loud crack, the head separated from the body, bounced off the tiles and rolled to a standstill on the living room carpet.

'What the hell's going on?' Brendan stood at the door.

'I can't deal with that thing being in here.'

'The fox?'

'That's right. It gave me the heebie-jeebies.'

'So you smashed it to bits?'

'The thing fell apart when I threw it.' I took a deep breath. 'I told you I didn't want those things in the house.' Feeling foolish, I picked up the pieces, took them outside and dropped them in the dustbin. Brendan followed me into the kitchen, where I poured myself a whisky.

'Dad, what's wrong? You're acting totally weird. Why can't you tell me what's going on? What did the psychologist say the other day?'

I'd told Ms Jenssen about my poor relationship with my father, thinking I'd have to give her something in case she told Occ Health I wasn't cooperating. I hadn't yet mentioned that my father had died in a fire.

'She thinks my mental health has been affected by stress –

the stuff going on at work, the skull threats... She thinks it is,' I made air quotes, 'exacerbating my vulnerabilities'.

I didn't tell him the rest. *It sounds like something happening in the recent past has reactivated a traumatic memory.* Something I hadn't wanted to remember, she'd thought, that held a lot of guilt for me.

'Has she said if you're OK to go back to work?'

'Not yet. I've got another session before she makes up her mind.' I was dreading the next one. The shrink was more astute than I'd hoped, despite the brevity of my replies; I'd worried that if I told her the truth, she'd immediately classify me as unfit for duty.

'What else did she say?'

'I need to forgive myself for things that happened in the past.'

'Things to do with my granddad?'

'Yes, to do with how he died.' I drained my whisky.

'There's something that's bugging me. It was summer when he died, right?'

'Yes, late July.'

'So it was warm outside?'

'Very warm, yes. What are you getting at?'

'Did you have your bedroom windows open?'

'Yes, I should think so.'

'So why didn't you smell the smoke?'

'I don't know.'

No. I had to tell Brendan everything, before it was too late and he stopped trusting me for good – even if he hated me for it.

'Wouldn't you have woken up? Your bedroom overlooked the garden, yours was the only one that did.' Brendan's voice was thick with emotion. 'Marcy told me. You would've smelt the smoke or heard the flames. You could've gone down and put the fire out before it got so bad. Then he wouldn't have died.' A sob broke from him. 'Then I might've known my granddad.'

'Bren. Please, don't go! There's something else I have to tell you.'

But he'd run upstairs, tears in his eyes. When I went to his room and tried to talk to him, he told me to go away.

———

On Boxing Day, Brendan slept past his alarm and ran out of the house without breakfast, refusing my offer of a lift to the airport. I spent the rest of day hanging around the house, feeling miserable, berating myself for being such an inept father. If only I'd told the truth, all those years ago.

27TH DECEMBER

Next day I decided to get off my butt and do something useful.

Thankfully, no one was in the office to ask what I was up to. I was supposed to be on annual leave 'til early January; the super wouldn't take kindly to me coming in surreptitiously to pursue my fanciful notions.

I switched on the computer and logged in to the system. It didn't take long to find and open the set of spreadsheets containing those phone numbers called and received by the phones of the Skull Crew members awaiting trial. We'd obtained records for the six months up until the date of arrest. This was evidence for the prosecution case which I was entitled to access, though until then I'd had no reason.

DS Freeman had gone through the data already, identifying the contacts of each gang member and highlighting all those phone numbers that weren't associated with any identified individual or company. There were twenty-six, not as many as I'd feared. Some numbers showed the false name in which the phone had been registered, others simply contained no name. Quickly but carefully, I copied the unidentified phone numbers into a new spreadsheet, 'Unidentified Numbers', moved it onto my flash drive and switched off my computer.

The first part of my plan had gone smoothly. The second part would require Sandra's presence. I needed to get my hands on the phone number of Sandra's private pay-as-you-go phone, without asking for it and without her knowing I'd got it.

Given I was SIO of Operation Rye, I had the private mobile numbers of all the officers on the Rye team, which I'd requested back in July – any numbers that they'd chosen to disclose, that was. Unsurprisingly, the private number ending in 028 that Sandra had disclosed to me wasn't among the unidentified numbers in my spreadsheet – I'd already checked. But there was a chance that the undisclosed phone number might be there.

Since our late-evening conversation a couple of weeks before, I'd been watching DS Hanna's movements carefully. I hadn't once caught sight of the clunky phone. She had left on time at the end of each afternoon, as if she guessed something was up.

I prayed she wouldn't cotton on to my suspicions before I could work out how to get what I needed. If she disposed of the phone before I managed to get its number, all this would have been a waste of time.

5TH JANUARY

On my third day back at work, four weeks before the trial of the gang members was due to start, DC Freeman approached my desk in a state of excitement.

'You'll never guess what's happened, sir! It's the mutt's nuts!'

'Try me.' I put aside my hummus-tipped carrot stick.

'Looks like a dog has found the murder weapon!' His eyes gleamed and a strand of drool hung from his lips.

An Irish Terrier on its way out for a walk with its owner had found a package under a tree on the Effra Lane estate. Inside was a thirteen-inch zombie knife wrapped inside two Waitrose bags.

'There's blood stains and fingerprints on the knife,' Freeman continued. 'It's in with Forensics. It could be the knife used to stab Nora Symonds and Solita Milton. The spot is out of view of CCTV cameras, coincidentally.'

I wondered who had left the knife. It had to have been put there recently, given the high visibility of the location. Someone had wanted us to find that knife.

An hour later, a phone call from Professor Singh confirmed my suspicions – the fingerprints found on the handle were Luke Delaney's. The news jolted me. Had the boy lied to us? The murder weapon was the one thing we still needed. We wouldn't know for sure if this knife was it until we had the DNA results on the blood, due in a couple of days. In the meantime, this development didn't look good for Luke.

———

I left work early. I needed to regroup and gather my reserves for the challenges that lay ahead. I'd been sleeping badly again; mentally, I was just about hanging on.

Brendan was due back from Ireland in two days. He'd agreed to stay with a friend until the trial ended, but visit me in the meantime. I'd promised him we'd sit down and I'd tell him everything that I'd been keeping from him about my father's death. My second session with the psychologist was coming up shortly too – I wasn't sure which I was dreading the most. If the assessment didn't go my way, sick leave was likely to follow soon afterwards.

I heated a carton of Moroccan chicken soup and was about to tuck in when my mobile rang. I reached for it, expecting it to be Brendan.

'DI Waverley? It's DC Grebe. You don't know me – sorry I didn't call back sooner, but I've been away in Tasmania. You wanted to know about DS Hanna?'

'Please, go ahead.' I'd almost forgotten about my request.

'We both joined the gangs team about eight years ago. I got to know her more than most I'd say. She kept herself to herself.'

'Yes, I've noticed the same,' I said. 'Did you have any concerns about her?'

'I never told anyone at the time, maybe I should have. But you know, you don't want to land someone in it.'

I repeated that the call was in strict confidence, and for background purposes only.

'It was at the end of a difficult day. This guy we were trying to arrest started shooting at us. We had to call for armed backup and the guy got shot in the leg. DS Hanna was obviously quite affected. She started telling me about her brother. He was a youth worker, never in any trouble – he got badly injured by a police officer in a drugs raid. It spurred her on to get involved with a guy who ran a local group against police brutality, stop and search powers and so on... She joined the police soon after that. She didn't actually admit anything but the whole thing sounded a bit like a confession, you know?'

'You don't happen to remember any names, do you?'

'No, she never said. The other thing that struck me... She knew an awful lot about gangs. I know, she was supposed to – but she knew more than most officers on the team. I joked with her once that she must know a gang member and she said that she did – used to, anyway. He was the brother of the activist guy.'

'That's very helpful, thank you.'

'Has she done something wrong, sir?'

'It's too early to say, to be honest. I'd rather not speculate at this early stage. And if you could keep this under wraps, for now...'

I ended the call, my mind buzzing. The pieces were coming together. Had DS Hanna joined up in order to right the wrongs of the past? Had she been using her position to help this activist – or perhaps his gang-involved brother?

7TH JANUARY

The results on the blood stains were back. The DNA profile of the blood on the zombie knife matched that of Nora Symonds.

'Brill!' DS Freeman smiled like a demented clown. 'We've got the little bugger.'

DS Harper looked upset. 'Luke lied to us,' she said.

'I know,' I replied. 'I believed him too.' The sense of betrayal I felt towards Luke was out of place, I knew. But Luke had told us that he hadn't touched the knife. The boy had some explaining to do.

Interviews with the three defendants were hastily arranged in order to clarify the new evidence.

Minty replied 'No comment,' to all of our questions.

I watched on the remote monitor as Dritan Deda was questioned by DS Rowan. He refused to answer any questions about the murder weapon and its subsequent disposal, and showed no emotion when told that it had been used to kill both Solita Milton and Nora Symonds.

———

I asked DS Harper to lead the interview with Luke Delaney. This was the crucial one. I wanted to be there too but I would keep my cool, I told myself, and not let emotion get the better of me.

'So, Luke, tell me,' Sam said after the preliminaries were over, 'why are your prints on the knife used to stab Nora Symonds?'

The boy shifted in his seat. He looked anxiously from DS Harper to me and back.

'I don't know.'

'You don't know?'

He looked down. Sam spoke more gently.

'Luke, we've found the knife. It's got your fingerprints on it.'

'I didn't do it.'

'You didn't do what?'

'I didn't kill Mrs Symonds.'

'Then why are your fingerprints on the knife used to kill her?' I couldn't keep the sarcasm from my voice. 'This time the truth might be a good idea.'

'Zom told me to get the knife after Minty dropped it. He told me to stab her.' His voice started to wobble. 'So, I picked it up and...' He closed his eyes.

Sam leaned forward. 'Then what happened?'

Luke shook his head, confusion on his face.

'Did you give the knife to Zom?'

'I-I don't remember.'

'Did you see who stabbed Nora Symonds, Luke?'

Again, a pause. 'Zom stabbed her. I know he did.'

'But you didn't actually see him stab her?'

'No.' His head sagged. 'I saw him afterwards, cutting her...'

I wanted to believe him more than anything else in the world. But a seed of doubt had crept into my mind.

'If Zom stabbed her like you say,' Sam asked, 'why weren't his prints found on the handle?'

'He was wearing gloves, I told you before. So was Minty.'

'And you weren't?'

'Zom said there weren't enough for me too.'

Luke had said in his previous interviews that the others had worn gloves. He had told us he hadn't worn any himself, but not why; we hadn't asked. I felt a slither of sympathy return. Deda had wanted Luke to do his dirty work, that was clear enough.

'Why did you lie to us, Luke?' Anger suffused Sam's voice. 'Why did you say you didn't touch that knife?'

'I thought if I told you the truth, you'd think I did it.'

'You thought we'd think it was you who killed Mrs Symonds?'

'Yes.' He looked at Sam and then me, biting his lip. 'I was scared. When you asked me where the knife was hidden, I guessed you hadn't found it so I decided to tell you I'd never touched it.'

We stared at Luke. He stared back, his lower lip trembling. I had an impulse to believe him but I wasn't sure if I could trust it.

'Is this the truth you're telling us now?' Bitterness spilled from my voice. Luke's brief shot me a warning glance, which I ignored. 'Or another lie to try to hide your guilt?'

'Please. You've got to believe me.' A tear ran down Luke's cheek. He swiped at it with his fingertips.

'Was it you who killed Nora Symonds, Luke?'

He lowered his head.

'No, I didn't. It wasn't me.' He leaned over the table and cradled his head in his arms.

———

We set to work preparing the crucial extra evidence regarding the murder weapon, for submission to the CPS. Deda must have known the knife would have Luke's prints and got someone to place it for us to find, to make sure the boy, as well as himself, went down for the murder.

The unexpected find impacted me deeply. Before the murder weapon was found, I'd expected there to be a reasonable chance that the jury might find Luke not guilty of the joint murder of Nora Symonds. That verdict seemed unlikely now. Although I knew very well that not telling the truth in one instance does not necessarily make someone guilty of a crime, my faith in this kid had been shaken. My faith in my own capabilities, come to that.

I'd let my judgement be clouded by my emotions. Running into a burning building to save Luke's life, and risking my own... I'd needed to save this boy and I'd never regret my actions. I hadn't figured that Luke would be the one to stab Nora, though. I'd wanted to see him as a worthy victim, not an out-of-control killer.

Soon, the trial of Vincent Edwards and the other defendants would begin. I was going to do my best to make sure that all the killers from his rotten enterprise were locked up for many years. And if Luke Delaney was among them, so be it.

10TH JANUARY

'Is there anything else you'd like to tell me about your father?'

Was there? My intention was to be as open and helpful as possible was withering under Ms Jenssen's scrutiny. This session had been way more challenging than the first. The psychologist's alert grey eyes had never left mine, at least that was my impression. My sense of being interrogated wasn't helped by the overly bright lighting.

'I'm getting a feeling that there's something else we haven't talked about, that might be central to what's going on for you.'

She angled her head in the manner of a crow assessing its

next meal. I grasped for something to say. Something big enough to satisfy, not so big she'd choke.

'He died suddenly,' I said at last. 'In a fire. I don't think I mentioned it.'

'No, you didn't. Tell me about that, please.'

I gave her the basics, not what I'd kept to myself for years. She pondered this, gently chewing the inside of her cheek.

'You've already mentioned the difficult relationship between you and your father. How did you feel about his death?'

Another bullseye from Ms Jenssen. She had a knack of zeroing in on whatever it was I didn't want to talk about.

'It must have been a terrible shock for you,' she nudged. 'To lose your father so suddenly like that.'

'It was difficult, yes.'

Ms Jenssen steepled her hands under her chin, not bothering to respond. I risked a glance at the clock. Ten minutes to the end of the session.

'Our time is running out. I was hoping we could dig further into the reasons underlying your current difficulties, and whether you might be ready to start addressing them.' She smiled sadly. 'Unfortunately, Callum, I have significant doubts as to whether you're ready to do that.'

A bolt of panic went through me. I wasn't ready to be sent home.

'Please, Ms Jenssen. Could we have one more session before you decide anything? If you decide I'm unfit for duty, I'll be...,' I searched for an acceptable word, '...scuppered. I'm the senior investigating officer of a serious inquiry. The case is going to court soon. I need to be there every day and give evidence.' I lowered my voice. 'Also, there's something else I have to get done soon. It doesn't just affect me; it affects the operation I'm heading and the whole of MIT55.'

The clock ticked louder than ever as I waited for her reply.

'That was the most you've ever said to me.' She smiled. 'I understand this is an emotional issue for you. But this has to be an objective decision. I can't give in to pressure.'

'I'm sorry. I've been under a lot of pressure myself, lately. The review into my operation is due to finish soon. They'll decide if I contributed to the death of my key witness. I already blame myself. If they tell me the same...' I trailed off. My shirt, drenched in sweat, clung to my back. This process is only adding to the pressure, I stopped myself from saying.

'It sounds as if you're struggling with guilt issues, Callum. Guilt can be a toxic emotion.'

I waited for something else. An acknowledgement of my situation, a small relenting.

'I know I need help to sort myself out. I want to do it for my son's sake, as well as my own.' That was one hundred per cent true.

She remained obstinately silent.

'Can I have another session before you make your decision?'

She tilted her head and studied me again like that damn bird.

'I'll think about it. You'll hear from me either way very soon.'

13TH JANUARY

Sam looked up from her ciabatta as I staggered past her to my desk with my coffee.

'You look like someone's dragged you through a dozen bushes.'

I gave DS Harper a wry smile back. It had been another bad night.

'I've been better, thanks.'

She carried on munching while tapping into her keyboard. Since our falling out we had hardly spoken to each other on a personal basis. This was a major thaw.

'I wanted to ask you about something, sir.'

I glanced around. We were alone, relatively – Freeman had a dental appointment and Rowan had probably overslept again.

She lowered her voice. 'Rob overheard Beetle and Smiley talking the other day. Something about you being assessed by a psychologist. Is it true?'

Great. Bailey had been having a chinwag with Pierce about my mental state... Anger flared inside me.

'Yes, it's true. I've been talking to a shrink so she can decide whether I'm psychologically fit for work. Probably not, by the looks of it.' I hadn't heard from the shrink yet.

'Sorry, sir. I had no idea.'

'I could be out of here any day now, twiddling my thumbs.'

'What about the trial? It starts in three weeks. Don't you have to go and give evidence?'

'This woman doesn't give a damn about that.'

Glancing around I saw Pierce behind the glass partition, looking curiously in my direction. I turned back to DS Harper.

'What are you up to later?' I whispered.

'Falling into bed with a mug of Ovaltine, probably.'

'Very wise.'

Sam turned back to her computer. Kicking myself for my lack of boldness, I parked at my desk.

———

At seven fifteen that evening I was alone in the incident room wondering whether to go home, when DS Freeman and DS Hanna entered the room. The pair had been helping local teams question three recently arrested Skull Crew members on drugs and weapons charges.

'What's happening?'

'Meal break,' Freeman replied. 'We start again at eight. Might head out for a burger.'

I watched Sandra switch on her computer and bring out an apple from her bag, followed by the clunky phone, which she peered at, frowning. My heart skipped a beat. So, she still had the pay as you go. It was now or never.

'Pizzas on me,' I announced with gusto. I phoned Lorenzo's and ordered two extra-large thin-crust pizzas, one vegetarian, one spicy chorizo. 'Sandra, come with me and help collect, will you?'

DS Hanna scowled, got unhurriedly to her feet, dropped the phone into her bag then picked up her bag and jacket.

Outside was dark, foggy and decidedly unpleasant. Sandra didn't reply to my attempts at small talk. As we approached Lorenzo's, her phone rang.

'I can't talk now,' she hissed, dropping her pace to let me go inside first.

I went up to the counter and asked for the pizzas. Sandra leaned against an empty table, still on the phone. Between the clatter from the kitchen area, I could hear her speaking.

'I told you, I can't do this anymore... I'll have to call you back, I'm in the middle of something.'

I took out my phone, which I'd switched to silent, as if about to make a call.

'Shit!' I stared at my phone in one hand while making a show of hitting my brow with the other, and moved towards her. 'My battery's dead, I forgot to recharge it. I need to call my son urgently.'

Before she could put her phone back into her bag, I held up my palm to stop her.

'Would you mind if I used your phone for a moment?'
Sandra frowned.

'I wouldn't ask but he's waiting for me to pick him up from

rugby practice, in a hell and gone part of London. I totally forgot about him.'

With a resigned expression she passed me the device. Its screen hadn't locked.

'Cheers,' I said as casually as I could manage. 'Grab the pizza, will you?'

Boxes were being laid out on the counter. I took a few steps away, angling my body so Sandra wouldn't be able to see what I was doing. As quickly as I could, I tapped the envelope icon on the screen, entered my mobile number in the message header that popped up and a random character in the message field, then pressed what I hoped was the send button. Sandra was scowling and shifting her weight from foot to foot, two large boxes stacked in her arms. I tapped in Brendan's mobile number and waited for him to answer.

'Hey, Bren,' I said loudly. 'I've been delayed at work. Get the bus back, will you?'

Goodness knows what he'd make of that, given he'd got home two hours earlier.

Fuck, Sandra was coming over. I selected the text message I'd just sent to myself and pressed the bin icon. Then I held out the phone, my heart thudding and a smile plastered over my face.

'Thank you, that got me out of a hole. My son might keep on speaking to me now, with any luck.'

She nodded, face stern.

Please, I silently prayed, let her not suspect anything. And let that message have got through to my phone and be deleted from hers.

———

Back at the stalag, no one spoke. Sandra ate her share of the pizza while scrolling through her computer screen; Freeman demolished nearly a whole pizza standing, scarcely pausing for breath. I was too tense to stomach more than a few mouthfuls. I'd plugged my phone into the charger and was standing guard in case Sandra were to stroll over and spot the battery level at a healthy ninety-five per cent.

Seconds after the pair left for their interviews, I grabbed my phone.

Thank God, it was there. An SMS message sent fifteen minutes earlier from a mobile number that wasn't in my contacts – a private number belonging to Sandra. It wasn't the number ending 028 that she had already disclosed, but one ending 041, that she hadn't.

Now, the moment of truth.

I opened the spreadsheet I'd set up with the unmatched phone numbers. Then I typed the 041 phone number into the search box.

Instantly, highlighted rows with the matching number came up. Ten calls from Karim Ali's phone had been made to Sandra's phone number, shown as unregistered, and twelve calls had been made from her phone to his. The calls had been made on dates throughout the tracking period, the most recent being on the morning of the arrests at Vincent Edwards's house. There were also several calls going to and from Edwards's mobile phone, the most recent made from his phone on the day of the arrests, just two hours before we turned up at his house – while Luke was being held in the cellar. Sandra must have called him from here.

I let out a long breath and closed my eyes. It was the clincher. I'd found the evidence I needed. Realisation broke over me like a huge wave.

DS Hanna had been in contact with the gang's top tier all along. She had known Edwards's phone number and his address too. She'd tried to stop us finding Vincent Edwards, despite knowing he was intending to seriously harm Luke. She had been in this room a few feet away when I mentioned that I hated foxes. She had heard me phone Luke when he was on the run. She had sabotaged my efforts to locate the gang leader's house, and as a result Jessamine Robbins had died and Luke had very nearly died. For all these months she had been here, relaying all that she knew to my adversaries.

Without further delay, I copied the crucial data to my spreadsheet, took a screenshot of it, copied the new files to my flash drive and deleted them from the computer. Then I began composing an email to my contact in the anti-corruption arm of the Met's Directorate of Professional Standards, attaching the spreadsheet plus the previous evidence I'd gathered showing the deletion of gang leader's address from our search list. I also added photographs of the fake skulls I'd received and the fox remains.

I have reason to suspect that an officer in the Operation Rye team that I lead, is working on behalf of the violent drugs gang that we have been striving to bring to justice, helping them threaten me and to obfuscate our investigation into serious crimes they have committed, including murder. Attached is the evidence I have obtained against DS Sandra Hanna.

Further evidence of her collaboration with the gang members was likely to be obtained on examination of DS Hanna's phone. Given the seriousness of the offence, I added, it might helpful for them to take swift action before DS Hanna attempted to destroy her undisclosed phone and the evidence contained within it. Deleted data on a SIM card could often be retrieved – unless, of course, it was burnt to a crisp.

I paused, about to type my name. Might it be better to post the evidence instead, so I could stay anonymous? What if they investigated and decided not to do anything, and word got back to Bailey that I'd reported one of his team to the funny farm?

No. Let Bailey do his worst. I typed my name and hit Send. Whatever the DPS decided, I would stand by my allegation against DS Hanna. This was no longer just inside my head – I had indisputable evidence.

17TH JANUARY

It was my third and final session with Ms Jenssen. I decided to take a risk and tell her everything about what had happened the night my father died. Whether it would make a difference, I didn't know. But going by the terse email I'd received confirming my appointment only two days before, I didn't doubt that she was ready to declare me unfit for duty.

It took me a while to get going. But I told her everything in the end, because I needed to. By then my voice was unsteady and my eyes were blurred with tears, and I felt cleansed. For the first time, I had admitted the truth.

Visibly moved, Ms Jenssen paused before speaking.

'Thank you for trusting me. I know that was hard for you.'

'You could say.' I looked up at the clock. There were five minutes of the hour left.

'I've changed my mind, Callum. I'm going to recommend that you continue in your job, on the condition you start weekly sessions with an approved counsellor, and you're re-assessed in six months.'

'Thank you.' I struggled to speak. 'I take it...' I tried to frame my question appropriately, 'you won't be passing anything I've just said on to Detective Superintendent Bailey?'

She tilted her head, observing me again in that birdlike manner.

'I'll need to think carefully about what you've told me and the implications. Medical information is normally confidential, though if there are grounds for believing a serious offence has been committed...' She rubbed her forehead, closing her eyes for a few moments. Then she looked straight at me with a brief movement of her lips that could have been a smile. 'But given the length of time that's passed since the events you've described, and the fact that you were still a child... I don't think there is a sufficiently strong reason for me to divulge details of our conversation to anyone.'

It was enough.

18TH JANUARY

I decided not to pour a whisky to calm my nerves. I'd do this properly. First, I'd fix dinner, then Brendan and I would talk. It was Saturday, so there was plenty of time before I had to drop him back at his friend's.

At five, Brendan stood sweaty and mud-streaked before me. He'd come straight from rugby practice.

'Hey, Dad. How did it go at work?'

I grimaced as a waft of odorous armpit reached me.

'Good. You'd better have a shower. Dinner in twenty, then we'll talk.'

It didn't take us long to finish the spaghetti. I sipped my water.

'You wanted me to tell you the truth,' I began, 'about what happened to your grandfather.'

Brendan sat back in his chair; hands clasped loosely over his belly.

'Go on then. I'm listening.'

'I warn you, you might find it upsetting.'

'Get on with it, Dad! If I'm upset, I'm upset, OK?' His voice was full of frustration. 'You always treat me like I'm a little kid!'

I launched in before I could change my mind.

'OK, I told you how it was with my father. The way he

reacted way over the top to things. There's a lot I haven't told you. He used to make me stand in the shed with the door closed. I must have been eight or nine. His animal figures were in there. I used to imagine them watching me, they freaked me out. He knew they did but he didn't care. He said I had too much imagination, they were just pieces of wood.'

Brendan raised his eyebrows. I pressed on.

'It got worse over the years – his need to control, to exert power over me. He'd punish me for the tiniest thing. He was strict with my sister too, but Marcy was calmer than me, and she always tried to please him. The day he told me I couldn't go on the trip, something broke inside me. I'd been looking forward to it for so long, to being with my mates and away from him. He didn't even give a proper reason; just said I'd been too cocky lately. I couldn't take it anymore. The anger grew inside me. I had to let it out, somehow... The idea came to me after dinner, when he lit up his cigarette. I decided I was going to take away his most precious things.'

I sipped my water. Brendan didn't move.

'I stayed in my room listening for Dad to come up to bed, around half twelve. I waited an hour to make sure he was asleep then went downstairs in my pyjamas. I took his lighter from the kitchen drawer and went into the shed. I scrunched up some old pieces of newspaper and put them among the rags he used to clean up after varnishing. Then I poured some of his bottle of white spirit on top and lit a piece of newspaper and dropped it on top. The flames started leaping up so quickly, I knew the place was going to burn.'

'Then what did you do?'

'I went up to my room to watch. The fire took hold much faster than I'd expected. I heard wood cracking and splitting and the roar of the flames through the open window... It was scary to watch. But it felt like a victory. At last, I'd got back at him.'

'What about your father?'

'I didn't hear him go downstairs. I stayed watching the flames, they mesmerised me. I wanted them to raze that place to the ground and everything of his inside it. Then I heard my mother screaming and I ran downstairs. She was in the kitchen in her dressing gown, holding the phone. There were charred carvings on the worktop. Marcy was there too, she said Dad had gone back into the shed to get more things and hadn't come out. I ran into the garden... I saw him behind the shed window. He was knocking on it, calling out. The flames were all around him.'

I closed my eyes, hearing him in there again.

'I didn't do anything. I just watched.' My voice faltered. 'I started the fire but I never meant for him to die. After they took him away, I told my mother and Marcy I didn't know how the fire started. I said I'd seen my father smoking in the shed, before I went up to bed.'

Brendan said nothing.

'I lied to the police too, and the coroner's inquiry. I kept expecting someone to challenge me, tell me I was an arsonist and I'd killed my dad. No one ever did.' Tears pricked at the back of my eyes. I dug my nails into my palms, struggling to hold myself together. 'I lied to everyone. I couldn't even tell my mother when she was dying.'

'No one ever found out the truth?'

'There was someone at the inquest – a forensic scientist I think – who said it was strange that the fire went up so quickly. But another one thought that was explained by my father dropping a cigarette stub onto a floor full of solvents. Whenever anyone asked me what happened, I stuck to the same story.'

'Marcy doesn't know?'

'No, but I think she suspects.'

'She said for me to ask you about the fire, when she brought the box of granddad's stuff over.'

'I'll talk to her,' I said. 'And your mother.'

Silence. I couldn't tell if Brendan was angry, upset or simply stunned. My heart hammered, a cold, panicky feeling spreading from my gut.

'Tell me what you're thinking.'

'Dunno. I sort of guessed it would be something like this. But now you've told me, it doesn't feel real.'

'Do you want to ask me anything?'

'Not really. It's a lot to take in. Think I might go to bed early.'

'See you in the morning, then. Love you, Bren.'

I stayed at the table, desolate. There was more to tell, when he wanted to hear it. But I'd said too much already. He was only sixteen. Had it been a mistake to tell him the truth? It could destroy our relationship, just when I'd thought we were back on track... It was impossible to take my words back, though.

LUKE

I GUESS I KNOW DEEP DOWN THERE ISN'T MUCH CHANCE OF ME being found not guilty. After the knife was found with my finger-prints on, my lawyer told me he'd do his best with my defence but I'd be lucky to get off the murder charge. Hope stayed alive inside me, even so.

The judge reads out Zom's real name and asks if they have reached a verdict. The rustles and whispering stop. The woman from the jury replies, Yes.

'Guilty.'

The judge says Minty's name and there's a sound like everyone in the courtroom is holding their breath.

'Guilty.'

Minty's mouth falls open.

'Luke Delaney.'

There's a *shhh* sound again. My hope soars, a kite without strings, beyond the reach of anything that might pull it down.

'Guilty.'

The kite crashes to the ground. A gasp comes out of me.

Below I see my sister hide her face in her hands. Kevin's mouth is an O. The DI grips the handrail.

I think of being locked up again inside that young offender prison.

It wasn't me! I want to shout it to everyone. I didn't kill her.

Now I know for sure.

CALLUM

ALL OF THE GANG MEMBERS WERE FOUND GUILTY AS CHARGED.

Luke's hopeful expression crumbled as Minty was found guilty of jointly murdering Nora. Then as he too was pronounced guilty, his face showed disbelief. Although I'd expected the verdict, I'd hoped it would be different, for Luke's sake. The sight of his youthful figure being led down to the cells was almost too much to bear. I picked myself up and headed out of the courtroom.

Outside the court building, Bev Milton approached me, her eyes wet. This was a moment I'd long ago imagined, yet feared might never happen.

'Thank you, for all you've done, Callum. I'll always be grateful.' I took her offered hand. 'I know the case was difficult... I'm sorry if that was partly my fault.'

I let that hang in the air for a second.

'That's how it goes sometimes, Bev. But we got what we wanted in the end.'

I wished her all the best for the future, loosened my tie and turned away. Everything had gone our way; this was the result I'd anticipated for so long. But now it had come, the satisfaction I felt was weighted with sadness.

4PM

'Going to the Green Man, sir?' DS Freeman called out. DS Harper and DS Rowan had their jackets on, ready to leave. 'We're off to celebrate.'

Operation Rye was over; all that remained for me to do was to go to court for the sentencing of the Skull Crew members next week. My team were being dispersed to other inquiries. Soon, I would be too.

'I'll give it a miss, thanks, Rob. You guys enjoy yourselves.'

I wanted to get home to see Brendan. A few hours ago, he had moved back into the house, as I'd promised he could once the trial was over. I wondered what sort of evening it would be. Since my admission that I had deliberately started the fire, Brendan had shut down again. I told myself to give him time. Secretly, I was scared I might have already lost him. I'd told Kate in outline what I'd told Brendan. She'd replied that she'd always known I was unbalanced and Brendan should live with my sister instead of me. I'd managed to hold in my reply, involving several expletives.

As I drove home, my thoughts turned to DS Hanna. She was coming into work as usual; I still had no inkling what the DPS were going to do in response to my email. If only I knew how long it would take for them to 'investigate the matter' as the officer who'd replied had promised. They might even have done so already, heaven forbid, and decided for some reason not to take things further.

I thought again of going to Detective Superintendent Bailey

and dismissed the idea. After his reluctance to believe that anyone in the murder team was involved in the threats, my self-respect demanded vindication by a neutral party that would investigate fairly and take action.

Hopefully, that would come soon. It was difficult to look Sandra in the eyes knowing what I knew. If this charade kept up much longer, I thought with a rueful smile, I'd be beyond help.

LUKE

KEVIN AND I ARE SITTING IN THE VISITING ROOM OF FELTHAM Youth Offenders, looking at each other over the table.

'You'll get through this,' he says.

He has to get two buses to get here which takes up all the morning. But he says he doesn't mind, he looks forward to seeing me. It's weird, we're getting on much better than when I was at home. He says I must take things a day at a time. Focus on doing something to help myself whenever I get down, like learning new skills. He even said meditation might help me adjust to this new life. I had to laugh. It's the sort of thing Mum would have said.

He puts his hand on the table between us. He's different from the old Kevin. His face looks older and he doesn't raise his voice when he talks to me. He's given up his waste supervisor job at the council and he's teaching boxing.

He says what happened to me made him see how he failed me. He blames himself for me going on the wrong path.

'That night at the hospital, when I didn't know if you was gonna pull through, I realised what a fuckin' awful dad I was. I know how I behaved to you was wrong. I know it's no help to you now an' I don't expect you to forgive me. But I'm sorry, son. I'm sorry.'

I can't speak. There's too much going on inside. I want to yell at him to go away and I hate him, and I want him to stay and hug me and be my dad for always.

Kevin puts his hand on my shoulder.

'I'll be there for you whenever you need me. Don't you forget.'

———

I get it, I do. I deserve to be punished. I've been here three months now, so I can imagine another twelve weeks or maybe even twelve months. But twelve years is impossible.

The lawyer said I shouldn't have been given more than the seven years minimum term, given my age and how I was treated by older gang members and this being my first conviction. But he doesn't think there's anything anyone can do.

V, Zom, Angel and Spicer all went to adult prisons. Minty is in Feltham with me. He got eight years. I saw him in one of the life skills classes.

The days are busy – we get lessons in all sorts. I've asked if I can take my GCSEs this year so when I come out, I can do something with the life I have left.

It's lonely in here. I wake up each morning forgetting where I am, then I realise. Sometimes when I look out of the window of this small room onto grey buildings and high walls, I don't know how I'm going to get through another week. I try to write things down when I'm sad, like Miss Collins said, all the things that I might forget and all the things I want to hold on to.

CALLUM

I ARRIVED IN COURT EARLY FOR THE SENTENCING, ALONG with an eager crowd of journalists and members of the public. Once again, the viewing gallery was full.

Relief spilled over the face of Bev Milton as the sentences were read out. Vincent 'V' Edwards, Dritan 'Zom' Deda and Damon 'Wolf' Banefield, all got life sentences. Edwards got a twenty years minimum term, Deda got twenty years minimum and Wolf got fourteen years minimum. Luke Delaney got life with a minimum term of twelve years and Tyler 'Minty' Cosgrove got life with a minimum of eight years. Karim Ali and Dale 'Spicer' Newton were each sentenced to fourteen years. Michael 'Angel' Gabriel got eight years. The lower-ranking gang members subsequently arrested were also sent to prison.

I shared Bev Milton's relief at the sentences for the thugs at the top tier of the gang, though the differing punishments meted out to Luke and Minty struck me. The difference was down to the discovery of the knife, I guessed, and Luke's admission that he'd lied to us about not picking it up.

'My team worked tirelessly for many months to bring some of these gang members to justice,' I said to the press waiting outside the court building. I put aside my prepared notes. 'I'm grateful that these men will now have to face the consequences of their crimes, which have devastated lives and caused much fear in the community.'

On the way back to Wood Green, something tugged at me. I'd joined the Met to make amends for what I'd done wrong, as much as to try to protect vulnerable people or apprehend violent criminals. But I had feet of clay. I had told my own lie, at Luke's age, every bit as serious as Luke's. How could I feel satisfaction at justice being upheld for others when I'd deceived others for so long, and escaped justice myself?

3.50PM

That afternoon I learned of the findings of the review into the investigation. The IOPC had cleared me and the rest of the Rye team of any wrongdoing in relation to the deaths of Nora and Jessamine. I didn't need any persuasion from my fellow officers to go with them to the pub to celebrate. I damn well deserved a drink. We all did.

Several rounds in, reminiscences abounded about the times during Operation Rye that I'd gone off on one, or returned in a foul mood after another confrontation with Pierce – needless to say, he wasn't at the pub. Nor was Sandra.

There was still no sign that the Met's internal investigations team had taken my accusation against DS Hanna seriously, though of course their investigation would be covert. But as I finished another pint, it stopped seeming so important. I could wait another week, another month – maybe I'd never know the outcome and Sandra would get to carry on doing the bidding of criminals... I tuned back in to the banter from the detectives gathered nearby. All were now merry-eyed and red-cheeked.

'Next job you're on, chief, make sure you don't let those granola bars out of your sight.'

'And watch out for the skull fridge magnets, boss. They're taking over London, so I've heard!'

Laughter erupted around me. I was being mercilessly ribbed about the so-called 'Granola Thief'. The whole of MIT55 and no doubt murder teams throughout London, knew all about that fake skull DS Rowan had found in the Mondeo's glovebox and my missing granola bars. I joined in with the laughter. Actually, under the influence of six or so pints of London Pride, the incidents were starting to have a funny side. I realised too, that I'd grown fond of the detectives working with me. Even their familiar quirks no longer seemed irritating – Rowan's dogged smart-arsed-ness and Freeman's unsubtle belches having pride of place. As for Sam... I didn't want to have to say goodbye to her, put it like that.

'Here's to all of you.' I stood unsteadily and lifted my glass. 'I'm not going to make a speech, don't worry. But while I can still get the words out... Thanks for all your hard work on Operation Rye everyone. Yes, and for putting up with me, thanks to whoever said that. Whatever is up next for you, the best of luck with it.'

That night I dreamed of Nora Symonds. She told me her death wasn't my fault and she was pleased she'd helped to bring the gang to justice. Even though it had taken an unexpected form, she'd had the quick end that she'd hoped for.

It was probably me kidding myself rather than a message from the spirit world, I thought next morning as I stirred from my worst hangover ever. But I'm grateful for that dream all the same.

LUKE

'ARE YOU DOING OK?'

'I guess', I say.

The DI says he's sorry I'll be locked up for so long. I'm choked up, can't reply. He hasn't given up on me after all.

The DI coughs.

'I'm sorry about what happened to Jez. I should have made sure she was safe.'

'Everyone makes mistakes,' I say.

He scratches his jaw, looks around the large echoey room that smells of disinfectant.

'This place must be tough to be in, day after day. But when you come out, you'll still be young. You'll have most of your life ahead of you.'

I know what he's trying to say. In twelve years I'll be twenty-eight, though. I won't be young anymore.

Suddenly the DI leans forward. His eyes look deep into mine. They are brown but close up you can see yellow strands in the irises.

'Did you kill her, Luke? Did you kill Mrs Symonds?'

'No.' I shake my head, push my tears down. 'I didn't kill her.'

He nods.

I want him to believe me. I'm totally certain now it wasn't me.

It was something in the trial that brought my memory back. The prosecution guy asked Zom how he knew what time it was when he got to her flat. Zom said he'd looked at his watch. That's when I remembered Zom was wearing his Rolex. An image flashed into my head of Zom's hand pushing the knife into her neck. His hand had the plastic glove over it but the glove didn't cover his watch. I could see the gold strap of his Rolex.

'Thank you, Luke. I wish you all the best.' The DI smiles and gets up.

I think of telling him what I remembered. Then he's walking out of the room, and I know I won't see him again.

CALLUM

THERE WAS LITTLE TO DO, OFFICIALLY; I'D YET TO BE ASSIGNED to another investigation. Unofficially, there was plenty. All day, I kept a watchful eye on DS Hanna. She seemed tense and quieter than usual. She hadn't been allocated to another case yet, either. When the others left for home she stayed at her desk, brought out a sandwich from a foil package and put her headphones on.

Something kicked off inside me. I shelved my plan to spend the evening with Brendan – I'd stay and see what DS Hanna was up to.

Six o'clock became seven o'clock. On my casual wander past her to the kitchen, Sandra was engrossed in her computer screen.

'Another late night?' I smiled. DS Hanna immediately clicked away the documents on her screen and looked up, startled. 'Fancy a lift home? It's looking stormy out there.' It was dark too, and starting to rain.

'No, I—' She cut herself off. 'Actually, yes. That would be

great, thanks, sir. If it's no hassle. Buses are pretty shit on Monday nights.'

As I drove fast along the Great North Road, radio on low, I sneaked a glance at Sandra. She hadn't spoken since getting in the car. Her shoulders were hunched forwards and she looked uncomfortable. Had she only accepted a lift in order to defuse my suspicions?

'Everything OK?'

'I'm good, thanks.'

'Better give me directions.'

Minimal directions were needed. A few minutes later we arrived at a small, ordinary looking block of flats.

'Stop here, will you?'

My mind raced. I needed to see inside her home.

'I'm sorry, would you mind if I came in a minute? I need a pee, must have had too much caffeine.' I smiled weakly as her reluctance gave way to resignation.

'Yeah, sure. No problem.'

I waited while Sandra unlocked the front door. As she stepped inside, a ball of white fluff appeared from nowhere and shot in ahead of me.

Nerves had made my bladder full, so I was able to use the toilet guilt-free. The bathroom exuded an air of neglect. The bath was piled with cat litter and DIY paraphernalia. The carpet didn't look very clean.

A melancholy squeak from just beyond the door interrupted my scrutiny. I emerged and tried to stroke the creature. It ran into the kitchen.

'That's Tiddles. He's not very friendly.'

Rather like his owner, I thought.

'I'll get out of your hair,' I said, loitering at the entrance to the kitchen. Sandra had removed her coat and was unpacking a shopping bag. 'Could I trouble you for a glass of water?'

The kitchen was smartly done out but also needed a thorough clean. In one corner, a few feet away from me, lay the cat's bed, strewn with white hairs.

'Thanks.'

I took the glass. Sandra removed a chopping board from a cupboard, got a piece of meat out of the fridge and put it on the board. The cat rubbed itself against my shins. As I lowered my hand and felt its soft, bushy coat, something clicked into place.

'What are you doing here?' Sandra's voice was suddenly tight and controlled. She took a knife out of the wooden block inside a drawer: it was an ultra-sharp Japanese type. With deft movements she began chopping the meat. 'Why are you checking up on me?'

'I'm not.'

'Someone's been following me. Did you ask them to do it?'

I didn't reply. Tiddles had hurried over to his bowl and was waiting, his ears and nose twitching, clearly excited about the prospect of dinner. DS Hanna kept chopping.

'You did, didn't you? What is it you think I've done?'

How to play this? I could feel her suppressed anger and wondered what was going through her head. Did she know that if she was caught for betraying her colleagues, she faced the prospect of several years in prison, in daily contact with people who hated police officers? Watching the blade cut through the meat with ease, my body tensed. That knife could do serious damage.

'I know there are things you haven't been straight with me about,' I replied. 'The reason you became a police officer, for one.'

'What's that got to do with you?' She pushed the blade against the meat, transferring the contents of the chopping board into the cat's bowl. Tiddles was ready.

I took a deep breath.

'Why *did* you join the Met, Sandra?'

'My brother's life was ruined because of two racists in the Met. They accused him of being a dealer because he sold four marijuana plants to a friend.'

She placed the knife on the chopping board. Its blade was wet with myoglobin. Her tone was hard, unyielding.

'He was just trying to get by, he needed the dope and he couldn't afford it out of his pay. He was a youth worker, not some Mr Big, for fuck's sake. But they didn't care. He tried to run away and one of them shot him in the leg.' Her mouth twisted. 'They never got punished. He couldn't walk properly after that. He's in a wheelchair now, in constant pain. Last year he tried to kill himself.'

'I'm sorry about what happened to your brother, Sandra. It's a tragic story.' I edged towards her. 'But it isn't any reason to turn against your fellow officers.'

'That's ridiculous. What are you talking about?'

She picked up the knife, took it to the sink and began rinsing it under the tap. I kept my eyes on the knife.

'Just admit one thing and I'll leave.'

'What's that?'

'Please, put that down first.'

She turned off the tap, picked up a tea towel and began to carefully dry the blade.

'The water leaves a mark if you don't dry it straight away.'

I took another step closer. She placed the knife down beside the draining board, still within her reach.

'You've been helping criminals, haven't you, Sandra? You passed on information about me to your friends in the Skull Crew.'

Her eyes widened. I carried on, my anger rising.

'You planted a skull in my car for my son to find, didn't you?

And you told the Skull Crew where I live so they could put mutilated animal parts through my front door. Isn't that right?'

Her chest heaved. 'Get out of here right now!'

'I'm right, aren't I?'

'Get the fuck out of here, Callum! I'm warning you.'

I did a quick mental calculation. If she were to pick up the knife now, what chance did I have of taking it from her?

'You knew Edwards's address all along, didn't you? You knew and you didn't tell any of us. Luke nearly died because of you.'

Her nostrils flared as her breathing deepened. For the first time, a whisker of fear showed in her eyes.

'You haven't got any evidence of that.'

It was time to get away.

'Have a good evening, Sandra.'

On my way out, I bent down to Tiddles, now curled up on his bed chewing on a toy fish, and gave his belly a rub.

Back in the car, I heaved out a breath. Thank Christ, I'd got out of there without being slashed by a sushi knife – and without DS Hanna noticing what I'd taken. My hands were unsteady as I transferred five white cat hairs from my unused tissue to an evidence bag, sealed the bag and placed it inside my jacket pocket.

LUKE

I GOT A LETTER TODAY FROM MISS COLLINS – IZZY, I HAVE TO call her now – saying she's coming to see me as soon as she's out of prison. She got six months for helping me escape from the police. It's less than it could have been as the judge said she has a good character. She says she knows one day I'll make my family proud and I must keep on writing things down.

Kirsty tells me she misses me and when they let me out we'll have the most fun ever and go on a long trip and do everything I've always wanted. I smiled and told her I'll start making a list.

Maybe one day I'll get to go on that trip. There's so many places I want to go, things I want to see. A whale, a kangaroo, the aurora borealis, the desert, mountains under snow – I could spend the rest of my time in here just writing them all down. And there's so many things I want to do before I die. Maybe one day I could become a vet or a racing driver, who knows. Or I could help kids like me who've taken a wrong turn in life.

Yes, I know it's only a dream. When they let me out, people will still see me as a murderer, won't they?

I hear from Mum sometimes. She tells me to keep on hoping, whatever happens.

There's only one person I haven't heard from.

I think about her at night when I'm alone with my thoughts. Sometimes I think about how things might have been if I never met her. Then I remember those nights when I held her close and how she tried to help me even though she was scared, and how she saved my life. I know she did some bad things – but who hasn't?

'I forgive you, Jez.' I say it under my breath in case she can hear, wherever she is.

CALLUM

2ND MARCH

BY LUNCHTIME THERE WAS STILL NO RESULT ON THE CAT HAIRS I'd taken to Professor Singh. It had been thirty-six hours; the lab would have the test result soon, surely. I uttered a silent prayer that a result, positive or negative, would come before the end of the day and put me out of my misery.

Around four o'clock, I headed to the toilets and returned via the coffee machine for another shot of wakefulness.

'Something's happening with Sandra. Come and see!' Sam waved me over.

Abandoning my coffee mid-stream, I ran into the incident room, stopping behind the small group loitering near DS Hanna's desk. Two plain-clothed female officers were standing over the detective, who sat looking up at them in astonishment, a half-eaten sarnie in her hand.

'DS Hanna, I'm arresting you on suspicion of perverting the course of justice...'

One officer clicked the cuffs over Sandra's wrists. The other removed her bag from her desk and pulled her coat off the back of her chair. Along with the others, I stepped back for the three to pass by. Sandra looked defiant. As she caught sight of me, her eyes glistened.

'They made me help them, Callum.' She kept her eyes on me as she was led away. 'I wanted to stop but they wouldn't let me!'

The seconds of silence stretched out. Acting DCI Pierce, watching the drama from the confines of his office, looked as dumbfounded as everyone else. Then everyone started talking at once.

'Shit! What was all that about?'

'Fucked if I know. Ferret, did you hear anything?'

'Whatever's she's done, she's going to wish she hadn't done it. That's five years if she's convicted.'

Sam looked at me with a question on her face.

Any semblance of work was abandoned while everyone began to speculate what exactly DS Hanna had done and when, and how she had been found out. I left them to it and headed to Lorenzo's.

My relief went beyond words. At last, I could get on with my life. Bailey could boot me out of the murder team if he wanted, I no longer cared. I'd proved I'd been right all along.

As I stood at the counter, downing my espresso, Professor Singh called.

'Suresh, what's up?'

'It's a match, Callum.'

The DNA from the white hairs I'd dispatched Wednesday evening, matched the DNA from the previously tested cat hair, with over ninety-eight per cent probability, he explained. Both sets of hairs had come from the same cat.

It was proof enough for me. DS Hanna had placed that skull in my car herself.

'Are you still there?'

'Sorry, I'm a bit emotional right now.'

'There's something else, Callum.' He hesitated. 'Last month I was contacted by someone in Professional Standards. He asked me to send over all the information we held in connection with Operation Rye as part of a complaint investigation, and not to mention it to anyone. Yesterday he rang and asked me to let him know the DNA profile result as soon as it came in.' He coughed. 'I thought you might like to know.'

'Thanks, Suresh. That might explain the burst of activity here this afternoon. You probably don't know, but two DPS officers came by just now and arrested DS Hanna.'

'Ah, did they now?'

I was smiling as I left the café. Had those five hairs finally prompted the DPS to take action? I'd probably never know.

My phone rang again. This time, it was the super.

'A word, Callum. Straight away, if you don't mind.'

Ten to five in the afternoon – an unheard-of hour to be summoned to Bailey's office. This must be serious.

———

'I don't need to ask if you're behind DS Hanna's arrest,' Bailey began.

'I am, sir. I had no choice but to follow through with my suspicions, despite knowing your views. I understand if you don't want me around anymore. I'm ready to resign.'

Bailey pulled gently at his moustache. He seemed bemused.

'That won't be necessary, Callum. I called you in to say well done. You followed your instincts and you proved me wrong.' He cleared his throat. 'In the light of that, and the IOPC clearing you of any wrongdoing... I'm going to recommend that you're promoted to the permanent DCI slot, instead of Martin.'

'Sir... I don't know what to say.' I'd not expected that. I'd even begun to wonder if the super himself might be involved in unwholesome activities.

Detective Superintendent Bailey explained that Andy wouldn't be returning to his old job as DCI after all; his application to transfer to a less demanding position in another unit had been accepted.

'It's not a done deal, so keep a lid on it for now. But I respect a man who sticks by what he believes – and has the wherewithal to prove he's right.' He lowered his voice. 'And in strict confidence, no one is particularly keen for Martin to stay on as DCI.'

My feelings towards Bailey warmed considerably.

'There's one condition.' Bailey's eyebrows lifted and joined into the familiar ginger caterpillar. 'That is, you and Martin bury your differences. I don't want any more nonsense between you two. Think it through, there's no need for a hasty decision.' He stood. 'That's all, Callum.'

————

'It was you who reported her, sir, wasn't it?'

Sam gave me a knowing look. Freeman and Rowan stared at me. The four of us were sitting around a table in the corner of the pub. Everyone in the Green Man was still gossiping about Sandra's demise. I'd managed to keep quiet about my role in her arrest, so far.

Sam smiled. 'Tell them boss, or I will.'

I gave in. 'OK, it was me.'

'You're kidding,' Freeman said.

'It was you?' Rowan was shaking his head. 'You reported her to Professional Standards?'

Sam lifted her glass. 'Well done, sir.'

Eventually, Sam and I found ourselves alone. I'd been waiting for this moment all evening. Now it had come, I was a bag of nerves.

Sam placed another pint on the table for me and a half pint for herself. She'd touched up her make up. Her lips were a striking shade of coral. Before I could say anything, she spoke.

'Callum, I just wanted say... Sorry I gave you such a hard time, when you were only trying to do the right thing. I was being a wally. I let my issues get in the way of rational thought.'

'And I'm sorry for being a total clod.'

I had an urge to kiss DS Harper on the lips, so firmly that every trace of her lipstick would be removed. But first things first.

'I've got a decision to make,' I said after a long swig from my pint.

'Whether to stay on in the murder team?'

'How did you guess?'

'I've got a psychic streak, didn't you know?' She smiled. 'Sorry, tell me more.'

'I've been thinking about leaving the Met. Maybe it's time to move on.'

'You're really thinking of leaving? Why?'

'I'm exhausted by it all. The run-in with Smiley. The review into the investigation. The people who died who shouldn't have.'

A wrinkle appeared on Sam's brow. 'And all that skull stuff?'

'That too.'

The sense that I needed to stay constantly alert hadn't gone, though there'd been no more disturbing incidents and nothing to arouse my suspicion. I wondered if I'd ever be free of it, even with weekly counselling for the next six months.

'You shouldn't leave because you were threatened, you know. That would mean Sandra and her gangster friends have gotten away with it.'

'It's not just that, Sam. It's everything: Bailey getting my fitness for duty assessed, thinking I was going to be sent home any day. I pushed myself to keep going 'til the trial was over and I got the bent cop out. Now both of those have happened... I'm not sure what I want.'

'I think a month off might be a good idea. I'm surprised you're still on your feet.'

'So am I, to be honest.'

'Are you still worried about someone trying to harm you?' Sam was serious again.

'Now the trial's over, that seems unlikely. Unless someone decides to take revenge on me for getting Sandra arrested, that is.' Hopefully that wouldn't be the case.

'You can't control everything, you know. You need to learn how to relax.' She flashed a mischievous smile. 'What have I been telling you?'

'Give me a break, you.'

I leaned closer. DS Harper's face, was angled towards mine, the colour of clear honey. She was beautiful. How had I not noticed before?

'You know what everyone's saying about Sandra?' Sam began. 'How they knew there was something dodgy about her all along. I never picked up on it. I know she kept herself to herself – but I thought it was because she felt left out. I used to feel a bit sorry for her. She told me how hard being a cop was with her back-ground... It just goes to show, anyone can surprise you.'

I nodded.

'Don't get me wrong, I don't mean that she doesn't deserve what she's going to get. Any cop who betrays their teammates and puts their own boss in danger... That's unforgiveable.'

I stared into my beer, my thoughts swirling into its cloudy depths. Was I any better than Sandra, really?

'There's another reason I'm thinking about leaving.'

'Go on.'

'Long ago, I did something I'll never forgive myself for. I've been forced to face it recently and it's making me question everything – who I am, what I'm doing in the Homicide Squad, why I'm a cop at all.'

I looked into Sam's brown eyes and wanted to lose myself in them.

'Callum, you have to do what's right for you – and that might mean moving on. But you're one of the best cops I've worked with – even with the grumpiness.' She looked at me sternly from under her eyebrows. 'It would be a waste if you gave up the job. Not to mention, if you go, I'll miss you like hell.'

Her hand rested on my forearm. I leaned closer, breathing in her warm scent.

'Whatever happens,' I found myself saying, 'I want to see you again. Outside of work.' Keeping a firm grip on her hand, I leaned across the table and kissed her, taking my time, the way I'd dreamed of doing.

Sam leaned back in her chair, her eyes wide.

'Where did that come from?' Her face crinkled into a huge smile. 'The answer's yes, by the way.'

Brendan came up to me holding two bottles of Corona. He held out one to me. It was chilled, a sliver of lime pushed into the neck.

'Great news, Dad, about the promotion.'

'Cheers.' I tipped some cashews into a bowl. 'It's not been formally offered yet, though; who knows what might happen in the meantime. Anyway, I'm not totally sure I'm going to accept. I might take some time off – I might take early retirement, even.'

'But you're only forty-one. You couldn't retire yet, could you?'

'Right now, I feel like doing absolutely nothing for a while.' I scooped a handful of nuts from the bowl before Brendan could gobble the lot.

Maybe Sam was right: I shouldn't quit because some gangsters and their bent little helper had tried to intimidate me. That would mean that they'd won.

'Are you OK, Bren? I've been worried. After what I told you...'

'It was a shock, after all this time.' Brendan swigged his beer. I could see something was on his mind. 'Did you never tell anyone the truth?'

'No, I didn't. I wanted to. Marcy, my friends at school, my mother... Your mother too. I tried to tell them all. But once you've told a lie, once people accept it as true, it's harder and harder to undo it.'

He'd been smoking in there. Perhaps in his last moments, my father had forgiven me for that lie.

'Did you want him to die?'

I stared at Brendan. It came back, as strongly as ever. How I'd crept downstairs, anger consuming me. Lighting the rolled-up page of the newspaper inside the shed. The *whoosh* of the first flames curling up from the floor.

Then those moments I'd spent years trying to forget. The heat on my bare arms as I approached the shed. My father inside, banging on the window, shouting my name. Standing outside for what seemed like hours, until I turned away... Then waiting under the tree for the smoke and flames to take him.

'Part of me wanted to save him,' I replied. 'But a bigger part wanted him gone.'

'Were you glad he died?'

I hesitated. 'After Mum told us he was dead... For a few minutes I felt so sodding happy, like no one could ever hurt me again. It was as if I'd been set free after years of being locked up.'

I'd almost been able to forget those minutes of joy, before the guilt took over.

Brendan began to cry, big noisy sobs, his shoulders heaving and tears rolling down his face. I forgot my own pain.

'Are you angry with me?'

'Yeah, I am.' He nodded, sniffing. 'Why didn't you tell me before?'

'I was scared. I didn't know if you could cope with the truth. I didn't want you to judge me, I didn't want to lose your respect. Starting the fire, then not helping my father...' I knew I had to tell him everything. For too long, shame had silenced me. 'I was ashamed of what I did that day. I still am.'

Brendan wiped his eyes.

'I get why you started the fire, Dad, why you didn't try to help him. He'd made you feel so bad for so long. Maybe I would've done the same, if he'd been my father.'

Gratitude clogged my throat. Maybe Brendan would be able to deal with this after all. I had a hunch he'd grow into a fine young man.

My thoughts drifted.

What would happen to Luke? How would he get through those long years behind bars, serving life for a murder he'd wanted no part of? I hoped he'd find some peace, whether or not he had been the one to stab Nora Symonds. But I'd believed him when he'd told me he hadn't.

Odd, I mused, how it turned out that Luke and I had so much in common. Though he'd been punished for something he hadn't done and I'd never been punished for something I had.

'I could go to the super and tell him the truth,' I murmured, mostly to myself. In theory, I could be prosecuted for the crime I'd committed as a sixteen-year-old, especially as the arson attack had led to my father's death.

'Why would you want to do that?' Brendan stared at me.

'Because I haven't been punished.'

'You have though, in a way.'

He was right, wasn't he? I play punched his arm.

'So, you don't think I should confess everything to the cops?'

'Dad, are you stupid?' Brendan pulled his most teenager-like face. 'You need to get your shit together and carry on catching the bad guys.'

I grinned and reached for my beer. 'I might just do that.'

In a rare moment of clarity, I decided not to say that from now on I wouldn't let my job get in the way of being a good dad. I knew myself only too well. Instead, I put my arm around my son and held him close.

ACKNOWLEDGMENTS

First of all, I want to thank Paul Dayes for his tireless help with all my questions and for putting me in touch with former gang members. Paul is director of the Exit Foundation (https://www. exitfoundation.org.uk), which helps young people to leave gang life and make a fresh start.

Thanks to all those who talked to me about their experiences within gangs.

Thanks to police advisor and ex-top cop Graham Bartlett for his invaluable advice on police procedure, and to the DC in the Metropolitan Police who helped with gang-related matters. Thanks also to crime and thriller author/Dark Edge Press publisher Louise Mullins, who helped me start my research into gangs.

Thanks to Jessica Norrie, author of The Magic Carpet for her advice on writing characters from many backgrounds and ethnicities that are different to my own.

I'm grateful to the teachers and former teachers who share with me their experiences in secondary schools, including authors Mandy James, Mandy Lee, Justine Gilbert, Bernie Steadman, Eileen W and Heleyne Hammersley.

Thanks to Simon Harding for one of the most helpful books I read on British urban gangs, *The Street Casino: Survival in violent street gangs* by Simon Harding (Policy Press, 2014). Another useful reference was *How Gangs Work: An Ethnography of Youth Violence* by James Densley (Palgrave Macmillan, 2016 edition). I recommend *Drug Wars: The terrifying inside story of Britain's drug trade* by Neil Woods (2019) for suspense-filled tales of undercover policing. *How I Escaped a Girl Gang: Rolling in a London Girl Gang* by Chyna (Coronet, 2011) also proved useful. Another invaluable book was *Blue: A Memoir: Keeping the Peace and Falling to Pieces* by John Sutherland (Orion Publishing, 2018).

Thank you to my publisher Hobeck Books, aka Adrian Hobart and Rebecca Collins, who believed in my book and brought it into the world.

A huge thanks to the early readers of *Silenced*, and the authors and bloggers who have helped to spread the word about the book, with a special mention to Linda Hill (Linda's Book Bag), Susan Hampson (Books from dusk till dawn), Michelle Ryles (The Book Magnet), Cathy Ryan (Between the Lines), John Fish (The Last Word Book Review), Lynda Checkley (lyndas_bookreviews on Instagram), Nick Wardron (The Untidy Bookshelf), Louise Cannon (Bookmarks and Stages), Deb Day (dds_book_reviews on Instagram), Donna Morfett (Donnas Interviews and Giveaways on Facebook), Miriam Smith and Lesley Wilkinson.

Lastly, thanks to all who have supported me over the many months of writing and rewriting this novel: friends such as Jacki Hall and many others online, my writing group pals Iris, Justine, Paul, Karen, Deb, Dorothy, Erica and Peter who gave me their unvarnished feedback, and my husband Stuart, who provided his insights and encouragement, along with a stream of links to BBC news articles about stabbings and violent crime in London. Thank you, the BBC!

ABOUT THE AUTHOR

A Londoner with Irish heritage, Jennie Ensor writes dark, gritty psychological suspense and thrillers as well as darkly comic fiction. She began her writing career as a journalist and loves to tackle controversial issues in her novels: Islamic terrorism, Russian gangsters and war crimes in her debut *Blind Side* (a thriller set in the year of London's 2005 terror attacks), domestic abuse and sexual exploitation in her second, *The Girl in His Eyes*. Her third book, a wander over to the lighter side of life, is *Not Having It All* – a wickedly funny, feel-good novel about love, lies and middle-age.

Silenced is Jennie's fourth book. Published by Hobeck, it is a crime thriller with a strong psychological element, venturing into the shadowy world of London drug gangs and police corruption.

Ms Ensor lives in north London with her husband and their Airedale terrier. She writes poetry as well as novels, some of which is published in UK and overseas journals; 'Lost Connection' placed second in its category in the 2020 Fish Lockdown Prize. In her spare time (?) she reads widely, sings choral music and practices yoga. She is a fiendish walker and regularly cycles the punishing local hills. Evenings she can often be found collapsed in front of a TV crime drama with a bar of chocolate/glass of strong alcohol.

For more information about Jennie and her writing, please join her website: **https://jennieensor.com** for details of her up coming books, price drops on existing books, offers and prizes.

Also see Jennie's Facebook page **www.facebook/ JennieEnsorAuthor** for her latest news, or follow her on Twitter @jennie_ensor or Instagram @jennieensor.

HOBECK BOOKS – THE HOME OF GREAT STORIES

We hope you've enjoyed reading Jennie Ensor's novel.

Jennie has written a short story prequel to this novel, *Saviour*.

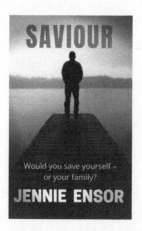

This story, and many other short stories and novellas, is included in the compilation *Crime Bites*. *Crime Bites* is available for free to subscribers of Hobeck Books.

Crime Bites includes:

- *Echo Rock* by Robert Daws
- *Old Dogs, Old Tricks* by AB Morgan
- *The Silence of the Rabbit* by Wendy Turbin
- *Never Mind the Baubles: An Anthology of Twisted Winter Tales* by the Hobeck Team (including all the current Hobeck authors and Hobeck's two publishers)
- *The Clarice Cliff Vase* by Linda Huber
- *Here She Lies* by Kerena Swan
- *The Macnab Principle* by R.D. Nixon
- *Fatal Beginnings* by Brian Price
- *A Defining Moment* by Lin Le Versha
- *Saviour* by Jennie Ensor

Also please visit the Hobeck Books website for details of our other superb authors and their books, and if you would like to get in touch, we would love to hear from you.

Hobeck Books also presents a weekly podcast, the Hobcast, where founders Adrian Hobart and Rebecca Collins discuss all things book related, key issues from each week, including the overseas and she's left without childcare, Bea turns to best friend Maddie for help.

Kurt, downing whiskies in his overheated hotel room, convinces himself that Bea is having an affair with Maddie. He persuades a neighbour to spy on the pair.

Maddie, meanwhile, longs for a child of her own with a man she can trust – and he must love cats. She meets divorced, risk-averse Colin in a lift. He's smitten, and resolves to displace Maddie's feline companions. But he starts to fear that Maddie sees him only as a 'handy stud with a fat wallet'...
Can Bea and Kurt find happiness again? Can Maddie and Colin risk falling in love?

"This is something different, and Jennie Ensor has totally cracked it." – bestselling author, Anita Waller ups and downs of running a creative business. Each episode includes an interview with one of the people who make Hobeck possible: the editors, the authors, the cover designers. These are the people who help Hobeck bring great stories to life. Without them, Hobeck wouldn't exist. The Hobcast can be listened to from all the usual platforms but it can also be found on the Hobeck website: **www.hobeck.net/hobcast**.

THE GIRL IN HIS EYES

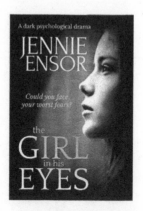

Abused as a child, a woman believes her father is grooming a new victim.

Laura, a young woman struggling to deal with what her father did to her a decade ago, is horrified to realize that the girl he takes swimming might be his next victim. Emma is twelve—the age Laura was when her father took away her innocence.

Intimidated by her father's rages, Laura has never told anyone the truth about her childhood. Now she must decide whether she has the courage to expose him and face the consequences.

Can Laura overcome her fear and save Emma before the worst happens?

"A must read." — James Jansen

"Compulsive." — Sebnem Sanders

"Highly recommended." — H.M. Holten

BLIND SIDE

Can you ever truly know someone? And what if you suspect the unthinkable?

London, 2005.

Despite her friends' warnings, a young Englishwoman can't resist her attraction to a charismatic Russian ex-soldier recently arrived in London. But, realising how deeply war-time incidents have affected him, she starts to suspect that he's hiding a horrifying secret...

Set in the year of London's 7/7 bus and tube terrorism attacks, Blind Side is a powerful tale of love and friendship, trauma and betrayal, secrets and obsession.

"builds suspense brilliantly" — Gail Cleare, USA Today bestselling author

"An absolutely stunning debut." — The Book Magnet

NOT HAVING IT ALL

Bea Hudson juggles her job at the 'Psycho Lab' with looking after her demanding five-year-old daughter, badly-behaved dog and ex-au pair. When her chief executive husband Kurt is sent